Spirits of Vengeance
The Stone of Spirits

ANDREW JOHN RAINNIE

Copyright © 2014 Andrew John Rainnie
All rights reserved.
ISBN: 1503091902
ISBN-13: 978-1503091900

Printed by CreateSpace

For more information:
www.andrewjohnrainnie.com

DEDICATION

For Irfan Javed and Piper Rainnie

Dear friends, sadly lost

My personal vengeance spirits

ACKNOWLEDGMENTS

Firstly I would like to thank my screenwriting mentor Rosie Cullen, who made me see that this story was far too big and too close to my heart to be squeezed into a screenplay. I would also like to thank Dickson Telfer for his invaluable insights, and Mike James, who helped edit the book into something slightly more elegant than what I had achieved on my own. I would like to thank those who have offered opinions on various drafts over the years, but I will single out Caroline, who read it cover to cover in a matter of days, offering a passionate and positive review that compelled me to see it published. I would like to thank my parents, John and Margaret, for affording me the upbringing that allowed such fantastic stories to evolve in my mind, and to my sister Lynsey, who is, and always will be, the Kamina to my Kaedin. And finally, to Lisa, for her patience and understanding while I disappeared for weeks on end into the world of Enara.

CHAPTERS

Part One

1.	The Ranger Returns	*Pg.3*	13.	Crossing Lake Comodo	*Pg.83*
2.	The Mists of Mytor	*Pg.9*	14.	The Intrigue of Gorran	*Pg.89*
3.	Death of a Ranger	*Pg.17*	15.	The City of Calisto	*Pg.97*
4.	The Elves of Elgrin	*Pg.29*	16.	Meeting of the Alliance	*Pg.109*
5.	The Town of Tilden	*Pg.35*	17.	The Black Tower	*Pg.117*
6.	The Grave Mistake	*Pg.47*	18.	The Seeing Spell	*Pg.127*
7.	Dreams and Awakenings	*Pg.53*	19.	Aftermath of Sight	*Pg.139*
8.	Bonds and Breaks	*Pg.59*	20.	Not Left Behind	*Pg.149*
9.	The Ruins of Anawey	*Pg.65*	21.	Nightmares and Discoveries	*Pg.161*
10.	Malenek Marches	*Pg.71*	22.	Men of Stone	*Pg.173*
11.	A Brief Escape	*Pg.75*	23.	Rain of Fire	*Pg.177*
12.	The Marauder's Cave	*Pg.77*	24.	The Lost Children	*Pg.189*

Part Two

25.	The Shores of Zalestia	*Pg.195*	33.	The Jalenari Jungle	*Pg.249*
26.	The Citadel of Zatharu	*Pg.203*	34.	The Tomb of Errazure	*Pg.257*
27.	The Relics of Zoren	*Pg.211*	35.	The Stone of Spirits	*Pg.265*
28.	The Ranger's Fate	*Pg.219*	36.	The Pit and the Past	*Pg.273*
29.	The Darosa Desert	*Pg.223*	37.	Soldiers and Sorcerers	*Pg.279*
30.	The Kindness of Rebels	*Pg.233*	38.	Fight or Flight	*Pg.287*
31.	The Ghost Town of Gorran	*Pg.239*	39.	The Pilgrimage of the Elves	*Pg.297*
32.	The Desert Storm	*Pg.243*			

Part Three

40.	Duru Umbin	*Pg.307*	46.	The Heat of Battle	*Pg.353*
41.	Flashback of a Farmer	*Pg.311*	47.	The Secret of the Stone	*Pg.361*
42.	The Wall of the Mind	*Pg.321*	48.	Risaar's Blade	*Pg.369*
43.	Light in the Dark	*Pg.335*	49.	The Ranger's Farewell	*Pg.373*
44.	The Great Divide	*Pg.343*	50.	Return to Elgrin Forest	*Pg.377*
45.	The Priest's Journals	*Pg.349*	51.	The Path of One	*Pg.383*

PART ONE

In the darkness, the four Elementals were united by Fate

Ygrain, God of Land
Aquill, God of Water
Whirren, God of Air
And Risaar, God of Fire
They combined to create the world ~ Enara

Ygrain brought forth the rock and soil
Aquill filled the rivers and the seas
Whirren whispered the wind and blew the breeze
Risaar let fire burn and the light flow bright

Their collective spark brought forth the gift of life
A myriad of children of many different forms
The Elementals retreated back into the æther
Forever watchful over their brave new world

Excerpt from the Orico, the common religious scripture among humans of the western continent of Amaros.

CHAPTER ONE

THE RANGER RETURNS

THE LIME GREEN GLOW FROM YGRAIN FUSED WITH THE PALLID, silvery light of Whirren, the larger of the two moons, casting eerie colours upon the cliffs of Caspia. The cragged coastline was a sheer drop, as though an ancient giant had long ago sliced the land with an axe as large as the continent of Amaros. A small, battered boat approached the foot of the cliffs through rough seas. The cloaks of two sailors, the boat's only crew, flapped in the night's bitter breeze. They watched as waves crashed against the rock face, struggling to discern the caves that they hoped to reach in the darkness.

"There!" shouted one, the master, his stoic voice carved by experience. "We must hurry. The tide has already risen!" They rowed in tandem through the choppy waves. The master's apprentice peered beyond the crashing surf and spotted the half-submerged hole they were aiming for.

"We will be scattered against the rocks!" he cried.

"The boat will," conceded his master, no stranger to sacrifice. "We will need to swim under the surface and into the cave. Are you ready?"

The apprentice nodded, his face stabbed by spray. They removed their cloaks in preparation. The master, an Amarosian, was tall and well-built, scraggly wet chestnut hair clinging to his white face, his jaw hidden by a sea-worn beard. A faded tattoo marked the back of his right hand. The apprentice was almost his opposite; a young slender Zalestian, his brown skin crowned by a head of short, black, springy hair.

The master tied a leather sack containing the last of their supplies around his body, and dived into the dark, angry waters. The apprentice stood alone on the boat, gazing up at the shadowy cliffs looming above him. There were none like this on the coast of Zalestia, his homeland now an ocean away.

He took a deep breath and followed his master into the spine-chilling sea. His muscles seized as he was enveloped by the callous darkness. The apprentice fought through the pain, struggling against the undercurrent. His lungs ached, desperate to breathe, but he was unsure if he had passed beyond the cliffs. If he surfaced too soon his gangly body would be strewn against the rocks, yet to not surface at all would mean a watery grave, and the total failure of his mission.

Before he could contemplate it further, something lunged for him. The last of his air was released in shock, filling his lungs with water. His master's tattooed hand pulled him up into the musty air of a dark cavern.

"Follow me," he said, barely allowing the apprentice to catch his breath. He tore strips from his robes and wrapped them around his hands, while his apprentice wiped the sting of the saltwater from his eyes. The older man climbed up into a small tunnel that ascended through the solid rock. Unlike the natural, sharp edges of the cavern, the tunnel was man-made, smoothed by industry, causing him to slip and slide back towards the sea. Water trickled down the tunnel, taunting him. The apprentice soon followed, cursing in his native tongue when he slipped.

"Do not worry," said the master. "It is only rain from above."

"What is this place?" he replied, the tight chamber echoing his voice upwards.

"Delivery shafts," said the Amarosian as they continued their arduous climb. "The miners of Northern Caspia are too far from Calisto or Lake Comodo to transport them by horse or by river, so they send the ore down these shafts in pots."

"But to who?" asked the apprentice. "No boat could enter that cavern."

"Several can, I assure you, but only at low tide." It had been part of the master's plan that they enter the caves when no-one else would. With the bitter thirty year war still raging on, he could not afford his Zalestian apprentice to be spotted or captured in Amaros. Those that had been caught in the past were treated to a cruel fate at the hands of the Amarosians. This had precluded any possibility of docking in the crescent circle port of Calisto. Their boat had been too badly damaged, and their supplies too low, to risk circumnavigating the continent to Rundhale or Heroshin.

No, this was their safest option.

This was their only option.

They climbed and slid for hours, until the master disappeared over the peak. A cool breeze greeted the apprentice as he neared the end of the stuffy tunnel. The constant patter of rain beat against the wooden shelter covering the exit, water flowing faster down the well. He clawed away at the final few feet, but stopped abruptly as loud, cantankerous voices filled the air. Had they been discovered by the Amarosian army? The apprentice lay still, trying to hear, but he was thwarted by the wind and rain and his own beating heart. He wondered what his master would wish of him. No doubt he would want him to remain hidden, but the apprentice had another agenda. He pulled himself over the edge, only to be confronted by the pointed tip of a sword. Behind the blade was a smirking, snivelling face.

"What 'ave we here?" asked the marauder, thrusting a flaming torch closer to the apprentice. "A Zalestian?" The marauder was a cowardly, wretched excuse of a man named Maulin Lamn, his face contorted like a Caspian rat. He grabbed the apprentice, dragging him out of the hole and dumping him in the mud. The Zalestian struggled as the marauder bound his arms with rope, but stopped when he glimpsed the corpse lying next to him. A dead miner, his clothes soaked in blood, stared back through glazed eyes. The apprentice tried to wriggle away from the body, but the marauder teased him, pushing him closer to the ill-fated man.

"We are poor travellers," said the master. "We are of no value to you." The apprentice tore his eyes from the corpse and saw his master kneeling nearby, a sword's cold steel kissing his throat. Two more murdered miners littered the ground, while a pair of marauders rifled through their belongings.

"Poor travellers would not risk their lives climbing through Caspia's cliffs at high tide," replied Maulin. "They would sail to Calisto and beg among the masses, unless they could not allow themselves to be seen," he added, eyeing the apprentice with a lecherous leer. "Nothing to say for yourself, you dark-skinned Zog?"

"He is my servant," said the master. "He will only answer to me."

"Or the Alliance," said one of the other raiders.

"It's true," said Maulin. "All Zalestians found in Amaros are prisoners of war, but then again, Lord Malenek is known to pay a handsome reward for Zogs that is still breathing."

"Malenek is alive?" inquired the master, unable to conceal his surprise. Before Maulin could answer, one of the other marauders interrupted.

"By the Elements!" exclaimed the scavenger. He unsheathed a sword of exquisite craftsmanship, the golden cross-guard curving inwards like two fiery pincers, encrusted with a large, red jewel at its centre. A broad blade erupted from the hilt, as if its maker had forged the steel from fire itself. The metal flame looked as though it were dancing in battle. It was inscribed with strange runes, which grew smaller towards the sleek upper edge all the way to the sharp point.

Maulin snatched the sword from his companion. His eager eyes admired its devastating beauty, the sheen of scarlet in its silver blade. He pawed at the glowing ruby, alive with undying fire, fused into the hilt.

"Poor travellers, aey?" he said mockingly. "Kill that one. We'll take the Zalestian alive and collect Malenek's reward."

The apprentice struggled to break free of his bonds as the men approached him, but his master had more success. Moving swiftly, with training and skill on his side, the warrior disarmed the marauders, leaving one gasping and the other unconscious in the mud. The master stepped towards Maulin, unravelling the strips of fabric from his hands. He stretched out his right hand to the marauder, revealing his tattoo, the mark of the Ishkava Rangers of the West.

"Return my sword and I will spare you," said Callaghan Tor.

Maulin let out a nervous cackle as he strengthened his grip on the sword's hilt. "You will spare me?"

"You have my word," replied the ranger, either oblivious or ignorant to Maulin's sarcasm.

"Why take your word when I will soon have your scalp!" With that vain, bald threat, Maulin charged at him with the sword raised above his head. He swiped it down upon the unarmed man. The ranger swiftly stepped aside. The blade struck the ground with a clang, momentarily wedged into a rocky outcrop. Maulin tugged at the sword, but it was stuck. Callaghan's fist flew through the rain and connected with the marauder's ugly face. He staggered backwards, dazed by the blow, but managed to remain on his feet. The ranger's hand slid over the hilt of his sword, twisting it and pulling it free. He raised the jewelled cross to his face, and whispered a secret enchantment only the sword itself could hear. Maulin, unable to accept defeat, picked up the sword of his unconscious companion and charged at the ranger again.

With the last whispered word from the ranger's lips, a searing hot flame burst from the jewel and along the sword's cold steel. The startling ignition caused Maulin to falter. The ranger took full advantage of his hesitation, and swung the flaming blade, slicing off the marauder's hand. The fleshy lump fell to the ground, the stump smouldering while his fingers still twitched.

Maulin could not feel any pain at first, or even the detachment of his hand. He used his remaining hand to feel where his other one should have been, passing his fingers through some phantom limb. As his brain caught up with his body, a glut of pain caused him to collapse to his knees. The marauder clutched the severed appendage in horror, the wound already cauterised from the heat of the sword's magical flame. Tears flooded Maulin's malicious eyes as the searing pain now took hold, so precise an agony that it prevented him from screaming.

The heat from the sword's blade radiated close to his head. Maulin glanced up, struggling to see the Ishkava Ranger behind the bright, unnatural flames licking the steel. Callaghan was no more than a dark presence wielding the weapon of a god.

"You... you're..." stammered the cowardly Maulin, but he could not bring himself to say the name of this living legend.

"Tell me all that you know of Malenek, or I will chop off your other hand and leave you to eat like a Heroshin dog," threatened the ranger.

"He returned several months ago," bleated Maulin. "Or at least, he appeared then. He may have returned sooner, or never have gone, no one knows for sure. He walked down from the mountains to the town of Morghen, seeking volunteers."

This made sense to the ranger. Malenek's castle was situated high in the Mytor Mountains, far away from the rest of the world. This had been the priest's wish, when his pessimism about the war had started to outweigh his sense of duty to humanity. Malenek had been so desperate to escape society that he had laid the first foundation stone himself.

"Volunteers?" asked Callaghan. "For what purpose?"

"I do not know," replied Maulin. "I am not in the habit of volunteering."

"Do not try my patience, marauder!"

"They said he was gathering an army," he confessed, sweating under the blade's flames. "But us marauders didn't think so."

"Why?"

"Some of our lot went to volunteer," he sobbed, "Malenek tested their mettle, and most were turned away. He chose Mytor farmers over hardened mercenaries."

He chose humble men, thought Callaghan. Loyal men.

"How many does he have?"

"How should I know?" cried the marauder. "What does it matter anyways? Its rubbish, I tell you. A priest don't need no army."

The ranger moved the blade closer, singeing Maulin's natty beard. "I know Vangar's thieves keep a watch on all things."

"A few dozen men," revealed the marauder. "A hundred at most."

"Then why is he paying a bounty for Zalestians kept alive?"

"Because the Alliance pays for them dead. Malenek loves the Zogs. Always has." Despite his deep-seated racism, the ranger was convinced that Maulin was telling the truth.

"Take your men and go," ordered Callaghan, calmly withdrawing his sword. "Leave everything else. And be warned, marauder, if we meet again in such a manner, my sword will claim your other hand."

Maulin snaked off to wake up his compatriots with a dutiful kick. As the pair sluggishly crawled to their feet, the one-armed bandit reached for his chopped off hand.

"Leave it," demanded Callaghan, replacing his sword in its sheath. The marauders ran off, Maulin cursing his companion's cowardice.

"Jaelyn, are you injured?" the ranger asked his apprentice. The Zalestian joined Callaghan in watching the marauders skulk off into the husk of night.

"Yes, but not as badly as that one," replied Jaelyn Zsatt, peering down at the severed appendage. "Does the code of the Ishkava Rangers not prevent you from killing?"

"We believe that death should only be considered as a last resort in resolving conflict," he stated, adding, "It is, however, a little ambiguous on amputation." Jaelyn was surprised to see a small grin appear on Callaghan's otherwise solemn face.

"But that man will surely die from his injuries?" questioned the novice.

"No, the flame cauterised the wound immediately. The only death will be his pride, if he has any left." Callaghan gazed upon the bodies of the three men killed by the marauders. "Times must be tough if Caspian miners are dealing with thieves. Gather what supplies you can carry. We will not be stopping here."

"But master," he protested, his empty stomach grumbling, "it has been days since we ate."

"The miners will soon find their murdered friends and demand answers," said the ranger, staring off into the distance at the tiny flickers of light from the mining town of Pacosi. He took the flaming torch the marauders had left, and set fire to the shelter over the tunnel entrance.

"Why are you lighting a fire?" quizzed Jaelyn. "You will alert the town to our presence."

"I will alert them to the position of their friends, who deserve a quick burial," he explained as the fire took hold and the shelter burned. "Now, let us head north to Mytor."

"But I thought the Ranger Temple lay to the west?" asked Jaelyn, heaving up his haul of marauder supplies, confused by this new geography.

"I am afraid your training will have to wait, Jaelyn," said Callaghan as he picked up his belongings. "I have to visit an old friend."

CHAPTER TWO

THE MISTS OF MYTOR

Callaghan Tor and Jaelyn Zsatt trekked for days on foot through the heavily-mined hills of Northern Caspia. They kept off any tracks or path to avoid members of the mining cooperatives, or marauder parties, or anyone else who may wish to collect the bounty on Jaelyn's dark head.

Soon after navigating through the series of stone columns known as The Thousand Fingers, they crossed the border of Caspia and entered the lands of Mytor. The boundary was marked by an ancient dry riverbed, like the scar of an old wound cut through the landscape, which quickly changed. The ground underfoot transformed from the rich, reddish brown hills brimming with minerals and ores, to steep slopes of black and grey rocks, jutting out at the travellers like blunt blades. Very little vegetation sprouted up from the derisory soil. Mytor was a land sparse of life, including people. Callaghan believed that was why Malenek had chosen to exile himself to this place, far away from the political reach of Calisto or the royal courts of Hylan. This was the region of the damned and the lost.

The two travellers eventually arrived in the small town of Morghen around dusk. Enara's bright red sun, Risaar, passed behind the hulking, mist-covered mountains of Mytor, casting the cloudy sky in a sea of scarlet. Aquill, the lesser blue sun, was barely visible in the bloodied skies. The ranger would have preferred to avoid the town, the residents known to be loyal to Lord Malenek. Some were celebrating their cult figure even now, as song lyrics featuring his name bellowed out from the town's tawdry tavern. However, the best path to Mytor Castle cut through Morghen, avoiding the razor sharp rocks that dominated lesser-used trails.

A few of the townspeople were milling around, and paused to throw the pair suspicious looks. Jaelyn, hidden by his hood, was surprised to see that it was his master, rather than himself, that was the focus of their unwanted attention.

"Is that Callaghan?"

"Can't be. He wouldn't dare show his face here."

Jaelyn sensed their eyes burning into his master's back as they exited the poor excuse of a town. The houses were slanted, slumped together as if the buildings were huddled in fear. He did not look back, following Callaghan through the broken stone arch that led north into the Mytor mountain range.

The slope they traversed was tricky at the best of times, but Aquill's faint indigo hue had washed Risaar's bloody light from the sky, making their climb even more difficult. The black rocky crags cast ominous shadows in the blue light wherever they turned. In the distance, the path levelled out and formed into a natural bridge leading over a deep chasm. On the other side lay Mytor Castle, built into the rock of the mountain itself, overlooking the ocean far below. Its bleak, lustreless walls were illuminated by bands of orange torchlight.

The pair crossed over the abyss, the perilous drop hidden by the hanging mists below. Before they were even halfway across, the grinding mechanism of the castle gates caused them to stop. An immense metal gate squeaked and groaned as it was raised. From the darkness emerged a single figure. In the last of the blue daylight Jaelyn spied a broad, beefy man, his face tucked beneath a bushy red beard. He paused a few feet from the pair, staring intently at the ranger. Callaghan stepped out to meet him. Both broke into a smile and gripped each other's arms. It was only now that Jaelyn spotted the same tattoo on the stranger's hand that Callaghan had emblazoned on his. This was another Ishkava Ranger.

"It is good to see you again, Callaghan," said the red-haired ranger. "There are few of us left as it is without losing you to the shores of Zalestia."

"I did not realise you had such little faith in me, Volan," said Callaghan.

"Aye, well, better sailors have drowned in Aquill's raging seas," muttered Volan Hesh.

"And better men yet on the spears of Zalestia."

"I see you brought one with you," said Volan, nodding toward Jaelyn. "Is he your captive?"

"My apprentice." The words turned the friendly atmosphere stale. Whatever Volan's thoughts on the matter, his years as a ranger had trained him better than to voice them.

"Come," he urged, turning to the castle. "Lord Malenek will be glad to hear of your arrival."

They followed Volan through the front gate and into a large antechamber. As they made their way deeper into the castle, the gate clanged shut behind them, trapping them inside. Callaghan glanced back at their blocked exit.

"You have nothing to fear," Volan assured him. Callaghan nodded, but did not drop his guard as they followed the burly ranger up a winding staircase.

"In what capacity are you here, Volan?" he asked.

"I am aiding Lord Malenek in his plans for the country." There was a hesitation in Volan's reply that made Callaghan ill at ease.

"Is the Alliance aware of this plan?" he probed. There was no reply from Volan, only a meek attempt to avoid Callaghan's gaze. "Do the other rangers know of it?"

"I am not... It is perhaps best if Lord Malenek explains it to you himself." Why is he being so vague and evasive? Callaghan wondered.

They reached a landing and walked along to an unassuming wooden door. Volan knocked three times. A voice on the other side bade them enter. Callaghan was unsure if it was Malenek's. Volan opened the door and ushered them into a modest study. The room was more cordial than the shadowy castle. One wall was dominated by a large map of Amaros, highly detailed in its design, a work of art more than of topography. Beside one of the many bookcases stood a tall, slender man with thinned silver hair, dressed in plain black priest robes. He replaced a heavy volume in its vacant slot, and turned to his visitors.

Callaghan was shocked to see Malenek standing there alive. He was sure it had been an elaborate ruse, but he had come anyway, driven by some misplaced hope. His wish had been answered as he stared upon Malenek in the very same room they had last exchanged some heated words. The priest was thinner now, gaunt with worry.

"Thank you, Volan," said Malenek. The older ranger took his leave, closing the door as he did so. Jaelyn felt uneasy, trapped in the room as the two men stared each other down.

"You seem surprised to see me, old friend," said the priest at last, breaking the silence.

"Where have you been all this time?" asked Callaghan, more angrily than he had intended.

"I travelled all over Enara, as I see you have as well." Malenek made a careful nod towards Jaelyn Zsatt. "Is this to be the first Zalestian ranger?"

"If he passes the Trials."

"Same old Callaghan. Do you still believe that this small, symbolic gesture will be enough to unite two lands that have been shedding each other's blood for over thirty years?"

"I believe it is the first step," replied the ranger earnestly, gearing up for another verbal spat. "No matter how small."

Malenek let a smirk cut across his face. "In all the years I have known you my boy, I have never thought of you as naïve."

"You think it naïve to hope for the best?" asked Callaghan. Malenek's smile dissipated into a sober, stony expression, a staunch façade disguising the warring ideas in his mind.

"I do not know what you glimpsed on your voyage across the oceans, Callaghan, but on my travels I saw two countries, both on the brink of self-destruction. Even when word of your new apprentice spreads far and wide, even if after his years of training he was offered your mantle of Ranger Elite, do you believe that it will be enough to stem the flow of anger and blood that has smeared a generation?"

"I can only hope so," said Callaghan.

"Honourable men like you have been clinging to their hope for decades," said Malenek, followed by a long, drawn-out sigh. "It has done nothing to steer us away from the destructive path mankind is on."

"And what path is that?"

"Complete annihilation," stated the priest, "unless we stop it."

"You already tried to unite these two lands through religion," noted Callaghan. Malenek's theories, that the divergent beliefs of the Amarosians and Zalestians were somehow linked, that they shared deities and fables, had been met with much derision in churches and kirks across the land. It was this failure that had driven Malenek to find solace in Mytor. Some of the smaller, rural villages such as Morghen had been more amenable to the priest's ideas, struggling to hold onto their faith after thirty years of war. Beyond the borders of Mytor, Malenek's attempts to marry two conflicting faiths had caused him to incur accusations of blasphemy. His ideals were described as the bastard offspring of two warring parents. Had it been another priest of the Elemental Church suggesting such things, they would have surely been stoned on the streets, but Malenek was special. Even as an exile, his council was sought by leaders of church and state, kings and queens, and men of other interests.

"That was an old dream of a younger man," conceded the priest. "A dream that died within these walls years ago."

Callaghan was glad to hear that Malenek had abandoned the passionate ideals that had poisoned their friendship. "So you do not believe that our gods and theirs are as one?"

"Oh no, you mistake me, Callaghan. I no longer have to theorise that these two lands are tied together by their beliefs. I now know it to be true. But even if people believed as I do, that these two religions are in fact opposite sides of the same page, they would take that principle and use it as a justification for more sinister acts, just as they do now."

What was this leading up to? Callaghan wondered, as the priest continued with his private sermon.

"No, I was a fool to think two warring lands could see their similarities when the creatures of Amaros do not even agree on interpretations of the Orico." He took his worn copy of the religious text from a shelf and flicked through it, perusing the words and symbols. "Caspians, Heroshins, the Etraihu tribes, the elves and the centaurs, we all worship different deities, or different aspects of the same ones. Man denounces the Nkar-Lek and Moltari as heretics, but no-one really knows what they believe, if they believe anything at all. Yet it is man who is fighting this war, and all men of Amaros, from the tips of the Tregorian Mountains to the cliffs of Caspia, know of the Orico. They know its stories, even if they have never read the book or even laid eyes upon its text. Religion is old, ingrained in people over eons, where stories of legends become myths, and then prophets."

"You know, for a priest you have a very skewed view of man and faith," said Callaghan. He hoped to ease the tense atmosphere with some friendly joviality, but it had the opposite effect.

"I was there, Callaghan!" exclaimed Malenek. "I was there when this war began!" The priest's fury flared, slamming his fist down upon his desk. "It started over a dinner conversation about gods! This war is nothing more than a measure of one's beliefs, throwing one set of deities against the other like children throwing wooden toys. It's a pissing contest!"

"Then what is this plan of yours that will change all that? The one that has my fellow ranger so ill at ease." Malenek turned his back on them, facing the map of Amaros.

"I intend to bring peace to every corner of Enara," he stated.

"If that were true, then why put out a reward for every Zalestian found in Amaros?"

"To protect them," answered Malenek. "The sons of Zalestia sent here to die by their errant Khan deserve a better fate. Do you know King Arthadian sends them off to that wretched Isle of Hanoya? They go there and hunt them with those bloody big volff hounds. However, my reasons were not entirely altruistic. I knew you planned to bring a Zalestian apprentice back with you, and I needed you to come here."

"Balen." At the sound of his given name, a name his servants and even his comrades rarely used, Balen Malenek turned and looked at Callaghan. The ranger laid his worn, heavy hand on the priest's bony shoulder, searching his eyes for answers. They were not the eyes of an old man, defeated by age in a bleak future. They had within them a spark of pure determination, marred only by guilt. "Enough riddles. Why did you bring me here?"

"I require the use of Ascara," he revealed, gazing down upon the hilt of the Callaghan's sword. The ranger withdrew from Malenek, his hand fingering Ascara's handle, almost to protect it from Balen's dogged eyes. "I require her magical fire to forge this land anew," continued the priest, "and to herald us into a new age."

Callaghan's concern grew quickly. Malenek was not the first to lay his sights on Ascara ever since Master Carrillo had nominated him as their Elite. He had been chosen over older, wiser rangers, yet none had objected to the decision, knowing he was worthy to wield her flame.

"I know others have desired its power, my friend," said Malenek, reading the ranger's sour expression, "but I am not them."

"That's what they all say, yet you are vague in exactly how you intend to use her," challenged Callaghan. "To rule perhaps?"

"Despite the title the Heroshin king granted me, I do not wish to lord over these lands like Dannen Gallo of Nimongrad once did. There was a time I could have made my mark as a member of the Alliance, but I did not. Ask yourself, Callaghan, have you ever known me to be a power monger?"

"Then why do you need Ascara?" Callaghan repeated, growing tired of asking the same question, troubled by the lack of a clear-cut answer.

"I need her fire, my friend. It will help guide us into a world where all people, north or south, east or west, light or dark-skinned, are equal. I can no longer live in a world where councillors and politicians get fat while sending scores of young soldiers to die, while kings and rulers make people breed purely to bolster their depleted armies. Now is the time for a purge!"

Callaghan stood his ground as Malenek shook his fist before him, the old man's speech still resonating around the room. The ranger saw through the façade. He had been wrong. There was no hunger for power, only anger, and guilt, and true belief. A greedy man could be struck down, but a man with total conviction in his ideas was a terrifying force.

"I will ask again for the last time, Balen. Tell me your plan or I will take my leave."

"I cannot tell you, old friend, for your sake," said Malenek, stung by the ranger's ultimatum. "You must trust me, and take a leap of faith."

"Then we are at an impasse." Why would he not tell him? Callaghan thought. Was the answer so horrific?

"So it would seem," agreed Malenek. The two men locked eyes for a moment, as the last shreds of their longstanding friendship disintegrated in a stalemate.

"Come Jaelyn," said Callaghan, "we have overstayed our welcome."

The apprentice, who had sunk into the shadows, followed Callaghan as he exited the room. Jaelyn glanced back at Malenek, who, with deep regret, politely nodded to the Zalestian.

"You knew he wanted the sword," Callaghan hissed at Volan Hesh, waiting for them at the top of the stairwell. Volan felt the betrayal of his ranger brother, and bore it with a heavy heart.

"I am sorry," he muttered. "I did, but it is not what you think. He is not a tyrant. He is a good man. A visionary."

"Then his words fail where his vision ends," barked Callaghan. "What is he planning?"

"I… it is… bigger than all of us," stuttered Volan, looking past Callaghan to Lord Malenek. "It is for the good of the people," he added, though Callaghan suspected the utterance was for his own reassurance rather than to try and persuade him. Was this really the wise ranger he once knew? Or had he been blinded by Malenek's mysterious vision for the future?

"If it were for the good of the people," whispered Callaghan, leaning closer so only Volan could hear, "why are you both so conflicted?"

"Would you rather we were blindly pursuing our goals, without any regard for the consequences? Like you, wandering overseas, and for what? One meagre boy?" Callaghan's dread deepened. These were not men driven mad by desire. They were reasonable men who were considering executing a plan that was, in their minds, both horrific and yet an absolutely necessity.

"I am assuming you act without the knowledge of the other rangers?" he asked Volan.

"The rangers are too few. We have lost many to the war. One man can no longer turn the tide."

"One man can always make the difference," said Callaghan. "You should know this better than anyone." Volan stepped aside, his fellow ranger's damning judgement too much to bear.

"Please, Callaghan," begged Volan, grabbing his arm as he brushed past.

"I will make sure Master Carrillo and the other rangers hear of this," warned Callaghan, shrugging of Volan's hand. The ranger and his apprentice hurriedly descended the spiral staircase. Malenek stepped out of the study and joined Volan as Callaghan disappeared from sight, leaving them only the echo of his footsteps.

"What do we do now?" asked Volan. "There are few tools of magic left in these lands, all under heavy guard, and all too delicate to wield. Ascara was to be the simplest path."

"Do not worry, Volan. He will return with the sword." Malenek said, as he strode back to his study.

"With all due respect, my Lord, I know Callaghan. He is a ranger, like me. His resolution will not sway."

Malenek paused, the flame of a nearby torch casting shadows over his face with a fiery forked tongue.

"Who said I was talking about the ranger?"

"My Lord?" asked Volan, confused.

"Follow them," instructed Malenek, ignoring him. "Force Callaghan to draw Ascara out."

"My Lord, I cannot," Volan stated, frustrated by the situation he now found himself trapped in. "He is my brother-in-arms. I will not attack him."

"You will not have to. Now go."

CHAPTER THREE

DEATH OF A RANGER

CALLAGHAN HASTENED THEIR DEPARTURE FROM MYTOR CASTLE, Jaelyn struggling to keep up. The chill of the sea breeze stung as they left the protection of the walls and crossed the gorge. Aquill had already set, the dark sky tinged with an aqua hue as Ygrain cast a cold green glow upon the mists. They were halfway across the narrow rocky bridge when Callaghan stopped, his hand on Ascara's hilt. Jaelyn spotted torch lights pursuing them from the castle.

"Master, they are coming."

"I know," replied the ranger, turning to confront Malenek's men. "Keep going. I will deal with them."

"I will not leave you to face them alone," said Jaelyn. Together, the master and his apprentice held their ground as the small party of Malenek's soldiers approached, led by Volan.

"Are you here to fight me, Volan?" asked Callaghan.

"I would never fight a fellow ranger," he replied. "I am here to beg. Please, give us Ascara."

Callaghan unsheathed his beautiful blade, slicing through the night air with an imposing shrill. "And if I do not?"

"Callaghan, do not do this," said Volan. "I will not fight you, but these are not my men." As if to back up his words, the small band of men withdrew their own weapons, though none as grand as Ascara.

"Jaelyn, stay close." Callaghan hoped he might scare them off with the sword's magic. He lifted the hilt to his lips, and whispered the incantation to the red jewel, within earshot of his Zalestian apprentice.

"Ascentio Risaar Emanos."

The flame spread out and engulfed the blade, the ancient symbols etched into the steel glowing brightly within the fire. The approaching men halted in their advance. At first Callaghan believed he alone had dissuaded them, but he quickly realised they were not staring at his sword, but at something that lay behind him. He could sense the change in the air, another spark of magic.

Jaelyn cast a spell in his native Zalestian tongue. Callaghan turned to see the façade of his apprentice disappear, an elaborate masquerade he had fallen victim to, replaced with a gleeful, contemptuous sneer. The sting of deceit pulsed through his body as silver light and smoke sparked from Jaelyn's fingertips. Callaghan tried to slice at the blast with Ascara, but the spell rushed at him, striking him backwards. He landed hard, his limp head hanging over the edge of the abyss. Ascara clanged beside him, her flame evaporating into the chilling night as the ranger lost his grip.

The Zalestian loomed over Callaghan's unconscious body. He picked up Ascara, admiring it closely for the first time. For months he had travelled with the ranger and his fabled blade, always within reach, but useless without the words that summoned forth Ascara's hidden beauty.

Volan snatched Ascara from the Zalestian's dark hands. He had enjoyed no part of this plan, and less so now seeing a Zalestian handling a sword that had been gifted to generations of rangers. He glowered a warning to the dark-skinned mage, one that required no words. Volan slid Ascara into his belt, before turning his attentions to Callaghan's body.

"Is he...?" Volan started, but he could not bring himself to say it.

"The curse I used was fatal," said Jaelyn.

"Could you not have disarmed him without bringing death with you?" barked Volan, his gruff voice shredded by guilt.

"I have spent weeks at sea alone with this man. He would have never agreed with our plan. This was the easiest way. It was a quick death."

"And what if I cannot conjure the fire?"

"Then what use is having a ranger at all?" retorted Jaelyn. Volan ignored his sneers, kneeling down by Callaghan's side to whisper a prayer.

"Gods of the Elements, you give us life through your powers. Ygrain forges our bodies. Aquill makes them clean. Risaar fills them with fire. Whirren lets us breathe. You have guided Callaghan through this life, and now you guide him into the next, as his body returns to the dust. May you find peace in Illyria, brother," he added, touching his forehead. "The Elementals know I never will."

"The gods will reward you for the part you play in our plan," said Jaelyn, as if it was matter of fact. Volan rose up, grimacing at the mage.

"No boy, they will not. I have accepted my fate. My ashes will be cast over Enara in a state of Ttarus for all eternity. There is no peace for me. You two," he shouted at the two closest soldiers. "Take the body to the castle. The least we can give him is a proper burial."

Before the pair could carry out the command, Jaelyn kicked Callaghan's body over the edge.

"What did you do that for?" screamed Volan, his hands clutching Jaelyn by his scrawny neck. Tears welled up in his eyes as he forced the Zalestian to the edge of the stone bridge, ready to toss him over so he could join Callaghan.

"We do not have time for the pleasantries of a funeral," hissed Jaelyn. "Release me, Volan. Lord Malenek is waiting." The ranger gathered his emotions and freed the young mage from his grip. Jaelyn marched back to Mytor Castle. The soldiers, sensing a change in hierarchy, followed him. Only Volan remained, peering down into the dark, ghostly mists below.

"Forgive me, my brother," the ranger whispered against the wind. Volan composed himself and hastened back to the confines of the castle, so that their plan could finally be put into action.

On the underside of the bridge, Callaghan clung to the rock.

"I forgive you, Volan," he whispered back. His muscles were burning at the sheer effort not to just let go and drop into the darkness. He panted and groaned as he started to climb back up with skin-torn hands, hauling himself onto the bridge. Blood streamed from his palms, the cuts soiled with dirt. As he gulped in the cold Mytor air, Callaghan mulled over Jaelyn's betrayal. How had he been so blind to the deception? He could make no sense of it, instead channelling his anger towards more pressing concerns.

Callaghan staggered to his feet. Mytor Castle loomed before him now, the black rock against Ygrain's green glow more unwelcoming than before. The ardent ranger tried to ignore the pain and approach the castle with stealth, but he was haggard from his brush with death. He could make out the minor movements of guards on the western wall, but part of the castle was built into the mountain itself. Callaghan tore some shreds from his cloak and wrapped them around his well-worn hands. It afforded him some protection as he scaled the castle's mountain side, aiming for a small, innocuous window.

The window led to a makeshift sleeping quarters for a large number of people, the bedding squashed tight together. A few of Malenek's volunteers helped each other with their armour, their spirits serious and proud, not the camaraderie Callaghan had come to expect of Amarosian soldiers. He counted the bedding, piled on top of one another. If Malenek did indeed have an army, the small castle itself was not big enough to support one for a long period of time. Callaghan gripped the wall as he waited for the last few soldiers to leave. Once they had gone, he slipped through the window.

The soldiers' voices echoed in the corridor outside. Callaghan stalked them, using the shadows and corners to conceal himself. The castle was scant of the ornate detail found in others, such as the exuberant Palace du Chatallis in Perhola, or the majestic Hamarhus Castle in Hylan. Malenek was a utilitarian, spending whatever wealth there was on his people rather than prizes and possessions.

The men he followed joined a stream of others headed towards the main banquet hall. Once upon a time Malenek had offered sermons here. Callaghan recalled the first time he had heard one. There had been only a dozen or so people in attendance in those days, and he had been a very different man, broken and without purpose.

The ranger crept up a staircase that led up to a small balcony overlooking the hall. From here he had a perfect view of Malenek's meagre army. They were roughly one hundred strong, just as the marauder Maulin Lamn had indicated. Barely a regiment, Callaghan thought, never mind a full-scale military force. The men sat hunched at two long tables, where a feast had been laid out. A curious thing, Callaghan noticed, was that very few of the men were eating. A heavy atmosphere hung in the air. It was like the aftermath of a battle, as if they had already survived the bloodied fields, rather than a hearty meal marking the start of a campaign.

If that had not been curious enough, Callaghan then caught sight of a creature that could not possibly exist; a giant carved from stone, roughly resembling a man, but one conjured by a sinister imagination.

A golem.

This truly was a castle of horrors, thought the ranger, as his attention was rapt by this beast of legend. At first he had mistaken it for an out of place statue, but the giant stone man had then moved as it heard Malenek enter, accompanied by Volan and Jaelyn. The small troop of men rose to their feet as the trio marched into the room.

"Gentlemen, our time is at hand," announced Malenek, holding up Ascara. He passed the sword to Volan. "Show them, Volan. Light the way."

The rogue ranger held the sword up as Jaelyn whispered the incantation into his ear.

"Acsentio Risaar Emanos," repeated Volan.

Nothing happened.

"Perhaps I should try," said Jaelyn.

"No!" hissed Volan, as he readied himself for another attempt.

"Clear your thoughts," said the mage. "Magic requires concentration."

"Acsentio Risaar Emanos."

Ascara's steel blade roared to fiery life, burning a bright silvery white, before returning to its normal orange hue. A chorus of murmured amazement resonated from the soldiers, but Malenek noticed that the flame's colour troubled Jaelyn.

"Is something wrong?" he asked the mage.

"No, it... it is nothing," Jaelyn replied. As Malenek stepped forward to address his men, the mage glanced out of the stain glassed window to the rocky bridge beyond. Could the sword have absorbed the spell? Jaelyn wondered, scanning the room for signs that Callaghan had survived, but finding none.

"As promised," proclaimed Malenek, "Ascara, the sword of Risaar, God of Fire." There was a roar of celebration and acclaim, but the priest hushed them with a wave of his arms. "Men, you are about to make the ultimate sacrifice," he said in a humbler tone. "It is my hope that you do this so that we may save our world. Do not forget to write your name in blood, or else your sacrifice will be in vain." Malenek produced a piece of parchment, and lay it down on the table along with a sharp quill. He turned to Volan, still clutching the burning sword. "You know what to do."

"Yes, my Lord." Even from the balcony Callaghan could hear the quivering uncertainty in Volan's voice. What was it Malenek required of the ranger that had him wrestling some inner turmoil?

The priest laid his hand on Volan's shoulder. "It is you that has the heaviest burden, my friend, but it is for all of Enara."

"Thank you, my Lord," muttered the rogue ranger.

"Gort," said Malenek, addressing the golem. Even from his hidden perch, Callaghan felt the ground tremble as the stone man stomped his mountainous feet across the floor.

"Yes," grumbled the creature.

"Remain here and watch over Volan."

"I could do this for you," said the creature eagerly. "I could wield the sword."

"No doubt," said Malenek, smiling as if Gort were an eager child, "but you are destined for greater things. I will need you when we march out upon Amaros. For the moment, this is your task."

"Yes, my Lord," said Gort with a resounding groan. Malenek and Jaelyn left the room, as Gort closed the double doors behind them, trapping the soldiers with himself and Volan.

"Who will go first?" Volan asked. After a moment of trepidation, a brave farmer named Martyn Keyll stepped forward. Callaghan watched as he took the quill and stabbed it into his own hand, before scribbling his name on the parchment in rich, red blood. Whatever the plan was, thought Callaghan, it involved blood magic. Old magic. There were so few mages left in these lands, Callaghan wondered how had Malenek devised such a plan? And who else may be in league with him?

Once Martyn had signed his name, he presented himself before a hesitant Volan, the first soldier in Malenek's new army.

"Are you ready?" Volan asked the farmer, although he could have been asking it of himself. Martyn nodded tentatively.

Even perched up high, Callaghan sensed the man's fear, bedazzled by the flames licking Ascara's steel. Volan raised the sword. Martyn Keyll closed his eyes and whispered a prayer. Callaghan could not drag his eyes away. He wanted to shout out and put a stop to this madness, this otherworldly magic, but he would be discovered and killed. He gripped the wall tight as Volan plunged the fiery blade through the soldier's heart.

The life force flowed from the farmer, still standing before Volan, his executioner. He wrested Ascara from the flesh of the warm corpse. The limp body flopped to the ground. Everyone - Volan, the soldiers, even the stone man Gort - were silent, afraid to breathe.

The errant ranger struggled with his emotions. A single tear escaped. It landed in the warm pool of blood, causing the faintest of ripples. Volan glimpsed his own reflection in the red puddle, that of a disgraced ranger. He was shocked to see a manifestation of Callaghan in the blood, hovering above him. Volan scanned the balcony, but there was nothing there. Perhaps the gods are judging me already, he thought.

"Next," Gort grunted, snapping Volan back to the here and now.

Callaghan, out of sight, chastised himself for being so easily spotted. He wanted to leap down and stop these deluded men from sacrificing themselves, but they would in all likelihood try and kill him for his troubles. As skilled as he was, there could only be a grim fate in fighting one hundred men unarmed. He had to uncover more details about Malenek's plan before it was fully achieved, and learn what pushed the plotters to take such perilous action.

The ranger retraced his steps back through the castle, avoiding Malenek's servants and minions. He made his way towards the study, his movement still stunted by his injuries. He rest within the safety of the shadows before attempting to tackle the stairwell leading up.

Footsteps stalked down the steps towards him. Callaghan broke from cover, doubling back to slip behind a nearby door that led to private sleeping quarters. He left the door ajar just enough to catch a glimpse of the man passing. Through the slit Callaghan spied a man he knew by the name of Salamon Silnor. Malenek's foul tempered horse-keeper reeked of fire and burnt flesh, his smooth bald head scorched and scarred. Salamon descended further down into the castle's depths, his footsteps trickling away. Callaghan wondered what in the name of the Elements was going on in this castle of horrors. Whatever Salamon was up to would have to wait; his master was the more pressing priority.

The window of the room he was in was almost directly below the study. Callaghan balanced himself on the window sill, and then scaled up the stone surface, a task made more difficult by his frayed fingers.

Voices spilled out of the window as he ascended. The ranger tried to overhear, but this side of the castle faced the black sea. The roar of the waves coupled with the cold wind whipping his face made it near impossible to listen in from this distance. He shifted his grip to try and better his vantage point, while at the same time aware that one wrong footing would lead to his certain death. The ranger had already appeared to die once today, he was unsure if he could dodge that inevitable fate again so soon.

"Those are my private journals," said the priest, still out of sight. Callaghan moved closer to peer through the window. As he stretched across, he spied Jaelyn standing beside one of the bookshelves, reading a volume he had plucked at random.

"I apologise, my Lord," said the Zalestian, placing the journal back on the bookcase, although it remained jutting out from the rest. "I was intrigued by your recollection of meeting Callaghan for the first time. How could a legend of your people be so troubled within?"

"It was his troubles that made him great," replied Malenek. "Remember that," he added as a warning.

"Yes, my Lord."

"Your deception and disposal of Callaghan was a turning point in this plot. You do your master's bidding well, Jaelyn."

Callaghan hugged the wall, striving to hear the conversation within over howling gusts of wind.

"It is regretful that he did not join us, my Lord," said Jaelyn. "An Ishkava

Ranger would have been a formidable ally."

"We are fortunate then to have Volan... for the time being," replied Malenek, his voice trailing off.

"The rangers will soon be a remnant of the past." Callaghan's eyeballs flared as Jaelyn announced the end of his brotherhood with such casual conviction.

"Indeed," said Malenek, "as will all things." Jaelyn moved out of the spying ranger's vision. Callaghan grabbed the ledge, sidling over to the other side for a better view. He could now see Malenek standing before the map of Amaros.

"Our first true test will be the royal city of Perhola," said the priest, his long, aged fingers tracing a path on the map. "From there we will make our way south to Gorran, taking on any resistance from the towns along the border between Heroshin and Legoria. After we take Gorran, we must follow the path along the Rundhale border, where we may encounter some resistance from the Etraihu or even the horse masters. They will be swiftly dealt with, before moving east to Calisto."

"What of the rest of the Heroshin region?" asked Jaelyn, noting the area Malenek had left out to the north-west. "What of the kingdom of Hylan? Or Barroch Bay?"

"We need not concern ourselves with Hylan," said Malenek, a subtle threat in his tone. "We will take Perhola. That sacrifice will be enough from Heroshin."

"But from what Callaghan told me of your land, Hylan holds a significant number of people."

"We will not attack Hylan!" snapped Malenek. The Zalestian did not wish to push the point, but it was crucial to his master's schemes.

"And what if our plan has not come into effect by the time we reach Calisto?" urged Jaelyn. "What if we require a greater number of souls?"

Souls? Callaghan thought. They talked in riddles the ranger could not yet unravel.

Malenek stepped over to the window, inhaling a calming breath of night air. Callaghan flattened himself against the wall, mere inches from the lord of this land. The priest stared over the dark world, Ygrain's pale green glow casting its aura over the eerie mists and murky sea, while Whirren shone bright in the opposite corner of the sky. From here Callaghan wondered if he could kill his old friend, if he could grab hold of him and send them both hurtling down to their watery graves. No, he thought, these two are not the only conspirators in this plot. He had to learn more.

"I will lead the army over the sea to Zalestia," answered Malenek. "Then we will have the beginning of the end." Callaghan tried to make sense out of this, but the schemers spoke in ambiguities while the wind lashed at his ears, intermittently deaf to their words.

"You should return to Zalestia, Jaelyn, and make sure the Stone of Spirits remains hidden," said Malenek. "Zahyr Zaleed Khan may yet discover it with his new contraption."

"The desert winds will keep it hidden in Errazure's tomb," assured Jaelyn, "although I dare not linger here any longer than I must. I have another task to perform for my master before you march from Mytor."

"What task?" quizzed Malenek, his face showing signs of doubt in his accomplice. "You mentioned nothing of this earlier?"

"It concerns the prophecy," revealed the dark mage.

"The prophecy cannot be fulfilled," said Malenek. "Your father and I have seen to that."

"My master believes there is one in Amaros who may yet hinder our plans."

"Surely with Callaghan dead there can be no other," said Malenek. "Oldwyn Blake perhaps, but he is locked away in Calisto's Black Tower, driven mad by a decade in his own company. Besides, without his staff, he is useless."

"While the future is never absolute, the divination my master had left little room for doubt," warned Jaelyn. "This individual could destroy everything we have worked so hard to create."

"Do you know who it is you seek?" Malenek asked.

"No, but my master provided me with a spell to lead me to them."

Jaelyn reached deep into his robes and produced a small knife. He murmured a spell while making a cut in the tips of each finger of his right hand. As he screamed the last words of the incantation, he flicked his hand towards Malenek's map with a wisp of silver energy. Specks of blood soaked into the parchment. The bloodstains moved toward each other, finally converging on one area of the map, in the expansive Elgrin Forest, near the town of Tilden.

"This is where our danger lies. What is this place, Tilden?"

"It is a small town, nothing but farmers and traders."

"Difficulties lie in all shapes and sizes. Surely you know this?"

"Yes, but… The forest itself…" Malenek paused, recalling a vague memory. "It is home to the elves."

"Elves?" asked Jaelyn.

"Creatures much older than man," explained Malenek. "They were once wise in the ways of magic, but they came to view it as unnatural. They saw how it perverted those who abused it, and so they abandoned it after the Legorian War. They are simple tree dwellers now. They covet their privacy, away from the other races of Amaros."

"Do they pose a threat to us?" he asked. "To the plan?"

"No, but they are best avoided," said the priest. "Anyone who trespasses in their forest is never heard from again. Just because they do not use magic anymore, does not mean they are not capable of defeating those who wield it. If you infringe upon their land, you risk alerting them to our plan."

"And if I do not go, the threat will remain unchecked," argued Jaelyn.

"This is my master's bidding. I must complete my task."

Malenek eventually nodded in agreement, succumbing to Jaelyn's logic. The mage offered the old priest his hand, which Malenek gripped in earnest.

"Good luck, Lord Malenek. May you bring peace to all of Enara."

"And to you, Jaelyn. Take whatever you need to complete your mission." He stared after the Zalestian as he left the study. A few moments later, the thundering doors of the castle creak open, and from his hidden vantage point Callaghan spied Jaelyn on horseback, crossing the rocky bridge.

Callaghan clung to the cold wall until Malenek had vacated the room. He clutched at the window ledge and hauled himself inside, his footsteps light on the flagstones. He gazed at the map of Amaros, the smear of red Zalestian blood still stained across Elgrin's green trees. Callaghan had brought Jaelyn here under the guise of teaching him the ways of the Ishkava Rangers. He had allowed himself to be deceived, but now was not the time for castigation. First he had to retrieve Ascara and stop Volan. Only then could he pursue Jaelyn and prevent him from assassinating the innocent life his mysterious master's aim was now centred upon.

Callaghan returned to the balcony within the banquet hall. He gazed down, aghast, forgetting the need to hide away. It took every ounce of self-control not to make a sound, wrenching any screams back down into his gut. One hundred corpses lay slain across the stone floor. The only people left alive were Gort and Volan. The desolate ranger clutched Ascara, the blade still burning in his hands. The double doors opened, and Malenek entered alone. Callaghan was surprised to see that the old priest shared his shock and terror.

"It is done, my Lord," muttered Volan, devastated by his handiwork. Ascara's fire evaporated, leaving her blade clean of any crime. The repentant ranger placed her on the table next to the parchment, scrawled with the signatures of the dead, written in their own blood. Volan picked up the list of martyrs and handed it to Malenek. The priest read the names, trying to remember each one.

"The people of Enara will remember your great sacrifice, Volan." Malenek's fist tightened around the blood-signed parchment, the red ink staining his hands. Malenek withdrew his own sword, a soldier's stock, not as decorative or as fascinating as Ascara, but that was the point. A bland weapon of man, untainted by the magic handed down by the Elementals. Volan closed his eyes and exhaled deeply.

Callaghan realised too late what Malenek intended to do. "No!" he screamed as the priest plunged his sword through Volan's heavy heart. Callaghan leapt from the balcony to the curtains and clambered down to the banquet hall. He rushed over to Volan, catching the ranger's body as he fell. Gort stepped out to stop Callaghan, but Malenek waved his stone servant back, somewhat stunned by the ranger's reappearance.

"I... see... them," Volan wheezed with his last breath. As the light left the dying man's eyes, Callaghan was aware of a disturbance in the natural order of the world. The room itself seemed to inhale a deep, ominous breath. A strange, bitter glow emanated from within, pulses of silver light surging over the corpses. Callaghan realised it was not one light, but one hundred. His eyes struggled to focus as the radiance took shape and form, slowly revealing the outlines of men, ghostly echoes cast in a morbid light, strands of silver energy dancing around them. Callaghan knew immediately what they were, but he could not bring himself to believe his own eyes.

"Spirits of vengeance," he whispered. They were only myths, and in all his adventures he had never yet seen one. They were those unfortunate souls killed by magic, yet granted a second chance by the person who had claimed their revenge. They were ghost stories told to children, and now they stood before him.

"It worked," Malenek whispered in astonishment. "It worked!" He dropped his sword and stepped forward to survey his supernatural creation. The old man was overcome with a flood of emotions; sadness, triumph, but mostly joy, thrilled that his plan was beginning to take substance and form in this army of spirits. They were growing used to their surroundings, focusing their energies on their individual forms, returning to what they had looked like in the physical world.

Callaghan watched in awe, as he carefully lay Volan's body down. How had the priest had discovered the secret of their resurrection? And how was he, the Ishkava Ranger Elite, going to stop them? With Malenek and Gort distracted, Callaghan retrieved his sword.

"Balen." Malenek turned, dismayed to find himself staring along the length of Ascara's blade into Callaghan's enraged eyes. The spirits' whispering grew louder as they fully enveloped their new lease of life. Malenek glanced over his celestial creations, his ultimate weapon. Callaghan sensed that somehow Malenek was communicating with these ghosts without speaking, as if they shared one mind. The army gathered behind their master and commander in formation. And it truly was an army now. Malenek could do little with one hundred soldiers, but with one hundred spirits he could breach any city wall, reach any ruler who did not submit to his plan.

The overheard conversation between Malenek and Jaelyn finally made sense. Even with a small number of these spirits, the priest could conquer all of Enara.

"I offer you one last chance to join me, old friend," begged Malenek, stretching his hand out to Ascara, edging the blade aside. "Events are already in motion; there is no stopping it now." Callaghan was still processing everything that was happening. The golem loomed beside Malenek, while the spirits drew closer. He quickly banished his fear of these unknowns, and focused solely on Malenek.

"I will die before I allow you to take this catastrophe any further," avowed Callaghan. "I swear it upon Risaar's name."

"Then so be it," said Malenek.

Before the ranger could strike, the spirits marched straight through their master, bearing down upon Callaghan. He retreated, slicing Ascara at the first spirit, but it was futile. The blade passed right through the ghost with little effect, briefly disrupting the spirit's energy like a hand through fog. Callaghan resisted the urge to flee. He needed to know for sure if the old myths were true; he needed to know exactly what he was dealing with. Withdrawing further, he brought Ascara's hilt to his lips and whispered the magical prayer. Her flame soon warmed Callaghan's face, while the oncoming spirits sent chills down his spine. One of the spirits had gained a little distance on the others. Callaghan thrust Ascara's flaming blade at the newly born ghost, aiming for the heart.

Let this work, he prayed. Let this burn them back to oblivion, and I will end it here and now.

The sword cut through the air and into the spirit's ethereal body. It stood unharmed, but Ascara's magical flame had wavered and extinguished before the blade emerged on the other side. If Risaar's sword could not stop these abominations, Enara was doomed. Callaghan's only hope now lay with whoever Jaelyn's had been sent to kill.

The leading spirit snatched at him with its transparent hand. Callaghan spun on the heels of his boots and sped towards the large stained glass window. He scooped up a battle shield that lay on the ground, thrusting it up as he exploded out of the castle in a throng of coloured glass. The ranger landed hard on the shield, using it to skim down the sheer slope. Even though his vision was shaken by the ride, Callaghan could see the approaching abyss that would soon swallow him whole. Sparks flew as he tried digging Ascara into the cliff, but she could not penetrate the black rock at this speed. Callaghan careered closer to the edge, the dark mouth of the narrow gorge ready to swallow him whole.

Just before the shield left the cliff, Callaghan sprung off, sailing over the gap. While in the air he gathered the sword in both hands. With little strength left, he stiffened his arms and managed to scream out the incantation.

"Acsentio Risaar Emanos!"

Ascara's blade burst with the fire of the Elemental once more. Callaghan hit the other side, directing all his momentum into the sword's hilt. This time, with the added heat, Ascara cut deep into the black rock. He lost his grip, managing to hold onto the sword with one hand. The shield fluttered down, battering off the side of the chasm.

Callaghan grasped at the cliff and found a steady handhold. He wrenched Ascara from the rock wall, before ascending the remaining distance to the top. Once he had heaved himself over the edge, he stared across the abyss to Mytor Castle. Malenek stood behind the broken window, with his stone bodyguard and his assembly of spirits. Callaghan alone could not stop them, of that he was certain, but whoever Jaelyn had been dispatched to assassinate may know something that could aid him in his quest. With the weight of the world on his shoulders, Callaghan did not spare a second for respite as he rushed down the mountain path. He stole a horse from the town of Morghen, and rode south-west towards Elgrin Forest to seek out this saviour of Enara.

CHAPTER FOUR

THE ELVES OF ELGRIN

THE SHORT BLOND TUFTS OF KAEDIN'S HAIR POKED OUT FROM under the bed sheet, as did the tips of his pointed elven ears. He snored softly, blissfully ignorant of the fact the other members of his clan had been awake since Risaar's red dawn. They carried out tasks and chores while Kaedin dreamed. The young elf did not care for tending to the trees that they lived in, or collecting sap from their bark-covered hides. He did not give much forethought to fetching water so that they may make bread or tend to the gardens. All Kaedin cared about, all he fantasised of, was journeying to Mount Ishkava. He wanted to overcome the gruelling trek to the Ranger Temple, submit himself to their training, and, after passing the trials, become the first ever elven ranger in all of Enara. Perhaps the mighty Callaghan would recognise Kaedin as his successor, and grant him the gift of Ascara, Risaar's sword of fire.

As Kaedin imagined such things in his slumber, his younger sister Kamina cautiously entered his room, her footsteps nimble so as not to wake him. Her long, shiny hair fell upon her simple Elgrin green tunic, its humble appearance hiding the expert stitching of her grandmother's hands. She crept over to the bed, making a game of trying not to wake her brother until she was standing right beside his big, snoring face.

"Kaedin!" she yelled, shaking him. He stirred, swatting her away with lucid hands, murmuring something inaudible before returning to his dreams. Kamina giggled, not only at Kaedin's reaction, but also at what the immediate future held in store for him.

She skipped out of their family tree house and waltzed gracefully along the path of rope bridges that connected the village. Generations ago they had lived as the other races did, in houses on the ground, but since retreating to the forest, they had remained out of sight from those who came looking, relying on the trees for home, shade, and nourishment. Kamina listening as they creaked and whistled and sang in the wind. The twin suns crawled slowly over the horizon, winking through the canopy of breeze-blown trees.

She reached one of the ancient trees, so wide it had been shaped into a stairwell, the central column still beating healthily with sacred sap. Kamina danced through the hollow and down the beautifully sculpted steps inside its trunk. She could hear the tree's roots sucking up the water to feed its leaves and blossoms.

The sprightly elf emerged from an entrance between two giant roots. Nearby, her grandmother Lashara was feeding some of the forest birds with leftover bread. Lashara's frail body was bent at a crooked angle, while her hair had silvered with age. Their race was blessed with longevity beyond all others on Enara, and she was one of the oldest, having been granted the title of Elder many moons ago. Kamina's grandmother often joked that she was alive when the elves had decided to withdraw from the hostile lands of Amaros to the sanctity of Elgrin Forest. Kamina often thought Lashara was teasing her with these tall tales, but every so often the old elf would reveal something that made it seem true. She enjoyed the evenings when Lashara told fascinating stories of her youth, sometimes using drawings she had made, collected in books of illustrations.

"Good morning, grandmother."

"Good morning, child." The old elf broke up the bread and spread the crumbs for the birds. They proceeded to peck away at the ground in a frenzied hunger. Kamina ran past, waving to the farmers tending to the unobtrusive patches of gardens dotted between the trees. They grew enough to feed their entire clan, while maintaining a delicate balance with the forest.

She reached her destination, an inconspicuous storage hut made by bending the branches of two trees together. Until recently, it was where her sister Talia had kept stock to sell to the humans of Tilden. However, a nest of wood snakes had taken residence and spoiled the provisions.

The inside of the hut was dank, covered in dust and the shells of dead insects. The light of the twin suns was reduced to slivers in this place, but Kamina could make out Talia in the centre. She was dressed in dirty rags, wearing thick gloves that stretched up to her elbows. In one hand she held a giant thick sack that wriggled and jerked in her grasp. Talia was hunting the last of the wood snakes, whose skins resembled tree bark, making them difficult to discern in the forest. She spotted it with her keen elven eyes and snatched for it. The creature hissed in panic, evading Talia's gloved hand, slithering away between her legs. Talia flipped back and dived for the snake, but it snuck into the darkness behind some storage pots.

Kamina admired her sister in that moment, for she had the ferocious anger of one the elders, those who had once lived as warriors, unable to forget the brutality of battle. That was not to say she was not beautiful, all elven women were, but Talia often neglected her looks. She worked harder at her tasks than many of the males, though never seeking out their companionship. Kamina knew that beneath the grime and dirt of those responsibilities, Talia was the most radiant elf in all of Elgrin Forest. The sisters often bathed together in a nearby pool next to a small brook, and to Kamina she was like a princess from one of Lashara's vivid drawings.

Talia struggled to move the storage pots to continue her hunt for the elusive wood snake. It pre-empted her and darted out of its hiding place. Talia's hands moved swiftly, seizing it by the neck. She wrestled it into the sack to join its family. The snakes squirmed inside, hissing and writhing with nowhere to go. Only now did Talia notice Kamina watching her from the doorway. The young elf's grin caused a triumphant smile to break upon Talia's tired face. It quickly faded when she realised Kamina was alone.

"I asked you to fetch your brother," said Talia.

"I tried to wake him, but he barely stirred."

"That lazy…" she started, fuming with anger. She was interrupted by the thrashing wood snakes. Talia glanced at the sack, and then surprised Kamina with a wicked smirk.

*

The elven Ishkava Ranger Kaedin Elloeth worked his way into the dark belly of Baron Norrek Melo's fortress, carving up the false leader's minions with the magical fire sword Ascara. The blade had been bequeathed to him, the Ranger Elite, the ultimate defender of Amaros, by his predecessor and mentor, Callaghan Tor.

Kaedin battled heroically up the narrow stone staircase, pulverising all those who opposed him. He kicked open the locked wooden door of the Baron's private court, shattering it into splinters. There the Baron stood, the coward sweating with fear as he held his daughter, the beautiful Lady Nyssa, in front of him like a human shield. The Baron forced her to guard him by pressing a dagger against her tender neck.

"Let her go, Norrek!" commanded Kaedin, his authoritative tone almost causing the Baron's hand to drop the blade.

"You cannot kill me," shrieked Norrek. "It is against your precious code of honour."

Kaedin held out Ascara and pointed it at Norrek.

"I will make an exception in your case."

Suddenly Norrek started laughing. He let go of Lady Nyssa, who also began to chuckle.

Kaedin suddenly realised he no longer held a sword in his hand, but a snake, which turned to face him with evil yellow eyes.

Kaedin snapped out of the dream. A wood snake hissed and snapped in his face. Norrek and Nyssa's laughter was replaced with that of Talia and Kamina. Kaedin dropped the snake, which quickly slithered under the green sheets. He leapt out of bed, screaming in a manner more suited to an elven girl. He wrestled with the snake and his sheets, whooshing out of the house in a whirlwind of panic. His sisters hooted hysterically, trailed him outside. They found Kaedin rolling around on the platform wearing little more than his undergarments, attracting the attention of some of their neighbours with his high-pitched squealing.

"Get it off me!" he yelled. "Talia, get it off me!"

His elder sister replied by holding up the wood snake in her gloved hand for everyone to see. "You mean this little thing?"

Kaedin stopped jerking around. He picked himself up as the chuckles of onlookers died away, a piece of early morning entertainment to break up the day. Kaedin tried to sulk back inside the Elloeth home, but he was stopped by Talia blocking the entrance, the wood snake still hissing in her hand.

"You have had your fun, Talia," he moaned. "Now let me pass."

"When I tell you to do something, you do it," she warned, "or next time, it will be more than a snake and a little embarrassment, understand?"

"I was… tired," he tried as an excuse.

"Dreaming about your Ishkava Rangers no doubt," she said. "The other elves do not care for your fantasies of swords and sorcerers."

"Well once I have celebrated *Dira Adolyn* tomorrow, I will be of age to leave and join them," boasted Kaedin. "Then the others will hear of my heroic deeds."

"Of age or not, the elders will never allow it," she advised him. "Would you choose to become an outcast from your kin?" Kaedin stared to his feet in response. "I thought not. Everyone here does a job so that we are afforded the peaceful life our ancestors granted us. There is no room for your laziness and daydreaming. You had best remember that."

"And you are not my mother, Talia. You had best remember that." Kaedin immediately felt sorry for stirring the memory of their deceased parents. He had said it out of spite and frustration; he hated this place, he hated his ancestors for giving up magic, for giving up on the outside world. Where Talia saw a peaceful existence within the safe haven of Elgrin Forest, Kaedin felt a smothering confinement, as if they had been coddled like children into this life. He barged past her, retreating to his room.

Talia stood outside their home, reeling from the shock of her brother's outburst. She dropped the snake, allowing it to slither away to its freedom. Talia did not have the heart to chase after it. She clutched the decorative wooden railing, routed by her brother's malicious words. She focused on the forest floor far below, trying not to cry. Kamina stood beside her, taking hold of her hand. Talia squeezed it, offering up a smile while wiping her eyes.

"I am fine," she said. "When Kaedin is dressed ask him to come down and help me load up the cart." Kamina nodded as Talia drifted away, still haunted by unhappy memories of the past. The young elf watched her sister leave, before storming into their home. Kaedin emerged from his room, shabbily dressed in his green tunic.

"What did she say?" Kaedin asked.

Kamina kindly kicked him in the shin.

*

Kaedin and Talia loaded up the cart with supplies to trade in the market town of Tilden; elven bread, vegetables, as well as sought after items like sap and resin milked from the trees. Talia sensed disapproving eyes watching her. She gazed up into the surrounding branches and discovered Endo Eredu spying on them. He made no effort to hide himself, or the disparaging expression etched across his face. Although the elders allowed her this indulgent interaction with the humans, there were those who failed to comprehend the benefits of the arrangement. Talia had argued that the day may come when they needed the help of the humans, and that it was better to be civil neighbours than warring creatures of legend. She secretly liked the change of temperament garnered from the townsfolk of Tilden, perhaps as a result of her own turbulent past. Apart from the eldest elves, she had spent more time than any other out with the confines of Elgrin Forest. It was in recognition of her past that they allowed her this ritual, if only to keep in place the uneasy peace they and their ancestors had strived so hard for.

Nearby, Kamina led the noble steed Eshtel toward the cart that he would soon draw. His large muscles worked under a skin of fine chestnut hair, his forehead marked with a blemish of white. Kamina spoke to him, her voice soothing to his equine ears.

"I thought I told you to ready Eshtel," Talia demanded of Kaedin. "Why is Kamina doing it?"

"Because she is better with him than me," he replied. "He hates me, yet obeys her every command."

"Who knew horses could be such good a judge of character?" she quipped.

"What is that phrase the men use?" Kaedin recalled, "Never look gift horses in the mouth?"

"What are you implying?" asked Talia, thudding a pot of resin down upon the cart floor.

"You know fine well what it means," he said. "What I mean by it is that Kamina will soon celebrate her own *Dira Adolyn*…"

"She has more than two years before she reaches that age."

"You should tell her the truth before then," urged Kaedin. "She is old enough to understand now."

"Enough!" barked Talia, drawing attention not only from Kamina, but other elves working nearby. "It is my decision, not yours," she continued in a lower tone. "I mean it Kaedin. Not. Another. Word."

Despite her warning, Kaedin opened his mouth to object. The words caught in his throat as Talia fetched her axe, a curved elven blade that had belonged to their father, Kaman.

"I promise, I will take it to my grave," he stammered. She caught his cowardly stare resting upon the weapon, letting slip a small grin at his misplaced fear.

"Do not worry little brother. When death comes for you it will not be at my hand." Kaedin sighed with relief. "I am sure it will be through your own stupidity."

"Then why do you need father's axe?" he asked.

"We may need it for the journey to Tilden," she explained curtly. "To chop down some deadwood."

"You have never had need of a weapon before," noted Kaedin. Talia paused, observing a change in wind direction. Something was stirring, some malevolent force, too close to them for comfort.

"It is a dire time in the world outside this forest," she said without further explanation. "Now go help Kamina with Eshtel." Talia watched as the steed kicked up a fuss when Kaedin tried to slip the harness over his neck. Kamina approached the horse and gently calmed his neighs. As Talia felt the warm glow of pride in her bosom, she could not shake the foreboding shadow that clouded her senses.

CHAPTER FIVE

THE TOWN OF TILDEN

WITH THE SMALL CART LOADED, THE THREE ELVES OF THE Elloeth family trundled along through the outer reaches of Elgrin Forest, towed by Eshtel. The journey would take several hours, wandering in the shade of the trees, then across the grasslands surrounding Elgrin until they met a rarely used barren dirt road. They were already late because of Kaedin's lazy slumber, but Talia was confident that they would arrive to catch the masses at the midday market.

The land immediately surrounding the forest was wild and overgrown. Despite the humans establishing settlements in Legoria after the elves had retreated into Elgrin Forest, superstition kept them from wandering too close. Some younger children ventured near in the warmer parts of the year, daring each other to step into the forest, defying their parent's fables and laws as they mistook bravery for foolishness.

Further along, the elves joined the dirt trail that passed by a farmer's field. In the decades after the Legorian War, it had been the poorest of men that had crossed the borders to claim the land. They had cast aside their fears, finding the ground fresh and fertile, just as the elves had left it. Now those poor farmers' descendants were prosperous land owners with stock and servants. Hired farm hands tilled the soil, using a meagre looking horse, a malnourished bag of bones. Kamina, sat next to Talia at the reigns, watched the men, their skin a curious shade of rust from their work. The elven girl waved to them. They made no gesture of reply.

"Why do they not wave back?" she wondered out loud.

"Because they are seasonal workers, not from these parts," replied Talia, narrowing her eyes sideways at the two men baking in the midday heat. "They are afraid of us."

Eshtel grunted in agreement. The mule-like horse, hearing the sound of his fellow equine, started to neigh and kick at the farm hands in protest. They whipped the creature, but the sight of Eshtel was inspiring. The lesser horse kicked and bucked, managing to break free of the poorly fastened harness. He ran free, gathering all of his strength into a gallop, until he had escaped over a small hill. The two farm hands stood scratching their heads, each secretly planning to blame the other when their employer enquired about the loss.

That is what you get for not waving, Kamina thought, a smug little grin weaved upon her face. She caught Talia bearing a similar expression. They smiled at one another with a certain understanding, as they trundled onwards to Tilden, its walls now visible on the distant horizon.

Torg Magnale, a brutish yet amiable guard, stood slouched at the top of the watch tower adjoining the entrance to Tilden. He scrutinized the elven cart as it wheeled its way up to the gate. The elven female stared back at him with those sharp green eyes, greeting him with a curt nod. He signalled down to his fellow guardsmen, who slowly dragged open the heavy wooden doors. Torg kept a suspicious eye fixed upon them until they were well inside the town and the gate was firmly closed. His trepidation was unfounded; he knew that if raiders or thieves were to infiltrate the town, they would not use the elves. But still, he was uneasy in their presence, those incisive eyes seeing everything, their pointed ears pricking up at every whisper. They drifted out of his vision behind the taller buildings of the town square.

Torg turned his attentions back to the road. A movement out on the plains caught the corner of his eye, but he shrugged it off as paranoia spawned by the elves. To calm his nerves, he filled a pipe with Heroshin angelica herbs, fresh from the market, and lit them with the contents of his tinderbox.

Tilden's market was a hectic throng of townsfolk, nearby villagers and farmers, a mass of humans engaged in shouting, selling and haggling. Some of them stared as the elves' cart cut through the crowd. Talia steered Eshtel into a lane by the market square, bringing him to rest in a free space out of the way of the other sellers. Kaedin leapt out of the cart, excited when he saw the children of men gathering around a puppet show used by wandering teachers. His adventurous mind enjoyed the tales they brought with them, despite the fact they were written for infants.

"I am going to listen to the travelling teacher," said Kaedin.

"Take Eshtel to the stables first," instructed his sister as she freed the horse from the cart. "And take Kamina with you."

"I would rather stay here with you," said Kamina, as she slumped out of the back of the cart.

"It will be interesting," insisted Talia. "Besides, I know you secretly enjoy the stories."

"I do not," Kamina protested.

"You have an inquisitive mind, much like Kaedin," said Talia. "You should allow it to grow." Kamina frowned at her, taking hold of Eshtel's reigns as she followed Kaedin across the square. With the strength of a grown man, Talia swivelled the cart around with ease. She unclipped the side panel to use it as a market stall, showing what goods she had on offer. Two sets of footsteps approach her over the ground littered with hay; a heavy tread man and a light-footed young woman.

"Good day, Talia," said a welcoming yet authoritative voice behind her.

"Good day to you too, Master Melo, Nyssa," she said, turning to greet the Master of the Guard and his daughter who, like Kaedin, was blossoming into adulthood. Norrek stood proud in his uniform, clean-shaven, his thin hair combed over his head. He had a similar look in his eye to Torg, but was more hospitable to the elves than his guardsmen were. Although it had not yet harmed him, Norrek Melo often wondered if being known as a friend of the elves would prove to be a blessing or a curse for Tilden. Had it not been thrust upon him, and had Talia not continued to make her trips to the market, the decades-old town might still be living in dread of Elgrin's creatures.

Norrek's beautiful daughter Nyssa beamed at Talia, her dusty brown locks dancing over her moon-shaped face. Her hazel eyes asked a question her mouth dare not in front of her father.

"Kaedin has taken Kamina to watch the teacher if you wish to join them," Talia informed her.

"Thank you," she whispered, prancing away to find them. Talia continued preparing her goods, aware that Norrek still loomed beside her.

"I wish you would not encourage her," he said solemnly. "No good can come of it."

"Would it surprise you to learn that I agree?" His reaction was answer enough.

"Then why promote it so openly?" he asked, puzzled.

"Would you rather ignore it, and have them sneak off in secret?" she countered. "That is what brought them together in the first place. If nothing is to come of it, then they must discover this for themselves."

"I would rather lock her away in a very tall tower until your idiotic brother dies trying to climb Mount Ishkava." Norrek paused, realising he may have stepped beyond the boundaries of his tenuous friendship with Talia. When the elf turned to face him, she cracked a wry smile.

"Some days, Master Melo, I also wish for this."

*

Kamina and Kaedin stood apart from the children of men as the travelling teacher busied himself setting up his small box theatre. Some of the more anxious mothers eyed the pair with concern. There were very few fathers; most had been recruited into the Alliance army, stationed in Gorran or even Caspia.

"I still do not understand your fascination with these infantile history lessons," said Kamina, her arms folded.

"It is not a fascination," he said. "I just like hearing stories. I have heard all the elven tales a hundred times over. The best stories are about the Ishkava Rangers, and we have none."

"Then perhaps you will be in luck. The teacher is from the Heroshin region," observed Kamina, pointing to the scarlet colouring and symbols adorned the teacher's cart and clothes.

"Stay here," he ordered, as he marched over to the teacher, a stout, bearded man by the name of Ivan Moffett.

"Master teacher," Kaedin said, startling the tense man who was rushing to start the show.

"Yes yes, I know I am late, the show will be on... momentarily." The teacher was lost for words as he gazed upon the elf's face. Although there were rumours that on rare occasions the elves visited the towns surrounding Elgrin Forest, Moffett had never actually laid eyes upon one before. It was almost like seeing one of the Elementals. He could not help but be stunned by their beautiful, sculpted face and graceful appearance.

"Are you from Heroshin?" Kaedin asked excitedly. Moffett indicated with a nod that he was, his awe equalled by his fear. The elf was overly eager, his quick, excited movements making the teacher tense. "Do you know the way to the Temple of the Ishkava Rangers?" he begged.

"No-one... well... it's... supposedly..." Moffett stammered syllables together, but there was not, as far as Kaedin could tell, an intelligible reply within them.

"Have you ever met a ranger?" tried Kaedin. "Like Volan Hesh, or Dash Cole, or even... Callaghan Tor?"

Moffett gathered himself, and recalled to Kaedin that while he had never actually met any of the wandering warriors, a fellow teacher had told him of seeing the legendary Callaghan fight with his magical sword of fire.

"He claimed to have seen the ranger best five thieves while struggling with a broken arm, slaying them all with his fiery sword," said the teacher.

"Ascara," whispered Kaedin, revering the tale of the fabled weapon.

Before he could question Moffett further, the teacher excused himself to start the show for the restless crowd of children baying for his blood. Kaedin wandered back to Kamina, but he found she was not alone. Just as the teacher had been speechless in his presence, Kaedin was momentarily overwhelmed by the appearance of Nyssa Melo.

"Hello Kaedin," she said, stealing his breath away.

"Hello." A welcoming, doting smile spread across his face. Kamina watched the interaction with a certain proud delight afforded to siblings in these embarrassing moments, until the silence grew stale.

"So," she said, breaking the lovers' gaze, "did the teacher know where the Ranger Temple was? Or how to reach it?"

"What?" muttered Kaedin, still distracted. "No, he spoke nonsense. I do not believe he has seen an elf before."

"I think you forget just how... mythical you are to us," said Nyssa.

"We may be mythical, but we are not as legendary as the Ishkava Rangers." Kaedin continued in the harshest whisper of secrecy. "He claims a fellow teacher once saw Callaghan fight off five thieves with a broken arm!" Kamina listened as Kaedin embellished the story. Talia had been right; while Kamina presented herself as only half-interested, deep down she was burning to hear every scrap of detail, every ounce of adventure. She chose to hide her enthusiasm for such things from the other elves, especially her own kin. They were a regular point of contention between her siblings. Their arguments were occurring more frequently as they approached Kaedin's *Dira Adolyn*. Kamina did not wish to encourage Kaedin further, worried that he might make good on his threat to leave Elgrin Forest, even as an outcast.

"His friend claimed to have witnessed him wielding Ascara, slaying the men where they stood. Imagine it! Risaar's sword of fire!"

As Kaedin revelled in the details, Kamina could not hide her disdain at the deaths the ranger had allegedly caused. She thought of her mother and father, two people she had known only as tombstones erected at the edge of Elgrin Forest. They had perished in an attack by raiders after travelling far beyond the safety of the trees. Kaedin tried to continue, but the story was spoiled for her now. Kamina shushed him as the teacher started.

"Today, I will tell you a story about the discovery of another land," Moffett announced. "Zalestia!" A few excited gasps escaped the younger children. When a sufficient hush had donned over the small audience, Moffett retreated behind the miniscule theatre. A small model fishing boat appeared on the unsophisticated stage.

"A fishing boat, the *Ulca Nores*, set sail from Calisto," boomed the teacher's voice from behind the box. "The fish had grown wise to the Caspian fishermen, and swam further out to sea. The *Ulca Nores* followed them, sailing out further than any ship had done before, hoping to return with a celebrated catch."

Just then the model boat collapsed in on itself. Moffett rose up from behind the box, muttering to himself as he tried to fix it, but the atmosphere was broken. The children laughed and jeered at his hopeless efforts.

"What use is a teacher if he cannot teach us what we already know?" chuckled a tubby boy near the back. Moffett faced his audience, hoping to turn the tide of disdain with calm, raised hands.

"Close your eyes children, and imagine that you are there, on the *Ulca Nores*. You can smell the sea air filling up your lungs, hear the flap of Whirren's winds filling up the sails. The small, rickety boat headed further than any ship had gone before, but soon found itself in more peril than anyone could ever imagine. They were chased by gigantic beasts into the expanse of storm-ridden seas known as the Badlands!"

Kamina closed her eyes as she imagined the smell of the sea, the spray on her face as the *Ulca Nores* chopped through the waves, manned by her fellow listeners. Apart from these trips to Tilden, the young female elf had never been beyond the trees of Elgrin Forest. However, her grandmother kept drawings and sketches of boats and ships and cities and the sea. In her mind, everything appeared as if illustrated by Lashara's delicate hand. Behind her she could see the massive forms of the beasts that lived below the water's surface, ferocious creatures with razor sharp teeth, far bigger than the tiny fishing vessel. Ahead of her, the sky quickly changed from a wispy blue to a dark, disheartening grey.

"The *Ulca Nores* had no choice but to battle through the Badlands," she heard Moffett say. The small boat braced for a wave as high as the tallest trees. Volleys of bright lightning scarred the black skies. Kamina peered through the frightful weather and spied a typhoon funnel spinning toward them. The entire crew spotted it. There was a sudden silence as they stared certain death in the face.

The raging funnel engulfed the boat.

As Kamina drifted deeper into her imagination, Kaedin found the courage to take Nyssa's hand in his. She smiled at him, indicating that they should slip away. While everyone else had their eyes closed, the young couple escaped, leaving Kamina alone in the company of her fictional seafaring shipmates.

*

Kaedin and Nyssa strolled along one of the town's few quiet streets. Nyssa listened as her elven companion moaned about the teacher.

"I cannot believe he would not tell me anything about the rangers. He just stood there, stunned, making no sense."

"Perhaps you are too handsome for your own good," she teased.

"What was the phrase you taught me? Beauty is in the eye that beholds it?" he said, taking her hand again, enjoying the feel of her fingers, smooth and delicate.

She paused in her stride. "Kaedin, do you still intend to leave Legoria when you are of age?"

"I do," he answered truthfully.

"I have heard rumours that the rangers are not allowed a partner, that they must be unattached, and give themselves to the noble cause of keeping the peace." Her fingers wrapped around his own, their bond now a trap.

"I have heard this also," he said, gazing down at their feet, at the space between, where awkwardness had just planted its seed.

Nyssa took his other hand. "Then perhaps I will become a ranger as well, and we can travel the lands together, like Flint and Sprong."

Kaedin laughed. "A female ranger?"

Nyssa dropped his hands. "Is it any more preposterous than an elven one?"

"No, but elves are naturally stronger than men, more agile and swift..."

"...and more arrogant," she added, "yet less adventurous. You live in the confines of a forest, locked away from the world. Why are you the only elf who wishes to walk away from all that?"

"Talia often jokes that I must have been dropped on my head when I was a child. She says I have a tendency for foolish, un-elf like behaviour."

"Like when we met?" she asked, smiling.

"Like when we met."

It was not uncommon for the children of men to become restless in their teenage years. Nyssa, being the daughter of the Master of the Guard, was more open to rebel in private behind her father's back, than throw a childish spat in his presence. Two years ago, before Talia had begun trading with the people of Tilden, Nyssa and some of the other children had trekked to the edge of Elgrin Forest, daring each other to wander within its bracken and trees. They had spotted an elf from the edge of the forest, gasping at his form. Their human chatter had disturbed him, and the elf had easily spied them hiding behind some bushes. They fled in fear, adrenalin pumping as they skirted through the trees and leaves. In her haste, Nyssa had fallen, twisting her ankle. The others ran, leaving her to the fate of the evil green-eyed elf.

Kaedin had approached the fallen human with a cautious curiosity. He had been visiting the graves of his parents, where he often sought solace after arguments with Talia. Like the humans, he too had been intrigued by the other beings of Amaros, those that lived beyond the forest. He often climbed the tallest trees to gaze at distant farmers or travellers. But now there was this girl in their forest, frozen in fear. Kaedin did not wish to take her back to the elves; they would be angry with the men and cause unnecessary antagonism between their two races.

The elf spoke to her, and while she did not understand his native elven tongue, his sounds were slow and smooth. She allowed him to examine her ankle, his fingers firm yet compassionate on her bare porcelain skin. He pointed out of the forest, towards Tilden. She nodded, understanding his intentions. With effortless grace, the elf lifted her up and carried her out of the forest, her face nestled into his chest. Nyssa was amazed by his strength; he was slightly taller than she was, yet raised her up as if she were made of feathers. He ran, faster than any man, speeding through the trees. She was so sure they would hit one that she closed her eyes, but soon they were out of the forest and trailing over the overgrowth and into the fields surrounding Tilden. Nyssa felt as if she were flying. The elven boy smiled as well, enjoying himself.

They reached Tilden shortly after nightfall. Rather than approach the gated entrance, Kaedin had leapt over an unguarded wall at the side. The girl had directed him to her father's house. He insisted on helping her inside, despite her pleading with him to go.

Nyssa's fears were not unwarranted, as Norrek caught them sneaking in. The guard was startled when he found his daughter with an elf. The furious father fumbled for his sword, ready to attack, but Nyssa stood in his way, defending her elven rescuer as she explained the events of the evening. Norrek begrudgingly thanked Kaedin, who repeated the words back in broken Amarosian. The elf had then fled, running full speed back to the forest, his heart fluttering, his thoughts captured by the human girl, and likewise, she with her elven hero. Meeting him was worth the punishment of chores and curfews her father handed down, although Nyssa took some pleasure in seeing the children who had left her helpless into Elgrin Forest suffer similar fates.

Kaedin's absence had not gone unnoticed. Talia, wishing to apologise, had searched for him at their parents' graves. She uncovered scenes of a struggle; human blood, and threads of Nyssa's clothing snagged on the bushes. Talia feared Kaedin may have been captured or kidnapped. Before she could return to the other elves with her alarming discovery, she spied her brother sneaking back to Elgrin Forest. Talia, driven by the panic that had seized her heart, forced the story out of him.

The next day, with the blessing of the elders, she rode Eshtel to Tilden carrying elven gifts for Norrek, an apology for Kaedin's intrusion on their land. The Master of the Guard was astonished by the quality and flavour of the bread, and suggested that, should Talia wish to trade, she would be more than welcome. Talia saw a certain logic in this; at the very least it may stop Tilden teenagers from wandering into their forest. Kaedin almost always accompanied her, if only to see Nyssa.

"Your Amarosian has improved a lot since then," she said, affectionately remembering that fateful day, "but I still like to hear you speak as you were meant to."

Kaedin stepped closer to her, their lips inches apart.

"What would you like me to say?" he asked.

"Anything," she replied, lost in his penetrating green eyes.

Kaedin spoke to her in his elven tongue, the smooth, captivating sounds sliding over her like Caspian silk. She closed her eyes, revelling in his nuances of his language. When he stopped, she opened them again. They were so close now that she could feel his hot breath on her face.

"I have a gift for you," she said. She reached into her pocket, and revealed a twine bracelet. "Happy Birthday. For tomorrow." Nyssa was disappointed when Kaedin did not accept the gift, as though it had affronted him. "Is something wrong?"

"We do not celebrate *Dira Nestyr*, our day of birth, in the same way that men do. We do not give gifts."

"Then I shall take it back," said Nyssa, feigning outrage.

"No. I am flattered. It is very kind of you. Tomorrow is not just any birth day; it is *Dira Adolyn*, the age of adulthood. Tomorrow I become a man. And we do receive gifts then."

"Good. I hope this will remind you of me when you stop being a child." She slipped the bracelet around his wrist. She smiled up at him, but he flinched in distraction, hearing something she could not perceive.

"You have to hide!" he exclaimed. Before she could argue, screams broke the peaceful calm of Tilden.

The warning bell tolled.

*

Kamina picked herself up from the wet wooden floor of the *Ulca Nores*. The ship was broken from its violent waltz through the Badlands. Her fellow crewmembers were battered and bruised, but they were alive and afloat, for now.

"Land!" bellowed one, a finger pointing at a vague phantom smudge on the horizon. The crew set about repairing the ship, limping toward the mass of land they assumed to be Amaros.

As they sailed nearer, Kamina could see a sharp reef protruding from the ocean, and beyond the blue lagoon they created, golden sun-kissed shores and a luscious green jungle of wild trees.

"Zalestia," she whispered.

"They were the first Amarosians to see that mysterious land," said Moffett, joining Kamina on the deck of the hand-drawn ship in her imagination.

"What did they find?" asked another child, bringing Kamina back to the reality of Tilden.

"Nothing," Moffett answered. "The little boat was damaged, and the captain decided to return to Amaros rather than strand his crew on unknown shores. They sailed around the Badlands, a significantly longer route. By the time they arrived back in Calisto, they had wasted away from hunger and thirst. Many thought them mad at first, talking of a land beyond the storm."

"When does Malenek appear?" shouted a podgy, impatient child, as Moffett fumbled with four model ships, props for the next part of the story.

"Well, around this time, Balen Malenek was only a young man, who wished to devote his life to the Elementals by joining the priesthood. However, his father was General Cabel Malenek of the Heroshin Army, Leader of the Guard in Barroch Bay. He wished for his son to follow in his footsteps, as he had done in his father's, and so Balen resigned himself to his father's aspirations. Cabel's position afforded him the luxury to grant his son any role he wished. He chose the royal guard to the king's ambassador."

"His first duty was to accompany the ambassador to the Caspian capital of Calisto. The Heroshin contingent had only been in the city a few days when the *Ulca Nores* returned. The news of another land sent shockwaves through all of Amaros, but perhaps none were more curious than young Malenek. An unprecedented union of countries - Heroshin, Caspia, Mytor and, of course, Legoria - decided that four ships, one named for each of the Elementals, would be built to journey across the sea and explore this new land. Balen Malenek was one of the first to volunteer."

Moffett set out the four finely detailed model ships. "Almost one year later, the ships were ready, the grandest ever constructed." His finger pushed one forward, bearing the symbol of the God of Air. "Malenek sailed on the *Whirren*."

"The *Risaar* was the first to be destroyed, struck by lightning in the Badlands." Moffett sparked some flint on one of the four model ships, setting it alight. The little model burnt quickly, leaving a pile of charred remains.

Kamina once again delved inside her mind, standing alongside Balen Malenek on the deck of the *Whirren* as they watched the *Risaar* burn. A typhoon caught the burning vessel, sucking the ship upwards in a vortex of fury. Kamina and Balen ducked as fiery debris rained down upon them. Balen ran to extinguish the fires.

"Next, the *Ygrain* was smashed upon the reef of rocks that surround the shore of Zalestia." Kamina could see the *Ygrain*, her hull bludgeoned on the deadly sharp rocks, her crew spilling out to sea, swimming for the *Whirren* and *Aquill*, both anchored at a safe distance.

"The crews of the remaining two ships navigated the rocks in longboats, eventually landing on golden shores." Kamina stood at the head of one of the scout boats, eyeing the approaching shores with anticipation. She jumped out of the boat and ran from the surf to the idyllic beach, the grains of sand sparkling like tiny diamonds in the daylight. The men behind her pulled the boats ashore, pausing to admire the wondrous new world that lay before them. The trees were unlike anything they had ever seen, ripe with wild, exotic fruit.

Rustling from the jungle alerted them to the fact that they were not alone. Kamina turned to see a man of dark complexion, dressed sparingly in an animal hide, carrying a spear.

"The Amarosians reached for their swords!" cried the teacher. Kamina was snapped out of her imagination, not by Moffett's entertaining exclamation, but by the sound of the warning bell.

*

Talia stood by the cart, half-emptied by the townsfolk. She studied the women of the village as they shopped, wandering here and there, usually on their own, until they came to see her. They would form into small groups of twos and threes before making their initial approach. Talia could almost smell the fear on their breath as they made forced conversation. She served a pair of young maids, each seeking a loaf of elven bread. The sale was interrupted by the clang of the warning bell. Talia forced the bread upon them as she armed herself with her father's axe.

"Hide!" she hissed at them, charging off towards the attacking invaders. They were marauders, criminals, creatures less than men. No, she would not demonise them; they were men who had cobbled together after being ejected from their own community, stealing from others to survive. As much as she tried to find wisdom in the little knowledge she had of them, her logic was always overshadowed by the unassailable truth; a band of raiders like these had killed her parents, and she hated them with every fibre of her being.

Her only thought now was to protect Kamina.

*

Kamina was surprised by the readiness with which the parents gathered their children and fled. She often thought of humans as clumsy and slow compared to her own kind. It dawned on her that this was a well-practised event. She was disorientated by the panic, unsure of her surroundings. In the ensuing chaos, Kamina failed to notice a marauder approaching her. By the time she turned and saw him, her legs were stiff with fear. The marauder seized her by the arm, scrutinized her. He touched her face with his other hand, which was not a hand at all, but a cold metal hook attached to the lump of limb where there had once been a hand.

"What have we here?" said Maulin rhetorically. "An elf? In a town of men? Oh, I imagine you'll be worth something." Kamina smelled the stench of meat and ale on his breath as he eyed her like a prized piece of meat.

The marauder tried to drag her away, but he was distracted by an athletic warrior elf, armed with an axe. She sliced through some of the less fortunate raiders with strength and precision, wielding the weapon better than any man would a sword. Her aim was now focused on Maulin, still holding the young elf with his grubby hand. She rushed at him, breaking his grip on the elf and crushing him against a wall. The marauder flopped helplessly as the elf gripped his jaw in one hand and her weapon in the other, the blade pressed against his scrawny neck.

"What audacity makes you think you can lay a finger on my kin?" she snarled. She jutted her arm back, ready to sever the marauder's head from his repugnant body.

"Talia!" yelled Norrek. She glanced in his direction to see that the fight was over. The marauders were retreating with their wounded, and whatever supplies they had managed to steal. Yet the townsfolk were more afraid of her. They crowded together, watching her with worried eyes. She lowered her weapon and released Maulin from her vice-like grip. He darted away, avoiding the awaiting soldiers by scrambling over Tilden's walls using his metal claw.

"You just let him escape," said Talia, still seething.

"We have no prison in which to keep them," said Norrek. "The Alliance has little concern with raiders. What would you have me do? Execute him?"

Talia could not bring herself to answer.

"Where is Kaedin?" asked Kamina.

They found him hiding with Nyssa in Norrek's house. Talia would be having stern words with her younger brother in private, making no effort to hide her disdain. They made their way back to Eshtel and the cart, but Norrek caught up with them.

"Talia. Please, I need your help," he begged. "One of my men was wounded during the raid. Your people... they have potions that can heal?" She wished to flee this forsaken town as fast as she could, to spirit Kamina back to the sanctuary of Elgrin Forest, but she could not in good conscience leave someone to die.

"Take me to him."

Norrek led her to a small guard house, where the injured Torg lay on a table, an arrow stuck in his thigh.

"About bloody time," he muttered, wincing through his words, feeling the life slowly drain out of him.

"Kaedin, fetch my supplies from the cart." Talia removed the arrow and treated the wound, using herbs and ointments from the forest to cleanse it. She fed the injured man a spoonful of medicine to ease the pain. Torg had lost the harsh look in his eyes towards her, replaced with what could have been misconstrued as gratitude. He fought to stay awake, but a deep sleep took hold of him, and soon his body went limp. His fellow guards exchanged worried glances.

"He is not dead," said Talia, allaying their fears. "Merely subdued. He will live, although in some pain."

"Thank you," said the Master of the Guard.

"Give him this when he wakes up," she said, handing Norrek a small cup of fine green powder. "Tell him to sprinkle a little in hot water to drink. No more than a pinch a day."

With the guard's life now out of danger, Talia gathered Kamina and Kaedin to make a swift exit from Tilden. Norrek caught up to them just as the guards opened the gate.

"I wanted to say thank you again," panted Norrek, struggling with his words. "We have very few guards. The war has taken most. If you had not been here, this could have been…"

"But I was here, and it was not," she said. "Although some of your towns people seem more afraid of me than the marauders."

"They fear what they do not understand," he replied. "We live in troubled times, fighting wars within our country and one across the seas. The Alliance is only concerned with defeating the Zalestians."

"And your people wonder why my kind retired to the forests?"

"A point well made," conceded Norrek. "But I hope you will return." Talia did not answer, merely offering a polite smile.

"Safe journey home," he said, standing back as Eshtel drew the cart out of Tilden. Kaedin glanced back to see Nyssa at the gates. She stood apart from her father, still in shock from the attack. Her hands were clasped at her heart, her face laden with sadness at their cruel separation. The heavy gates closed, and she was blocked from his vision.

CHAPTER SIX

THE GRAVE MISTAKE

THERE WAS A TENSE, BITTER MOOD BETWEEN TALIA AND KAEDIN on the journey back home, as the afternoon cooled into evening. They sat as far apart as they could on the front seat of the cart. Eshtel's hooves battered the ground ahead of them. Kamina slumbered in the rear amongst the unsold stock, drained by her ordeal. Kaedin could sense his older sister's animosity, her features rigid with controlled rage.

"If you wish to chastise me, I suggest you do it now," he whispered, as the welcoming green leaves of Elgrin Forest grew near.

"You abandoned Kamina to indulge in your meaningless relationship with the human." Despite her anger, Talia's voice was low, her words detached.

"Her name is Nyssa," said Kaedin, "and it is not meaningless."

"Kamina is your family!" hissed Talia, the reign on her emotions slipping. "She comes first! Not Nyssa. Not anyone else."

"You best watch your words, sister," whispered Kaedin. "It is not me who lies to Kamina about…"

Talia slapped him hard across his face. Kaedin held his red cheek, glaring at her. She realised she had stepped too far. She moved to comfort her brother, but he recoiled. Her hands had loosened on the reigns, the distraction causing Eshtel to buck. Talia regained control and ordered the horse to an abrupt halt.

The jolt shook Kamina from a nightmare, her mind plagued by the marauders. She gazed out, scared to see they had not yet arrived home.

"What is wrong?" she murmured. "Why have we stopped?" The young elf was confused by the concentrated silence between her older siblings.

"There is nothing wrong," said Kaedin, climbing into the back to fetch the axe. "I am going to collect some deadwood from the fallen trees." Kaedin slid off the back and headed for the forest.

"Kaedin, do not be foolish," urged Talia. "It is almost dusk."

"There is time yet before the first sun sets," he replied.

"Can I come?" Kamina asked, already hopping off alongside him. Talia watched them stroll off together. Kamina waved back at her as the pair disappeared behind some foliage. Kaedin stalked away without any such farewell. Talia felt ashamed for lashing out at him; for all his faults, she had to remind herself that Kaedin was still young. She whispered to Eshtel, who started again along the dirt trail, soon enveloped by the forest.

*

Callaghan had ridden his stolen steed without rest until they reached the hilly grasslands of Legoria, where the poor creature had slowed to a crawl, exhausted by the chase. He left the horse close to a nearby farm, hoping it would be cared for as he continued on foot. His body screamed at him through his aches and pains, run ragged in his dogged pursuit of Jaelyn. The ranger could see the mass of trees that made up Elgrin Forest on the horizon. It was so wide that the dark green leaves hung like a heavy cloud over the land. This was where Malenek's target was, the potential saviour of Enara.

There was a brief shimmer of movement on the next ridge.

Jaelyn.

The sight of the traitor quashed the ranger's aches and reignited his pursuit of the Zalestian. By the time Callaghan was upon him, they were almost within reach of the forest. An unusual silence descended upon the field, unbroken by animal calls or chirping insects, only Callaghan's heart pounding in his chest. He drew Ascara, his eyes darting around, trying to weed out the hidden mage.

A twig snapped, breaking the eerie quietude. The ranger swung his sword round, but her wanting blade found nothing. He scanned his surroundings for any sign of Jaelyn, the hair on the back of his neck standing on end as the air fizzed with magic.

The silver flash of a deadly spell sparked towards him. The ranger rolled out of its path, exposing himself to attack. Jaelyn cast another incantation. Callaghan caught a glimpse of his dark, disdainful face. He ducked the second spell and lunged to where Jaelyn had been. Once again there was nothing tangible for his sword to strike.

"Do you know now how I defeated your pitiful tests in Zatharu, ranger?" echoed Jaelyn's voice. Callaghan swung round, but its source was indefinable, calling out from all directions.

"You cheated," replied the ranger. "With magic."

"I thought it would be harder to deceive an Ishkava Ranger," boasted the mage, his voice ricocheting off the trunks and branches of the forest itself. "You are not worthy of the reputation the Amarosians see fit to grant you."

"Just as you believed you had killed me," shouted Callaghan, deriding him, hoping to draw his adversary out.

"Jaelyn?" There was no reply. "Jaelyn!"

The Zalestian was gone.

Callaghan hovered hesitantly at the cusp of the mighty forest. He hoped the elves would somehow sense the danger that was about to descend upon them. They had once been wise in the ways of magic, yet he feared the forest folk would be blind to Jaelyn's presence, just as he himself had been. He had to pursue the man he had unleashed on these lands, and hope the elves would forgive his trespass. He stepped into the shade of the trees, tracking the traitorous apprentice deeper into the shadows of Elgrin Forest.

*

Kamina struggled to keep up with Kaedin as he traipsed through the forest, his fist tight around the smooth handle of the axe.

"Are you and Nyssa going to be bonded?" she asked.

"What?" said Kaedin, surprised. "No. I do not know. It is complicated."

"But you love her?" teased Kamina.

"I care for her," admitted Kaedin. "But she is of man, and I am elf kind. Even if we were allowed by the elders, as an Ishkava Ranger I would not be permitted a partner."

"So if you had to choose, you would choose the path of a ranger?" she asked, disappointed in Kaedin's lack of romance.

"Yes," he answered sharply, his pace quickening. Kamina huffed along, struggling again to keep up with her brother's longer gait.

"But why?" she continued. "No elf has ever become a ranger before."

"That is no reason why one cannot be. Callaghan was once just a man."

"Why do you admire him, him above all other rangers? Why not Dash Cole, or Mondo Blake, or Volan Hesh?"

"How do you know so many names?" he asked.

"I listen," she replied. Kaedin smiled, impressed by her knowledge.

"Callaghan is the Ranger Elite, but before that he was a brave and fearless hero."

"You always talk as though you have met him," she said, joking to herself.

"I have." Kaedin continued to march quickly through the forest, but his were the only footsteps on the leafy floor. Kamina had stopped dead in her tracks behind him.

"You met Callaghan Tor?" Kamina was dumbstruck. How was it that she had never heard of this encounter before? Why had her brother kept it hidden from her?

"He stayed with the elves once, seeking refuge," revealed Kaedin. "I was very young. It was before you were even born." Kaedin kicked himself for unlocking this bittersweet memory, for slipping up after keeping this fact a secret for so long.

"Before mother and father were killed," said Kamina.

"Yes." He needed to stem her thoughts before the whole truth unravelled. He retraced his steps back to her, lifting her melancholy face with his hand. "We should go and visit them."

Kamina nodded, smiling as they changed direction, Kaedin's pace now in line with her own.

They reached a towering black willow tree as Risaar began to set. The last streams of the reddish daylight illuminated two elven graves, arranged side-by-side at the foot of the tree. Each burial was marked by a circular band of stone, carefully inscribed with symbols, wishing them peace in the next life, in Loria. A new tree had sprouted up from the hole in the centre of the stone. The saplings, while still young, towered over the two elves. The one planted on the grave of Kaman, their father, was growing an unusual blossom of blue flowers. That of his wife, Shara, was beginning to show small white okal berries. Kaedin closed his eyes and mouthed a silent prayer to them both.

"I do not want you to leave the forest," said Kamina. He opened his eyes and looked down at her young, innocent face as she pleaded with him. "I do not want you to leave me. I could not bear it if you were away. I do not want you to leave like they did." Tears welled up in her eyes. In that moment she reminded him of Talia, but without her remoteness or anger. Talia would never cry, or allow herself to be seen doing so. Kaedin knelt down and swept Kamina up in his arms. She sobbed on his shoulder.

"Turn your mind from such thoughts, Kamina. We... we are family. You will always be a part of me." He let her go and held up the axe. He made a small incision across the palm of his hand. He turned the blade to Kamina. She withdrew, but Kaedin coaxed her into offering him her hand. He made a similar cut on her palm, and then grasped her wounded hand in his.

"There," he said. "We have a blood pact. No matter how far apart we are, we will always be a part of each other."

"But what if..."

"...when," he corrected her.

"What happens when you become a ranger?" Kamina asked innocently.

"Then I will take you with me as my trusted apprentice!" Kaedin laid his hand on her shoulder. "You are my kin. No distance can break that bond."

Kamina sniffled, wiping away her tears with her sleeve. Kaedin rose up, smiling so that she would smile too.

A cry of unfamiliar, foreign words cut through the forest. The air snapped and fizzled. A flash of silver light surrounded Kaedin. His limp hand dropped the axe. He fell to his knees, collapsing on top of Kamina. His face pressed upon her, only it was not his face. She looked into her brother's eyes, but they were without the spark of a soul. She tried to fathom what had just happened as the weight of his body slumped against her. The startling speed of the occurrence prevented Kamina from grasping the harsh, horrific truth.

Kaedin was dead.

*

Talia arrived back to the settlement, steering Eshtel to an alcove where she hid the cart. She started to remove his harness when the horse kicked uncontrollably without warning, neighing and snorting at her. Talia tried to calm him, but he bucked and shrieked in a wild frenzy.

Another scream pierced the air nearby. Talia snatched for the axe, forgetting Kaedin had taken it. Lashara stumbled towards her as fast as her crooked body would allow. She fell before she reached her granddaughter, tormented by a terrifying affliction. Talia ignored Eshtel and rushed to Lashara's aid.

"Grandmother, what is wrong?" pleaded Talia, kneeling beside her. The old woman's hands clenched the ground, digging deeper into the dirt.

"Kaedin. A shadow has fallen over him. I cannot…" Lashara's words were silenced with a gasp, gazing beyond the trees with an unnatural sight.

"Grandmother?"

"There is nothing," she whispered finally. As other elves began to gather around, Lashara was struck by another vision.

"It nears her… it is almost upon her!"

Talia's heart stopped.

Kamina.

Behind her, Eshtel's strong legs managed to destroy the cart, freeing him of its weight. The angry steed galloped straight for them. Talia shielded Lashara as the mighty beast vaulted over them. The horse landed hard, bolting off through the forest, pieces of harness crashing to the ground in his wake.

*

Kamina was unable to breathe, tears frozen in her eyes. Footsteps approached her, the crunch of leaves under their feet. Whoever drew near was hidden from her view by Kaedin's dead body, still slumped before her on his knees. Kamina realised that she too was hidden from this assassin's line of sight, but not for long.

A twig snapped as he neared. Panic and adrenalin surged through her. She moved swiftly, Kaedin's falling corpse offering her enough cover to dart behind the thick trunk of the black willow. The murderer moved across the forest floor until he was on the opposite side of the tree. Kamina trembled as she boldly peeked around the bark. A thin man with dark skin loomed over Kaedin's body.

A Zalestian.

He kicked the corpse over to look at the dead elf's face.

A glint of light caught Kamina's eye. The tree axe lay by Kaedin's feet, its blade reflecting the last slivers of daylight. The blood from their silly pact still stained the edge. She looked down at the fresh cut on her hand, the blood trickling down her fingers. Kamina closed her fist tight until it shook, summoning the courage she would need.

She had to avenge her brother.

*

Jaelyn paused over the elf's body longer than he should have allowed, but the creature captured his curiosity. It was not because he had never seen an elf before, but that he could not believe this young, pointy-eared tree dweller lying dead at his feet could ever have hindered his master's plan.

Something moved behind the mage. He spun quickly, summoning a spell, but his words were cut short when another elf, a young female, buried an axe deep in his chest. He felt his insides burst and explode as he drew his last breath. Jaelyn slumped to a heap in the leafy soil next to Kaedin. The last thing he saw was the timid, blonde elven girl who had killed him, quivering with a mix of adrenalin and fear.

*

Kamina gulped the forest air in short, sharp swells of panic. She was fixated upon the axe protruding from the Zalestian's body, her culpable, bloody handprint plastered upon the handle. Nausea overwhelmed her as the severity of her situation finally struck home.

Kaedin was dead, but she had avenged him.

No. She was a murderer. A killer.

She knelt down, stretching her fingers out to touch his body, to make sure that this was real and not some nightmare, hoping she would once again wake up in the back of the cart.

Rustling sounds from the bushes nearby startled her. A lone warrior rushed into the clearing. He surveyed the scene, looking past her panicked face at the dead Zalestian. Kamina was petrified, unable to escape the scene of the crime. The man's eyes fixed upon her now. Kamina's guilty conscious drove her deeper into her paranoia. Who was this man? A friend of the Zalestian? Was he going to kill her now, in revenge for her vengeful act?

The man stepped towards her, but paused as the thunder of hooves careered through the forest, heading straight for them. Eshtel surged out of the trees and bore down upon him. He moved with almost elf-like agility, avoiding the horse's flailing attack.

Kamina seized upon Eshtel's diversion and fled, but the warrior was quick to give chase. He shouted to her in Amarosian, but the rush of speed as she ran away deafened his words. Eshtel once again came to her rescue, rearing himself on his hind legs in front of her pursuer, who jumped back to avoid the brute force of the horse's hooves. Her eyes lingered too long on what was behind her. She lost her footing and fell to the floor, cracking her head against a large dead branch. She lay still, her vision fading, the forest a blur of greens and browns. People shouted, Eshtel neighed, and the trees mourned. Before she succumbed to the unconscious dark, she thought she heard Kaedin whisper her name one last time.

"…Kamina…"

CHAPTER SEVEN

DREAMS AND AWAKENINGS

"...Kamina..."

It was a dream. Of that Kamina was certain. It had the resonance of something more, yet not quite as vivid or as coarse as reality. Every detail was serene and yet insubstantial. Light shimmered off every surface. She was younger here, sat in Talia's lap as her sister read from a book. Kamina's fresh eyes were enchanted by the colourful pictures painted on the pages. She recognised the four Elemental Gods drawn in a style similar to Lashara's; the blue watery form of Aquill; the green, stony hulk of Ygrain; Whirren, depicted here as a creamy white hurricane blur; and the fiery, burning shape of Risaar. At their centre, the spherical world of Enara, formed from the marriage of their magical elements.

It was the story of Origin.

"The four Elementals came together and combined their wisdom and power to create Enara," read Talia, her voice tranquil and joyous, a voice she had rarely used in the years since this moment, this altered memory. "They created the land, the sea, the wind, and the fire. They breathed life into every living creature."

Talia turned the page. The new illustration depicted the Elementals leaving Enara and becoming the two suns and two moons. "They left the world to watch over us from the stars."

"Why did they leave?" Kamina asked.

"Because they had wished to create a peaceful world, full of life, but their different creations warred amongst one another. They left because one of them committed the ultimate sin."

"What did they do?"

"They took another's life."

The last words were not Talia's, uttered in a husky and authoritative voice. A man's voice. Kamina twisted her neck up to see the warrior from the forest, staring down at her with judgemental blue eyes.

*

Kamina gasped as she woke in darkness, wrapped in strange sheets in a bed that was not her own. A rabble of raised voices rumbled beyond a door, slightly ajar on the opposite side of the small room. She slumped down from the bed, still dazed from her fall. Kamina slinked over to the sliver of light streaming through the gap. The voices grew louder, more distinct, angrier. She could make out Talia's above the rest.

"You brought this upon us!"

The young elf peered out to see her sister pacing across the floor, arguing with the human warrior from the forest, the same man from her dream. He remained calm and collected, in contrast to Talia, choosing to speak with a clear and composed voice.

"The mage was my mistake, but I did not bring him to you or your people, Talia. He was sent here."

He had called her by her first name, Kamina noted. Who was this stranger? And how did he know her sister?

"By whom? And for what?" demanded Talia. "To kill an innocent boy?"

"Talia," said Norrek, stepping between them, a mediator to the madness. It dawned on Kamina that they were in Norrek's house. "Let the man speak."

"I do not know who sent Jaelyn. His purpose was to eliminate a threat to his master's plan."

"Kaedin? He was no threat!" exclaimed Talia. "He was a boy! Tomorrow is his *Dira Adolyn*. He was to enter adulthood. He had dreams of joining the Ishkava Rangers. Yes, your presence in our lives spurred him towards that path. He wanted to be you!"

Kamina's mouth fell open. The man arguing with Talia, the man who had seen her kill the Zalestian, was Callaghan Tor, the Ishkava Ranger Elite.

"I do not know what the Fates had in store for the boy, but Jaelyn was directed here to remove someone who could jeopardise their plans."

"He succeeded," said Talia bitterly.

"Not completely," remarked Kaedin.

Kamina was frozen stiff as she heard the voice of her brother from beyond the grave. She was sure she had imagined it, but then Kaedin himself stepped into view from the corner he had been crouched in. She threw open the door and ran to grab him, but she passed through his body, clattering against the opposite wall. She would have hit the ground, had it not been for the ranger's quick reactions. Kamina looked up from his arms into his eyes, warm and blue, just like her dream. A smile almost appeared on his unshaven face.

Callaghan raised Kamina back to her feet. She faced Kaedin as if it were the first time they had met, studying his form, confused by his appearance. He was here, present in this house, but yet not quite alive. The colour had drained from his face, now ghostly and elusively transparent. His clothes were drabs of grey and silver, while his skin radiated a pale white glow. She could see from his expression that he was just as equally confused.

"Kamina. Kamina," repeated the ranger, kneeling by her now, his face level with hers. She turned to him in a daze.

"What... what is...?" The words would not come, lodged in her throat. Kaedin turned from her, upset. She looked to Talia, and saw her staunch sister shed a tear.

"Kaedin has been brought back to life... as a vengeance spirit."

"Preposterous," muttered Norrek. Callaghan continued, regardless of what the Master of the Guard thought.

"Kaedin was killed by magic," he explained. "An unnatural death, an abuse of the power of the Elementals. You avenged his murder with his blood wet on your hands. It was this bond that brought back his spirit." Kamina stared down at her hand, at the scar forming across her palm. Kaedin held up his ethereal hand. The scar on his hand glowed silver, as though it were more tangible than the rest of him.

"This is madness!" Norrek pleaded. "Talia, you cannot believe what this man is saying?"

"There are ancient stories among our people, of creatures who returned as ghosts," she explained. "We call them the *ackran-fay*. According to legend, their lives were extended by the will of the Elements, because their death had been a perversion of the natural order."

"They were killed by the power of the Elementals. By magic," said Callaghan, casting a glance down at Ascara hanging by his side. "Power no mortal creature was intended to wield."

"Why are we in Tilden?" whispered Kamina to Talia.

"I did not wish to take Kaedin to the elders like this," was all she said, before they were interrupted by a commotion from outside.

"Father! Father! Let me in!" Nyssa screamed. "I demand to know what is happening!" She managed to wrestle her way through the two guards outside her home, catching a glimpse of the secret tryst surrounding Kaedin's spirit. She could not grasp what her eyes were seeing. The guards let her go as she stopped fighting them. Kaedin approached her slowly, his spectral hand stretching out towards her.

"Nyssa," he said, but even his voice had changed. It was unsettling to hear, echoing out as if he were speaking from a dark cave. The sound sent shivers across Nyssa's skin. Kaedin's true love retreated, stumbling into the guards. The contact scared her, recoiling from them before tearing off into the twilight. Kaedin stood still, watching her disappear, lost in a world of solitude.

"Fetch my daughter. Tell her I will be there shortly. And close the door for gods' sakes!" barked Norrek. The two guardsmen hastily complied.

Talia tried to comfort Kaedin by placing a sisterly hand on his shoulder, but her fingers seeped through his body as if it were made of dust caught in the moonlight. She stared at him, her face contorted by a weird smile, both amazed and apologetic. Kaedin withdrew back into the corner where he continued to sulk.

"Tell us all you know," Talia said to Callaghan. "You said this Jaelyn had a master? That he had a plan?"

"I do not know who his master is, only that he colludes with Lord Malenek."

"Malenek?" quizzed Norrek. "Then he is not dead?"

"No. Malenek has also discovered how to bring spirits of vengeance into this world. He has exploited this disparity by creating an army of them."

"Why did you not mention this before!" exclaimed the Master of the Guard. "How many of these things does he have?"

"One hundred strong," revealed the ranger.

Norrek let a nervous laugh pass his lips. "But that is nothing! Even in its weakened state, the Amarosian army is a thousand times that."

Callaghan quickly drew his sword and sliced the blade through Kaedin's ghostly torso. The spirit glanced down as the sword passed right through his ethereal body, striking the brickwork behind him. The metal disrupted his aura, as if his mind had been ripped apart before springing back together. It was not painful, but certainly unpleasant. He checked that his form remained whole, but the only mark left by the sword was a nick on Norrek's wall.

"A hundred thousand, a hundred million. It does not matter," said the ranger, sheathing Ascara. "Almost nothing can stop them."

"But why create spirits at all?" asked Norrek.

"Malenek believes the war between Amaros and Zalestia has broken Enara beyond the point of salvation. He intends to use this army to purge the land of life, to start again."

"You said almost nothing," noted Talia.

"Malenek mentioned an artefact. The Stone of Spirits. I believe this may be the key to stopping their plan."

"Never heard of it," said Norrek. He glanced at Talia, who shook her head.

"Nor had I," continued he ranger. "From what I overheard, I believe it to be somewhere in Zalestia."

"Well that's just great," Norrek grunted. "What does it do anyway?"

"I did not know," admitted Callaghan. "I am out of my depth. I need help from someone who may be able to shed more light on the spirits."

"Is there such a person?" asked Talia.

Callaghan paused on the question for a moment, trying to think of those he knew that may offer some information or guidance. He could only think of a single name, one that Malenek himself had mentioned, and one that presented a major problem. "Oldwyn Blake," he said eventually.

"The cyclops!" exclaimed the Master of the Guard. "The council have him locked up in Calisto's Black Tower, and with good reason. He killed Ambassador Ramiro's son! They will never let him go free."

"I only need to speak with Oldwyn," said Callaghan, eyeing Kaedin. "I think the Fates did have a purpose for you, Kaedin. Jaelyn was sent here to kill the one person who threatened his master's plans, and in doing so, may have accidentally gifted us the very person he was meant to destroy."

"Kaedin?" quizzed Talia in disbelief.

"Me?" said the spirit, stunned. "Really?"

"Yes. I believe the gods have granted us a gift, a small chance to save not only this land, but the entire world." Even though he was now a vaporous spirit, Kaedin beamed with pride.

"Please do not encourage him," said Talia. "He was bad enough when he was alive."

"I must take Kaedin to Calisto. The council must be warned about what is coming so they can prepare. They will require proof so that I can speak to Oldwyn."

"When do we leave?" Kaedin asked, but Talia stepped in front of him in protest.

"You said Perhola will be the first city Malenek attacks. You must ride there and warn them."

"I alone cannot fight this army," stated Callaghan. "I must find the Stone of Spirits. A messenger can be sent."

"They will not believe a humble messenger," argued Talia.

"It is true," grunted Norrek in agreement, as he poured himself a drink. "The Lord Steward's men are unlikely to swallow such a tall tale. There is a spirit standing in my own house and I barely believe it."

"Then send someone persuasive," he replied.

"Kaedin cannot go with you," challenged Talia. "We know nothing about what has happened to him."

"You have not asked me what I think!" shouted the spirit, silencing their squabbles. Kaedin glanced between his sister and his hero. "Callaghan is right. I must journey with him to Calisto."

"If that is what you wish," she muttered, trying to play down her brother's betrayal. "As the new day dawns, you will be beyond *Dira Adolyn*. The decision is yours." All she had ever tried to do was protect them both. She wanted to blame someone, but it was not Kaedin's fault the mage had targeted him.

No, she thought, the blame is mine.

"Master Norrek," said Callaghan. "I require a horse, one with speed. I promise you I will repay the debt should we make it through this alive."

"And if not?" asked Norrek.

"Then none of this will matter." Norrek nodded in the face of the ranger's bleak logic. He stepped outside to relay the orders to his men. Callaghan watched as Kaedin and Talia whispered in their elven tongue. Even as a ranger he was not versed in the ancient language of Legoria, but from their posture, he assumed Kaedin was offering an apology.

Someone tugged on his shirt. Callaghan discovered Kamina standing by his side, vying for his attention. He had almost forgotten about the spectre's younger sibling, despite the important role she had played in his resurrection.

"What is it child?" he asked, kneeling down beside her.

"The man I... the Zalestian?"

"Jaelyn?"

"Was he a bad man?" she asked sheepishly. Callaghan's life had, for many years, been haunted by death. He had not considered how taking the life of another, even to protect herself, would affect one so young. Her moral compass was only able to deal in absolutes, the ranger thought, while the lines on his often blurred together. It should have been him that was racked with guilt over Jaelyn's death, so Kamina did not have to suffer it.

"My master says there are no bad men, only bad deeds, but Jaelyn had performed many bad deeds. You did a very brave thing." He stroked her blonde hair from her face, searching for acceptance in her emerald green eyes.

The whispering between Talia and Kaedin had stopped. The pair watched him as he comforted Kamina. The ranger rose up and patted her on the head, before following Norrek to make sure he found a suitable horse for the long journey ahead.

The three elves stood in silent discourse. Kamina stared at her brother's spirit, unable to hold him or even touch him. For the first time in forever, Kaedin was going to leave her.

He was breaking his promise the same day it was forged in blood.

CHAPTER EIGHT

BONDS AND BREAKS

THE HORSE WAS READIED AS RISAAR'S BRIGHT LIGHT BEAMED OVER the horizon. Callaghan had hoped to depart under the cover of darkness. He had no doubt Kaedin's ghostly appearance would bring with it hysteria to those who caught sight of him. Norrek had drafted a few loyal men to help them make a hasty departure, men who were not so superstitious, men who could keep a secret. He led Callaghan to the horse he had procured; a white mare, her coat and hair blemished with spots of grey.

"The horse is Torg's, a guardsman injured in a recent raider attack. He will have no use of her in the near future," said Norrek, patting the mare's grey speckled hide. "She is strong, fed and watered, just liked you asked." The words Callaghan would have used were overindulged and old. He soothed the horse's snow-white head, warming her to his sight and presence. He whispered to her in a tongue unfamiliar to Norrek, but one the horse itself recognised, or at least responded to.

"You speak the words of the centaurs?" quizzed the Master of the Guard. Callaghan nodded.

"What name do you give her?" he inquired.

"Plagacia," replied Norrek.

"What a horrible name for a creature of Rundhale," muttered the ranger.

"Torg named her after his wife," stated Norrek. Callaghan grit his teeth, feeling foolish in his error. He turned to apologise, but he noticed a slight grin at the corner of Norrek's mouth. "Do not worry, ranger" he whispered. "Torg often says the creature reminded him of her long, whining face." Callaghan smiled briefly, but it soon faded, a moment of levity before the challenging journey ahead.

Callaghan mounted the horse as Norrek left to fetch the spirit. Plagacia was at ease with the ranger on her back. Talia accompanied Kaedin as they emerged from Norrek's house. The trusted guardsmen held their breath as they caught sight of him, forcing them to re-evaluate their beliefs.

"In the name of the Elements!" a young guard whispered, clutching the silver cross that hung around his neck. The guards were not the only ones to react. Plagacia backed away from Kaedin, sensing his unnatural presence. As he neared the mare, she began to kick and buck. Callaghan tried to pacify her, but to no avail. Norrek grabbed her reigns, steadying her while the ranger quickly dismounted. Plagacia broke free, darting away from Kaedin just as

Nyssa had the previous night.

"Fetch that horse back!" barked Norrek. The young guardsman, still clutching his cross, did not hesitate to follow the horse in fleeing.

"It seems this journey will be more difficult than I had anticipated," said Callaghan.

"Eshtel will take him," replied Kamina. The ranger turned to find the spirit's sibling guiding her steed towards them. The horse showed no fear of Kaedin. He even tried to nudge him, and would have succeeded had his nose not passed through the spirit.

"Eshtel, do not do that," moaned Kaedin, stepping backwards. "It feels strange."

"Are you sure, Kamina?" asked Callaghan. "It is a dangerous road ahead."

"The road to Gorran is hardly fraught with danger," said Norrek.

"Time is of the essence, Master Norrek," explained Callaghan. "I plan to ride through the Gauer Plains to Finsing Falls, and then down through the Crymyr Pass."

"But that's suicide!" exclaimed Norrek. "Never mind the beasts that roam the plains, there are marauders hiding in the caves surrounding the falls. And even if you avoid them, the Crymyr Pass, well…"

"It is the quickest route, despite the dangers," insisted Callaghan. "So I ask again Kamina, are you sure?"

"Eshtel wants to help Kaedin," said Kamina, glancing up at Talia. She could not deny Kamina this one opportunity to help, and nodded in agreement.

"Thank you," said Callaghan. "Since you are giving me something, it is only right I give you something in return." The ranger produced the twine bracelet Nyssa had gifted Kaedin. "The men took it from Kaedin's body. I thought you might like it as a keepsake."

Kamina took the bracelet and placed it around her wrist. Callaghan was surprised when she sprang on him, hugging his torso. He allowed himself to comb his hand through her beautiful, blonde hair. She truly is a precious child, he thought.

We must depart," he said, breaking her hold on him. Talia pulled Kamina away, allowing the ranger to mount Eshtel. The sisters gathered awkwardly around their ghostly brother, unable to hug him goodbye.

"Do not do anything foolish," was all Talia could bring herself to say.

Kamina could not find any words. He was leaving her, and although it was the way Kaedin had always wanted, in the company of a ranger, she was still upset. Kaedin knelt down in front of her and held up his hand, showing the bright cut on his palm. Kamina did the same with her matching wound. Their hands hovered together, almost touching. She closed her fingers around his, but they melted through him. In spite of herself, Kamina started to cry.

Kaedin tried to leap on Eshtel behind the ranger, but only ended up falling through the horse and onto the ground on the other side. It snapped Kamina from her melancholy, causing her to laugh.

"It is not funny!" bawled Kaedin.

"I guess you will have to walk, spirit," said Callaghan with a grin. Kaedin picked himself up. "I hope you can keep up."

"I can run as fast as this flea-bag," boasted the elf, becoming increasingly narcissistic as he adjusted to the advantages of being a ghost. Eshtel merely snorted at him.

"Come, we must depart." Callaghan tried to turn Eshtel, but the horse refused, instead strutting over to Kamina. The horse nuzzled her with his wet nose. She placed her arms around his neck and gazed into his big brown eyes.

"No, Eshtel. You must take the ranger to Calisto without me." The stubborn steed lay down in protest. Callaghan had never seen such loyalty in a horse before, except to the fellow hooved centaurs in Rundhale.

Kamina cuddled Eshtel's head tight and placed her lips by his ear, whispering, "You must do this. The lives of many depend upon it. But come straight back, back to the forest. Do you understand me?"

Eshtel did not move.

"Well?" she demanded. Eshtel rose with a protesting neigh.

They trotted to the main gate, the spirit keeping pace by their side. The small party of onlookers followed them. Norrek's men opened the gate, avoiding direct eye contact with either the ranger or the ghost. Kaedin turned briefly to wave goodbye. Talia, Kamina, and Norrek had gathered at the entrance to the town. Kaedin was looking for someone else, but she was not there. He retracted his ghostly hand from the air. With his head hung low, the sorrowful spirit ran to catch up with Callaghan.

Despite the recent turn of events, accompanying Callaghan while running alongside Eshtel felt freeing to the wayward elf. It was not exactly how he had imagined meeting the legendary ranger, but the details did not matter. He was going on an adventure. However, as they journeyed away from Tilden, Kaedin struggled to move. It felt as if the air had solidified, each step forward taking more effort than the last. Eventually it became so painful that the spirit fell to his knees, grunting in agony. Callaghan quickly doubled back and leapt off Eshtel.

"Kaedin? What is wrong?" The ghost grew more transparent, almost disappearing out of existence.

"I do not know… I feel weak." As Kaedin faded in and out of this world, another commotion occurred at Tilden's gate. Callaghan saw Norrek urgently waving him back. Kamina was slumped in Talia's arms.

"Can you walk?" Kaedin nodded. With some effort, Callaghan and the spirit returned to Tilden. As they neared, Kaedin's glow grew stronger. They found Kamina wrapped in Talia's arms, wiping a cold sweat from her pale forehead.

"What happened?" Norrek asked. Talia glanced up at Callaghan, who nodded, almost reading her thoughts.

"They must be bonded spiritually," Callaghan surmised. "Where one goes, the other must follow. This is good news."

"Good?" questioned Talia. "She nearly... they both nearly died!"

"Malenek," remembered Norrek.

"Yes, Malenek," said Callaghan. "He is physically linked to his spirit army. He cannot simply orchestrate their movements from Mytor. He must accompany them, which will slow their march and manoeuvring considerably. However, if I am to reach Calisto with Kaedin, I will need to take Kamina as well."

Kamina, still pale and woozy, hid from the ranger's gaze behind her sister. The sudden sweep of excitement dissipated now that she was directly involved in his plans.

"No!" declared Talia. She changed her stance, spreading herself wider, like a wild animal protecting her young.

"She will be safe in my care," said Callaghan.

"You are a harbinger of death!" exclaimed the elf. "I will not let you take her."

"Talia, what is wrong?" Kamina asked. She had regained her strength and colour, but was more concerned with the harsh tone Talia invoked.

"Nothing," she said, her jaw clenched in anger as she turned to Callaghan. "We must talk in private." The elf and the ranger stepped aside. The others watched them converse in animated whispers.

"What are they talking about?" asked Kamina, but Kaedin either did not hear her, or chose not to answer. The way they interacted made her suspect Kaedin was not the only elf who had met Callaghan before. Had Talia known the ranger in the past? Kamina wondered. Before she could give it more thought, the pair returned back to the gate.

"I will go alone to Calisto," said Callaghan, having acquiesced to Talia's demands. "Hopefully they will take me at my word as a ranger, although I suspect they will demand more proof."

"But, what about why this happened?" begged Kaedin. He could not believe it. He had waited all his life for this moment, and it had taken his death to reach it, only to have it quashed by Talia and her over-bearing nature. "You said this was fate?"

"Your sister believes that you and Kamina will be safer within the confines of Elgrin Forest. However, she has granted me Eshtel." Callaghan winked at Kaedin, and then glanced towards Kamina and Eshtel. Kaedin, understanding the ranger's hidden message, replied with a subtle nod.

"I wish you well in your quest, Callaghan Tor," said Talia as he mounted Eshtel.

"And I apologise to you, Talia Elloeth."

Before she could ask why, Callaghan kicked Eshtel into a quick gallop. The ranger stretched down and snatched Kamina's arm, whipping her up onto the horse in front of him. The young elf cried out in surprise.

"I am sorry, but this is the only way," Callaghan whispered to Kamina as she tried to wrestle out of his grasp. "Hold on."

"Kamina!" screamed Talia, ready to give chase.

"Talia." She paused, glancing sideways at Kaedin, who offered her a weak smile.

"Kaedin, do not do this," she pleaded, reaching out to grab him. Her hand only pierced a blur of silver as the spirit shot off after Callaghan. Talia released a short burst of speed in pursuit, but eventually stopped, realising how futile it was.

"Talia, take Plagacia," Norrek yelled, running after her. "You can catch up to them,"

"It is no use, Norrek. Eshtel is faster than your best horse. He was bred by the centaurs." They watched as the trio very quickly became dots on the outlying grasslands.

"Please protect her," prayed Talia.

"What now?" asked the Master of the Guard.

"Evacuate your village." Talia returned to Tilden, spotting the young guard still trying to calm Plagacia. She marched over, Norrek running at her heels. Talia comforted the mare before mounting her.

"I assume you have a plan?" he asked.

"I need to inform the elves what has happened here," she explained. "I will then ride west to Gorran and north to Perhola, warning every village in between. If the ranger is right, each and every one of them is in danger."

"Talia, let me send one of my men to Perhola," he offered.

"It is as the ranger said. If a mere man is the messenger, the people may not believe him."

"But they'll take heed of an elf? Their old enemy?"

"They fear what they do not understand," she recalled him saying. "What would you think if an elf had left Elgrin?"

"I pray to the Elements that you are right," he said.

"I have to do this. I have to help somehow. Take care, Master Melo."

"And you, Talia Elloeth."

She kicked Plagacia's hide, and the mare bolted out of the town. Norrek stood with the young guardsman, watching the elf ride off, her blonde hair whipping behind her.

And then she was gone.

"Your orders, sir?" asked the guardsman.

"Knock on every door," he commanded. "Tell them to prepare to journey to Calisto. Pack only what they must."

"And if they ask why, sir?" Norrek gazed into the distance as the dawning twin suns cleared the horizon. "Sir?" repeated the guard.

"Tell them an army marches from the north. No more." The guardsman quickly saluted, scurrying away to spread the word. Norrek climbed the guard tower by the main gate and rang out the warning bell.

CHAPTER NINE

THE RUINS OF ANAWEY

THE TALL WILD GRASS BREATHED WITH THE STRONG BREEZE, flowing back and forth like water. Kamina gazed out over the fields as they blurred past. Kaedin ran beside them through the grass. His pale silvery glow was like the fin of a fish darting through water, but the grass did not part for him like it did the wind. It was an unnatural sight, beyond comprehension.

The little elf buried her face deep into her sleeves. Kamina could still feel the damp of the tears she had shed after being unceremoniously ripped from the ground in Tilden. Eshtel thundered along faster than she had ever seen him go before. It comforted her, as if he somehow understood the urgency of the situation and wished to be done with it so they could return home. Kamina thought of Talia, how she would be angry with Kaedin for this. She hoped her sister was in close pursuit of them, chasing her foolish brother and her kidnapper. Kamina closed her eyes and imagined the safe green leaves of Elgrin Forest. The memories of its bold colours warmed her in the cold evening, everything around them dull and tepid.

She said nothing to the ranger as the journey wore on, and he said little to her. Callaghan had tried to comfort her at first, but he accepted her silence as a tolerance of their situation. They rode hard, the landscape changing from the flat farm lands surrounding Tilden to the uneven hills and valleys of the Gauer Plains. This was the Legoria of the past, untouched by man, who had only encroached on the outer rim of the region. The route was more direct, but it was also more demanding. Eshtel struggled ascending some of the steeper hillocks, while Callaghan directed him away from herds of wild creatures.

"Bismun," he informed her, noticing her curious gaze. "They are of the gentler variety. You can tell by the pale stripe along their back. The fiercer bismun have a red marking."

They broke away from the plains, Callaghan choosing to take them through a wide valley. The ranger slowed their pace, allowing Eshtel to trot along and catch his breath.

"There was a teacher in Tilden who said you had killed ten thieves while nursing a broken arm," recalled Kaedin. "Was that true?"

"It was only three," corrected Callaghan. "And I did not kill them. I merely delayed them until some soldiers happened upon us."

As Kaedin gushed over the ranger, Kamina spotted some rocks up ahead, positioned in an unusual formation. She soon realised that they were not rocks, but carved stones and statues, eroded by age and weather. When they were nearer she observed symbols etched upon them. Even though they were worn, she recognised some of the characters. Kaedin took the opportunity to stop and study them.

"These are ancient elvish," she said. The ranger nodded as they passed by. "But where did they come from?"

"From there." Callaghan pointed to the ridge ahead of them. There were more stones, half-buried in the ground, layered with dirt and moss. There was a structure at the peak Callaghan had indicated, or at least the ruins of one. They made their way up the slope of the valley towards it. Kamina was amazed to find that what had appeared to be a solitary building from the valley was in fact the start of a crumbling city. It now lay broken, a dead relic of her ancestors.

"Anawey," she whispered quietly, out of respect for those who had perished here.

"I did not know if you were aware of it," said the ranger.

"I have heard my grandmother speak of it," revealed Kamina, "but rarely, and always with sadness."

Kamina leapt down from Eshtel and placed her light feet on a smooth flagstone. It chilled her through the soles of her boots. She gazed across the carcass of the city, realising it had not merely been abandoned when the elves receded into Elgrin Forest, but attacked, razed to the ground.

"Something terrible happened here," she managed to say, her minute voice carried across the decimated landscape by a sudden gust of wind.

"There was a battle," explained the ranger. "The Last Battle in the Legorian War. In those days, the entire region belonged to the elves. The armies of men assembled on all sides, wishing to destroy their enemy. The attack was pre-emptive, born out of fear and greed. Both sides suffered many casualties, and so the elves retreated, abandoning this city, but not before they demolished it."

"The elves did this?"

"To stop the city and the power it held from falling into the hands of men. They scarred the lands so no man would dare rebuilt here. It acts as a warning, far more powerful than the treaty agreed to afterwards."

As this new knowledge sank in, Kamina watched Kaedin's ghostly figure wandered among the ruins, his intangible body passing through walls where once their people had thrived. Overwhelmed, she let a tear escape. It fell from her face, seeping into the desecrated ground.

"We shall make camp here," announced Callaghan, dismounting Eshtel. As he led the horse to a small puddle of water, Kamina crossed through the ruins towards Kaedin. She found him staring at the weathered statue of an old elf, the name worn away.

"Kaedin, what are we going to do?" she asked.

"What do you mean?"

"We have been kidnapped," she hissed. "By a ranger."

"I know," he turned, beaming at her. "Is it not exciting?"

"This is not funny," she said. "This is not one of your games. This is real!"

"I know it is real!" he snapped. "Look at me. Do you not think I know?" Kamina gazed down at her feet in shame. For all her brother's faults, he was coping with his afterlife remarkably well.

"Kamina," he said, kneeling down, unable to touch her, his hands passing through hers. "We have to do this. You heard Callaghan. This is no longer about you or me, or even the elves. This is about all of Enara."

Kamina nodded, but as she watched him rise up and drift off to explore some more of the ruined city, she wondered if the world as it was deserved to be saved.

*

Night fell upon them, chilling the barren landscape. Callaghan built a fire in the corner of what was left of two joining walls, hoping to trap some of the warmth within the ancient stonework. He withdrew Ascara and whispered the enchantment to her fiery, red-eyed jewel. The blade burst into flames, and Callaghan stuck it under the construction of twigs and branches, until the gathered timber was able to maintain the fire. Forks of amber flickered in the darkness, casting shadows of ghouls and ghosts in the ruins. He noticed Kaedin studying Ascara as he sheathed her blade.

"It was the sword of Risaar, or so they say," said Callaghan, answering the question glowing in the spirit's eager eyes. "Legend says that each of the Elementals left a weapon to be wielded by a deserving mortal, but no-one was judged worthy, and so they were stolen instead."

"Have you found any of the others?" quizzed Kaedin.

"No, no one has. It is only a legend."

"How do you make the blade turn to fire?" asked Kamina. It was a secret Callaghan had kept hidden since it was passed down to him by his master and mentor, Hiron Carrillo. But given recent events, he could not tell anyone the secret to Ascara's power, even an innocent elf.

"I command her to do so. She only responds to those who are brave enough to wield her power, and noble enough not to abuse it."

"Like a ranger," said Kamina. Callaghan nodded, thinking of Volan. That was why Malenek had needed him, he realised now. And yet she had worked for the rogue ranger.

"How many men have you killed with it?" asked Kaedin. "Ten? Twenty? A hundred?"

"With Ascara? Four."

"But the stories…"

"…are exactly that, my elven friend. It is an illusion. The stories are exaggerated and embellished with every re-telling."

"But you do not stop them spreading," said Kamina.

"No. There is something to be said for fear and notoriety. They often allow for situations to be resolved before the first sword is even drawn. In most circumstances words are often more useful than weapons."

"Our current circumstance is not one of those." Callaghan found himself disarmed by the young girl's curt comment.

"No," admitted the ranger solemnly, "no it is truly not."

"If you had to kill Malenek to ensure the safety of Enara, would you do it?" she asked?

"Would you, little one?" the ranger replied. Kamina did not answer.

Callaghan shared out the food that Norrek had gifted him for the journey. Among the items was some of Talia's elven bread. Kamina would only eat this, its rich taste reminded her of home, of her sister's hands kneading the dough, mixing with it the herbs and spices of Elgrin Forest. It warmed her stomach.

Kaedin ate nothing, prowling around the campfire. Callaghan studied the spirit as he crunched into an affel fruit.

"Kaedin." The ranger's finished fruit core flew towards him. On impulse, he reached out to catch it. The affel core passed right through his fingers and body, but it slowed, changing trajectory as if caught by a sudden gust of wind.

"Why did you do that?" Kamina insisted. "It was not fair on him!"

"It was not my intention to make fun of your brother, Kamina," he said. "It was merely a test. I have noticed Kaedin is able to interact with this world."

"How?" asked the ghost. "I cannot touch anything."

"Yet you walk on solid ground," noted Callaghan. "Perhaps the spirit world mirrors Enara in this respect, but I think it is more plausible that you are acting on instinct. I believed if you were forced to act, to rely on your natural reflexes, you may just forget that you are a spirit."

"It did slow down," said Kamina. He glanced down at the fruit core by his feet, as if his body had deflected its path.

Suddenly Kaedin found himself sinking into the very ground on which he stood.

"Kaedin!" exclaimed Kamina, reaching out in vain to grab hold of him.

"What is happening?" yelled her brother, his ghostly limbs scrambling to grab the ground and stop himself sinking under the surface, but it was hopeless.

"Kaedin, concentrate," ordered Callaghan, now on his feet. "Imagine you are alive, you are real, whole, and should not be sinking into the ground."

"I cannot!" screamed the spirit, sinking deeper with every second.

"You are not trying! What sort of ranger will you be if you cannot even focus?"

Pushed by his hero's sharp criticism, Kaedin closed his eyes and concentrated. His spirit body gradually stopped subsiding into the ground, with only his head and shoulders visible.

"Good, now take hold of my hand. Kamina, take the other. Do not think about it Kaedin," said the ranger, seeing the doubt seep over the spirit's face. "Just do it."

Kaedin's ethereal limbs emerged from under the ground. Callaghan tried to grab one, but Kaedin's fingers flailed through his outstretched arm.

"You can do this, Kaedin," Kamina said encouragingly.

The spirit tried again, but with the same result.

"Kaedin, please," she begged, her eyes welling with tears. He looked at her, and realised all the things that were at stake with his life, such as it was, were hers to share. If he fell down, deep within Enara, Kamina would be unable to follow, and she would die.

Kaedin's hand lurched out towards her. She snatched at it with both of hers. Kaedin gripped Callaghan's arm with the other. The warrior ranger and the elven girl worked together and dragged him out of the phantom hole he had imagined himself falling into. When he had fully emerged, Kamina lost her grip of the ghost and fell backwards, as did Callaghan. They looked up to find Kaedin's spirit once again standing on solid ground. For one brief moment Kamina forgot that she had been kidnapped. She laughed at the surreal predicament they found themselves in. She was surprised to see Callaghan shed his serious demeanour, grinning at them both.

"I think we have had enough excitement for one day," said the ranger as he picked himself up. "We had better get some sleep. It will be an early rise tomorrow."

"Kaedin does not do well with early rises," said Kamina. If he had been able to, Kaedin would have blushed. The ranger provided Kamina with a thick shawl, which she wrapped herself up in, lying close to the fire. Kaedin stayed awake all night watching his sibling sleep. He found the fruit core Callaghan had hurled at him and tried it pick it up. The first few times he managed to raise it off the ground. Soon he was able to keep it hovering in his palm for short periods of time, before it fell through his skin, back down into the dirt. After hours of practise, he finally clasped it in a fist. He hurled it away into the darkness of the night.

CHAPTER TEN
MALENEK MARCHES

Balen Malenek's bloodshot eyes stared intently at the map of Amaros that adorned the wall of his study. The blood spell that Jaelyn had cast was still in play upon the parchment. Unfortunately, Malenek suspected that Jaelyn himself was not. The dot of blood was on the move from the town of Tilden, heading south-east towards the ruins of Anawey. Malenek guessed that Callaghan had disposed of the Zalestian mage, and was now accompanying whoever Jaelyn had failed to assassinate to Calisto. The ranger had chosen the most direct route, past the Finsing Falls, through the Crymyr Pass and around Lake Comodo, but it was also dangerous territory, a land of thieves and other savage beasts.

The priest clasped his hands around his cross and said a prayer for Jaelyn. His fingers were worn and still dirty from helping Gort bury the bodies of his ghosts. His hand was shaking. His entire body had been weakened by the birth of the spirit army, as if he had given each of them a piece of his soul, leaving little for himself. He was stronger when they surrounded him, but even then it felt as if his essence was spread further than it was ever meant to be. It could prove to be a hindrance in battle, thought the priest, as he struggled to take the map off the wall, rolling it up in a protective hide.

He drifted silently along the darkened corridor to his personal chambers, sparse and empty of possessions, unlived. His battle armour and chain mail were laid out on the bed, the polished plates a parting gift from Volan. It lay there like an empty shell, as if the being within had died in his sleep and withered away into nothingness. Malenek picked up the closed helmet, gazing down, meeting the stare of its empty eye slits, fingering the pattern of tiny holes that would allow him to breathe when he took on this armoured form. He pushed the pivoted mouth guard back over the helmet, half expecting to see a spirit residing within. All he found was his own dull reflection hiding in the darkness.

Salamon knocked on the door, interrupting his thoughts. Malenek snapped the mouth guard shut, turning his attentions to his servant. The gaudy man carried with him the sulphuric stench of fire and death.

"The... men are waiting, my Lord."

"I will be there momentarily," replied Malenek. Salamon closed the door behind him, leaving the priest to dress for war.

A short time later Lord Malenek clanged down the stone steps in his battle armour, the polished metal a far sight removed from his usual religious attire. The sound itself was like death bells marching on, growing louder. He paused on the steps, surveying the small spirit army that awaited him. Their silver ethereal glow illuminated the entire hall. Gort towered in front of them, his mighty stone body tougher than any forged armour. Salamon stood next to him, dressed in worn chain mail, holding a barbute under his arm, his hair greasy with sweat.

"Salamon, you will remain behind."

"But my Lord…" Salamon's protests were quelled by Malenek's raised steel hand.

"We may have need of the beast. You must remain and play your part. I will send word when the time comes."

"Yes, my Lord," muttered Salamon with a sigh. He bowed to Malenek, taking his leave to unburden himself of the chain mail.

"As for the rest of you, our time has come," he announced. "There is no going back. Like me, you believe that this world is too far-gone, that we have spilled too much blood on our lands and in our seas for even the gods to cleanse. We must believe that our sacrifice will bring a new age of peace to all corners of Enara."

"For Enara!" shouted Martyn Keyll. The soldiers cheered the words again in reply. The collective scream from the spirits sent a shudder down Malenek's spine as it reverberated around the room. The priest could not allow himself to question his resolve. He gazed down at the gauntlets that gloved his hands, clenching them into fists. This is what he had to be; hard, uncompromising, resolute.

The large castle gates swung open, and Malenek emerged, riding his armoured steed Shento. Although a prime breed of horse, even he had been riled by the spirits. Shento had grown somewhat accustomed to being in their presence over the last few days, just as the spirits had become inured to their own form. They had learned how to focus their energies and manipulate the physical world in which they were now only echoes. Still, Malenek could feel the agitation in Shento's muscles as they started off down the mountainside.

It was dark when they set off, reaching Morghen in the dead of night. The air was so calm, still and cold, as if Death had already visited this place a thousand times over. Perhaps it will be a blessing, thought Malenek, to ride an army of spirits into a ghost town.

A few of the townsfolk emerged from their homes, tired and bleary eyed, armed with their blunt tools of agriculture. They were disturbed from their sleep by the commotion from the streets, and the strange, eerie lights that illuminated the buildings. The same instinct that Shento felt crept across their skin, that something was wrong with the natural order of things. Upon recognising Malenek, the visor of his helmet raised, the townsfolk were somewhat eased, but not entirely.

"My Lord Malenek?" one called out. "What is happening?"

Malenek opened his mouth to speak, but found he could not answer them. These people trusted him. Many of the spirits called this place home. Their town was under the care of Mytor Castle. They farmed the roughest terrain and lived a meagre, quiet existence. They did not deserve to die in such a way. But if the plan worked, they would all see the other side and bask in the tranquillity of Illyria.

"My Lord?" cried another, a woman this time. Again, Malenek did not answer. He lowered his visor, diminishing his view so he could not see them all at once. In the silver glow of the spirits, his metal mask was truly terrifying, as was the hollow voice that emerged from within.

"Do it," he ordered. The spirits advanced on the townsfolk, some of whom ran, while others were frozen in terror. Malenek watched through the visor as the first spirit reached into the flesh of a man and severed the sacred link between body and soul. The victim fell to his knees, his limbs contorting in agony. The man's skin seized up tight and turned a morbid grey, his eyes losing all colour until they were dead white orbs. His dry, bloody mouth let out a ghoulish scream that made Shento whine, rearing up on his hind legs. Malenek soothed the horse, unable to tear his eyes away from the abomination on the ground. They wore the shape of a man, but twisted in torment and rage. It was nothing more now than a savage beast, a prison of flesh for the broken soul trapped within.

An ætherghoul.

CHAPTER ELEVEN

A BRIEF ESCAPE

Kamina woke to see the red sun peek over the horizon. Her kidnapping ranger was gone. Kaedin stood nearby, spying on Callaghan a short distance away, on his knees, in prayer to Risaar. He held Ascara pointed down, the tip of her blade sunk into the topsoil. He whispered the incantation, setting the sword ablaze. The first light of day combined with the magic of the fire to create something almost musical. The ranger was a silhouette to them, lost in the shadow of his contemplations.

He had his back turned to them, Kamina thought.

She gathered her senses and glanced around. There was a small clump of crimson-leaved trees on the other side of Anawey's ruins. They could outrun the ranger and hide there, and then double back along the route they had travelled, back to Elgrin Forest. Back home to Talia.

"Kaedin, we have to go," she hissed. "Now!"

"Go?" asked the ghost. "Go where?"

"Home!" she pleaded. He hesitated, so she made his decision for him, running towards the distant trees, stretching their nauseating bond.

"Kamina," he called out, his fading ghostly form speeding after her. Good, she thought, he will follow until he has caught up. She dashed through the ruins of her ancestors, leaping over crumbling walls and through desolate buildings. It was nothing but a scab of stone on the landscape. Soon the stone underneath her feet changed to grass. Kamina careered down a gentle slope towards the trees until she her feet cracked the scattered twigs on the forest floor. The red, leathery leaves slapped against her skin, their surface cool with morning dew. She paused beside a thick trunk, waiting for Kaedin to join her.

"Where are you going?" She jumped as he appeared behind her.

"Home!" she exclaimed. He laughed in disbelief.

"Kamina, do you not understand what is going on?"

"I do not care!" she cried out. "This is a matter for men, not elves!"

"Kamina," he said softly, kneeling next to her. "If we do not play our part in this task, there may not be a home to go back to. And even if there is, even if we could just go back and live our lives in a veil of ignorance, what would I do? Am I to remain this way forever?" As if to prove his point, he moved his ghostly fingers through hers. He focused his energy, and she felt a spark of pressure, tingly like fire, yet worryingly cold.

Kaedin's spirit was holding her hand.

The thrilling sensation only lasted a few seconds, before her fingers passed through his. Kamina withdrew and looked up into his eyes, surprised to find her own fears reflected in them.

"Why did this happen to us?" she asked.

"I do not know, but everything happens for a reason. And right now, our path is with the ranger. Agreed?"

Kamina nodded sullenly, wiping away tears of stupidity. Before she could say the words, they were startled by a ghastly, yet familiar voice.

"What have we here?" sneered Maulin, emerging from the small forest. He took Kamina by surprise, his twisted metal hook pressed against her delicate neck. "Seems the fates have decided your path is with me, precious elfling."

"Let her go!" screamed Kaedin. The elven ghost had gone unnoticed by Maulin until now, obscured by a tree. The marauder backed away from the spirit, his grip still tight around Kamina.

"What in the name of the Elements is this?" he gasped. Kaedin readied himself to attack the marauder, but Maulin pressed his cold steel hook into Kamina's neck, just enough to puncture her skin and draw a sliver of blood.

"Stay there, or she dies!" warned Maulin. "I swear she will!"

"Do not dare harm her!" Kamina was signalling him with her eyes, flicking over to her left, back to Anawey, back to the ranger. Kaedin shook his head; they both knew he could not make it across the ruins with her held here as his anchor. Kamina squeezed her eyes tight, nodding just enough to make him understand, without driving the hook any further into her flesh. Kaedin realised that if he waited any longer, the marauder would retreat further into the trees. Fighting against every fibre of his ghostly being, Kaedin reluctantly dashed through the trees until he had cleared the forest.

Maulin fled in the opposite direction, clumsily crashing through the bracken while carrying his elven prize. Kamina tried to break free, but her energy was already draining as she was spirited away from her ghostly sibling.

Kaedin darted up the hillside toward Anawey, but he too soon suffered the strain of their bond being stretched so far. He collapsed at the edge of the crumbling city, his form fading away. He looked at his outstretched arms, watching as they diminished, almost invisible.

Kamina struggled to keep her eyes open, her senses on fire as she fought to remain conscious. The passing trees became blurs of browns and reds whizzing by. The heavy breath of the marauder rasped in her ears as he barged through branches, splintering like bones. In the distance she could make out the gargling of a river.

"Kaedin! Kamina!" called Callaghan.

Kaedin, now completely transparent, tried to scream out for the ranger, but all he managed was a deathly croak.

"Callaghan. Callag…" he tried, but the ghost disappeared out of existence. As he did, Kamina finally lost the battle to keep her eyes open, drifting into unconsciousness as her kidnapper lugged her towards the rush of water.

CHAPTER TWELVE

THE MARAUDERS' CAVE

"I'M TELLING YOU I SAW A BLEEDIN' GHOST!"

Kamina recognised the scratchy voice of her abductor as she was roused from the dark void she had slipped into. Her back was cramped against a damp, rocky wall, water trickling down its surface. She overheard a conversation somewhere to her right.

"Have you been drinking?"

Kamina's eyes slowly cracked open. The room was actually a cave, a chilled morning breeze blowing through its mouth, partially hidden by a waterfall.

"That's not the point."

The waterfall wallowed into a larger river gargling nearby. If she could reach it she may stand a chance of escape, but as her senses returned, she felt the coarse rope binding her wrists and ankles.

"It is if you claim to have seen a spirit walking around among the living! What were you doing near the elven ruins anyway?"

Kamina struggled to free herself from the rope, scraping her hands against the rock at her back, but it was not sharp enough to fray the threading.

"I thought I could smell a fire."

The blurry form of the two men standing at the cave entrance came into focus. One was her nefarious abductor, while the other was his opposite; tall, muscular, an ex-soldier perhaps. He was younger than Callaghan, but a brutal scar ran down his face over his right eye, half-hidden by a patch. The other eye was intact; steel blue, still showing a glimmer of youth, but the disfigurement aged him, his expression harsh and cold.

"You have the nose of a blood rat, Maulin," said the scarred man. "Apparently, you also have its blind eyes."

"I know what I saw. Maybe... maybe it was an elf trick. Magic."

The man with the eye patch glanced round to study the elf. Kamina quickly shut her eyes, hoping she had been swifter than the man's singular sight. She kept them closed, pretending she was still unconscious. She focused on the sounds of the cave, trying to pinpoint her captors. However, she was still dazed, and could hear nothing but the rushing wind and flowing water.

"What say you, little elf?" the man whispered callously into her ear, his hot, foul breath wafting over her face. "Was this ghost the result of elf magic? You can open your eyes, I know you're awake."

Kamina elected to keep feigning sleep, her eyes firmly shut. She was surprised by the cold steel of Maulin's hook against her chin, causing her big green eyes to burst open. The faces of the two men filled her vision, compelling her to lean back against the hard cave wall. The scarred man took a hold of Maulin's wrist and forced him to draw his hook away from the elf.

"That's better," he said. "What's your name, child?"

"Kamina."

"I am Vangar." The name sounded familiar to her. She felt sure she had heard it whispered in hushed conversations in Tilden. Kamina recalled gossip about a soldier returning disfigured from the war, and refusing to return to Zalestia. Was this him? He was a deserter, now a marauder, leading the raiders who operated between Legoria and Caspia.

She could now hear the echoes of other marauders deeper within the cave, snoring, eating, and jeering. In another section, someone was grinding and sharpening blades.

"What is a young elf doing so far from the trees of Elgrin?" Before she could decide whether to answer truthfully or not, Maulin interrupted.

"Ask her about the ghost," he hissed hurriedly, waving his hooked hand at her accusingly.

"I already have one scar on my face," said Vangar, placing his hand purposefully on Maulin's metal appendage. "I do not need another." He pushed the hook down until it was safely tucked away by the marauder's side. Vangar turned his attentions back to the young elf.

"Kamina, Maulin claims that you were in the presence of a ghost. Is that true?"

Presence of a ghost.

Kamina realised that she was awake, that she was alive and feeling strong, which meant Kaedin must also be alive, and close by...

...Or perhaps he had faded so far that their bond had snapped.

Perhaps her brother was lost forever.

"Answer him!" urged Maulin.

"Yes," Kamina admitted meekly.

"See! She does not deny it! It is elf magic. That is why they remain hidden in the trees. They commune with the dead!"

"Maulin, could you try and be a little less melodramatic?" asked Vangar rhetorically. "Can you explain what this ghost was, Kamina?"

"He was my brother, but he is now a spirit of vengeance."

"They're nothing but a myth," cried Maulin.

"Then what is that standing behind you?" said Kamina. Both men spun round to find Kaedin's spirit staring back at them with a face of fury.

"By the Elements!" breathed Vangar. Maulin, seeing the spirit for the second time, fled deeper into the cave.

"There's a ghost! A ghost!" he screamed.

"Stay back!" Kaedin warned Vangar, as he manoeuvred himself towards his sister. She was unharmed, but he could do little for her, incapable of untying the ropes. He pointed a reproachful, ghostly finger at Vangar. "Untie her now!" he demanded.

Vangar, normally a man of action, was flustered by the spectre's appearance. In his career as a soldier he had seen some truly strange things, but this was a new realm of wonder, one that rendered him immobile.

Maulin's loud retreat had alerted the other men to the danger. They emerged from the cave tunnel with their weapons raised.

"I told you!" howled Maulin hysterically. "Didn't I tell you?" One of the marauders, Slavek Istin, quickly assessed the scene. While the others struggled with their fearful apprehension of the spirit, Slavek's base instincts kicked in. The marauder charged at the elven ghost, his sword held like a lance. Kaedin realised that the weapon would pass right through him and strike Kamina. On impulse Kaedin stretched out his arm to stop Slavek. His hand flowed through the man's chest and snatched at his beating heart.

Slavek stopped abruptly, the sharp point of his sword hovering right in front of Kamina's eyes. The marauder's whole body shivered. He struggled to breathe as the spirit held his soul. The ghost tried to remove his hand without harming him, but something snapped within the man's body. Slavek dropped his sword, clanging on the rocky floor. He staggered backwards, collapsing in the cave. He wailed like a wild animal, clutching at his chest. He clawed at it, scratching away clothing and skin, as if trying to rip himself open. The others stepped back as he writhed around, screaming in agony.

Slavek suddenly stopped moving.

"Is he dead?" asked Maulin?

"Slavek?" said Vangar. The only reply was a low, ferocious growl building slowly in the back of his throat. Slavek picked himself up, but his limbs moved awkwardly, his body creased, like an injured animal. His face was deformed, the grey reminder of a man.

The undead creature lunged at one of the marauders, attacking him, mauling him with a supernatural brutality. Most of the others retreated into the cave, unprepared for an attack. Vangar watched with wide, unflinching eyes as the thing feasted on the dead man's warm flesh. Slavek's head snapped up, his nose sniffing a different, sweeter scent.

An elf.

He pounced for Kamina. She watched as Slavek's rotting face jutted towards her, but then she felt herself moving away. A hand snatched the elven girl and dragged her out of the cave, a hand marked by the symbol of the rangers.

Callaghan threw himself and Kamina through the waterfall onto the waiting Eshtel. The steed sped away, leaving the creature that was once Slavek Istin screeching in disappointment. The echoes of screams and clashes of weapons reverberated off the walls of the cave. They heard one final, inhuman shriek over Eshtel's galloping beat, as the marauders managed to mortally wound the abomination.

"Hold on!" screamed Callaghan. Eshtel sprinted along a narrow path carved out halfway up a ravine, the rapid river running below. She could not see Kaedin, but sensed her spiritual sibling was not far behind.

A whistling sound pierced the air. Eshtel neighed in pain, bucking as he lost his balance. Kamina tumbled down the ravine wall, hot blood on her hands as she scrabbled at the side. She landed hard in a puddle by the river's edge. Everything was happening too fast and with too much pain. Eshtel bleated in agony, an arrow embedded in his hide. Kamina crawled over to him and held his head in her hands. She kissed him, crying. He could not move. Her tears wet his face as she gazed into his large, frightened eyes. Hands groped around her waist, dragging her away from her beloved Eshtel.

"Kamina, we have to go, now!" grunted the ranger, but she fought him off.

"We cannot leave him!"

"We must!" he barked, dragging her away.

"Eshtel!" The horse neighed after her, trying to find the legs to follow, but they buckled, his bones fractured. Eshtel collapsed to the ground.

"Kamina! Please!" begged the ranger

"They are coming!" Kaedin screamed somewhere behind them.

Another arrow sliced through the air, burying itself in the ground between Kamina and Eshtel. Kamina caught a glimpse of the archer, a slender man with a long dark prison of hair covering most of his face. A pair of black eyes peered out at her between the strands. He was of the Etraihu tribes that lived in Rundhale, making the crime against Eshtel even worse.

"I am sorry," cried Kamina, over and over, as she finally gave in to Callaghan's will. She took one last glance at her brave injured steed, before turning her back on him, blocking out his agonising wails.

The trio clambered along the water's edge, fleeing from the pursuing marauders, now baying for blood and revenge. Kamina was distracted by flashes of movement in the trees above them on both sides of the bank.

"Kamina, move!" shouted Kaedin, as a well-aimed arrow zinged towards her. He leapt in front of her, his intangible form deflecting the path of the arrow before the ghost crashed right through her.

"Kaedin, hurry!" she yelled, pausing as the ghost picked himself up, running through the water without making a splash. Callaghan, lagging behind his elven ward, screamed after them.

"Keep going!" he ordered. Callaghan turned to cover their escape, but was tackled to the ground by Maulin Lamn. He slashed at the ranger with his hooked hand.

"Remember me, ranger?" he hissed. "I knew I would have my revenge, just not so soon!"

Callaghan dodged his deadly hook, kicking Maulin away. They rose to face one another, but Callaghan could hear the other marauders coming for them. He had to end this quickly.

"Remember what I promised?" he asked the marauder. As Maulin tried to figure out what the ranger meant, Callaghan swiftly withdrew Ascara and chopped off his other hand, sending it flying into the water. He left Maulin kneeling by the river's edge, watching as his remaining hand waved goodbye from the white rapids.

Kamina splashed her way through the shallows of the river, as arrows and men continued to scream after them. Kamina avoided another arrow, wading further into the widening river, but the flow proved too much for the young elf. Callaghan caught up with them splashing through the shallows, spotting Kamina being sucked away by the undertow.

"Kamina... no... the edge!" She could barely hear him between the gurgling and lashing of water. The rush grew louder. Kamina realised that the river was carrying her towards a colossal waterfall.

The Finsing Falls.

She grasped for a rocky outcrop, but missed, smacking her head against it. The current carried her under the water. The young elf fought to the surface again, just in time to see the edge of the water disappear. A large weathered outcrop jutted out from the peak of the waterfall, dividing it in two. Kamina managed to seize hold of the slimy rock. The water pulled at her, trying to suck her down and over the edge. She dug her nails into the rock, hanging over the waterfall. The drop was so vast that the bottom was hidden below a cloud by vapour. Kamina struggled to keep hold as her strength dwindled. Her nails scratched into the stone as the water rushed all around her, pushing her over the edge into oblivion.

Callaghan caught up to her, making a leap from the riverbank to the outcropped platform. He caught Kamina's wet hand just as she lost her grip, dangling over the edge. The ranger heaved her up before she slipped from his sodden grasp. As they caught their breath lying on their backs, they discovered Kaedin staring down at them, completely dry.

"Do not just lie there!" he urged "They are coming!"

Callaghan dragged Kamina up onto her feet, but it was too late. The ranger thought about trying to reach the opposite side, but there was a rush of feet on both banks. The armed marauders had caught up with the trio, emerging from the slopes and trees. Kamina's rapid heartbeat punctured the silence of the stand-off. In between her heavy gasps she could hear fists tighten around the worn handles of swords, the reverberating tension of the strings on their bows. All the while, the reaping rush of the Finsing Falls poured into the unseen pool below.

Kamina caught sight of the Etraihu archer who had murdered Eshtel. She glared at him, his cold black eyes staring back along the arrow aimed at her. Perhaps he sensed her accusation, for his eyes lost their sharpness, and he lowered his aim away from her.

Vangar stepped away from the crowd he had led, following Callaghan's path, leaping from bank to rock to outcrop, sword in hand. Callaghan withdrew Ascara and her steel met Vangar's, defended himself and the elves from the former soldier's attack.

"I do not want to fight you, Vangar" shouted Callaghan.

"You attacked us!" he screamed back, swinging his sword again. "You killed one of my men, turned him into that thing."

"You brought that upon yourself when one of your men kidnapped a child in my care."

Vangar paused in his attack. "Why is a ranger travelling with an elf and a ghost?"

"I do not have time to explain. All I can tell you is Lord Malenek is marching with an army of spirits, and these elves may hold the key to defeating him."

"Malenek?" quizzed Vangar, almost laughing. "The priest?"

"He marches from Mytor. He will reach Perhola soon, before heading south to Gorran. Vangar, you must let us leave. You and your men should travel to Calisto."

"Calisto?" spat Vangar. "We would be arrested on sight. They would hang us all!"

"It will soon be the safest place in all of Amaros."

"Why? Because of those things?" asked Vangar, pointing his sword reproachfully at Kaedin. "What did you do to Slavek?!"

"I do not know," begged Kaedin. "I did not mean to."

"Liar!" Vangar swung at the spirit, but the blade passed right through him, heading straight for Kamina. She stepped back to avoid the blade, but found no solid footing, only air. She tumbled backwards off the edge, plummeting into the mists of the Finsing Falls.

"Kamina!" screamed Kaedin, diving after her, leaving Callaghan to face off against Vangar and the marauders alone. The ranger glanced over the edge to see Kamina and Kaedin disappear into the vapour of the falls.

"Vangar, go to Calisto," advised Callaghan, sheathing Ascara. The leader of the marauders was astonished when the ranger leapt after the elves to an uncertain fate. He watched as Callaghan was enveloped by the spray, deafened by the rush of the falls.

The pool at the bottom was suddenly upon him. Callaghan flopped into the water, dragged down in a daze. The current wrenched him along the as he fought against its watery grip, eventually breaking through to the surface, gasping for air. He heard Kaedin calling for his sister further along the rapids.

"Kamina!" Kamina allowed her body to be dragged along the rapids, trying to avoid the spate of rocks jutting up from the frothy waters. She tried calling out for Kaedin but her mouth clogged with water. She was dragged and battered along the course of the swirling river, until she was unceremoniously spat out into the air. Kamina glimpsed the magnificent sight of Lake Comodo, a great expanse of water, so far and wide it could have been mistaken for an ocean, before plunging into its dark depths.

CHAPTER THIRTEEN
CROSSING LAKE COMODO

KAMINA CRAWLED FROM THE CHILLING WATERS OF LAKE COMODO onto the gritty shore of a small island near the waterfall. She tried to walk, but her legs were exhausted. Instead she tumbled to her knees. She rubbed her frozen body with shaking arms in an attempt to warm up. Kaedin appeared at her side, unscathed by their perilous passage through the rapids. He spoke to her, but she could not hear the words, her head buzzing with pain, haunted by the memory of Eshtel's cries of agony.

"Are you hurt?" asked Callaghan as he sloshed up beside them. Kaedin shook his head, but Kamina was too cold to answer. The ranger withdrew Ascara and called forth her magic, allowing the fire to consume a dead log. He beckoned Kamina to dry off next to the flames. The elf rose up and marched towards Callaghan with all her might. Water dripped from her tightened fist as she punched him square in the face.

"You killed him!" she yelled. "You killed Eshtel! "This is all your fault!"

The ranger clasped her wrists, preventing her from lashing out again. Kamina's emotions struggled for a release as the grief consumed her. Her frail body convulsed as the tears ran over her face. Callaghan wrapped his firm arms around her. His soothing voice whispered an apology. Grey clouds above them cried too, as it started to rain, extinguishing the flames. Time drifted endlessly as they stood there, the dead fire's steamy smoke rising up behind them.

"Callaghan," interrupted Kaedin. The ranger followed the ghost's gaze and spotted a small sailboat tacking towards them.

"Kaedin, can you vanish?" The ghost nodded, disappearing into thin air as he made himself transparent. Only if you were looking hard enough for him could you see the distortion of light in the vague shape of an elf.

"Ahoy there!" shouted a rotund man with bright, rosy cheeks. He dropped the sail, allowing the boat to drift towards the island.

"Hello," replied Callaghan.

"I saw the smoke," explained the sailor. "Thought it was a bit of an odd place for a picnic."

"Our boat sank," lied the ranger. "Would you be kind enough to transport my ward and I to the shore, master…?"

"Link's my name," he called out. "Link Raliss. As for ferryin' ye across the Comodo, what you got in the way of payment?"

"We were robbed by a gang of marauders. We have nothing left."

"So your boat sank after you were robbed by a bunch of thieves?" Link asked sarcastically, peering closer at Callaghan. "Yet you still have your sword. Marauders would have taken a fine weapon like that I suspect."

"It is how we escaped," said Callaghan. "Please, we have urgent business in Calisto."

"The sword for the ride," bartered the man.

"Enough!" boomed a voice from an unseen source, like a deity watching from the sky. "You will take us wherever we wish to go." Link's head twitched around like a bird's, trying to discern the source of the sound. Kaedin materialised, sitting opposite him on the boat. The tubby sailor leapt up, nearly falling overboard. He swung one of the oars at Kaedin, with no effect, the paddle passing right though him.

"By the blue beard of Aquill!" Link muttered, dropping the oar and staring suspiciously at the corked jug of mead rolling around the hull by his feet.

Callaghan and Kamina waded out towards them. They climbed into the boat, while Link contemplated leaping out. However, there was nowhere to go, save for the island, and there was little chance anyone would pass by here for days. Link cursed himself for having sailed this far west on the lake to indulge in a spot of fishing, away from the timber traffic between the town of Comodo and Calisto.

"Please, don't hurt me," Link begged, but Callaghan allayed his fears.

"Master Raliss, we are not going to harm you," he said. "All we require is transport to Calisto."

Link's gaze now fell on the little girl, staring intently at her pointed ears. "What happened to your ears, lass?" he asked. Kamina conscientiously felt her ears to make sure they were okay.

"She is an elf, Master Raliss, as was the boy, although as you can see, he is now a ghost." Link glanced back and forth between the pair, reaching for the jug of ale.

"So why should I take you to Calisto?" he asked, taking a swig. "It's a bad enough omen having a woman on board, let alone a bloomin' elf and the ghost of one!"

"Because you will have the thanks of a ranger," said Callaghan, showing his tattooed hand. "One who will owe you a favour."

Link eyed Callaghan, weighing up his options. "Well, I do have to sail down the Ico to Calisto," thought the sailor aloud. "It's my job you see."

"You are a log runner," said Callaghan.

"Aye, that I am," confirmed Link. "Suppose it would be nice to have the company of a ranger. It's becoming a more dangerous run these days."

"Because of raiders?"

"Worse," warned Link. "Ogarii. Creep out from the swamps on unsuspecting sailors. Used to be an attack was rare, but now…" He trailed off, taking another drink.

"Then I offer you my protection in exchange for safe passage to Calisto," said Callaghan, sticking out his hand. Link begrudgingly accepted it, having his heart set on the sword.

"I'll have to stop in Comodo first to pick up some supplies," explained Link. "I was trying to save some crona by fishing out here, but luck wasn't on my side."

"No, we must avoid the town," said Callaghan.

"Given you company I can see why you'd want to," replied Link nervously, uncorking the jug again and taking a deep swill. His mouth erupted with a gaseous rift that repulsed Kamina's heightened sense of smell. "But I have to eat, and I suspect you and your pointy eared friends might wish to do so as well."

Callaghan glanced at Kamina, shaken and weak after their escape from the marauders. "Very true, Master Raliss."

"Righty ho then. Welcome on board the *Tepona*. Let's get going, shall we?" The sailor was careful not to touch Kaedin as he moved to the bow of the boat to unleash the sail. Soon they were tacking their way east across Lake Comodo's great expanse. Link minded the sails while Callaghan sat at the stern, steering with the rudder. They neared the edge of the lake, where a small town stood near the opening of the river.

"Comodo," announced Link, who up until this point had been entertaining himself by singing songs rather than asking questions. "Town only exists because of the loggers. Without them, it would be a ghost town. No offence."

"None taken," said Kaedin.

"And that," said Link, raising a fat finger and jabbing it towards the waterway, "that is the River Ico. Pretty much the fastest way to Calisto from these parts. We float logs downstream, but us log runners sail down too, making sure none get stuck or stolen. Can't afford that to happen at the moment, supply outstrippin' demand."

"Because of the war?" asked Kamina.

"Aye, lass, 'cause of the war." Link grimaced at the mere mention of the crusade that had spanned an entire generation. He gazed across the water to try and curtail a crushing memory.

The rain lessened as the grey clouds drifted north. Link docked at the furthest jetty he could find. Kamina eyed the hills behind the ramshackle town, pocked by the stumps of the thousands of trees cut down to feed the hunger of the war.

"Stay here," said Callaghan, as he helped the sailor tie up the boat.

"And don't touching anything," warned Link, before the pair paced along the boardwalk to the town. Kamina kept staring at the treeless hills, the rows of stumps like gravestones.

"It is not his fault," whispered Kaedin in their natural tongue. Kamina offered no reaction. "The ranger," he continued, "Eshtel's death is not his fault."

"He kidnapped us," hissed Kamina in an equally hushed tone, despite this particular dock being deserted.

"What other choice did Talia leave him?" retorted Kaedin.

"He could have left us there. We could have gone home."

"Are you so selfish that you would stand by and watch as darkness consumes the world? We have been given the responsibility of helping Callaghan defeat it."

"I did not ask for this," she said timidly.

"No, you ran away, and Eshtel died saving you. If his death is anyone's burden to bear, it is yours." Kamina turned away from her cruel spirit's stinging criticisms. She would not give him the satisfaction of seeing more tears roll down her cheek. They were tears not of sorrow, but of self-pity, for she knew there was some truth is what Kaedin said.

The two men returned. Callaghan carried a basket of food, while all Link Raliss seemed to have procured was more ale. They hastily set sail again, the wind now in their favour. Callaghan caught the sailor eyeing Kaedin with a fearful fascination that was becoming standard around the elf spirit.

"Kamina," said Callaghan. "Take the rudder for a while."

"I do not know how."

"It is simple. I'll show you." Kamina stepped over to the ranger and sat next to him. He took her hand and gently placed it on the tiller.

"Now, aim for the river," he said, his arm stretched out straight in front of them. "Push the tiller in the opposite direction of where you want to go. Like that. See?" Kamina nodded, veering the boat to the right before correcting it. "Good. Why don't you try it for a while." Kamina directed the ship towards the river as Callaghan moved to the bow, planting himself opposite Link.

"Don't leave her there too long," hissed Link, "or we'll all be meeting Aquill at the bottom."

"You are curious about the boy," said Callaghan.

"Curious, aye, but I knows when and when not to pry. Ghosts, rangers, elves – I've heard tales of them all, but never in one story, and that doesn't bode well. So if it's all the same to you, ranger, I'd rather get ye all off my boat, collect some of Calisto's finest brew, and head back upstream none the wiser to your business."

"Ignorance will not prevent what is coming," said Kaedin loudly, having overheard their conversation. Kamina knew his words were directed not only at Link Raliss, but also at her.

"That might be true," retorted Link, "but ignorance has served me fairly well for over sixty years now, while you're a boy with one foot in the grave." Kaedin sneered at the sailor, staring off into the distance.

From the source of Lake Comodo they headed south along the River Ico, cutting straight through the landscape. As they sailed further downstream, the hills flattened themselves, the clumps of trees on the banks growing sparse.

"I could go ashore and scout ahead," Kaedin suggested. The ranger realised he was eager to leave the boat, still smarting from Link Raliss' remark.

"Do not let anyone see you," he shouted after the spirit. "And do not go too far ahead." Kaedin nodded as he waded out to the shore, vanishing into thin air.

The clouds were cast in brilliant shades of pinks and lilacs by the setting suns, heralded the evening. Link attempted to light a small oil lantern by sparking two worn pieces of flint. After the sailor had cursed all four Elementals, Kamina glanced over to Callaghan, indicating Ascara with a discreet nod of her head. The ranger softly shook his head in reply. Before the girl could approach him to ask why, Link finally won his scuffle with the flint, sparking the oil alight.

"Thank Risaar for that," he huffed, hanging the lantern out in front of the bow on a bendy stick. Before he did, he lit a splinter of wood and stole a light for his smoking pipe. Link lounged back and relaxed as the gentle evening breeze carried them gradually down the river. Ygrain and Whirren's celestial bodies hung high above them. The ranger, the elf and the transparent spirit wandering the shoreline listened as the old sailor sang a shanty about the seas.

"A poor old man comes riding by,
And we say so, and we hope so.
A poor old man comes riding by,
Oh, poor old horsey boy.
Says I, 'Old man, your horse will die,'
Says he, 'Young man, this horse will cry.'
But if he dies we'll tan his skin,
And if he don't we'll ride again.
For one long month I've rode him hard,
For one long year he's beat the bard.
But now my month is up, old boy,
Get up, you swine, and ride for joy,
Get up you swine and look for graft,
While we lays on this dingy raft.
He's as dead as a nail in the door,
And he won't come worrying us no more.
We'll use the hair of his tail to sew our sails,
And the iron of his shoe to make deck nails,
Oh, poor old horsey boy…"

Kamina shut out the silly song and its awful lyrics. She wrapped her weary body in a warm bismun hide Link had dug out, ignoring the pungent odour of fish trapped within the fur. The day's excitement still stirred her thoughts, forcing her to lie awake, staring at the stars. Link eventually forgot the words to the shanty, humming along to the tune instead.

"You get some shut-eye as well, ranger," said Link, manoeuvring his bulk beside the tiller. "I'll keep an eye on the water, and an ear out for your sulking spirit."

Callaghan sat his weary body down across from Kamina. He stared at the young elf, watching her on the verge of sleep, yet struggling to cross the threshold.

"Kamina," he said in a hushed tone. She flicked her eyes open. "I am sorry about Eshtel. He was a very noble creature." Her words caught in her throat, so she simply nodded, closing her eyes to prevent any more tears being shed that day.

The ranger's condolences afforded her the peace she needed to sleep. That night she dreamed she was riding Eshtel, only he was made entirely of water, prancing across the surface of Lake Comodo.

CHAPTER FOURTEEN

THE INTRIGUE OF GORRAN

AFTER WITNESSING THE ELVES AND THE RANGER PLUMMET OVER the edge of Finsing Falls, Vangar and the marauders returned to their cave. Slavek's disfigured body lay still on the dirt floor. He ordered a handful of men to take the corpse and burn it on the banks of the river below.

As daylight faded, he watched the burning carcass from the mouth of the cave, blurred by the curtain of the waterfall. The flesh popped and sizzled in the fire, dulled by the rush of water. The sombre, elemental sounds were broken by Maulin, whining and yelping as Creevy, a former butcher and therefore the closest the marauders had to a doctor, attached Maulin's second hook in as many months. As Vangar partook in a passing jug of mead, a toast to Slavek, he found it only fuelled his anger toward the misbehaving marauder.

"Quit your whining, Maulin!"

"Perhaps you hadn't noticed, but I just had my bleedin' hand chopped off!" he cried back.

"With your luck you should have just asked the ranger to kill you to spare you any more pain," said Vangar, goading him.

"This is not my fault!" he shrieked, holding up his two hooks. Vangar launched himself across the cave and swiped Maulin's legs away from him. His body landed hard, coughing up a layer of dust. Before Maulin could catch his breath, Vangar pressed his boot down upon the man's chest.

"Who took the elf? Who brought the ranger and the ghost upon us?" He removed his boot, allowing Maulin to breathe. "You bring this cursed luck upon yourself and upon us. If you lose a foot we will leave you for the dogs."

"I want my revenge," sulked the handless marauder.

"From a ranger?" asked Vangar in disbelief, trying not to laugh. "Are you that dumb? Even if he did not die in the Finsing Falls, even if he crippled himself on impact and lost his sword to the rapids, and birds had pecked out his eyes, and an Ogarii had ripped him in half, he would still manage to carve you up like Creevy back when he was a butcher!" The other marauders scoffed and jeered at Maulin.

"What are you laughing at?" barked Vangar. "This dim-witted fool brings death to our door and you dare laugh?" The men were subdued into silence. Vangar had never been elected their leader; this was no democracy, there was no Council or Alliance here. He was the best man for the job, a good soldier and a natural captain. He kept them within the boundaries of some vague moral code, but they had never witnessed such behaviour in him as this.

"What did the ranger say?" asked Creevy. A state of unease had gripped Vangar's men. He shared a glance with the Etraihu archer, Ariel Atari, who had been mysteriously absent since the attack. There was an understanding between these two brothers-in-arms, familiarity with no need for words. This was just as well, as the archer had not said so much as a syllable since his return from Zalestia over a decade ago. He let his arrows do most of the talking. Ariel nodded a brief reply to Vangar before disappearing back into the night.

"The ranger claimed that Lord Malenek has an army of those spirits." There were some low grumbles of disbelief. "I do not believe he was lying," said Vangar above the mumbled protests. "Rangers rarely do, and if that was not proof enough, do not forget he had a spirit with him. We all saw it."

"It could have been magic," suggested a superstitious marauder named Tig Norden. "The elf, she could have been casting the spell. No-one knows what witchcraft they are capable of."

"We cannot be sure," conceded Vangar, "Which is why I will ride to Gorran. The ranger said Malenek would attack there after he sacks Perhola."

"If all this is true, if Malenek is leading some army of spirits and demons, better we not be heading in the opposite direction?" Vangar was not surprised to hear the cowardly comment come from Maulin.

"We must be certain. If Malenek attacks Gorran, we will retreat to Calisto. The ranger suggested that it would be the last safe haven against the spirits."

"Yeah, we'll escape the spirits by sending ourselves to the gallows!" joked Dappin Creig. This was true, thought Vangar. Most of the marauders were wanted men, with considerable bounties on their heads, whether those heads were attached to their bodies or not. What they lacked was an alternative.

"Why not simply outflank him, ride north?" suggested Maulin, thinking it was now safe to speak.

"I would rather face a trial than one of those demons, and you can bet the spirits are leaving them in their wake," answered Vangar, anger seizing him again. "You have followed me many times before, and I have done good by you when you were outcast and rejected by the Alliance, abandoned by the army, no longer wanted in the cities and towns you once called home because you were injured and infirm. Perhaps we should not care, but we… but I am not the monster they make me out to be. Just because my country gave up on me does not mean I gave up on it. We break the laws of the land to keep ourselves alive, but these are very laws of existence that are being broken, and if I can help prevent that then I will at least try." Vangar paused, his long-lost soldier's pride striving to take over, to find purpose.

"The choice is yours," he said solemnly. "You can follow me and control your own fate, or you can remain here and cower inside this cave, waiting for spectres to transform you like Slavek. Those of you who wish to join me, get some rest. We ride out at dawn."

*

Plagacia's hooves clapped along the well-worn track towards Gorran. Talia was barely aware of the beating rhythm, or the breaking dawn of the twin suns. Her head was lost in thought, as Endo's last words echoed in her ears.

"What if the end justifies the means?"

From Tilden she and the borrowed horse had headed straight to Elgrin Forest. She had steered Plagacia through the thick trunks of the approaching trees, an agent of urgency. By the time Talia reached the Tree of Edku, the tallest and most sacred tree in the entire forest, many of the elves had already gathered in its hollow. News had spread like fire throughout Elgrin, whispers of a dark intrusion upon their territory. Those elders with memories of magic from the days of Anawey had sensed the death of one of their kin.

"Talia!" Lashara spotted her as she dismounted the horse, directing a young elf to tend to the mare's needs for a long journey. "What is going on? Where have you been? Where are Kaedin and Kamina?"

"They are safe, for now." Before Lashara could interject, Talia added, "Please grandmother, it is a long story, and I am afraid I do not have time to tell it all." They cut through the crowd and into the Edku Tree, passing through the throng until they reached the dais at the centre where the other elders were congregating. Among them was Abbal Eredu, the oldest of them all, and his grandson Endo, being groomed as the future leader of their people. He had tried to court Talia on more than one occasion. Even now she could see his affection for her shine in his light green eyes. Her continuous rejections had raised a formal wall between the pair. Though the elves showed restraint with their emotions, Talia always felt Endo's words were tainted with hurt when directed at her.

"You should not be among the elders, Talia Elloeth," he said as he blocked her way, his voice tainted with false authority. Talia forced her way past, fixing her sights on Abbal, bowing before him.

"Abbal, if you would allow me to address our people, I believe I will be able to allay some of their fears." Despite his grandson's postured protest, the old elf nodded. Talia stepped up to the podium. The assembly of elves turned to her, although the fact that it was Talia and not Abbal who addressed them sparked as many whispers as it silenced.

"Be at peace my friends," stressed Abbal, stepping next to her. "Talia Elloeth has something to share." A tense hush rose up within the vast hollow of the Edku Tree. Talia suddenly realised how dry her mouth was.

"The rumours are true," she said finally. "Kamina and Kaedin were attacked by a mage from the Other Land. He was being pursued by the Ishkava Ranger Callaghan Tor. The mage... he killed Kaedin." There was a collective intake of breath. Lashara had to rest against Endo as the grief struck her heart. "Kamina, fearing for her life, managed to defeat this intruder." This caused even more concern among the gathering. "With the help of the ranger, we carried the bodies to Tilden."

"You should have brought them back here," said Karris Kolt, one of the elders. His view was echoed by several of the others.

"There is more!" Talia snapped back, with a furore that shook the bark of the Edku Tree. The crowd of elves scrutinised her. After the death of her parents, Talia had always been somewhat estranged from the elves, and her recent association with the humans had done nothing to resolve this. "When Kamina killed the mage," she continued, "Kaedin was returned to this world as an *ackran-fay*."

"Impossible!" roared one of the crowd.

"They are nothing but legend!" screamed another, until a wave of silence unfolded from Abbal's hand.

"You will grant Talia Elloeth the same respect you would grant me," he said. "If she says the *ackran-fay* exist, then I believe her."

"But father, how is this possible?" asked Endo.

"Old magic," whispered the eldest elf. "Blood magic." A brief nod from Talia affirmed Abbal's suspicions.

"Where are Kaedin and Kamina now?" begged Lashara.

"The ranger Callaghan has taken them to Calisto to warn the human Alliance. There is a bigger plot at work here. Kaedin is not the only *ackran-fay* to be summoned to these lands. The priest known as Balen Malenek marches from the north with an entire army of them."

"With what purpose?" asked Endo.

"That remains uncertain, but the ranger believes Malenek wishes to use them to cleanse Enara of any more bloodshed. You must take our people and leave Elgrin Forest. Go to Calisto," urged Talia. "The *ackran-fay* will not pay heed to warnings or borders."

"The matter will have to be deliberated amongst the elders," Abbal reasoned. "I sense, however, that you wish to travel a different path."

"The humans deserve to be warned," she said.

"Then let their own kind spread that warning," remarked Endo.

"By then it will be too late," argued Talia.

"Child, I understand what drives you to do this," said Lashara, taking Talia aside. "It is not your fault."

"I know grandmother," Talia whispered as she hugged the old elf. "But someone has to. Find Kamina. Keep her safe."

Plagacia had been well taken care of in the short interim. Talia mounted the mare, but the call of her name delayed her journey. Endo had followed her from the Edku Tree. The horse eyed him precariously as he approached.

"Talia, they will not leave the forest."

"Then they will die, Endo." Her curt words stung him.

"You may not agree with it, but Abbal believes it is for the good of our people to remain where we are. Malenek has no reason to come for us. This is a human concern." Over the years, Endo had watched his grandfather make hard decisions, listened to his stories of their war with the humans. He was moulded by them into a leader whose only concern was his own race.

"This evil will touch every living creature in Enara," she insisted. "We can no longer hide and do nothing, like we have done for over a hundred years."

"You said Malenek had created the *ackran-fay* to bring peace to Enara. Have you considered the possibility that he might be right?" asked Endo.

"How can you ask that?" begged Talia.

"Because you have not. If it is true, if Malenek can indeed deliver true peace to this world, then perhaps we should not stand in his way." Talia shook her head in disdain, lost for words, as Endo continued. "I too am tired of hiding. A world without war, without men fighting amongst themselves, or with the centaurs, or Moltari, or even us. A world where every race is at peace. Does that sound like such a horrific idea?" Talia found that Endo was holding her hand, felt the unrequited love on his fingertips as they graced her skin.

"You are talking about the death of innocents," she said, moving her hand away from his.

"Men have always killed men," argued Endo. "It is ingrained in the very nature of their being. Let them exterminate one another so that we may leave the confines of this forest without fear, into a world unburdened by man's need for battles, free from the plagues of war and death."

"Unlike you, Endo, Malenek does not seem to care what race you belong to. He has already killed Kaedin and countless others. He claims these lives in the name of peace, but at what cost?"

"What if the end justifies the means?" he reasoned. Talia felt sick at how cold and calculating Endo could be, tainted by his grandfather's ancient memories of man. She kicked Plagacia's thick hide. The horse thrust forward, propelling them both through the trees and away from Endo Eredu.

They had ridden throughout the night, Talia able to see where the horse could not. All along the dark path, Endo's words had haunted her.

"What if the end justifies the means?"

Talia could not accept that, as she rushed to warn the elves' once sworn enemy about the impending danger of Malenek and his *ackran-fay*.

Over the next ridge she caught her first glimpse of Gorran. It was nestled on the edge of Caspia's borders not only with Rundhale but with Heroshin as well. The city's heavily fortified stone walls were triangular in shape; one side facing each region, including Caspia, for Gorran had not always belonged to the country it now occupied. Beyond the walls, the surrounding lands were poked and scarred from past battles and skirmishes. Far to the southwest, Talia could make out the ruins of Duru Umbin, a great wall that had been built along the border of Rundhale and Caspia. It had fallen centuries before, but parts remained, a reminder of man's need to divide and conquer.

Talia slowed Plagacia on the trail up to the gates, aware of the sights of numerous archers upon her.

"State your business," shouted one from behind a parapet.

"I request an audience with your highest authority." They mumbled nervously to one another, trying to decide who would stay. The quick footsteps of the more cowardly guard faded as he ran to fetch a superior with the courage to face a lone, female elf.

"Get down from the horse," bellowed a voice.

As soon as Talia had done so, the double gates were opened. Four guards armed with crossbows approached her, fingers tense on the triggers. Behind them, a fifth man emerged; a soldier of a higher rank, a sedcoran, with short rusty hair and a kind, trusting face. He was however apprehensive at the unexpected appearance of an elf.

"Do not make any sudden moves," he commanded. Panic and mystery marred their faces. "What brings an elf this far from the forest of Elgrin?"

"I come as a friend, with a warning," said Talia. "I must speak to whoever is in charge."

"For the moment that would be me," replied the sedcoran. "Our ataincor has journeyed with Duke Garstang to Calisto."

"Then I would speak to you in private," she suggested.

"I do not have the authority to do so," he said curtly.

"Then take me to someone who does."

The sedcoran considered this for a moment, arriving at a solution. "Disarm yourself," he ordered, indicated her father's axe. The strings of the crossbows remained tense. She offered the weapon to the sedcoran's waiting hands. "May I also ask that you wear your hood," he muttered. "I am sure you understand."

Talia, too tired from the journey to fight for her pride, covered up her elven features with her green hood. They made their way through the city gates, while one of the soldiers led Plagacia to be fed and watered.

It was still early and most of Gorran was still asleep, although Talia saw a few curious faces pop out of windows and from behind doors. The troupe made their way through the cobbled streets, the walls of the buildings casting cold morning shadows upon them.

"What is your name?" she asked the soldier.

"Sedcoran Fleck."

"Where are you taking me, Sedcoran Fleck?"

"To see someone who you can pass your message on to," he replied.

They approached a small castle crammed into the centre of the city, and beyond that, she could hear the early calls of the soldier's barrack. Sedcoran Fleck moved in the opposite direction, towards a building with a domed roof, marked by a cross, each end decorated with a different coloured piece of glass.

This was a church of the Elementals.

Fleck ordered his men to stand guard at the door and let no one enter, while he escorted the elf inside. The interior of the church was dark, the twin suns not yet high enough to penetrate the high stain glassed windows. Four candles flickered at the far end of the church near the pulpit, each one positioned under the effigy of an elemental. A figure moved past them, having just finished lighting their wicks. The flames waltzed with the wind of his movements as he turned to see who had entered.

"Who is there?" asked an aged voice.

"Engel, it is Anton." Priest Engel Larson lit a candle and carried it along the aisle to meet them. He wore black robes, but his skin and hair were both a sallow white.

"And who is this with you?" he enquired, straining his eyes to see. Talia removed her hood. The priest stepped back in shock. His frail hand dropped the candle. The elf reacted quickly, catching it before a single drop of wax could reach the ground. Fleck was on edge. With speed like that, she could have disarmed him and his men before the first bolt had been fired.

"My name is Talia Elloeth," she said, handing the candle back to the priest's shaking hand. "And I have come to deliver a warning."

"I should leave you," uttered Fleck, still weary of the elf.

"Are you so afraid of what I may say?" she asked. Anton paused in the aisle, but did not leave. "Then stay, and listen."

"You said you have come to deliver a warning?" asked the priest. "From your kind?"

"No. As we speak, an army marches from the north, led by Lord Malenek."

"But Lord Malenek is a priest," argued Engel. "He has been blessed by the Elements themselves."

"I understand your affinity towards him," said Talia, trying to appease the priest, "but he has come to believe that this land is broken and needs to be purged."

"Even if it were true," interrupted Fleck, "his army cannot be any greater than that of the Alliance?"

"Not in number, no," she offered vaguely.

"Meaning what?" asked Priest Larson. "What are you not telling us?"

"Malenek has raised an army of ghosts. They cannot be damaged by conventional weapons."

"This is absurd!" he hissed.

"I assure you it is true," protested Talia. "I would not have come all this way if it were otherwise."

"And what would you have us do?" asked Larson in a mocking tone.

"The Ishkava Ranger Callaghan is on a quest to find a way to defeat the spirit army, but until he does, he believes it would be best to evacuate to Calisto. It will be the last city Malenek strikes."

"Evacuate, just like that?" he said, sneering. "And while the city is left empty, perhaps the elves will take it over? Or the centaurs? We all know the pointy ears are friends with the hoofs!"

Talia thrust her face firmly into Engel Larson's so he could see her pupils flare. The priest witnessed the dark holes engulf the emerald green of the elf's irises, like deep wells filled with anger.

"I am risking my life to warn you puny men that you are in danger and you dare to insult me!" she seethed. The priest backed away, afraid of her.

"Sedcoran Fleck, arrest her. Get her out of this house of worship."

"Please, come with me," said the sedcoran, trying to diffuse her rage. He did not wish to provoke her further by manhandling her. The livid elf stormed past him and out the door, Sedcoran Fleck following at her heels. Priest Larson returned to the four statues and fell to his knees.

"Why? Why did you send this mendacious creature to my house?"

They did not answer.

*

Sedcoran Fleck emerged from the church to find Talia challenging the four guards, all of whom had their crossbows aimed at the elf.

"Put your weapons down!" he commanded.

"Sir?" said one of the corans, not wishing to let his guard down.

"Trust me, coran, she could kill you before your finger even pulled the trigger." The men complied, lowering their crossbows. Sedcoran Fleck offered her the hilt of her father's axe.

"The priest told you to arrest me?" she inquired.

"Engel Larson is not my superior. You, fetch her horse." The coran Fleck indicated quickly saluted, speeding off to find Plagacia.

"But you cannot evacuate either."

"No, not until I receive an order to do so. I will send word to Duke Garstang in Calisto. In the meantime, I will organize my people and send spotters north."

"Why do you believe me?" she asked.

"I am not sure that I do, but I am a soldier. We prepare for the worst, and hope for the best."

"Your logic is sound, Sedcoran Fleck," she said. "When you send a messenger to Calisto, be sure the Duke has spoken with the Ranger Callaghan Tor. He will hopefully arrive there soon."

The coran charged with fetching Plagacia returned. Talia took hold of the reins and once again mounted the mare.

"Where are you going now?" asked Sedcoran Fleck.

"To warn the people of Perhola, although I fear I will be too late."

"Why are you so concerned?" he asked. "I mean no disrespect, but you..."

"I am an elf," she interjected. "That does not make me ignorant to the plight of others."

"I wish you a safe journey, Talia Elloeth."

"And to you, Sedcoran Fleck."

Talia sped out of his sights, down the streets to the already open gates, charging north into Heroshin territory.

CHAPTER FIFTEEN

THE CITY OF CALISTO

RISAAR AND AQUILL WERE HIGH ABOVE THE HORIZON BY THE TIME the ranger nudged Kamina awake. The *Tepona* was tied up at a riverbank near some swampland. Curtains of creepers hung from the branches of the dull trees all the way down into the bogs below.

"We require your help, little one," said Callaghan.

"I am not so little," she protested as he helped her into the mud.

"In this case it is an advantage," he reassured her. Callaghan guided the elf to where Link stood, next to a large log trapped between two rocks.

"Oh aye, she'll fit for sure," said the old log runner. Kaedin's ghost grinned beside him.

"Fit where?" Kamina asked, although she soon wished she had not.

"There is a small space underneath the log," explained Callaghan. "We need you to crawl under and push up to try and free it."

Kamina examined the space they expected her to wriggle into. Not only was it tight, but it was also teeming with large bugs and insects. "Under there?" she protested. The others nodded. "Can you not do it?" she said to Kaedin.

"The ghost tried," said Link with a laugh. "He's useless." Kaedin shrugged off the insult as Kamina sighed and grudgingly lay down on the ground. She shimmied under the log until her face was almost pressed against the bark. Callaghan and Link stood on either side of her.

"On three," said Callaghan. "One, two, three!" Kamina's little arms pushed as the two men heaved up on either side. The log broke free with a sudden jolt.

"Well done," said the ranger, but his thanks were cut short as the ground shook. An ugly, hunched beast, double the size of a man, burst through the trees, snarling at them.

"Ogarii!" screamed Link, letting go of the log and running back to the *Tepona*. Callaghan could not hold the weight of the trunk alone, losing his grip of the log. It fell back between the rocks, further than before, pinning Kamina underneath.

"Kaedin!" she tried to yell, but the wind had been knocked out of her lungs. Callaghan withdrew Ascara and quickly summoned her fire in an attempt to scare off the Ogarii.

"Callaghan, help!" shouted Kaedin as he tried to move the log. He could not concentrate long enough to lift it, tumbling through the wood. The ranger noticed that the Ogarii's vision had shifted to the spirit.

"Kaedin!" he commanded. "Run into the swamp to draw its attention. But do not engage it." The last thing they needed was for Kaedin to transform an Ogarii the same way he had the marauder Slavek Istin. Kaedin followed Callaghan's instructions, manoeuvring away from the log and into the swamp. The primitive Ogarii followed his ghostly glow into the gloom. As soon as the beast turned its back, Callaghan rushed to Kamina's side.

"Help," she squeaked.

"Things might get a little hot," he warned, taking Ascara and grooving her fiery blade into the bark. Her magical flame quickly charred the healthy timber to ash. Kamina could feel the heat singeing her legs. The ranger hacked away through the disintegrating wood until it was split in two. He helped Kamina roll the smaller section off her tiny frame. Despite the stench of the swamp, Kamina gulped at the air.

"Come, we are still in danger!" He sheathed his sword and slung Kamina over his shoulder, rushing back to the *Tepona* as fast as he could. Link had already released the boat from its moorings, pushing off into the river. Callaghan waded into the water and unceremoniously dumped Kamina inside before climbing over the hull.

"Where's the bleedin' ghost?" yelled Link.

"There," said Callaghan, pointing through the swamp. The spirit sprinted towards them, the Ogarii lumbering behind him. The ghost skipped over the surface of the water and into the boat, leaving the angry swamp dweller fuming on the shore. It roared at them, livid at losing its luminescent prize.

"That was a close one!" panted Link, rubbing the sweat from his brow.

"Close one?" exclaimed Kaedin. "You nearly got my sister killed. Over a log!"

"I'm the one doing you lot a favour here," snapped the sailor, "I said I'd get you to Calisto, and sure enough I will, but these logs are my livelihood."

"Get down!" yelled Callaghan. The Ogarii had picked up the burning log and launched it at the *Tepona*. The flaming missile collided with the mast. It broke off into the water along with the sail. The attack almost caused the boat to capsize, but Link threw himself against the port side, his bulk correcting the balance.

"Grab the sail!" he cried out. Callaghan and Kamina reached for the material, catching its edge, but the mast was towed under by the current. Half of the sail ripped off in their hands. The Ogarii gave a snorting last laugh from the shore before trudging back into the swamp.

Link sat in silence, surveying the damage to the *Tepona* as they drifted along the river. "Well, at least we got half the log back," he said, indicating the burnt block floating beside them. None of the others shared his enthusiasm. "Right then, I suppose we better try and fix her."

At Link's insistence, Callaghan manned the oars, putting distance between the boat and the swamp dwelling Ogarii. Kamina helped the sailor construct a makeshift sail from the piece they had salvaged, along with some fishing line and a spare oar. It was much smaller than the original, but it caught enough wind to propel them along the River Ico until the breeze faded. Callaghan voluntarily manned the oars again while Link relaxed and uncorked a jug of ale. The elves watches as they passed by farmlands, fortified against attacks from the wildlife of the nearby swamps.

"You're doing a fine job there, ranger," said Link "I think you missed your calling."

"It is you who should be rowing," remarked Kaedin. "You have the honour of having the Ranger Elite in your boat."

"Kaedin, Master Raliss has allowed us passage to Calisto. I am happy to repay the favour," said Callaghan.

"I meant no disrespect, spirit," said Link, weary of the ghost elf. "He's got us here in record time. See."

As the *Tepona* rounded the next bend, the elves cautiously stood up and saw the seaport of Calisto for the first time. Although still some distance along the river, the city was a wonder, the stone buildings stretching across the cliff edge, encapsulated by a protective wall. Somewhere in the centre Kamina noticed a crooked structure that jarred with the picturesque skyline. The black bricks of the solitary tower had been weathered down to a gloomy grey.

"It is magnificent," she breathed.

"Aye," chimed Link, "and that's only the half of it."

A healthy wind picked up and propelled them along the wide river. The upper docks of Calisto were bustling with activity, with many boats moored along both banks. Most were transport barges carrying timber and ore from the quarries north of Lake Comodo, or food from the farms they had passed. Some had been transformed into makeshift houses, with potted plants and herb gardens decorating their decks.

"Kaedin?" Kamina asked. The spirit had cloaked himself now that they had reached Calisto. Even though Kamina knew he was nearby, but she was unnerved by the fact she could not see him.

"I am here," he whispered behind her, making her jump. If she focused hard enough, she could see the light refracting differently around his aura. "Callaghan insisted I remain invisible."

"And I suggest you wear your hood," said the ranger, not so much a suggestion as an order, forcing the point by pushing it over her head.

"Stay close," she said to the spirit. A feeling of alienation crept upon her as she spied large, burly men unloading cargo and supplies.

"I will," he replied.

Callaghan helped her disembark as Link tied up the *Tepona*. "What are your plans now, Master Raliss?" enquired the ranger.

"Well I won't be going upstream until I get the old *Tepona* repaired," he grumbled, grimacing at the makeshift mast.

"Here is some crona to help." The ranger gifted the sailor with a small bag of Caspian coins. "But even when the repairs are completed, I suggest you remain in Calisto for the time being."

"See, this is why I don't ask no questions."

"I would be deeply offended if you did not take my advice," said the ranger.

"Well, I ain't making any promises," replied the old sailor, "but I've got a few friends in the city who owe me a drink or three. Maybe I'll look them up."

"I hope that you do." Callaghan offered Link his hand, which he shook. "Thank you, Master Raliss. I am in your debt."

"Yer welcome," he said, grinning. "You take care now. You too, Miss Kamina."

"Thank you," she shouted back as she followed the ranger's quick pace.

"And tell that bleedin' ghost to behave!"

Callaghan led them along the river edge, where teams of men snared the logs with ropes and scooped them out of the water. They crossed a bridge, but Kamina paused by the railing. She spotted the black tower again, much closer now, built near the river next to an equally repulsive building. Together they looked like a closed fist, save for one poisoned finger pointing at some horror in the sky. Callaghan grabbed her shoulder and pushed her forward.

"There is no time for sightseeing," he said as they continued their journey into the heart of the city. The streets here were narrow and dingy. Odd men lurched in doorways, while all of the women wore too much face paint and too little clothing. They twisted and turned through the maze of streets, Callaghan constantly checking to see if they were being followed.

"Is someone behind us?" whispered Kamina, as the ranger glanced back.

"I am not sure," he replied, "but given the circumstances, it is best to be cautious. I am not entirely sure who we can trust here."

They emerged into a wide street near a throng of people, gathered at the gates of the army barracks. The citizens peered through the railings to see the soldiers marching and performing drills, proud mothers, wives and children among them. Kamina noted that different divisions wore distinctive colours, signifying the region of Amaros they were from. The Caspians were dressed in blue and white, while the Heroshins wore scarlet and gold. She presumed the small group clad in black and silver were from Mytor, and that those in brown and orange were from Rundhale. The elf was happy to see the humans of Legoria displaying Elgrin green and grass yellow.

"Can we trust the army?" asked Kamina. Callaghan did not reply. They skirted through the crowds until they reached the bustling town square. Kamina spotted old men sitting across from one another, moving carved pieces of wood across a chequered board. Mothers lazed on benches and gossiped while their little soldiers and princesses ran around them. The children paused in their play as Callaghan marched past.

The ranger led them under the archway of a grand building and across a street. They were suddenly transported into a different world, one of green grass, prim kept bushes, and flowers of every colour. At the centre of the grounds was a tall, circular structure. Two guards were positioned by the entrance. They eyed the approaching party suspiciously.

"State your business," said one.

"We are here to see Ambassador Hesh," replied Callaghan.

"And you are?" he asked, peering inside the ranger's hood, unable to see his face clearly.

"An old friend," he said. He removed his hood, deliberately showing them his Ishkava tattoo.

"Follow me," said the guard. He led them inside, cutting through the debating chamber in the centre. The floor was engraved with the familiar cross of the four Elementals. A statue of each deity stood at the edge of their respective symbols, all four pointing a giant hand upwards. Kamina followed their almighty stone digits and gazed in wonderment at the levels of public galleries above. A mural was etched into the ceiling at the very top, her sharp elven eyes noting the painstaking detail to colour. It was a representation of Creation, the four gods bringing together their individual elements to create Enara, here depicted as a baby enveloped in a sphere.

"Kamina," called Callaghan from the doorway. She hurried along and caught up to him as they ascended a staircase. Kamina paused again beside a circular window, overwhelmed by the view beyond. The Ico poured out over the edge of the crescent-shaped cliff into the cove below, where a bounty of ships gently bobbed in the bay. From the top of the cliff men operated a series of ropes and pulleys, lowering materials and boat parts down the height of the rock face to the shipbuilders below. She now realised what Link Raliss had meant when he had said "that's only the half of it."

Callaghan placed a friendly hand on her shoulder. "Welcome to Calisto." He could do little else but grin at Kamina's wide-open expression of wonder. "This way."

They followed the guard around the outer ring of the building. He stopped at one of several doors, chapping on it three times in quick succession.

"Yes?" beckoned an old voice from behind the door.

"You have some guests, ambassador," announced the guard as he swung the door open.

"Who is it?" called out the old voice. The guard invited them to enter. Inside was a small study, and sitting at a sun bleached wooden desk was an old man, in formal, Heroshin dress. "Callaghan, my dear boy!" exclaimed the old man. He rose up slowly and greeted the ranger with a gentle hug.

"It is good to see you, Cohen," he said.

"You may go," Cohen said to the hovering guard. The soldier stole one last glance at Callaghan, unaware he had been escorting the Ranger Elite. "I heard rumours you had travelled to Zalestia." Only now did Cohen notice Kamina, still hooded. "And you have a guest." Worry suddenly filled his face.

"Callaghan, please tell me you have not brought a Zalestian here?"

"No, although I doubt you are going to be any happier," replied Callaghan as he closed the door behind him. "Kamina, you can remove your hood now." The old man's expression turned from fear to astonishment as she pushed back the cloth, revealing her perfect blonde hair, her pointed ears, and her sparking green eyes.

"In the name of the Elements!" Cohen nearly choked on his words, raising his hands to his mouth. "Callaghan, why have you brought a child of Elgrin to our city? Is there a threat from the elves?"

"The elves are not our enemy, ambassador. The truce still holds. I will tell you everything I know, but I would prefer to address to all members of the Alliance at the same time. How soon could you convene them?"

"Well," the old man stumbled, trying to gather his thoughts, "I believe there is a meeting of the Caspian Council scheduled for tomorrow morning with Duke Garstang and Craecoran Gemmel. Ambassador Messer will also be attending. He has never truly been able to give up his place on the council…"

"I need to interrupt that meeting," said Callaghan. "Invite the other Alliance members to do the same. Tell them it is a matter of urgency."

"And what of the Duke?" inquired Cohen.

"This concerns him also," replied the ranger.

"Ramiro will not like his meeting interrupted," he warned.

"After he hears what I have to say, his council meeting will be the least of his concerns."

"For your sake and that of my reputation, I hope so," cautioned Cohen, throwing on a scarlet cloak. "I must go at once if I am to gather them all."

"Cohen, please wait. There is something else I must inform you of. A personal matter." The aged ambassador already had one foot out of the doorway. He paused with a grim expectation of what the ranger had to say.

"Volan?" he asked. Callaghan nodded.

"I am afraid your brother is dead."

"How?" Cohen uttered eventually.

"Lord Malenek killed him," said Callaghan without further explanation. "It was a swift death."

"The priest?" begged Cohen. "Callaghan, what in name of the Elements is going on? What are you not telling me?"

"Please, ambassador…"

"As you wish," he said, realising he could not squeeze an answer from the ranger. "I will make sure they are all in attendance. Wait here, I will organise some private accommodation for you and your guest within the confines of the chambers." With one last glance at the little elf, his face crushed by grief, Cohen left them.

"Kaedin?" said Kamina. The spirit materialised, sitting on Cohen's desk.

"Who was that?" he asked. "And who was his brother?"

"That was Cohen Hesh, the Heroshin ambassador," explained Callaghan.

"His brother was..."

"Volan Hesh," said Kaedin, interrupting. "He is a ranger, like you."

"He was a ranger," corrected Callaghan. And nothing like me, he thought afterwards.

"Malenek killed him?" asked Kamina. The ranger, wearied by the last few days, merely nodded. The elves remained silent, leaving him to his remorse as he slumped into a chair against the wall. Kaedin inspected the room while Kamina gazed out of the window, fascinated by the world below the cliffs.

"Is this where the four ships were built?" she asked. "The ones that sailed to Zalestia?"

"Many ships were built here that sailed that path. Where did you learn about the Great Ships?"

"A wandering teacher in Tilden started telling about us about how the Great War began, but he did not finish his story."

"There is nothing great about this war," grumbled the ranger. Callaghan caught sight of Kamina, fearful she had said something wrong. "Where did your teacher end his lesson?"

"The crew of the *Whirren* had just arrived on the shores of Zalestia," she recalled, "including Malenek. You know him, perhaps you know the story better than the teacher."

"It is not a story for young girls, human or elf kind," he warned.

"But it is one I now find myself a part of," she replied.

"I cannot argue with that." The ranger stood up and joined her by the window. "I want you to remember there is only one account of these events from the Amarosian side. Malenek's. They may not have transpired quite how he recalled. Close your eyes."

Kamina did so, and found herself once again standing on the sparkling golden beaches of Zalestia, as if drawn by Lashara.

"The landing crews of the ships made it to the shores. The jungles were populated with strange trees sporting large, leathery leaves. The branches bore strange fruit which the men were all too hungry to taste, despite orders not to." Kamina imagined the soldiers daring one another to take a bite of the odd fruits.

"Suddenly the men were on alert as they spotted a lone figure studying their boats. Quite how he had snuck past them was at first uncertain, but the Zalestian was a hunter, skilled in stalking prey. But was discovered, so surprised by these men as pale as Whirren that his skills escaped him."

Kamina imagined the reaction of the soldiers, all reaching for their swords, a whole squad against one Zalestian, armed only with a spear. "As you know by now, Zalestians are dark skinned. The hunter's strange appearance would have only made the soldiers more uneasy. But it was Malenek who prevented a catastrophe, or at the very least, delayed it."

"No!" Malenek yelled. Kamina watched as he dashed forward, ahead of those eager to draw blood. He cautiously stepped toward the native.

"Unlike many of the soldiers, Malenek was well-educated, and managed to communicate with the hunter. He led the Amarosians through the dense jungle. They found it rich with life, home to creatures both dangerous and astounding, large reptiles that towered above them."

Kamina cowered under the dark forest, following the crew. An almighty roar echoed through the trees, causing the nearest branches to shake. Kamina ran on, breaking through the edge of the forest to behold the greatest sight her imagination had ever conjured. The giant Citadel of Zatharu, an amazing structure of huge stone blocks, decorated with statues of the Zalestian gods, of which there were many.

"The citadel is far larger and grander than Calisto or even Perhola," Callaghan informed her.

Kamina broke from her imagination by opening her eyes.

"Have you seen it?" she asked. "Zatharu?"

"Yes," he said. "Now close your eyes and do not interrupt again." Kamina did as she was told. "Now, the Amarosians were invited to meet the royal family, Jada Zhan... the queen, and her three sons, the princes, or kharie as they are called, Raztan, Qeuzz, and her youngest, Zahyr."

Kamina spied on the proceedings, as the Amarosians bowed before a tall dark woman, wearing an elegant, colourful headdress. The three princes were dressed with richer cloth than any of their subjects. They carried by their side large swords with bloated blades that put the Amarosian arms to shame.

"The guests were treated as kings, or khans as they are known in Zalestia. After weeks of exchanges, when a dialogue had been established, the crews of the *Aquill* and the *Whirren* were honoured with a grand feast. Young Malenek discussed religious and philosophical ideas with the shamen, mages of sorts, who it was said could commune with the dead."

"Like Oldwyn Blake?" enquired the elf.

"Not quite," continued Callaghan. "The Zalestians believe that one god, Gianna, gave birth to the world, and her many offspring watched over it and her creations. These demi-gods lived in worship among men, and the progeny of their relationships with the mortals became mythic heroes and villains. The royal family, the Zaleeds, are said to be a direct descendants of the Goddess of Beauty, Jazintha. Malenek noted that some of these gods had direct equals in Amarosian mythology. For example, The Goddess of Wind was matched to Whirren, our Air Elemental."

In her imagination, Kamina wandered behind Malenek and the shamen, touring the many statues of the Zalestian gods.

"Likewise, the God of the Seas, Seychalla, was similar to Aquill, the Water Elemental. Malenek noted with some apprehension that Risaar's equal was to be found in Azik, God of the Underworld."

"There is a world under this one?" she asked.

"It is a figurative place, a fiery dungeon where evil men go when they die." Kamina closed her eyes again, coming face-to-face with an ugly demon statue.

She ran along a dim corridor to catch up with Malenek and the shamen.

"Finally, they showed Malenek the most magnificent treasure he has ever set his eyes upon. The Jewel of Gianna."

Kamina found herself standing before a large, polished clear gemstone, as big as a man's fist. Malenek reached forward to touch it. The white light within swirled and glowed, as if sensing his presence. Kamina watched as wisps of energy danced and dazzled inside the jewel.

"It was said that the jewel contained within it the power of Gianna herself."

Kamina was back among the crew of the *Whirren*, still feasting and gorging themselves on wine, displaying unruly behaviour. The Zalestians sat in silence, unhappy with the proceedings. Quezz rose up from his seat and deliberately barged through them, looking to start a fight.

"The three young kharie were arrogant in their beliefs, and dared to mock the Amarosians and their Elementals as they drank more wine. Qeuzz suggested that their guests bow down to Gianna, but the Amarosians refused. An argument ensued, and the guests decided it would be best to leave."

"You're lying," interrupted Kaedin, having heard the story before. "They were slaughtered."

Although Callaghan had tried to save her from it, Kamina imagined the entire Amarosian delegation, cut down by the Zalestians, but not before one of them killed Qeuzz.

"But Malenek survived?" she asked.

"He managed to escape with the help of the shamen he had befriended." Kamina imagined herself tearing through the jungle in the dark, close on Malenek's heels. Behind them an army of Zalestians pursued, led by the royal siblings Raztan and Zahyr.

"Malenek reached the *Whirren*, but he was its sole occupant." The elf watched Malenek from the desolate *Whirren*, unable to help him as his young hands burned climbing the anchor rope aboard.

"He clambered onto the deck, but now that he was truly alone, he realised the impossibility of returning home. No one could sail a ship that size on their own, but Malenek had faith in the Elementals." Kamina watched as he hoisted the sails with great difficulty, but once they were raised Whirren herself filled them with a strong wind. She joined Malenek at the stern of the ship, as he watched Zalestia disappear behind them.

"Without supplies, his only choice was to head straight through the Badlands. It is nothing short of a miracle that he emerged from that endless storm." Callaghan paused, deep in his own thoughts.

"What happened then?" she asked.

"The ship managed to find its way home, crashing into the cliffs of Caspia. They found Malenek injured within the wreckage. He was delirious, malnourished, and with fever. His solo voyage was a bad omen for the council." Kamina could see Malenek, morbidly pale, carried ashore amidst a great commotion.

"Days later the *Aquill* appeared on the horizon, right there." Callaghan pointed out the window and beyond the bay. She conjured up the *Aquill* in her mind, manned by Zalestians. Raztan Kharie paced up and down the deck, shouting orders at his crew.

"The Zalestians were smart and did not attack Calisto. They sailed round the continent until they spied an easy target."

"Barroch Bay," said Kaedin.

"The *Aquill* was eventually destroyed, but the attack on Barroch Bay was seen as an act of war. It brought together the squabbling regions of Amaros, including Rundhale, and together they formed the Alliance of Nations."

"And what of Malenek?" Kamina asked Callaghan.

"People believed he was saved by the Elementals. He received a commendation and promotion, but he resigned his position as a sedcoran. He followed his true calling as a priest, eventually moving to Mytor, as far away from the war as he could. With the help of his small community, he built his castle in the mountains. His reputation matured as he did, offering sage advice beyond the words of the Orico, his insight sought out by kings and leaders alike."

"Is that why Ambassador Hesh did not believe you?" asked Kaedin.

"Reputation is a powerful weapon," was all he could think to say in reply.

"You said it was a miracle Malenek survived the journey back, yet you made it there and back," pointed out Kamina, thinking she had found a telling flaw in the story.

"I did, but I took a small boat and a very long route. Even then, it was a journey fraught with peril."

"What happened to you in Zalestia?" she asked. "Did you meet the Queen?"

"Zhan," he corrected, "And no, I met her son, Zahyr, who is now khan, king of all Zalestia. He would have killed me, had I not offered my services in rescuing his daughter, Jazintha."

"Like the Goddess of Beauty?" asked Kamina.

"You were paying attention," praised Callaghan. "The zharie is named after her."

"Is she beautiful?" asked the elf. "What happened to her?"

"Beauty is in the eye of the beholder," said Callaghan coyly. "She was kidnapped by a small band of rebels…"

"Like marauders?"

"In some ways, yes. I managed to rescue her, and in doing so persuaded Zahyr Zaleed Khan to allow one of his subjects to accompany me back to Amaros, to train as my apprentice."

"Did you sail back through the Badlands?" quizzed Kamina.

"You are the most inquisitive elf I have ever met," he laughed.

"How many elves have you met?" she asked, hoping he would reveal how it was he knew Talia.

"More than most men, and no, we did not sail through the Badlands."

"But you are planning to this time." It was not a question so much as an intuitive remark.

"Yes," admitted the ranger. "Like Malenek many years ago, time is not on my side. But first I will need to seek out a captain brave enough to sail through them."

It was late in the evening when Cohen returned. Although Ramiro had protested, the meeting had been changed to accommodate the ranger. Cohen showed them to an empty room, which one of his servants had furnished with temporary bedding.

"It will not be as comfortable as one of the city's inns, but I thought it wise that your elven friend not leave the chambers. If her presence becomes known it will start a frenzy, but I suspect you are here to do so anyway."

"Thank you, Cohen," said Callaghan. The ambassador bid them goodnight. From the window, Kamina gazed down on Calisto bay, the stars and moons reflected in the vast ocean. Ygrain and Whirren were tinged with an orange arc as they caught the last of Risaar's light, although the great sun had settled long ago.

"Do not let anyone see you," said Callaghan, standing nearby the ledge that Kamina leaned precariously over.

"It is beautiful," she whispered, reeling herself back from the balcony in case any Caspians strolling along the cliff edge path happened to glance up.

"I sometimes forget that the elves have seen so little of Amaros," said the ranger.

"There is a small pool in Elgrin next to the river, where the young are blessed soon after they are born, but it is barely a teardrop compared to this," she said, indicating the twinkling expanse of ocean.

"Kaedin?" called the ranger. The ghost revealed himself. "Tomorrow is very important. This is why I brought you here. I need you to appear before the council."

"But I do not know anything," Kaedin confessed.

"Not speak, Kaedin," stated Callaghan again. "Appear."

"Are you sure?" asked the ethereal elf. "Your friend does not look as though he could handle the shock of seeing a spirit. In fact, he looks closer to the grave than I am," he added as a joke.

"Cohen Hesh has many years left in him, believe me," warned Callaghan.

"Sorry," said the spirit.

"Now, I suggest we all get some rest." Kamina lay down the sheets that had been gifted to them by the ambassador, but with all the excitement of recent days, the little elf could not sleep a wink.

CHAPTER SIXTEEN

MEETING OF THE ALLIANCE

THE NEXT MORNING A SOLDIER KNOCKED ON THE DOOR OF THEIR guest room. Following his instructions from Ambassador Hesh, he guided the two guests to the meeting that had been hastily rearranged. The flurry had caused much speculation to fly around the barracks, fuelled by a rumour that one of the guests was a Ranger of Ishkava.

The closed council chambers of Caspia were located in the top floor, above the public debating chamber, although these days Alliance meetings took precedence over any regional affairs the local councillors may have had to discuss. Kamina and Callaghan sat outside the large doors, along with two posted sentries. They tried to hide their curiosity about the ranger and his companion, but in vain. With the help of the unseen ghost whispering in his ear, Callaghan caught one of the guards spying on them, returning a deadly stare that told the guard to keep his eyes front and centre.

Eventually the doors opened, revealing the frail form of Ambassador Hesh. "We are ready for you now, Callaghan."

"I doubt that," whispered Kaedin to Kamina, who scowled at the thin air she guessed the spirit was standing in.

Callaghan and Kamina were ushered into the council chambers. They faced a semi-circular table where the five ambassadors of Amaros were seated, the flags of their respective regions draped behind them. Kamina could feel the eyes of the only female councillor upon her. She had long jet-black hair, with a single grey streak running down one side of her face. Her black eyes reminded Kamina of the Etraihu archer who had killed Eshtel. She also noted a well-groomed man sitting in a lone chair by the wall. From the formal attire adorned with medals, she guessed that he was Duke Garstang.

"I call this emergency meeting to order," declared Ambassador Ramiro Messer, former Chief Councillor of Caspia. "We have been summoned by the Ishkava Ranger Callaghan Tor, who has an urgent matter he wishes to bring to our attention."

"Thank you, Ambassador Messer," he said, ignoring the hint of sarcasm that spiced Ramiro's words.

"Do not thank me, ranger," remarked the ambassador. "You have interrupted a meeting of the Caspian Council. If it were up to me, we would not be dealing with your haphazard intrusion."

"I come on a matter of grave urgency," said Callaghan.

"Urgency?" retorted Ramiro. "We have lost our stronghold in Zalestia's southern islands, and must now work to reclaim it. So unless you and your wandering bunch of rangers have any suggestions how to win this war…"

"Zalestia is half a world away," proclaimed Callaghan, silencing Ramiro with his interruption. "You have more immediate concerns on your own soil."

"Callaghan, please enlighten us," said Cohen.

"But first explain why you travel in the company of an elf," interrupted the Etraihu female, Rundhale Ambassador Arkes Da'ri. Her acute observation surprised both Callaghan and Kamina, while the other ambassadors chirped in astonishment. With a nod from the ranger, the elf lowered her hood, her striking features startling the leaders of Amaros.

"Explain yourself, ranger!" demanded Ramiro. "Why you have brought this… creature into our chambers?"

"I present to you Kamina Elloeth." Kamina did not know the customs among men, so offered a small curtsey. "She has become entangled in a plot that would see not just the end of Amaros, but all of Enara."

"These are bold words, ranger," said Arkes Da'ri. "I hope you have brought proof to corroborate your claims."

"Please, Ambassador Da'ri, allow me a moment to explain from the beginning." The Etraihu ambassador yielded the floor as Callaghan continued. "Lord Malenek has gathered an army that marches from the north."

"This is preposterous!" exclaimed the Mytor ambassador, a pallid man named Miden Lome. "Lord Malenek has no army. He is a priest, a man of peace who brought light to my land long after the downfall of Nimongrad."

"I must agree with the honourable ambassador from Mytor," said Ramiro. "Malenek is a priest, a dreamer, his head stuck in Illyrian clouds. He could not possibly form an army that hoped to defeat our combined forces."

"And yet he has," stated Callaghan. "He was in league with a Zalestian mage sent to Elgrin Forest to kill the one person that may have been able to thwart this plan."

"And this is her?" enquired Arkes again. "You stopped him?"

"Not exactly," answered the ranger. "Now, Kaedin," he muttered quietly under his breath. Callaghan stepped back and waited.

Nothing happened.

"Kaedin, now" he muttered again, louder this time.

Again nothing happened. The ambassadors stared at the ranger.

"Master Ranger, what is a Kaedin?" asked Arkes Da'ri.

"I'm afraid I do not have the time nor the patience to find out…" muttered Ramiro as he stood to leave, but a booming voice cut him short.

"Sit down!" commanded a chilling, eerie voice. Although Kamina had grown used to Kaedin's ghostly state, she recalled the sensation of hearing his spirit voice for the first time, the cold, echoed tone having made her skin crawl. It was a feeling the ambassadors now shared.

"Who said that?" asked Ramiro, slowly returning to his seat. "What trickery is this?" He gazed around him, trying to spot the intruder hidden in the room.

"This is no trick," whispered the voice behind him, causing Ramiro to spring back up from his seat.

"Ranger, stop this foolishness!" urged the ambassador.

"Kaedin, reveal yourself." The ghost materialised before the Alliance, its members gasping in horror. Duke Garstang rose from his seat, grasping for his sword, but Callaghan's calming hand reassured him that the spirit was not a threat.

"Callaghan?" begged Cohen, "what in the name of the Elements is this?"

"A former elf," he replied. "Kaedin was killed by the Zalestian mage, but returned as a spirit when his sister Kamina avenged him."

"It is magic?" Ramiro asked.

"Blood magic," replied the ranger.

"But what has this to do with Malenek?" enquired Miden Lome.

"Malenek has exploited this unnatural occurrence, and now commands an army of these vengeance spirits. They can walk through the walls of your cities and homes. They can reach into your body and separate your soul from your flesh."

To demonstrate the ranger's claims, Kaedin drifted through the table at which they sat. Three of the ambassadors jumped from their seats until their backs were against the wall, Miden Lome knocking over the Mytor flag. Both Cohen and Ramiro remained seated. He suspected the former was unable to rise due to old age, while he imagined the latter had not flinched through sheer stubbornness, embarrassed by Kaedin's earlier antics.

"As if that were not enough," continued Callaghan, "they cannot be harmed by conventional weapons." He unsheathed Ascara and cut her blade through Kaedin several times, doing nothing other than momentarily disrupting his aura.

"Is this a trick meant to intimidate us?" demanded the Caspian ambassador.

"No. I brought Kaedin before you today to demonstrate the power Malenek wields," replied Callaghan, sheathing his sword.

"If what you say is true, then what can we do?" asked Arkes Da'ri.

"I would request that you consider two courses of action. The first would be granting me permission to lead an expedition to Zalestia. I believe the instigators of this plot are to be found there, along with a weapon that may be able to stop Malenek's spirit army."

"And the second?" asked Ramiro, growing more irritated by Kaedin, who continued to breeze through the table.

"I humbly request the release of Oldwyn Blake."

"No!" roared Ramiro, his voice like thunder. He erected his full body in outrage, his chair crashing against the wall. Unfortunately, Ramiro rose up at the wrong moment, colliding with Kaedin's hand, his ghostly fingers passing inside Ramiro's head before he could withdraw or whisper a word of warning.

The spirit was bombarded by an onslaught of images and sounds. The council chamber disappeared in a sudden mist. When it dispersed, Kaedin found himself standing next to Ramiro, somewhat younger, more composed. An old man with long grey hair sat with his back to them, reading through a mountain of scrolls. A wooden staff lay by his side, with a green crystal embedded at its crest.

"My son is of the opinion that we need magic to win this war," said the younger Ramiro, his voice not as harsh as before. "We know the Zalestians have banned its use. It is our only advantage. We need you, Oldwyn."

"And I am needed by others," replied a wise yet troubled voice.

"You are the only mage left in these lands."

"Not the only one, no, but certainly the most approachable, and equally the most dangerous. Meddling with magic, using it in an unwarranted war, will come at a heavy price, one neither you nor I are willing to pay, Councillor."

Kaedin's vision was once again clouded as an unseen force hurled him through the mind of Ramiro Messer. Kaedin slammed into a wall inside a luxurious house, decorated with extravagant pieces of art and history.

"The mage refused," said Ramiro.

"But he is a citizen of Calisto!" exclaimed another, younger voice. Kaedin followed the sounds, discovering the speakers in the next room. Ramiro was conversing with his son Reynard, an ataincor, high in the ranks of the Caspian army.

"He is a law unto himself," explained Ramiro.

"So he will not help us defeat the Zogs, which he could do with one wave of his beloved staff, yet he will cure the ills of individual soldiers as easily as he breathes?"

"He said these were small acts that cause small ripples. A big act will cause a splash that will hit us all like a giant wave."

"Then we will stand far away," said Reynard. "We do not need him, only his weapon."

"Son, that staff was once wielded by the Witch of Anawey. It is not a toy to be trifled with. I believe the only reason Oldwyn is able to control it is due to his heritage." Ramiro noticed his son seem to be lost in his own thoughts. "Are you listening to me?"

"Yes, father."

"It was a good idea," reassured Ramiro. "This is why you are they youngest ataincor in the history of the Caspian army, but let us close the door on this avenue of thought."

Reynard nodded half-heartedly as the mists descended again, and Kaedin was yanked through Ramiro's memories. He was left with a sickly feeling as he landed on the cold cobblestones of one of Calisto's streets, wet with rain. There were people shouting and yelling, but the details were vague and unclear, the memory distorted. Ramiro ran past him. Kaedin tried to follow, but the ambassador's mind was tilting and turning, making it impossible to keep up. Ramiro halted outside the army barracks, currently under attack. Towers of rock shot out from the ground as a group of low ranked corans tried to tackle Oldwyn Blake, at the epicentre of the magical disturbance. A pile of dirt rose up and formed a hand. It seized one of the corans, hurling him against a building. His limp body splashed down in a puddle near Ramiro. The councillor dared to glance through the fence. Kaedin joined him and spotted Reynard silently sneaking up behind Oldwyn, ready to snatch the mage's staff. Oldwyn, however, had sensed the stealthy attacker. A spike of stone shot out of the ground and staked the ataincor, hoisting him into the air.

"Reynard!" screamed Ramiro. Kaedin felt the extreme sense of loss as if it were his own. The fighting men lost their motivation as their leader bled out on the spike and died. His father fell to his knees below, gazing up at his son's lifeless face hovering in the air.

"I warned you of this," Oldwyn lamented, standing by Ramiro. Gripped by rage and powered by vengeance, Ramiro snatched Oldwyn's staff and ripped it from his ancient hands. The ambassador swung at the mage's head, knocking him out with a single strike of the green crystal.

"Seal him in the top of the Black Tower," seethed Ramiro.

"What are we to do with the current prisoner, sir?" asked the most senior sedcoran on the scene.

"Execute him," he grunted. The soldiers dragged Oldwyn's unconscious body away, leaving Ramiro to grieve while clutching the staff, succeeding where his son had failed. Kaedin stood beside him, overwhelmed as he shared in Ramiro's sorrow.

Once again Kaedin was thrust through a thick mist, suddenly finding himself in a darkened room with a low ceiling. He could see the staff amidst the gloom, hanging from one of the walls like a trophy. Ramiro was slumped on his knees, weeping before it. Kaedin could feel the deep river of grief that threatened to swallow the ambassador whole. Ramiro turned to him sharply, now able to see the spirit invading his mind.

"Get out of my head!" he screamed.

Kaedin fell to the floor of the council chamber, the energy holding his ethereal spirit together dancing erratically around him. It fluctuated for a few moments, stabilising when the spirit overcame the shock of the mind meld. Ramiro sat down in a similar state, deeply disturbed by the bitter memories the spirit had unlocked. Kaedin was relieved when he saw that the ambassador was unchanged, at least physically, not the snarling beast Slavek had turned into after their interaction. The other ambassadors attended to Ramiro, who gasped for water. Kamina tried to do the same for Kaedin, but Duke Garstang withdrew his sword and pointed the blade at the spirit.

"What did you do to him?" the duke demanded.

"Duke Garstang," said Callaghan, "the blade cannot hurt the boy."

"Then what about the girl?" said Garstang, shifting the aim of his blade towards Kamina. Callaghan's fingers edged down to Ascara's hilt.

"I am fine," coughed Ramiro, although he was still clearly out of sorts. His words defused any potential swordplay between the ranger and the duke. Ramiro stared at the ghost, and Kaedin wondered if he had experienced the same memories at the same time. Had it been Ramiro driving them to those chosen moments? Or had they both simply meandered along a random path? Was it possible Ramiro had seen Kaedin's memories, like some sort of trade?

A sharp knock on the door broke the excitement of the spirit's manifestation. Callaghan opened it to reveal the burly form of Craecoran Gemmel, Caspia's highest ranked soldier, second only to the duke himself.

"There is a messenger here for Duke Garstang," announced Gemmel. The duke sheathed his weapon and joined the ranger in the doorway. Standing behind Craecoran Gemmel was Sedcoran Anton Fleck.

"Sedcoran Fleck? Why are not at your post in Gorran?" demanded Duke Garstang.

"I have already reprimanded the sedcoran for leaving his post," said Craecoran Gemmel, "but you should hear what he has to say, sir."

The duke's role in the army was largely ceremonial, a remnant of the Heroshin rule over Gorran. Technically he was the highest ranked soldier in Caspia, and due to the Alliance, all of Amaros. He was a pseudo-politician, charged by the Caspian Council to run Gorran, now home to the largest army barracks and training grounds in Amaros. He had never fought in any war, but treated the men with respect, and in matters relating to the Amarosian army, laid his trust in his immediate subordinates.

"Go ahead," ordered Duke Garstang.

"A lone rider arrived in Gorran with a warning," recounted Fleck. "She claimed that Lord Malenek marches from the north, with an army of... well, ghosts, sir."

"It seems you were right, ranger," said Garstang, glancing sideways at Callaghan with a hint of an apology.

"There is more, sir," added Fleck. "The messenger... she was an elf." The duke turned his eyes back into the closed chamber, staring at the small elven girl and her ghostly companion.

"Thank you, Sedcoran Fleck, Craecoran Gemmel." The men saluted and left, the craecoran closing the door behind him.

"Duke Garstang, you have to order an evacuation of Gorran," pleaded Callaghan. "Everything I have told you is true." The duke considered all the information presented, his eyes drawn back to the spirit. The ambassadors interrupted before he could come to any conclusion.

"What are we to do when all these refugees arrive here?" asked Ambassador Lome. "How long can we be expected to house them?"

"For as long as you can," answered Callaghan, no longer attempting to mask the disgust in his voice. "These people require shelter from the storm of spirits that is soon to blight this land. And there will be more people fleeing than just those from Gorran. Calisto is the last city Malenek's army will reach. This is where we need to make our stand."

"All of this is assuming your story is even true, which I still doubt," said Miden Lome. "Lord Malenek is simply not capable of what you charge him with."

"There was a time when I would have agreed with you, ambassador," confessed Callaghan, "had I not seen him raise the dead himself." The ranger was aware that Cohen Hesh was staring at him, but avoided his gaze for fear of giving away his brother's implicit involvement.

"And yet you also have a spirit under your control," noted Miden. "How do we know it is not the rangers who lead this army?"

"Because I am telling you the truth," repeated Callaghan, irritated by the mulish objections being raised by the Mytor ambassador.

"And we are merely to take your word for it?" asked Miden Lome.

"Yes!" Everyone in the room, even Callaghan, and especially Kaedin, was taken aback by the outburst from Kamina, who had now risen to her feet. "We have travelled for days, we have fought marauders and Ogarii to warn you about this threat. Why do you doubt the truth when it is staring you in the face? Why do you question the word of an Ishkava Ranger?" Kamina's chest heaved as she regained her breath.

"There is no-one in this room who doubts the resolve of a ranger, child," said Isan Narain, the ambassador for Legoria, finally contributing to the proceedings. But it is a fantastical story. You have showed us the existence of these vengeance spirits, but that does not prove there is an army out there, or that Malenek is the one who leads them. We require more."

"Release Oldwyn Blake and you will have it," said Callaghan. "He can cast a seeing spell. Some of you have seen it done before."

"No, no magic," muttered Ramiro, but he was still subdued from the spirit stumbling through his memories.

"We will put it to a vote," said Cohen, who had been waiting for the perfect moment to intervene. "All in favour?" The Heroshin raised his hand. Arkes Da'ri followed suit, clearly influenced by Kaedin's appearance. Miden Lome refused to raise his. Isan Narain also remained irresolute.

"There," said Ambassador Lome with a smirk. "Your request has been denied." As Miden gloated, Isan Narain glanced over at Kamina and Kaedin. Although the elves would probably argue against it, Elgrin Forest fell under the purview of the region of Legoria. The elves had vacated the lands, and those humans unhappy in Heroshin or Caspia had left to resettle in the hope of a more peaceful life, until the war had begun. Isan stared at the girl who had risked her life to deliver this message, and at the boy who had already given his. As Kamina met his gaze, her eyes pleading with him, Isan realised that, as their Ambassador, he owed them this much. Finding the strength of character, he raised his hand, wiping the smirk from Miden Lome's face.

"The Alliance rules three to two," stated Cohen. "Your request is granted

Callaghan. Oldwyn Blake shall be released into your custody."

"Be warned, ranger," Ramiro rasped. "If he does anything that places a single citizen of this city in danger, you will be held solely responsible."

"I understand. What of the ship to Zalestia?" asked Callaghan. "Or the evacuation of Gorran?"

"That will depend upon the proof your prisoner provides," said Ramiro. The ambassador brought a spherical gavel down against a sound block. "Meeting adjourned."

CHAPTER SEVENTEEN
THE BLACK TOWER

TWO CORANS GUIDED THE TRIO TO THE PRISON IN WHICH OLDWYN Blake had been confined for over a decade. Kamina discovered it was the greyish black tower she had spotted from their approach along the Ico, built upon a small outcrop that jutted into the flowing river. It loomed above them now, like a dead tree trunk stripped of its branches and leaves, filled with the worst of men and left to rot.

They ascended the sole spiral staircase, occasionally passing a thick door, heavily barred from the outside. Those interned here bayed and scratched at them from the confines beyond. Kamina followed Callaghan closely as the corans led them upwards, round and round until her head was dizzy.

After the final step they faced a solitary black door. One of the corans unbarred it while the other produced a ream of keys. He flicked through them, eventually finding the correct one to slip inside the lock. The bleak key twisted with a screech of rust. The corans stepped aside, not daring to enter the cell of Oldwyn Blake. Callaghan sidled by them and pushed the door open. Kamina followed him cautiously with Kaedin behind her, invisible and taciturn.

Thin rays of light struggled to seep through a series of narrow slits cut around the wall, no thicker than a thumb. The walls themselves were covered in layers upon layers of writing, scratched into the stone by fingernails. Fragments criss-crossed over one another where the maddened author had ran out of space. The different styles of writing varied wildly, from tiny, illegible scribbles to wide, frantic scrawls.

Callaghan stepped into the room, unblocking Kamina's view of the prisoner. He was malnourished, a mere bag of bones and hair, slumped in the centre of the room with only a ragged loincloth left from his original prison garb. His overgrown grey hair stretched down beyond his shoulders, covering his face like a drab veil. His head was hung low, facing the floor as he scratched words into the stonework with bloodied, broken fingertips.

The ranger knelt down next to the once powerful mage. "Oldwyn. Oldwyn, do you know I am?" he asked quietly.

"I told you, stop distracting me," mumbled the mage.

"When did you tell me this?" he asked.

"Yesterday, and the day before that. But you always come, as persistent as the real ranger, but I know the difference." Callaghan realised the mage was gripped by the madness of incarceration, distraught by the welts and cuts that scored the wizard's withering body.

"Get this man some food, water, and fresh clothing!" he demanded of the guards, who were hesitant to comply. While the Ishkava Rangers were respected in most circles, they were not ranked in any army. "Now!" roared the ranger. His tempered ferocity was enough to scare the guards back down the spiral staircase at speed. Once they were gone, Callaghan turned his attentions back to the beleaguered mage.

"You will be looked after, old friend," said Callaghan, placing his warm hand on the weak man's shoulder.

Get out of my mind!" shrieked Oldwyn, glaring up at them for the first time with his one giant eye. Kamina gasped at the deformity. Kaedin was so shocked that he lost all focus on keeping his transparent camouflage. His silvery form shimmered and reflected in Oldwyn Blake's naked eye. The anger that had surged through the cyclops dissipated when he saw the ghost. He tried to stand, but his legs were unsure, trembling as he tread across the worn prison cell floor. He reached out a quivering hand and tried to touch the spirit's face. His skeletal fingers passed right through, disrupting the flow of Kaedin's being. Oldwyn stared at his hands, as if recalling some long forgotten memory trapped in the labyrinth of his mind.

"No, no, no, no…" Oldwyn repeated as he backed away from Kaedin. "No magic here! I forbid it! This is my domain!"

"Please, Oldwyn, calm down," urged Callaghan. "Kaedin is a friend."

"He is magic!" cried the mage. "The worst kind of magic!"

"Oldwyn, listen to me. There is an army of spirits that will soon descend upon us," revealed the ranger. "We need your help."

A strange noise rumbled from Oldwyn's chest; a guttural sound that gathered strength, until a chaotic laugh emerged from his throat, echoing around the room.

"You're already a spirit! You're all spirits!" He suddenly lost the strength to stand, falling on all fours. Callaghan moved quickly to help him. "All I see is spirits," the mage mumbled under his breath. Oldwyn rubbed his fingers against the ground, before he started crying in Callaghan's arms.

The guards pounded back up the steep steps carrying water and clothing. "There is food on the way, sir," one managed to say. Callaghan nodded his thanks, taking the shawl they had brought and wrapping it around Oldwyn's frail body. The other handed over a jug of water. They took their leave to find the food that had been promised. Callaghan carefully placed the jug in Oldwyn's bony hands.

"Drink, old friend." The ancient man guzzled down on the water. "Slowly," Callaghan advised as the mage choked. When the jug was empty, he helped Oldwyn sit up, resting him against one of the walls. The cyclops' large eye gazed out from behind a mop of wet hair, staring into the distance, far beyond the walls. The ranger returned to the elves, who had retreated to the safety of the doorway.

"I thought you said he could help us," said the spirit, contemplating Oldwyn Blake with a denigrating look.

"Kaedin!" Kamina shot him a reproachful glance that would have killed him were he not already dead.

"He can," replied Callaghan solemnly, glancing back at the cyclops. "Or at least, he could have done so in the past. His mind has been broken by this place. We have to find his staff. The magic it holds will remind him of who he once was."

"But he said he does not want magic," noted Kamina, confused.

"I do not believe Oldwyn knows what he wants. Ramiro's torment has seen to that," cursed Callaghan. "The staff is what he needs if he is ever to escape the malady that has festered in his mind."

"Well where is it, then?" asked Kamina.

"I do not know," he confessed "It disappeared soon after Oldwyn was imprisoned. I had hoped he would be able to tell us."

"Is it made from a branch of dark Elgrinwood, with a shiny green emerald at its peak?" asked Kaedin. The ranger's expression was answer enough.

"You have seen it," said Callaghan. Kaedin nodded. "Where?"

"In Ambassador Messer's memories."

*

The guards had insisted on locking Oldwyn's cell after they left. Callaghan had argued against it, but given the cyclops' current state, the ranger had conceded it was for the best. They now marched through the city towards Ramiro's estate, which lay on the edge of one of the crescent cliffs. It was a luxurious white-brick villa overlooking the ocean, with a small garden filled with colourful fruit trees. A two-man guard detail was posted at the main gate leading up to the house. Both brandished ceremonial Caspian swords, the hilts flourished with flecks of blue and white. Callaghan approached them with Kamina by his side, her face hidden by her hood. Kaedin was once again transparent, shadowing them.

"State your business, ranger," ordered the lead guard.

"I seek an audience with Ambassador Messer," replied Callaghan.

"He has not yet returned home. Perhaps you can find him at the council chambers."

"That is where we have just come from," said Callaghan. He neglected to tell the guard that Ramiro was indeed there.

"Then you shall have to wait." Callaghan moved to step past the gate, but found a sword thrust across his path. "Outside," added the unwavering guard, sneering slightly. These soldiers were handpicked by Ramiro for their loyalty to him. They had clearly been warned about the ranger's presence in the city.

"As you wish," said Callaghan, bowing politely. He and Kamina retreated until they were out of the guard's vision. "Kaedin," whispered Callaghan, pausing as if to admire the view of the bay.

"Yes," answered the invisible elf.

"I need you to go inside and find the staff. Do you think you can manage that?"

"Yes, but the house is a good distance from here."

"I will be fine," said Kamina. "Go."

Kaedin hastened back to the gate and passed through the wall that surrounded Ramiro's property. He drifted over the deserted gardens and breezed through the front door.

The rooms within Ramiro's house were surprisingly empty. Gone was the colourful décor Kaedin had witnessed in his fleeting encroachment upon the ambassador's mind. The interior was now barren, home only to a few utilitarian pieces of furniture.

The spirit had trouble concentrating, the bond with Kamina stretched tight. He dispelled with his transparency as he floated up to the rooms above, but these too were scant and bare. The room from his vision was not here. Kaedin tried to recall what it had looked like. It was small, dimly lit, with a low ceiling.

A basement.

Ramiro would not keep the staff out in full view of whatever guests he may entertain. No, he had been revering it in private. Kaedin drifted back downstairs to a large study. He noticed a fine rug crafted by the Etraihu people, a gift from Ambassador Da'ri, spread across the floor. Kaedin poked his head through the threads into the ground below, revealing a set of stone steps that led to a hidden vault.

The spirit sunk through the floor, descending the steps into a treasure trove of artefacts. His ghostly luminescence sparkled on something reflective at the other end of the room. As Kaedin stepped closer, he found the staff of Oldwyn Blake, suspended in time on a purpose-built shelf. The staff itself was not sleek or sanded down. To Kaedin it looked like a small, elongated tree. At its tip a green jewel was held in place by a small mesh of twigs sprouting from the top.

Kaedin returned to the room above. He had easily slipped through the floor, but how could he retrieve a solid and weighty object from the hidden basement? He would have to do it as a corporeal being would. Taking a moment to mentally prepare, he suddenly snatched out at the rug with one hand. It took a few attempts, but eventually he managed to grasp it long enough to whip it away. In its flight it struck an oil lamp. It wobbled on its stand. Kaedin quickly dived and grabbed for it as it fell off, but the lamp slipped right through his ghostly fingers and smashed upon the floor. He watched the door intently, waiting for guards to burst in, but they did not come.

Now he had to contend with the basement door. Unlike the rug, it was heavy and would require a longer period of contact to pull up. He positioned his hands by the iron handle, focusing all his energy into his fingers as he pried it up. The thick wooden door lifted slightly, but Kaedin lost his grip and fell backwards, the door thudding back into place. Kaedin picked himself back up and tried again.

"Come on, Kaedin," he whispered, goading himself. He strained himself as the door lifted higher, but again he failed. The door slammed shut, louder than before. The spirit summoned all his strength for another attempt, but was stopped by the creak of the front door.

The guard entered, alerted by a smash followed by several thuds. He drew his weapon, convinced that he saw a brief flash of silvery light. He crept through the house, eventually discovering the source of the disturbance inside the study. A lamp was smashed, and a rug had been thrown away. The guardsman also noticed the secret basement door. He had been through the house many times on duty, but he had never once suspected that another room lay hidden beneath his feet. He peered over his shoulder at the front door ajar, deciding whether or not to have a peek at whatever treasures or secrets the ambassador kept concealed below.

His decision was made when a child wailed from inside the basement.

*

Callaghan peered round the corner, keeping a watchful eye on the house and the remaining guard. Kamina tugged at his robe, drawing his attention to Ramiro and his entourage approaching the house. The ranger manoeuvred himself in front of the armed escort, trying to secure the spirit more time to complete his task.

"What is the meaning of this, ranger?" demanded Ramiro. "Have you come to my home to gloat? Is it not enough that you have won the freedom of the man who murdered my son?"

"His treatment while incarcerated under your orders has driven him to insane," said Callaghan.

"It was magic that drove the cyclops mad. I merely contained it before he could harm anyone else." The ambassador turned to his bodyguards. "If the ranger does not leave this area, then remove him by force," he ordered, storming off towards the gates of his residence. The four guards surrounded Callaghan, their hands itching to withdraw their weapons. He could only hope that Kaedin had discovered the whereabouts of Oldwyn's staff.

*

The guard aimed his sword at the vault door as the voice called out again.

"Please, is someone there?" begged a muffled voice from below. "Please let me out!"

"Who are you?" asked the guard.

"My friends and I... we were just playing, but they trapped me down here, and I can't get out!" The voice started to blubber, wailing and sobbing from underneath his feet.

Aware that Ambassador Messer was due back to the residence soon, the guard wished to resolve this situation quickly and with minimum fuss. He reached down and hauled open the bulky basement door. He peered down the stone steps into the gloom. It appeared deserted, but there was an object lying on the steps; a long wooden staff, with a green emerald shining at its peak. The guard picked it up, mesmerised by the magical jewel.

I'll take that," said Kaedin, now standing behind the guard. The spirit snatched the staff, juggling it through the house. He managed to throw it out of the open door before he lost contact. The guard was so scared that he ran straight down into the dank basement, pulling shut the sturdy door for protection. Kaedin toyed with the idea of showing the guard just how little shelter it offered against a spirit, but he had the more pressing matter of the mage's staff to deal with.

*

Ramiro had just passed the guard on gate duty when he saw Oldwyn's staff leap out of his home, seemingly of its own volition. It was quickly followed by the infernal spectre who had dared place his unnatural fingers inside his mind.

"You!" he cried at the remaining guard at the gate. "Seize that staff!" As the guard hurried towards the house, Ramiro spun on his heels, pointing an accusing finger at Callaghan. "The rest of you, arrest the ranger."

Callaghan readied his hand around Ascara's hilt, but one of the bodyguards grappled with him, forcing his arms behind his back. The ranger fought them off, kicking one square in the face, but the guard wrenching his arms back kept hold, determined to make a prisoner out of him.

With the guards focused on bringing down Callaghan, they ignored his companion. "Kamina!" he yelled. "Get the staff to Oldwyn!" One of the four bodyguards turned his attentions to the elf. He lurched for her, but Callaghan wrapped his legs around the guard's head. The ranger twisted his full body sideways, tumbling to the ground in a mesh of flailing limbs. "Go!" he screamed again, fending off another attack from Ramiro's men.

In the garden, one of the guards charged at Kaedin, who lingered over the staff lying in the grass. The ghost focused all his energy into his foot. He chipped the staff into the air and over the man's head. The guard's momentum carried him forward, and had Kaedin been alive the elf would have been crushed. Instead, the guard careened right through him, tripping on the front steps of the villa and cracking his jaw as he fell.

The airborne staff sailed through the skies, heading towards Ramiro. He stretched his arms out to catch it, but was robbed by the elven girl as she leapt up and plucked it from the air.

"Give that back, thief!" he snarled at her. She was caught in his garden, Ramiro the only person standing between herself and the gate. She charged towards him wielding the staff. It had been locked away for so long, thought Ramiro. He could not allow it to fall back into the hands of Oldwyn Blake. He could not allow more people to be killed be the cyclops' magic.

Kamina ran towards the gates, but Ramiro spread his bulky arms out, blocking her way. She deliberately dropped to the ground, skidding along the path and under Ramiro's legs. She was almost free when Ramiro managed to grab her cloak. The sudden shunt backwards caused her to drop the staff. Kamina wriggled out of her shawl and scooped up the staff again. She bolted into the city, leaving Ramiro holding her green hood within his tight grasp.

The ranger's scuffle with Ramiro's bodyguards had drawn a crowd, but many within the mob now took notice of Kamina. Without her hood to hide her elven features, she became a target for their peering eyes, the subject of their gasps and gossip.

"Child," shouted Ramiro, running after her. "That is no toy. Return it to me immediately."

"Kamina, take it to the Black Tower!" grunted Callaghan, as he broke a bodyguard's nose with his elbow. The elf tore through the crowd, who quickly parted for her. The luckless guards grasped at her swift outline, but she managed to dodge their reach. She hurtled herself through the streets, pirouetting off walls and leaping over the humans. Her acrobatic escape astonished the citizens of Calisto while confounding the guards that gave chase. Shouts and whistles called for more soldiers to join the pursuit.

The young elf charged through the grounds of the council chambers, but she found her path blocked by a contingent of corans. She darted across the bridge immediately above the waterfall, crossing over into the divine grounds of the Grand Elemental Cathedral. Kamina pushed herself on, her heart caught in her throat as she attempted to navigate this strange human city. She could see the Black Tower rising up before her, but on the opposite side of the river. The first bridge led directly to the army barracks, from which more soldiers were pouring out to join the hunt. She sprinted by them, flitting through the timber yards, avoiding the various men carrying crates and planks of wood. The soldiers were not so agile, crashing straight into them, sending the less observant ones splashing into the river.

Kamina reached the last bridge, only to be met by another blockade of guards. She leapt onto the railing with a keen sense of balance, honed from leaping between branches in Elgrin Forest. She streamed across the metalwork, avoiding their grasping, outstretched arms.

As she reached the opposite bank, she remembered that this was the path Callaghan had first dragged them along when they had arrived in Calisto. She ran through the poor looking buildings, frightening the painted ladies away. Kamina paused to catch her breath, lost in the urban maze. She had not been paying attention to the route Callaghan had taken that day. Her eager eyes glimpsed the top of the Black Tower down a narrow alleyway. She had taken a wrong turn, and so doubled back, dodging and diving through the trail of guards, who were not so quick to alter their direction.

Kamina hurried into the barracks and headed straight for the prison. She could see it now, the entrance, as well as the guards standing on duty. They spied her approaching, their comrades in pursuit close behind her.

They braced their weapons.

"Keep going!" Kaedin yelled. He materialised in front of the guards. They dropped their weapons as the blood rushed from their faces. Both attempted to flee, but Kaedin managed to pin one against a wall with his presence alone.

"Keys!" demanded Kaedin The remaining guard frantically snatched for the jingling jumble of keys and tossed them towards the spirit. They keys passed right through him, but Kamina caught them at his back. "Go," said the ghost. "I will hold them here."

She unlocked the door and dashed up the spiral staircase before the rabble of guards reached them. Pandemonium erupted below as the soldiers contended with Kaedin's spirit. Kamina ran round and round the spiral staircase until there were no more steps for her feet to find. The black door loomed in front of her, the only thing now separating her from the cyclops. She fingered the keys with a quivering hand. Callaghan had asked her to do this, she thought, to free this mage. But what if the ambassador was right? What if magic was evil? It had been magic that had killed Kaedin, after all.

The decision was made for her as some of the guards evaded Kaedin, battling their way up the stairs towards her. She stared at the mass of keys on the large ring, trying to recall which one opened the lock to the cyclops' cell. She had no choice but to try them all. Kamina inserted key after key, but to no avail. The guards' footsteps echoed up the stairwell, pounding towards her. They turned the corner as she slotted in the correct key. She twisted it in the lock.

Kamina barged through the door. Oldwyn was slumped on the floor where they had left him. The old man spotted the staff with his bulging eye. He scurried away from her like a frightened spider, clawing at the walls.

"No! No, I told you, no magic! Get it away!" Kamina did not care for his protests. The guards were almost at the top of the stairs. She marched up to Oldwyn, urging him to take the staff.

"Take it!" she demanded. "Now."

"Please, do not make me. I cannot… not again…"

The contingent of guards reached the landing, but halted as Kaedin's head emerged from the flagstones, rising up to block their way. Ramiro scrambled through the throng of men to the doorway, displaying no hesitation by marching right through the spirit. He stalked into the chamber, accompanied by the small contingent of loyal corans. The elf had goaded the cyclops into a corner, imploring him to take the staff.

"Move away from him, child" pleaded Ramiro. "He is dangerous."

Kamina stepped back from the weary old man huddled against the wall. Tears spilled from his lonesome eye. Was this who Callaghan wanted to save them? Kamina wondered. Could the staff's power really heal the manic delirium that possessed the mage?

"I am sorry," she said, her arms sagging down under the weight of failure. The cyclops looked down at her with pity. As he dropped his guard, Kamina swung the staff straight at him.

"No!" cried Ramiro, but it was too late. On instinct, Oldwyn grabbed it. With the staff in his hands, the green jewel started to glow bright. A fierce energy flowed down the wood and through Oldwyn's fingertips, buzzing at the forgotten feeling of magic. The surge of power flourished his weary body, rejuvenating him, healing his wounds. He shuddered as the elemental force reclaimed his soul. He grew taller and more brooding in front of Kamina as his crooked back straightened out. Behind her the soldiers stepped away, some scuttling back down the steps. Ramiro remained steadfast, ready to face the man who had stolen his son from him.

Oldwyn finally opened his large eye, staring down at Kamina. She could see herself reflected in its thin film. The pupil switched focus from her to Ramiro. The ambassador retreated as the mage marched towards him, but he was unable to escape through the tight troop of soldiers choking the stairwell.

"I order you to put that weapon down," said Ramiro. His voice faltering as he faced Oldwyn Blake. The mage loomed over his jailor, seething with rage.

"You have kept me prisoner for over ten years without charge or trial. I should kill you where you stand."

"Like you did to my son," rebuked Ramiro, finding the strength to stand up for himself in the face of Oldwyn's threats.

"I warned you about the dangers of meddling with magic, and yet you persisted," growled the one-eyed mage. "You are as responsible as me for the death of your spawn, and the other soldiers who you seem so quick to forget."

The broody wizard barged through the contingent of guards, descending the spiral staircase to freedom. He was swiftly followed by the elf who had returned his staff. The soldiers eyed the ambassador with contempt, as the filed back down the steps. Ramiro Messer was left alone in the highest cell of the Black Tower to contemplate the mage's words.

Far below, Oldwyn emerged from the doorway of the prison. The gathered soldiers of the five nations of Amaros stopped and stared. He dirtied his feet on the hard ground, soaking up the power of Ygrain from the soil. The surrounding citizens, who had gathered after witnessing Kamina's chase, felt the reverberations of his steps through the soles of their shoes. Oldwyn knelt down and kissed the dirt, blessing it with a prayer.

Callaghan forced his way through the crowds, his veins throbbing with adrenalin after his victorious clash with Ramiro's men. The cyclops rose to his feet. Callaghan stepped out to meet him, offering his hand, but Oldwyn refused to take it.

"You should not have freed me, Callaghan."

"Amaros needs you," he said, taken aback. "There is an army marching…"

"I know of Malenek's plan," said Oldwyn coldly. "Even I cannot stop an army of vengeance spirits."

"I need you to cast a seeing spell," said the ranger. "I need you to show the Alliance that the army exists, so they will grant me passage to Zalestia."

"This I will do for you," said Oldwyn. "But first, I need a horse." He marched through the crowds and snatched the reigns of the first horse he happened upon. The owner would have argued that this constituted theft, were he not so scared.

"Oldwyn, time is of the essence," stressed Callaghan as the mage mounted the steed, calm under the wizard's enchanting influence.

"Time, ranger?" he said in disgust. "I have lost over ten years of time. I have lost more time than there are leaves in Elgrin Forest, or flakes of snow in Araneque. One more day will not turn the tide in your favour."

The mage whispered strange words into the ear of the steed, which sped off through the city. "I will return before morning," he called to Callaghan.

The ranger was offered little respite. No sooner had Oldwyn thundered off on the back of a stolen horse than the crowd burst into a hysterical chatter. Only now, in the wake of the cyclops' release, did they fully register the presence of an elf and her bonded spirit, framed in the doorway of the Black Tower. A few fainted, while others cried out and cursed at the pair. Callaghan snatched Kamina from the throng, whisking her away while Kaedin evaporated into thin air, confusing the citizens further. A blizzard of shrieks burst from their beaks.

"Never a dull moment in this city!" cracked one of the mob, accidentally bumping into a slender man clad in a long brown coat. "Sorry, friend," he said, but the slender man did not reply, or even acknowledge the impact. He was too busy staring after the ranger.

CHAPTER EIGHTEEN

THE SEEING SPELL

In an unreachable cave within the coastal cliffs of Caspia, the green glow of Oldwyn's staff illuminated the deep cavernous walls, long suspended in darkness. There were signs that someone, or something, had once resided here. The ground was grooved with large footprints, while the walls were poked with holes where giant fists had raged.

Oldwyn ran his fingers over the ridges, troubled by the ferocity resonating from them. The brute force that had punctured the thick rock was not merely venting frustration. This was a fight between two souls. He could still feel the antagonism within the walls, hearing the echoes of screams that had accompanied this violent clash. But whatever beings had inhabited this cave were now long gone, and all they had left behind was destruction and dust.

"I am sorry," whispered Oldwyn, to the wind and the memory, as he gazed out at the night sea.

*

Kamina lay slumped under the window of their makeshift quarters. She no longer dared to gaze outside, hiding from the panicked Caspians who picketed the council chambers, demanding answers after the day's strange events.

Callaghan returned with a plate of food and a jug of fresh water. "Where is Kaedin?" he enquired. Kamina had not noticed the absence of her brother, growing accustomed to his invisible state while they were in Calisto.

"I do not know," she muttered, gazing around, hoping to spy him, as if hiding in plain sight. "He cannot be far."

The phantom elf was perched on the roof above them, fixated on the cathedral on the opposite side of the Ico. It was so packed full of people that any stragglers had been forced to crowd outside, a mob of shadowy faces partially illuminated by torchlight. He strained to hear the words of the arch-priest's hastily written sermon above the horde's hateful chattering and the rush of the river as it descended into the crescent bay. Elves, ghosts, wizards, and rangers; these were all omens of some ominous threat the Alliance could not reveal or had no knowledge of, depending on the citizen's level of paranoia. They were terrified, and as Kaedin dissolved through the roof into the chamber below, he thought they had every right to be.

*

Callaghan left Kamina sleeping under Kaedin's protective gaze. The ghost, eternally awake, eyed his snoozing sibling with a sliver of jealousy. The ranger ventured through the sleeping city's quiet streets. He arrived at the northern gate, where he awaited the dawn of Risaar for his daily prayer, as well as Oldwyn's promised return. He had fears about the mage, but not doubts. Callaghan knew Oldwyn would come back to Calisto, but whether it would be to help them or seek revenge for his incarceration was still to be revealed.

As the dark sky melted into a canvas of reds, oranges, and pinks, Callaghan withdrew Ascara. He knelt down, jabbing the sword into the soil, the large ruby level with his face. Risaar peeked over the horizon as Callaghan whispered the enchantment. The ranger closed his eyes as his sword burst into flames. He prayed to the Elementals that this day would provide some ease. He could feel the heat of the sword, so hot it was scorching his clothes, but he carried on with his prayer, suffering Ascara's intensity for as long as he must. It reminded him of his training in the Ranger Temple, the arduous trials undertaken in the unbearable heat of Mount Ishkava's lava chambers.

It reminded him to endure.

He allowed the fire to die, rising back to his feet. He was about to return through the gate when he heard a distant neigh and the clatter of hooves. The silhouette of a lone rider haunted the rising orb of the red sun.

Oldwyn Blake had returned.

"Still praying to the gods, Callaghan?" he asked, halting his stolen horse.

"Every day," replied the ranger.

"Do they ever answer?"

"Not with words," he said, trying to judge Oldwyn's temperament.

"Pray they never do," warned the mage with a grim voice. "I fear you will not appreciate what they have to say." Oldwyn patted the horse as he trotted back to Calisto, the ranger following at a brisk pace.

"Did you find what you were looking for?" inquired Callaghan.

"Who says I was looking for anything?" he deflected.

"Oldwyn," said Callaghan earnestly, wishing to avoid a quarrel.

"No, I did not," said Oldwyn with a sigh. "Nor did I find what I feared." The mage took solace from this. "Do not concern yourself, ranger. You had the young elf free me for a reason. Explain it to me."

"I need you to cast a seeing spell wherever Malenek's army is," he said as the pair made their way back to the city. "I have to prove to the Alliance that this threat is real."

"The gift of sight is not to be squandered," replied Oldwyn abruptly. "The Alliance will claim trickery."

"It will not just be the members of the Alliance who are watching."

*

Talia trekked through the hills that marked the border between Heroshin and Legoria. The elf took some comfort in being able to spy the distant green of Elgrin Forest far to the east. Its thick trees and fauna were far removed from the Hyru salt flats that lay west beyond the looming hills. The ground here was gravelly and hard, although every once in a while she glimpsed the strange structures of salt that tarnished the otherwise flat whites of the west. The region was known for its hot springs and geysers, heated by Mount Ishkava. The brooding volcano was not visible from here, located on the opposite side of Heroshin.

She descended down the steep slopes, straddling the border as she rode along the length of the River Hertince. The opposite bank was lined by a series of stone markers, more relics from when Legoria belonged entirely to the elves. The town of Onassis appeared on the horizon, nestled near the river on the edge of the region. The settlement had been the first of man's intrusion into the elves former territory after the war. Most had come from the distant city of Perhola, disillusioned by the royal court and the wealth it hoarded. As she arrived at the town gate, she once again felt herself in the aim of human archers perched above.

"State your business," shouted one from behind his helmet.

"I have an urgent message for your leaders," she yelled, opting to use anxiety rather than diplomacy, given the discouraging outcome in Gorran and the several other towns she had visited along the way. The heads disappeared, and after a hushed conversation, the gate ground aside. They revealed Andis Wahl, Onassis' Master of the Guard, a heavy set man whose face was consumed by a grizzly ginger beard. The townsfolk stopped and stared, eyes veering towards the gate. A troop of guards had been called, taking up various positions around the town.

"I have heard rumours of elves wandering into the township of Tilden," he said, "but never this far from Elgrin."

"I am Talia Elloeth," she said.

"Andis Wahl," he said dryly, not extending any formal greeting. "My guards said you had an urgent message to deliver."

Talia quickly recounted her tall tale to Andis, placing emphasis on Malenek and his army of vengeance spirits marching from Mytor. "They will soon be upon Perhola, and after they decimate that city they will begin their journey south to Gorran, wiping out every village and town that stands in their path." Andis took some time to let Talia's tale sink in. The elf grew frustrated by the man's silence. "You do not believe me."

"I do not know what to believe," he admitted. "This is a strange story you share, yet you offer no proof."

"Is it not enough that she is here?" A waif of a woman carrying a burden of clothes marched towards them. A young soldier tried to stop her but she shook him off.

"Poppel, this is none of your concern," said the Master of the Guard.

"An army marches towards the city where our friends and neighbours are currently making trade, yet it is none of my concern?" she snapped. "It is all of our concern!" Her exclamation caused unrest among more of Onassis' population, now gathering in number, the rumour of an elf visitor having spread swiftly through the town.

"I have a sister in Tilden," said Poppel, turning to Talia. The elf was slightly surprised by her prattling personality. "She has bought goods from you. She spoke very highly of your bread, last we met, and I will trust anyone who can make that miserable biddy pass a compliment." Talia twigged that this woman suffered some human eccentricity, but if she was the only person willing to listen, then so be it. "What is the plan?" Poppel asked. It was Talia's turn to be stumped. "The Alliance does have a plan?"

"I am sure by now they do," said the elf. "I rode from Tilden to spread the warning. The Ishkava Ranger Callaghan Tor journeyed to Calisto to alert your Alliance. He advised that people should evacuate there."

"Then that is where I shall take my children," said Poppel. "Thank you." Talia watched her run off, pausing to relay the brief conversation to her friends and neighbours.

"They will all want to leave now," said Andis Wahl with a heavy sigh. "Most of them have never ventured further than Perhola."

"Then you had best guide them," she said, mounting Plagacia once again.

"That horse needs rest," noted Andis. The nag was wheezing, ready to collapse at any moment. Talia had stopped during the night to allow them both a brief respite from their task, but it was not enough for either of them.

"She will have some soon," shouted Talia, riding away. Andis grimaced when she swiped a sheaf of arrows and a bow left lying by a lazy sentry.

"Guard!" yelled Andis, marching towards the man currently looking for his pilfered weapon. The guard stood to attention, his cheeks flushed with guilt. "You left your weapon for the elf to steal. Go after it."

"W-what?" he stuttered, unsure why he was being castigated.

"Follow the elf and retrieve your weapon. That's an order."

"Alone, sir?" begged the timid guard.

"No. You!" Andis screamed at an unfortunate passing guard. "Go with him. Follow the elf and see if what she said is true."

"And if it is, sir?" asked the first.

"Then I imagine your stolen weapon will be the least of your worries."

The guards stumbled around, preparing their steeds to pursue the elven thief. Despite Plagacia's fatigue, they were already far from Onassis. Talia slipped the soldier's bow around her body, ready for use at the first sign of danger. After days of travelling she felt that there was a purpose to her journey. The woman named Poppel had provided her with a glimmer of mad hope. She was sure the woman would flee, and in that, Talia had saved one family, or at the very least stayed her execution at the hands of the dead.

*

"I wish I was the ghost," muttered Kamina to an invisible Kaedin, as she lugged two buckets of dirt into the main hall of the council chambers. Even though she could not see him, Kamina knew her brother was grinning. She dumped the buckets by Oldwyn's feet, wiping drips of sweat from her forehead. The mage was busy completing a circle of soil almost as wide as the room itself, outlining the circular cross mosaic embedded within its floor. Callaghan followed her, carrying two significantly larger buckets with seemingly effortless strength.

"Is that it done?" she wheezed, as Oldwyn patted the dirt together, finishing the ring.

"Done?" asked Oldwyn in disdain, rising up to his full height.

"The circle is finished," she noted.

"No, my dear, dim-witted child," he said with a patronising smile. "We must also fill the circle." Kaedin chuckled softly from the shadows. Kamina sagged as she and Callaghan picked up their empty pails.

"When you find this Stone of Spirits," she grumbled to Callaghan, "I want you to choke him with it."

"I will bear that in mind," he replied with a grin. Despite himself, he was enjoying the company of the young elves, even though he knew it was only temporary.

As they reached the exit, Kamina was swept aside by the whirlwind force of Ambassador Ramiro. His bodyguards trailed close behind, caught in his wake, sporting bruises from their altercation with Callaghan.

"What in the name of the Elements do you think you are doing?" he blasted. "This is a desecration of the cross!" Ramiro moved to kick apart the circle, but Oldwyn launched himself across the room.

"If you so much as brush one grain of soil out of place, I will take you out of this city, bind you to a post, and leave the spirits to ravish your broken body," warned the mage.

"Are you threatening me?" said Ramiro, his nose almost touching Oldwyn's. "An ambassador to these lands? A former councillor of this city?"

"Yes I am, you repugnant fool." This blunt answer momentarily stumped Ramiro, who was more used to the long-winded rhetoric of politics.

"You have... you have no right to..." he stumbled.

"Ambassador Messer, you asked me to provide proof of the spirit army," said Callaghan, stepping between the ambassador and the mage. "Oldwyn will do so with a seeing spell."

"Did he have to drag all this dirt in here?" asked Ramiro, lamenting over the dirty floor.

"It is a suitable location," replied the ranger.

"Just make sure you and your friends brush this blasphemy up once this spectacle is over." Ambassador Messer marched around the circle of dirt, venting his frustrations at this staff as they ascended to the upper levels.

Kamina finally stepped outside, filling her bucket from the cart of dirt that Callaghan had acquired. Oldwyn had made it explicitly clear that the soil used in the spell must be untainted and fresh. They had ridden a safe distance out of the city and gathered the load before morning was over. When they had returned, the protesting swarm that had surrounded the temple and chambers the previous night had dispersed. Now that Oldwyn Blake was present, Caspia's citizens were steering clear of the council chambers, not bold enough to protest and shout in daylight as they had been under the cover of darkness. Only the duty bound guards dared to wander in the vicinity, while the surrounding streets were eerily deserted.

"The spell will be ready before the two suns descend," Kamina overheard Oldwyn say as she returned with more soil, the wizard's words tainted with trepidation.

"You worry it will not work?" inquired Callaghan.

"The spell will work as it is intended to. My fear lies in what we will see."

"Well, at least one good thing has come of all this." Oldwyn glanced at Callaghan, not comprehending the ranger's meaning. "Your freedom."

"Only history will show if that is true," mused the mage.

"Oldwyn," said Callaghan, placing his solemn hand on the wizard's shoulder, "I should have acted sooner, perhaps created a ruse that required your expertise."

"And yet you did not, because deception is not in your nature," said Oldwyn. "It is not your burden to bear, Callaghan." Only now did the ranger notice Kamina standing nearby.

"If it will be ready before nightfall then I must go," said Callaghan. "I will need to take Kamina and Kaedin with me."

"Where are you going?" asked Oldwyn.

"To find you an audience," replied Callaghan. "We seem to have scared everyone off."

"But who will help me finish here?" he demanded.

"I am sure you will find someone. Kamina, come with me." The thankful elf swiftly followed the ranger out of the council chambers. Oldwyn followed them to the entrance and tapped one of the guards on the shoulder. The guard stood attentive to his post, ignoring him.

"I require you two men to carry the rest of that soil inside," said Oldwyn, using the staff to indicate the cart, half full of rich dirt.

"I am sorry sir, we cannot leave our posts," replied the soldier automatically. Although he could not see the mage, he sensed him move closer, felt the warm flow of his ancient breath on the back of his neck.

"Move that dirt," rasped the old, gravelly voice, "or I will bite off your ugly, little ears."

The gentle tide sloshed and sucked around the posts holding up the long esplanade that curled around the base of the crescent-shaped cliff. They had descended from the council chambers into the complex system of steps and platforms carved into the sheer cliff face. Callaghan guided them through the caverns, some natural, others man made, finally emerging out at the oceanic underbelly of Calisto. Kamina was now able to see the multitude of boats she had glimpsed from above in much greater detail. They came in all shapes and sizes, from rickety looking dinghies to grand ships of war, built to carry hundreds of men across the vast ocean. Large pulley systems craned over one section of the bay, delivering constructed parts from the shipbuilders' yards above to the launch ports below. Callaghan led her along the boardwalk, past shops and stalls built into and above the stone. She noticed they were receiving much undue attention, her ears catching snippets of conversation.

"It is him, the ranger…"

"…an elf? My great aunt would turn in her grave…"

The crowds parted for Callaghan as he continued along the gantry. He led Kamina to the epicentre of the marina, a large circular viewing platform raised above the walkway, where a single tree was planted. Behind them, the Ico descended into a massive waterfall, having eroded the cliff away over time. Callaghan stopped by the small tree. Upon closer inspection, Kamina realised that the trunk was growing from the centre of an elemental cross, etched with Amarosian writing.

"What does it say?" Kamina whispered.

"The Four Elementals empower us to enlighten our enemies," translated the spirit.

"Very good, Kaedin," said Callaghan.

"Nyssa taught me," said the invisible elf, basking in the ranger's praise.

"It was planted after the first Zalestian attack on Calisto. It destroyed part of the docks," he explained. By now those on the platform were curious about the ranger and his companion, while others had paused on the walkway below.

"People of Calisto," he announced, addressing the crowds. "I am Callaghan Tor, Ranger of Ishkava. I know some of you were frightened by yesterday's events, but you have nothing to fear from myself or my companions."

"She's an elf!" spat a loud-mouthed woman. Kamina naturally hid away behind the ranger.

"She is a child!" he shot back. "Would you hound a human child in such a manner?" This silenced the heckler, but as one shrank away, another voice arose.

"You set Oldwyn Blake free!" exclaimed a bitter man. "He's a murderer!"

"Oldwyn Blake acted to defend himself, as any man would, and he has lain in that cell for over ten years without trial." Callaghan's words did not appease the crowd, which erupted into a rabble. The man who had denounced Oldwyn hurled an affel fruit at Callaghan, but it never hit its intended target. The mob was stunned as the piece of fruit halted abruptly in mid-air, hovering above their heads. Kaedin slowly materialised, shedding his transparency, his outstretched arm holding the affel fruit. He tossed it back to its thrower, but the bitter man was too scared to react. The affel fruit fell to his feet, rolling along the planks of the boardwalk until it splashed into the bay, bobbing on the surface of the water.

"Hello," said Kaedin.

"What are you?" cried one.

"Are you a wizard?" begged another?

The crowd erupted into a cacophony of questions. Callaghan smiled. With this one act, Kaedin had secured an audience for the seeing spell.

"Citizens of Calisto!" he yelled over the barrage of voices. "Everything will be explained in the council chamber this evening. Please do not be afraid to attend."

His vague summons did not satisfy the crowd. They pushed on, reaching for the ranger, pleading for answers and promises of protection. Callaghan grabbed Kamina's hand and escaped through the masses, following Kaedin who opened up a path through the swarm of people. Unbeknownst to the trio, they hurried past a curious old boat captain named Braydon Pike, who was had already resolved to accept the ranger's invitation.

*

Torches were placed on the floor surrounding the soil circle as evening crept upon them. The debating chamber was packed to the upper tiers, a mass of faces squashed over the balconies. The doorways were blocked by bodies desperate to glimpse what the ranger had teased. Every seat on the steps surrounding the seal was taken, the cross mosaic itself now completely covered by a thick layer of dirt. The front seats were reserved for members of the Amarosian Alliance, the council of Calisto, and others of high rank or persuasion. Everyone was abuzz, chattering away like a flock of birds.

Oldwyn stood next to the circle with his staff, his one eye closed in concentration. Behind him, Callaghan was seated with an inquisitive Kamina. Kaedin had elected to remain invisible, but she could just see his vague outline sat on the floor in front of them.

"How will it work?" Kamina asked Callaghan.

"Imagine everything in Enara is connected," he said. "The surface that Malenek and his army walk upon feels him, and through the ground this soil can feel it also. With Oldwyn's help, the connection will act as a window, and reveal them to us."

"I do not understand," she said, pressing him further.

"You will," he replied.

"I am ready," announced Oldwyn, opening his giant, singular eye, casting it in the direction of those still nattering until they hushed themselves. The mage brought the staff before him, muttering to the green gem, which glowed brighter as he spoke. His chanting grew louder as he waved the staff in the air, casting it around in a circle. A strong wind picked up, as if emanating from the vortex created by his magical cane.

Oldwyn swiftly arced it upwards. A green orb of magical energy floated slowly out of the crystal tip. The crowd gawped as the bubble of magic drifted over the circle. As soon as it reached the centre, gravity grasped at it. The sphere smashed down into the soil, shaking the building to its foundations, causing more alarm than actual damage. A wave of green energy rippled out over the dirt surface. It dispelled as soon as it reached the edge of the circle, discolouring the flames of the surrounding torches from their standard orange to a bright, leafy emerald green. The agitated audience watched in anticipation, but nothing happened.

"Did it work?" Kamina began to ask, but Callaghan placed his finger over his lips, instructing her to be silent. Oldwyn gently grazed the staff against the topsoil. The magic-infused dirt burst to life, moving like the ocean, rising up in waves, structuring itself. The final form was a perfect scale model of a city. Many within the audience recognised it as Calisto. Oldwyn conducted the dirt like an orchestra, with the city growing larger until the circle of dirt showed a replica of the council chambers. The walls fell away, revealing the people within; a mass of small bodies constructed from the soil, sitting watching a circle, miniature flames of the torches floating above the soil. As if demonstrating that this was real, Oldwyn waved his arms. His dirt equivalent mimicked the movement.

"What does this prove?" asked Ramiro.

"That the spell shows what is happening in the here and now," replied Oldwyn. He waved the staff over the dirt, and the landscape changed, as if they were flying over the length of Amaros. Eventually the soil slowed and settled, revealing the replica of another city, one perched on a large outcrop.

"What is this we are seeing?" asked Ramiro.

"It is the Heroshin city of Perhola," answered Cohen.

"And it is under siege," said Oldwyn, indicating one side of the city with his staff. It was being attacked by a small horde of creatures that were once men. However, there was another squad, further back, which glowed with the same green magic Oldwyn used for the spell.

"The spirit army," he announced. The mage controlled the circle, descending closer to the spirits. At their centre the audience spotted a knight in armour upon a horse, and another creature of legend, a golem. Braydon Pike, having squeezed his way to the front with some of his crew, focused on the man of stone intently.

"Captain, that looks like..." whispered Oran Cobb, Pike's first mate.

"Not here," hissed the captain.

With a strained movement of his hands, Oldwyn brought their view back so that they could better see Perhola. The citizens, comprised of grains of soil, were pouring out of its walls. Many were attacked by the creatures and dragged back to the spirit army, where they were transformed into the ghoulish abominations. While the majority of the audience focused on the small band of spirits, Kamina noticed a flicker of movement at the edge of the circle in front of her. As she peered closer, she discerned a lone rider on a horse, galloping at speed straight for the city.

"Talia."

*

The elf rode fast, digging her heels into Plagacia's grey-speckled hide, unable to comprehend what she could see in the distance. A legion of hunched, snarling creatures grabbed at the fleeing Perholans, dragging them back to the cluster of spirits. The ghosts delved their hands into the bodies, snapping their souls and trapping them within the flesh. The victims screamed as they contorted and died, mutating into those vile things. Amidst the silver glow of the spirit army, Talia could see Malenek's armour at the core, reflecting their eerie radiance.

Her keen eyes spotted two children who, against all odds, had made it through the gauntlet of ghouls. Talia raced towards the survivors, a boy and a girl. One of the undead beasts was bearing down upon them. She whipped up the stolen bow and strung an arrow, aiming at the morbid demon while Plagacia galloped forward. Talia let the arrow fly.

The beast raised a mutated hand, ready to claw at the young girl. An arrow whizzed past her head and caught the creature square in the chest. The force lifted it clear off its feet, sending it crashing to the ground. The children changed course and scrambled towards the archer on horseback, pleading for help. As they neared, they were taken aback by the sight of the elf.

"Do not be afraid," Talia reassured them, dropping from Plagacia. Unnatural screams from Perhola howled in their direction. The children's yelling had attracted the attentions of the spirits. Talia saw the ghosts point at them, ordering their undead servants to advance. The savage creatures snarled and thundered towards them. She plucked the children from the ground and onto Plagacia's back.

"Listen to me," she said. The children were in shock, their bodies wrought with fear. Talia took the boy's face in her hands, gazing deep into his eyes, trying to reach beyond the absolute dread that they drowned in. "Listen to me!" the elf snapped again. The young human gazed into her eyes, hypnotised, his panicked panting gradually slowing down. "Ride south-west. Do not stop until you reach Elgrin Forest."

"But…" the boy began to protest.

"Do not stop for anything," she said. "Ride deep into the forest. The elves will find you. Tell them you were sent by Talia Elloeth. Tell them everything that has happened here. Do you understand?"

"Yes," nodded the boy. "Talia Elloeth."

"Now go!" Talia slapped Plagacia's hide. The horse dashed off on the long, unbeaten road to Elgrin. The animal paused, neighing back at her. The children heard her shout something they did not understand, words from the elven language. The horse neighed back a sad reply before leaving her, carrying the children to safety.

Malenek's forces quickly descended upon the elf. She could outrun them, but for how long? After trekking halfway across Amaros, Talia was tired of running. She loaded another arrow and aimed it at the stampeding hordes.

The two scouts from Onassis watched from a small hillock to the south. They were shocked by the terrifying scene playing out before them, and dared not progress any further.

"By the Elements, she's doing it," whispered the soldier without a bow as they witnessed Talia take down another of the spirits' ghastly disciples. "She's winning."

*

The entire council chamber cheered as they watched the soil representation of Talia shoot one arrow after another, slaying Malenek's army. Oldwyn had managed to enlarge the scene, focusing on the elven warrior, as half as tall as she was in real life.

"She is doing it!" Kamina exclaimed to Callaghan, grabbing his arm. The ranger's face remained solemn. The creatures Talia had shot down were rising up again. They snapped the arrows from their fleshy hides as if they were nothing but tiny thorns.

"The arrows are not enough to free the soul trapped inside," murmured Oldwyn. The crowd chattered in fear as a vengeance spirit entered their view. The apparition, a floating man shaped by the glowing green magic, had outflanked the elf and approached her from behind.

"No!" screamed Kamina.

*

As if hearing Kamina's scream from the other side of Amaros, Talia spun round, confronted by the vengeance spirit. She quickly let loose an arrow, but it shot straight through the spirit's head. She felt its cold, vaporous fingers enter her body, clenching her soul in its cursed hand. It gazed at her, not with indignation or malice, but with sorrow.

With one final twist of its arm, it broke her in two.

*

Kamina drifted closer to the circle, watching helplessly as Talia was consumed by the ghost. She was so close to her sister's avatar that she could almost touch her. As Talia fell to her knees, Kamina reached out to comfort her, to cradle the miniature version of her sister in her arms, but the dirt crumbled away in her fingers. The young elf gazed up at Oldwyn. The light in the staff's crystal was waning. The mage was as tepid now as when she had first laid eyes upon him in the Black Tower.

"Do something," she begged. "Get her back!" The ranger hastily stepped over to Oldwyn.

"I do not have much strength left," he muttered.

"Let me help," said Callaghan. He placed one arm around the mage, and the other over Oldwyn's hands that held the staff. Callaghan felt Oldwyn drawing life-force from him, as their combined energies flowed into the crystal. The shapes in the soil began to reconstruct themselves. Talia's avatar lay on the ground, curled up in a ball, while the attacking spirit loomed over her. The spirit's head shifted, as if it could see Kamina kneeling at the edge of the circle. The miniature ghost then turned and faced the ranger and the mage, the green glow of the magic captivating them.

"Talia?" whispered Kamina, sobbing over her sister's body. However, it was no longer her sister. She had been transformed into one of the ghastly, contorted creatures. It roared up and dived towards her. The young elf was sprayed by a blast of soil as it left the circle, losing cohesion and form.

The glowing green spirit raised its arm and pointed at the mage, mouthing unheard words. Oldwyn lost consciousness, collapsing against Callaghan. The staff fell from his hands and struck the soil. The dirt was set aflame, an intense, magic-fuelled blaze that extinguished itself just as suddenly as it had appeared.

The seeing spell was over.

*

The two scouts from Onassis felt Talia's failure as if it was their own. The brief hope she had granted them now seeped away into sorrow and angst.

"We have to leave," said the second guard. "Now!"

They turned their horses back in the direction of Onassis, but were confronted by a trio of the ætherghouls. The creatures leapt up and snatched the guards from their saddles, dragging them kicking and screaming along the harsh ground until they were unceremoniously dropped before the spirit that had broken Talia.

In their last moments as men, they whimpered.

CHAPTER NINETEEN
AFTERMATH OF SIGHT

A DISCONCERTING SILENCE STRANGLED ANY THOUGHT OF SOUND in the council chambers. The spectators stared at the scorched dirt that tarnished the seal on the floor. None were as close as Kamina, paralysed in her place beside the circle. A tear formed in the corner of one of her green emerald eyes, rolling down the curve of her porcelain cheek. It clung to her skin, but as with all tears, it eventually fell, exploding upon the soil.

A tsunami of screaming and wailing shook the chambers. Waves of panic lashed over the people of Calisto. They tried to flee, but found the exit blocked by armed guards. The crowds began to bottleneck, fighting and stampeding as they tried to break free.

"This is madness. Why are the exits blocked?" Cohen demanded as the crowds jostled them.

"I ordered it so," said Ramiro insistently. "We must control this. They will spread rumours. The city will riot."

"I fear this is far beyond our control," stated Isan Narain. He glanced over at Callaghan, who fought to protect the unconscious Oldwyn from the stampeding feet of the wild mob. The ranger dragged the cyclops onto the circle of soil, where even the most panicked of citizens did not dare set foot upon. He grabbed Ascara and whispered the incantation. The flaming sword proved enough of a distraction to halt the baying herd.

"People of Calisto! Calm yourselves and listen to me!" he commanded.

"Let us out!" cried one, a sentiment supported by the mass of spectators.

"And where will you go?" Callaghan asked the man. "To Gorran? Hylan? They are all in the sights of the spirit army now. Calisto is the furthest city from Perhola. At the moment, this is the safest place in all of Amaros."

"For how long?" yelled another. A few of the crowd grumbled in agreement, but the majority waited for the ranger to answer.

"You are right," he said. "They will eventually reach these walls, and the spirits will walk right through them. But I believe that there is a weapon in Zalestia that will help defeat this army. Many of you are the owners of the ships in the bay below. Who among you is willing to traverse the Badlands and take me there?"

The crowd chattered amongst themselves. Captain Pike jostled his way through the masses. One of his crew, a brutish man named Darien Yore, grabbed his arm, holding him back.

"Captain, you can't be serious?" said the crewman. Pike shot a warning glance at Darien's hand, which he quickly removed. The captain forced his way to the forefront of the gathering Darien following in his wake.

"Even if we were willing, the Alliance have forbid it," said Pike.

"And you are?" asked Ramiro?

"Captain Braydon Pike, ambassador."

"Under the circumstances," said Cohen, stepping away from his peers, "the Alliance will bow to the wisdom of the Ranger of Ishkava."

"Well, captain?" asked the ranger. Darien nudged up next to Pike, whispering into his ear.

"Captain, do not do this," pleaded the contentious crew member.

"Captain, do not do this," pleaded the contentious crew member.

"Silence your tongue," hissed Pike. All eyes were on him now, including those of the ranger. Callaghan stepped towards him, sheathing his sword.

"Captain Pike, what say you?"

"I volunteer my ship, the Arad Nor, and her crew," said Pike hesitantly. "She is a small fishing vessel, but swift in the water."

"Good," said Callaghan, shaking Pike's hand. "Speed is essential if we are to return in time to stop this threat."

"We have just returned to port," added Pike. "It will take us at least a day to resupply for the journey." Callaghan thrust a small leather purse of coins into his hand. The old sea captain shook it, liking the sound that jangled from within.

"You have until dawn," stated the ranger. Captain Pike nodded his acceptance of the challenge. The mob made a path for him as he left, followed by his crew, although the guards remained staunch at the exits. They looked to Ramiro for orders. The ambassador merely waved his hand, and they moved aside for the crew of the *Arad Nor*. With the exits unimpeded, the calmer crowds began to file out, although some remained, struggling to digest the existence of the spirit army and the sacking of Perhola.

The chamber was almost empty, save for the rulers and dignitaries who were locked in heated debate. Callaghan discovered Kamina kneeling at the edge of the dirt circle where Talia's avatar had leapt out at her. She picked up a handful of soil, still warm from the fleeting fire, and watched it trickle away between her fingers.

"We have to go and save her," she said, finally registering the ranger looming at her side. He knelt down to face her, seeking words to comfort her, but he stumbled as hot tears streamed down her sorry little face. "Please, Callaghan, you can save her, I know you can. I am sorry I ran away from you. I am so sorry. Please, just save her."

"Talia is gone," said Kaedin. The spirit was now visible, slumped on a step nearby.

"You do not know that!" cried Kamina.

"I do know!" he screamed back. He could still feel Slavek Istin's soul breaking in his ghostly hand. The vivid memory would haunt him forever. "She is one of those things now."

"Ætherghouls," said Oldwyn, waking up in the circle. Callaghan moved to help him up, but he refused, using his staff to leverage himself to his feet. "The creatures you speak of are known as ætherghouls. I believe the elven word is *gwann'gul.*"

"They are nothing but stories," said Kaedin.

"Like ghosts?" retorted Oldwyn. "The old stories of the vengeance spirits tell that they could reach into a person and break the connection between body and spirit, leaving the soul trapped within, helpless. Without this light to guide it, the body is nothing but an undead prison, a frenzied, tortured ghoul and mindless slave of the vengeance spirit who sired them."

They all turned to look at the spirit sitting amongst them.

"Why are you looking at me?" he pleaded. "I did not mean to make an… ætherghoul." Oldwyn snorted sceptically.

"We know, Kaedin," said Kamina softly.

"I overheard Jaelyn say they needed souls for their plan to succeed," recalled Callaghan. "Could it be that he meant these ætherghouls, and not the spirits?"

"There can be no doubt the spirits are but a tool," Oldwyn surmised. "The ætherghouls are Malenek's purpose. That is why he marches across Amaros."

"He said he was going to bring peace to all of Enara," said the ranger. "Is this what he meant? To transform us all into those things? What is he hoping to achieve?"

"That I do not know," professed Oldwyn. "I will need to visit the university's library to learn more. Callaghan, when you faced off against Malenek, did you see his bodyguard?"

"The stone man?" remembered the ranger. "Malenek referred to him as Gort." A flash of panic appeared on Oldwyn's weary face. "Is something wrong?"

"Besides an army of ætherghouls and spirits descending upon us?" remarked the mage. "No. I must go."

"What about Talia?" Kamina asked as he hobbled away. "Can we save her?" There was no answer from Oldwyn as he disappeared into the night.

"Kamina, I fear Kaedin is right" said Callaghan eventually.

"What about the Stone of Spirits? Perhaps it can bring her back?"

"Perhaps," was all Callaghan could muster. He could not bear to kill off the girl's one glimmer of hope so soon after seeing Talia transformed. He knew nothing of the stone's power, but he held little hope that it could restore the souls of the ætherghouls.

"This is all your fault!" she screamed, angry at his one word answer. Kamina pushed the ranger with enough force to send him sprawling to the floor. "You brought this upon us. You brought Jaelyn to Elgin Forest. To our home! You killed Kaedin! You killed Talia!" Tears once again streamed down the elf's young face. She escaped the council chambers to hide her sorrow, the ranger helpless to stop her.

Kaedin was sat staring at the scorched soil, shell-shocked, dwelling on his encounter with Slavek Isten. He had created an ætherghoul, watched as the man was twisted into that ghastly fiend. Talia had experienced that same pain before she died, only she was not dead, just trapped. Was this somehow his fault? Kaedin wondered. Was this why Jaelyn had been sent to assassinate him?

"Kaedin, I am sorry about Talia," said Callaghan, picking himself up. The spirit did not respond. "Kaedin?"

"What?" The ghost was beginning to fade, as his bond with Kamina was stretched.

"Find Kamina, make sure she is… just find her." Kaedin wandered off after his distraught sibling. "Invisibly," added Callaghan. Kaedin melted into the air before he reached the exit. He went unnoticed as he ran through the crowds of people outside the council chambers, including Captain Pike and his crew.

"Buy whatever we need, and do it quickly," ordered Pike, handing the ranger's purse to Oran Cobb. "Tell the crew to get some shut-eye."

"Aye, captain," said the first mate. He dutifully marched away to carry out his orders, taking most of the crew with him. Only Darien Yore remained behind.

"This is a bad idea, captain," said the stubborn sailor.

"When I want your opinion I'll ask for it, Darien. Now stop lingering around me like a bad smell and help your crewmates."

"They are no longer my crewmates. I quit."

"Darien…" pleaded Pike, but he was quickly cut down.

"No, captain, this is a fool's errand, as well you know. If the Badlands don't kill you, the Zogs will, and I won't have any part in it. I've lost enough family to that wretched place."

"Would you rather cower here in Calisto waiting to be violated by one of them spirits?" hissed Pike. Darien, whose arms were as thick as the average man's thigh, squared up to the wiry old captain.

"I won't be cowering," he growled, but Pike did not flinch. Darien turned his back on him, sauntering off towards the town square.

"We leave at dawn," Pike shouted after him. "We won't wait for you, or that chip on your shoulder." Darien waved Pike's words away with a bat of his hand. The captain carried his disappointment away towards the docks.

Their heated exchange was overheard by the slender man in the brown coat. Something chirped menacingly from within his coat. He peeled back one of the flaps until he could see the black, winged creature that resided in his inner pocket.

"Don't you worry, my sweet," he whispered to the herk. "You'll be flying soon enough." The man fed the creature some dried worms from another pocket. When it was satisfied, he closed over his coat and started to shadow Darien through the darkening streets of Calisto.

*

Oldwyn had elected to visit the Grand Elemental Church before heading to the library. After the seeing spell and his journey the night before, he wished to offer a prayer to the deities. As he crossed the bridge, he spied a throng of citizens struggling to gain admittance, hoping to receive forgiveness before the end of days. The mage remained on the bridge, ignored by passers-by as he watched the last slivers of daylight fade.

His ominous eye observed the city workers rushing to light the beacons and twin lighthouses that adorned the crescent cliffs. This chore was made more difficult by a sudden shower of rain. He watched the raindrops descend, smacking off the railing of the bridge, dripping down with the rest of the River Ico into the bay below, becoming one with the ocean. He gazed out beyond the cliffs into the depths of the sea, until it was lost in the darkness. From the gloom of the wet evening an epiphany emerged in his mind.

Oldwyn knew what Malenek's plan was.

*

Servants skirted around the debating chamber, relighting the torches while a heated battle of words raged between members of the Alliance.

"It was a trick!" denounced Ambassador Lome, pointing an accusing finger at Callaghan. "A trick you and your cyclops friend conjured up to create mass panic and tarnish Lord Malenek's good name!"

"It was no trick," said Ramiro before Callaghan had the chance to defend himself, "and we all know it." This silenced everyone except Miden Lome.

"But Ambassador Messer..." he protested.

"Do not say another word in favour of that man, Miden, or I will have your resignation." The Mytor ambassador, realising he was now in the minority, capitulated. "We have allowed Balen Malenek certain freedoms over the years in exchange for his religious guidance. It is clear now that this was a mistake. Ranger, what is your plan?"

"I will journey with the crew of the *Arad Nor* to Zalestia," said Callaghan. "I will seek the aid of Zahyr Zaleed Khan in finding the Stone of Spirits." The mere mention of the leader of Amaros' enemy raised a few eyebrows and low whispers. "I will also attempt to discover the identity of the Zalestian who is conspiring with Malenek."

"How do you know it is not Zaleed Khan himself who helps Malenek?" asked Duke Garstang.

"When I overheard Malenek discussing the stone, it was said that even Zaleed Khan would not find it."

"Ranger, you claim this mission is for the greater good," said Glin Corag, chief councillor of Caspia, "yet from my perspective it looks as though you are running away."

"If I had wished to flee, chief councillor, I would have not brought unwanted attention to my departure."

"Then why not stay here and fight?" challenged Corag. "You possess the fabled sword of Risaar after all."

"Ascara is of no use against the spirits," said Callaghan firmly. "And I have a certain understanding with the Khan that offers me a unique advantage."

"You have been to Zalestia?" asked Ramiro, slightly shocked. "Against the orders of the Alliance?"

"Yes," admitted the ranger. Not wishing to recount the story of his false apprentice, Callaghan cut to the chase. "There is an army marching upon us while we stand doing nothing. I am afraid the pleasantries of the Alliance's discipline will have to wait."

"Assuming we survive," said Ramiro.

"I will travel to Zalestia, but you, the leaders of these lands, must prepare the city to receive the refugees who are fleeing Malenek's forces."

"Agreed," said Ramiro. Callaghan was thankful to be working alongside Ramiro instead of fighting him. While he was stubborn in his grudge against Oldwyn, Callaghan knew he cared for his city and his country. "Duke Garstang. Send the evacuation order to Gorran."

"Yes, sir. Craecoran Gemmel left ahead of me to prepare for such an eventuality. He awaits my word."

"Then send your fastest man," ordered Ramiro.

"I will go myself," said Garstang with a swift salute.

"Duke Garstang," said Callaghan, "I would ask that you take Ambassador Da'ri with you."

"You wish me to ride to Gorran?" she croaked, sitting idly on the steps.

"And beyond. The tribes of the Etraihu must be warned. Malenek may march straight here, but he can send his minions across Duru Umbin and into their lands. All the tribes will listen to you, as will the centaurs."

"The horse masters listen to no human, man or woman."

"Then seek out an Ishkava Ranger by the name of Dash Cole," suggested Callaghan. "He was in Rundhale last I heard. He has dealt with the centaurs before."

"Why seek them out at all?" she asked.

"They are older than man or elf. Perhaps they know more about the spirits than we do," said Callaghan.

"As you wish," she replied. The duke and the Rundhale ambassador hastened away while the argumentative Chief Councillor raged on.

"And what are we to do with all these refugees?" stressed Glin Corag. "We do not have the resources."

"We will ration supplies," insisted Ramiro.

"Might I remind you that you are no longer Chief Councillor, Ambassador Messer," said his successor.

"No, but as you just pointed out, I am an Ambassador of the Amarosian Alliance, which is in charge of this country's affairs of war. Now go and organise the representatives. Speak to the merchants and farmers…"

"I know how to do my job," grumbled Corag, abruptly leaving the chambers.

"Ranger," said Isan Narain. "The elf who we saw…" At a loss of words, the ambassador pointed to the circle. "Was it she who warned Gorran?"

"It was. Her name was Talia Elloeth. The elves I travel with are her kin." Ramiro overheard this, and felt pity for the elves, even the ghostly one. "She was privy to the knowledge of Malenek's plan when I departed Tilden. I am sure she has warned every settlement she passed in your ward."

"I pray to the Elements she has," said Isan. "I do not wish to send a messenger out to their death. What I do not understand is why Malenek would attack Perhola, yet not attack the kingdom of Hylan?"

"I do not know. He was very specific that Hylan was not to be touched." Callaghan glanced at Cohen Hesh, his friend and the Heroshin Ambassador, who was comforting Miden Lome. The Mytor ambassador was slowly accepting the reality of the situation, and that everyone in his home town of Morghen was most likely dead, or worse, turned into ætherghouls.

"You suspect King Arthadian to be in league with Malenek?" asked Isan.

"No," replied Callaghan. "Malenek's route is the most decisive. It would take him days to trek across the salt flats with his army in tow." Cohen overheard the subject of conversation. He left Lome to join the fray.

"Poor fellow, everyone he knows is from Mytor." They each regarded the pale figure slumped on the steps. "Callaghan, is there anything else we can do to bolster Calisto's defences?"

"Not that I can think of," he replied. "The spirits can walk through walls."

"Never trust a ranger to do a wizard's work," announced Oldwyn as he reappeared. Ramiro's unpleasant demeanour returned upon sight of the mage. "I believe I may be able to cast a defensive spell around the city, one even the spirits cannot penetrate. It will take time to prepare."

"We asked you for aid once before and you turned us down," said Ramiro. "What has changed?"

"You are not asking, or holding a sword to my throat," said the mage with impunity. "I am offering my services of my own volition, Ambassador." Ramiro wrestled with his emotions, strangling his fury before he could unleash it upon the cyclops.

"I can never forgive you for the death of my son," he hissed as he stepped closer to Oldwyn. "You and your magics are dangerous, but if they can help protect this city from the threat of annihilation, then do so." The very words stripped Ramiro of his energy. "Please, excuse me," he murmured as he staggered out into the rain.

"As well as Oldwyn's spell, is there no way we could take Malenek out ourselves?" asked Isan. "Longbow archers may be able to shoot him."

"Malenek is a former soldier, ambassador," said Callaghan. "We saw his strategy in the seeing spell. He lingers at the rear with the majority of the spirits for protection, while the ætherghouls invade and drag the victims back to the spirits."

"Callaghan, I must prepare the protection spell in the library," interrupted Oldwyn. "Would you be so kind as to help me?" The ranger and mage made their way out of the council chambers.

"What do you need my help with?" asked Callaghan.

"What? No. Nothing. That was a ruse to be rid of the politicians. I do not trust them. But I believe I have fathomed what Malenek's plan may be."

"Well? What is it?"

"Not here," whispered the wizard.

*

Kamina wilted on a neglected decorative bench in the grounds of the council chambers. She could barely feel the cold of the rain, or the fact she was soaked through to the skin. The only thing she felt was the swollen sense of loss that consumed her heart.

Her sister was gone.

"Kaedin?" she asked softly.

"I am here," he said, perched quietly and invisibly next to her.

"I need to see you." The spirit's form appeared next to her. His ethereal energy shone in the rain, creating a colourful glow that Kamina tried to touch. It was beautiful, although she could not bring herself to say such a thing. She turned her attentions back to the curtains of rain beyond the edge of the cliff.

"She is gone," Kamina said. Kaedin could do little else except nod and try and hold Kamina's hand.

Ramiro Messer watched them from the exterior of the council chambers. With Oldwyn's resurgence, his mind dwelled on his dead son, on his own sense of loss. He pitied the elves to have to deal with that burden so young. He considered approaching them and offering his condolences, but Callaghan and Oldwyn emerged from the building. The ambassador departed with his men as the ranger crossed the grass to the elves.

"Come, Kamina," he said, "let us get you out of the rain."

*

Darien was slumped at the bar of the Sto Tavern. News of the spirit army had spread throughout the city. Most of the citizens had taken the ranger's advice and descended upon the Elemental churches to pray, rather than trying to forget the impending doom by inebriating themselves, as Darien was in the process of doing.

"Barkeep, another ale!" he bellowed, followed by a hearty belch. The scrawny barkeep shook his head as he fetched the order.

"Make that two," said a newcomer. The slender man in the brown coat sat next to Darien. "I'm buying," he added, spreading a few crona across the bar. Darien strained to focus on the stranger, but was sure they had never met.

"And to what do I owe this generosity?" he slurred as the barman brought their tankards, sloshing with foamy beer.

"If the world is going to end, I might as well spend the crona while I have it," said the stranger.

"I'll drink to that!" roared Darien. They clapped their tankards together in a toast. "Ceilu!"

"Ceilu!" repeated the stranger.

Darien held out his hand. "Darien," he said. "Darien Yore."

"Bosk Finney," he replied, shaking the sailor's hand.

"Finney," repeated Darien. "That's funny!" he said, laughing loudly at his own joke.

"No, Yore funny," said Bosk, joining in with the laughter. Whether it was because of Darien's drunkenness or his terrible jokes, the peeved barkeep soon called time on their evening.

"Come," said Bosk, finishing his beer, "I know of an inn that stays open until Aquill lights the skies." He helped the larger man out of the tavern, and together they staggered through the soaked streets. They passed by a small church, brimming with bodies, the priest's preaching echoing late into the night.

"This way," urged Bosk, turning Darien down a gloomy alley.

"Don't think I've ever been this way before."

Those were the last words spoken by Darien Yore.

A short time later, Bosk emerged from the shadows of the alley alone. The herk twittered in his pocket. Bosk delved into his coat and removed the winged creature. From another pocket he produced a small note he had prepared and tied it to the herk's claw. Bosk gazed deep into its eyes, enthralling the herk so its head did not jut around.

"Find Lord Malenek," he said clearly to the creature. He threw it up into the air. The herk flapped its wet wings against the rain. It disappeared into the night sky, its winged shape briefly seen as it passed in front of Whirren's silvery moon.

CHAPTER TWENTY
NOT LEFT BEHIND

THE OLD LIBRARIAN WAS DEAD BEFORE HIS TIME, THOUGHT Kamina, as he strained his eyes so far his eyelids were almost shut. Like him, the library itself was a relatively small building that perhaps once had been home to students, scholars and philosophers, but at present its halls were deserted.

"I wish we were in Hylan!" gurned Oldwyn under his breath. He led the small party past the librarian and down a stone spiral staircase into a sub-basement level, the oldest part of the library. "King Arthadian has a wonderful library, or at least he did. Quite exquisite. Is he still alive?"

"Yes, and in good health, last I saw," answered Callaghan, "despite the political plotting of his court." The mage had been locked up for so long, had missed so much, and yet at the same time, with the ongoing war, very little had changed.

They descended further now, down a creaky set of wooden stairs, Oldwyn leading the way with his glowing green staff. The ever-cautious ranger carried a flaming torch lit by Ascara.

"Do you believe the stone man, this Gort, is tied to Malenek's plan?" asked the ranger eventually. Given Oldwyn's reaction in their last conversation, Callaghan had deliberated whether or not to broach the subject, eventually deciding he needed answers.

"I do not believe so," said the mage. "It is possible that he is a golem, a soldier of stone created by the Moltari during the Mytorian Wars."

"Then the Moltari could have some hand in this," said Callaghan.

"The thought did cross my mind," said Oldwyn swiftly, "but seeing as there is only one, it would infer that it is a remnant of that ancient war, found or captured by Malenek to do his bidding. I would not dwell on it."

They arrived at the lowest level, a narrow room strewn with scrolls of parchment, as if it were a graveyard for ancient written words. Oldwyn shook his head as he started to search through the mess.

"No, the priest's plan lies not with the stone man or the spirits," continued Oldwyn. "It is the ætherghouls that hold the key. Let me show you. And Callaghan, please put that torch somewhere safe before you burn everything."

The ranger placed the torch in a rickety holder hanging on the wall. Oldwyn slammed down the staff, breaking its base through the tiled floor into the ground below. He removed his hands and the staff remaining standing, fixed to the floor. Oldwyn chanted a spell, and a pale green light cast out in all directions from the staff's emerald, forming a basin made of magic energy.

"Do you have some water?" Oldwyn asked. "I would hate to make the elf run and fetch some." Callaghan complied, offering Oldwyn a full skin of water. The mage poured its contents into the newly formed bowl. Kamina was amazed that it did not leak through the thin layer of energy. Green wisps appeared to float within the water, making it shimmer as it swirled.

"Now what?" asked Callaghan.

"Oh, yes, the most important bit." Oldwyn reached inside his cloak and revealed a large round fruit known as a cangerin, burnt orange in colour. "Could you cut this in half, Callaghan?" The ranger took the fruit and unsheathed his sword. "Exactly half," warned the mage. Callaghan tossed the fruit into the air, and then slashed with Ascara. Two perfect halves fell to the floor. Callaghan grinned as he handed them back to Oldwyn.

"Suppose you think that's impressive?" moaned the mage. "Here, you can eat that one." Oldwyn scooped out the juicy fruit of the half he held, offering it to Kamina.

"No, thank you," she said.

"Please yourself," shirked the mage, gobbling it all in one go, the juices dripping down his beard. "Now, imagine this almost-half cut fruit skin is our world, Enara." He placed the skin on the water face down, so that its semi-sphere bobbed above the surface. "Now imagine the water is the place our souls travel to after our bodies cease to be."

"Illyria," whispered Callaghan.

"We call it Loria," mumbled Kamina.

"Illyria. Loria. Whatever you wish to call it. It is not made of substance, as our world is," he explained, delving his hand into the water, glowing as he let it drip from his fingers, "but of ethereal energy, like our ghostly friend here."

"And the other spirits," added Kaedin.

"Exactly. Now, normally, we start life on Enara." Oldwyn illustrated this by placing a few drops of water on the surface of the fruit skin. "Say this is you, me… Well not me… But your average being. They are born on this world, they live their lives, but when they die…" Oldwyn's finger followed a drop as it trickled down the fruit skin, all the way to the ocean of water, where it became one. "…they return to the afterlife."

"What does this have to do with Malenek?" asked Callaghan.

"Everything!" exclaimed the mage. He reached into the basin, and turned the fruit skin upside down. It still floated, but with the hollow facing up, like a round boat. "Now, imagine that for some reason the energy released in death, the soul, the spirit, was trapped in Enara." Oldwyn delved his fingers into the water, and allowed drops to fall inside the hollow fruit skin, weighing it down. "For example, a mad priest forms a spirit army, who then turns the population into ætherghouls…"

"…Trapping the spirits within the bodies," said Callaghan, realising what conclusion Oldwyn had arrived at. The mage continued to pour water from his hand into the hollow fruit skin.

"And as more and more souls are trapped…" The fruit skin, overcome by the weight of the water within, submerged under the surface, sinking down.

"He is pushing us into Illyria," surmised Callaghan.

"I think he is in fact drawing Illyria here," corrected Oldwyn. "My analogy is somewhat backwards, but essentially, yes."

"What happens then?" asked Kamina. "What happens if Loria and Enara meet?"

"We all become spirits," said Kaedin.

"Precisely." Oldwyn removed his staff. The magical basin disappeared. The water and the submerged fruit skin splattered on the broken tiles.

"A new age, where everyone is equal," recalled Callaghan. "That is what Malenek said. Is it even possible?"

"Anything is possible, my dear boy," surmised Oldwyn, drying his hands on his cloak. "Although the forces involved will tear this world apart."

"Had the Elementals wished this," stated Callaghan, "they would never have created Enara in the first place."

"Who can know what gods wish for?" posed Oldwyn, his one eye glancing at Kamina.

"What of the Stone of Spirits?" she asked. "How can that help us?"

"I have never heard of such an object," stated Oldwyn, "which is why we are here." He indicated the ancient scrolls and texts that surrounded them.

"What are you looking for?" asked Callaghan.

"Anything related to this stone that you speak of, or the spirits and ætherghouls," replied Oldwyn, as he started digging through scrolls. "Myths, legends, stories, anything that may help me keep them outside the walls of… oh, what have we here?" As Oldwyn lost himself in the runes of an old scroll, Callaghan took Kamina and Kaedin aside, away from the busy mage.

"My elven friends, you have done your people proud. The men of Amaros… of Enara, will be forever in your debt. But this is where we part ways."

"No," protested Kaedin.

"Please, stay here and help Oldwyn sort through this mess," implored the ranger.

"But we can help you find the Stone of Spirits," he pleaded.

"I have no doubt you could. You have both been very helpful these last few days. If it were not for the two of you, Oldwyn would still be locked in the Black Tower. But the next step of this journey is fraught with far greater dangers than marauders and politicians, and I promised your sister I would keep you safe."

"Please Callaghan," begged the spirit.

"Kaedin," whispered Kamina, but he ignored her.

"We will not cause any trouble…"

"Kaedin," repeated Kamina.

"What?"

"Let him say goodbye," she said softly. Callaghan gazed down at the girl. She had receded within herself after watching Talia taken by Malenek's forces. She looked away from him, avoiding eye contact. The ranger felt her pain as his own personal failure.

"It is not goodbye," said Callaghan. "I will return with the Stone of Spirits, I promise."

"Do you honestly believe that?" asked the spirit solemnly.

"I will if you will." Kaedin considered this, and then nodded in agreement. "Be good for Oldwyn," he said in parting, making his way towards the steps.

"Callaghan," whispered Kamina with a weak voice. He paused on the steps as the elven girl approached him. "I am sorry for saying this was all you fault. It is not. I should have trusted you from the start. I am sorry I ran away from you at Anawey." He knelt down, running his rough hand over her innocent face, wiping away the tracks of her tears.

"Do not run away from Oldwyn," said the ranger. "He is too old to chase you." He kissed her forehead. He clumped up the steps, and then he was gone.

The two elves sulked in silence, save for the vague sounds of Oldwyn mumbling as he read. The cyclops drifted further and further along the long narrow passage as the night wore on, investigating old, often illegible texts. Kaedin, forever awake, had never known Kamina to be so subdued, except when Eshtel had died. Now Talia was gone too. She had left them both, but she had left him with her secret, one he could no longer keep.

Kamina could not even consider sleep, constantly reliving the horrific episode of the seeing spell. In the early hours of the morning she tried to steer herself away from such thoughts. She wondered what Callaghan was doing, how he was preparing for his journey across the sea, whether he was sound asleep, or wide awake like her, reliving the past.

"Do you think he will succeed?" asked Kamina.

"I am not worried about Callaghan," he replied. "He is a ranger, he can look after himself."

"Are you angry with him?"

"No," said the spirit. "Not with him."

"Then who?" Kaedin evaded her questioning eyes. "Me?"

"No," he mumbled.

"Oldwyn?" she hinted.

"Talia," he said finally. Kamina was aghast.

"If you were alive I would slap you right now," she said, scowling as she stood up. "Talia gave her life to protect the people of this land!"

"Kamina…"

"All she has ever done is look after us," she continued. "She even convinced the elders not to banish you after you went to Tilden with Nyssa."

"This has nothing to do with Nyssa!" he hit back.

"Then what?" demanded Kamina. "Why are you angry with Talia. She was our sister…"

"She was not your sister!" he blurted out. Kamina stood gaping at him, wondering if she had heard him correctly.

"What?" was all Kamina managed to say eventually.

"I cannot believe she left me to tell you this," he said, bitterness tainting his words. "All the times I asked her, begged her to tell you the truth and now…"

"Kaedin, you are scaring me." Her body trembled. What truth had Talia kept from her?

"Talia is not your sister," he stated with a heavy heart. "She is your mother."

"But… but… our parents… Kaman and Shara…" she stuttered, her mind stumbling through a barrage of questions. How was this even possible?

"They are my parents, but your grandparents," said Kaedin, trying to untangle the truth from the lies Kamina had been raised to believe.

"But Talia… she is too young… Kaedin, none of this makes any sense…" Kamina's heart raced, her mind refusing to function as her world was turned upside down.

Her whole family had hidden this secret from her, she thought.

Even Kaedin.

"Kamina, please sit, and I will try my best to explain." Kamina curled up on the steps, Kaedin kneeling opposite. "I was too young to remember any of this. I learned the truth from Lashara."

"Grandmother knew? When did she tell you?"

"Not so long ago," he replied ambiguously. "When I found out, I begged Talia to tell you. It should not have fallen to me."

"Kaedin, tell me what Lashara told you." Kamina bore him down with her eyes. He sighed, shaking his head as he started to recount the story for her.

"When Talia was younger, before she reached *Dira Adolyn*, she fell ill. Kaman found her fallen upon the forest floor, taken by a fever. He had heard her scream out in pain, before collapsing in the leaves."

"Was she attacked?" asked Kamina.

"No. There were other footprints, but they led nowhere. The strange part was what Talia had screamed out a name. Malenek."

Lord Malenek? Kamina could not believe that this was a coincidence.

"Kaman knew of Malenek from Lashara. She had been one of the few elders who met with men from the Alliance, trying to recruit the elves in the war against Zalestia. The men had told the elves of the crossing to the new land, of the betrayal, and the sole survivor, but their plea for help was rejected."

"I knew nothing of this," mumbled Kamina. "Why did Talia say Malenek's name?"

"I do not know. None of the elves do. But Kaman was desperate to save his daughter, who grew weaker with every passing day. He decided that they must seek out Malenek in the hope that he may offer some insight into her illness, and hopefully a cure."

"But the elders forbid it. With little choice, Kaman and Sharla fled Elgrin Forest with Talia. I was little more than a baby, so they left me in Lashara's care."

"They never returned, did they?" Kamina was piecing the truth together, working out where the fabrication ended and the real story began.

"No," said Kaedin. "It was believed they had met an uncertain fate. The elves scouted the roads in secret for weeks. Eventually, near the Mytor border, they found Kaman's cart. His body was inside, along with Sharla and several raiders. They had been ambushed, but Talia was not with them. The elves feared the worst - that she had been kidnapped, sold, or killed."

"Months passed, but then one day Talia returned to Elgrin Forest, a child growing in her belly. She had no memory of what happened, only that a human farmer had found her and nursed her back to health. Then, on her *Dira Adolyn*, Talia gave birth. To you."

Kamina took a long time to absorb everything that Kaedin had told her. Finally she asked the most burning question.

"If Talia is my mother, then who is my father? Was it the farmer?"

"Lashara would not tell me," said Kaedin. "It was a sore subject with her, and I dared not broach it with Talia herself." Kaedin could see the devastating toll this news was taking on the young elf. "Kamina, however you came into this world, all that matters is that you did."

"Then why all the secrecy?" she asked. "Why tell me lies?"

"Talia was so young, too young to be a mother. Given the extraordinary circumstance, the elders decided it was best if you were raised as our sibling. When I found out I begged Talia to tell you the truth, but she always said she was waiting for the right time."

Kamina sifted through the story, but kept returning to the fact that it had been Malenek's name Talia had shouted out; a man she would never have met, or had any knowledge of. Now he marched across Amaros with an army of spirits, and her brother, no, her uncle had been targeted by the very same man.

Kaedin was her uncle. That would take a lot of getting used to.

It had to all be linked together, thought Kamina. It was like trying to solve a riddle without hearing all of the clues. Talia. Malenek. Callaghan. The Stone of Spirits. Kamina could not see the connection, but it was clear now that her family was somehow central to this plot. She believed, however foolish it was, that the Stone of Spirits was tied to Talia's fate, that it could restore her. It was the missing piece of the puzzle. Kamina wanted answers, and she would not get them by hiding in a library.

"We have to go to Zalestia," she whispered, not wishing Oldwyn to overhear.

"You heard what Callaghan said," hissed Kaedin.

"We have to go to Zalestia and find the Stone of Spirits," she stated defiantly. "Then we will work out how to use it to bring Talia back."

Kaedin could see the intensity at work in Kamina's eyes, focused now on this single ambition, blocking out everything else. He quickly stole a glance at Oldwyn. The mage's nose was still buried in ancient scrolls, muttering under his breath as he scanned endless lines of symbols. Kaedin nodded in agreement, and indicated for her to make her way up the steps as he made himself transparent.

A few seconds later, the scrolls and parchments were scattered around the room, blown about by a sudden wind. Oldwyn busied himself picking them up, cursing the gods. Kamina seized the opportunity Kaedin had created and leapt up the wooden steps.

When he was sure the elves were gone, Oldwyn Blake stopped pretending he cared about the clutter. He turned to face the steps they had just ascended.

"Good luck my little friends. You will need it."

*

The black sky was at its darkest before Risaar peaked above the horizon. Captain Pike leaned over the stern and gazed out as the sunrise glistened over the ocean. The dawn was something he rarely registered on most days, but there was something strange and poetic in this one. He realised he was thinking it may his last in Calisto.

"This is very dangerous, captain," said Oran Cobb, joining Pike on the deck of the small skimmer.

"You don't need to tell me of the risks," the captain grumbled in reply.

"I was not talking about the journey." Pike turned to face his first mate as Cobb continued. "I meant letting the ranger on board this ship. You saw the same as I did when the wizard conjured his spell."

"I will make sure our guest does not venture into the cargo deck," said Pike.

"No offense, captain, but he is a Ranger of Ishkava. They go where they please, and they will often do so without you even knowing."

"I'm more concerned with Darien," said Pike, shifting the conversation away from the secrets that lay below the deck.

"He will return before the second sun dawns," assured Cobb, but his captain grimaced with uncertainty. His first mate had not witnessed Darien's brooding departure as Pike had.

"Captain," interrupted Irvine Burr, a crewman currently loading supplies from the dock. "There is a man here to see you." Pike expected to see the ranger with his ears burning, but even in the dim morning light he could tell the man standing next to Burr was not Callaghan. Pike made his way to down to the dock, but even up close he did not recognise the stranger.

"State your business," he said sternly, acutely aware they were soon to set sail. It was a fact most of the city knew, with many of its citizens descending to the esplanade to see them off.

"My name is Bosk Finney, captain…"

"I said state your business, Mr. Finney, not your name."

"I heard there may be a position on your ship," said the stranger. "If this is true, I'd like to offer my services."

"I'm afraid you've been misinformed. I'd find whoever sold you such a notion and take the back of my hand to them." Pike turned and walked back over the plank to his ship.

"I would do that sir, but he was significantly larger than me. His name was Darien Yore."

Pike stared back at the man. He crossed the plank again so he could look Bosk straight in the eye.

"Darien sent you?" quizzed the captain.

"He did not wish to take up such a dreaded journey, sir. We got to drinking, and he offered me his place, his contract with you."

"You're lying," said Pike. "Darien may be many things, but a coward is not one of them."

"Then where is he?" asked Callaghan, who had managed to sneak up on the dispute with his usual brand of stealth. Pike thought back to the comment Cobb had made about the rangers. "Captain, where is your missing crewman?"

"I do not know," replied Pike.

"Sir, if I may," said Bosk, addressing Callaghan. "The last I saw of the man, he was being kicked out of a tavern where we met, with the intention of finding another."

"I will send my first mate to fetch him," stated Pike swiftly, signalling for Cobb to join them. "Which tavern was it?"

"We do not have time for this, captain," said the ranger. "If this man wishes to take up the vacancy then let him."

"May I have a word in private," said Pike. Callaghan acquiesced as the surly captain led him away from Bosk.

"Ranger, I do not know this man, nor have I ever heard of him, and I know nearly all of the sailors that rush in and out of this place."

"Mr. Finney," Callaghan called out, "where are you from?"

"Barroch Bay," Bosk shouted in reply.

"You see, captain, he is a sailor, just not from this port."

"I still don't trust him," murmured Pike.

"You don't need to, but we do need a full crew to have any hope of surviving the Badlands, so I insist that you take him."

"Be it on your head then, ranger." The captain marched past Bosk and onto the deck of the *Arad Nor*, barking orders in preparation for launch.

"Come," said Callaghan, leading Bosk Finney to the boat, "we best get on board before Captain Pike changes his mind."

"Yes, sir," he said, following the ranger.

"I am curious as to why you would volunteer for such a mission?" Callaghan asked Bosk as they crossed over onto the ship.

"I have seen the horrors of an entire town being sacked by the Zalestians," he replied. "I was just a young man when they turned Barroch Bay into a ghost town. So if I can stop that happening to my country, then I will." For an older man he had the zeal of a young soldier, something the ranger admired.

When Bosk Finney finally set foot on the *Arad Nor*'s deck, he smiled at the irony that it was the ranger who had managed to win his place on the ship he was sent to sabotage.

*

Kamina rushed from the university to the peak of the crescent cliffs where they had descended into the bay the previous day. Kaedin trailed her, invisible to the naked eye, calling out for her to slow down, but there was no time. From above she spotted the small crowd that had gathered to wish the *Arad Nor*'s crew a safe and successful journey. The ship had already cast off, and was slowly gliding through the calm waters of the bay, heading for the entrance between the two curved cliffs.

"Kamina, he is gone," said Kaedin. "Let us return to Oldwyn."

"We can still make it," she declared, without stopping to gather her breath.

"How?" he asked, but Kamina was already speeding along the cliff edge, towards the ship building yards and supply houses sprawled along the top. Sailors and work men were shocked to see an elf dashing through their domain, but they were too slow and clumsy to stop her. As she ran, Kamina kept one eye on the *Arad Nor*, drifting across the bay, powered by three oars poking out of either side. She realised there was not yet enough wind to raise the sails, that they would not do so until they reached the mouth of the bay.

There was still a chance.

She reached the last of the supply buildings, with only the lighthouse between her and the narrowing point of the cliff's end. The *Arad Nor* would soon escape the shallow bay into the freedom of the endless ocean. One of the pulley ropes from the supply houses dangled far down below, while another was already wound up. She found a pair of thick gloves lying by the unmanned pulley. She slipped them on and grabbed the end of the rope.

"Kamina, do not be so foolish!" urged her ghostly sibling.

"Run through the lighthouse and jump to the ship," she said, ignoring his protests. "Now!"

Before Kaedin could respond, Kamina dashed off the edge of the cliff, in the opposite direction of the bay's entrance. She fell fast, until the rope tensed and tightened, jerking her back through the air in a wide arc. She swung back towards the mouth of the bay. The *Arad Nor* was almost in open waters. The men on board were preparing to hoist the sails.

It was now or never.

She let go. For a moment, Kamina felt like she was flying. As she soared towards the ship, the crew of the *Arad Nor* raised her sails, providing the stowaway elf with the perfect cover. Kamina clattered against the side of the stern, hanging on by one hand, the roaring water below her. With the sails raised, the ship picked up pace. It passed between the cliffs and out into the vastness of the ocean. Kamina found another grip with her flailing hand. She heard a curious crewman step towards her, having heard the thud of her landing. She kept her body pressed tight against the hull. The crewman glanced over, but not enough to see Kamina clinging to the side of the ship like a barnacle. He shook off his concerns and continued with his duties.

When she was sure she would not be seen, Kamina climbed over the railing and onto the deck of the *Arad Nor*. She glanced back at Calisto, caught off-guard by the beauty of the outer cliffs, pure white in colour. They were decorated with giant carvings. A statue of Whirren, almost as tall as the cliff face, stood on one side of the bay. He stared out over the sea, granting ships wind in their sails. It looked as if there had been another statue on the opposite side, but only the legs remained, the rest destroyed in an attack by the Zalestians. She guessed it would have been Aquill. As they sailed further out, she spied fleets of large warships in the open waters, anchored and empty. These were the next wave that would attack Zalestia.

Her sea-gazing was cut short by Captain Pike bellowing instructions to his crew. Kamina found shelter behind some barrels, but knew she would soon be discovered. It was only now that she realised Kaedin was not with her.

"Kaedin?" she whispered. There was no answer. "Kaedin!"

"Here," he said, poking his ghostly head from below the deck. "There is a cargo hold underneath, you can hide there."

"How do I get down?" she asked.

"Most of the crew are up on deck. I will distract them. When I do, run for the door." He faded away. Soon she heard a fracas at the bow of the ship, as some barrels broke loose. Kamina snuck along the side, and dived down the short steps below deck. She made her way along a narrow corridor, uncertain which door she should attempt. She placed her hand on a handle.

"No," hissed Kaedin. "The one at the end."

As he spoke, the door Kamina was about to attempt shunted open. She moved quickly along the tight corridor and shimmied through the cargo hold entrance before she was spotted. However, she did not have time to close the door. Ellis 'Cook' Roe, a plump, sweaty crewman, poked his head out of the galley, having heard voices.

"Someone there?" he asked, but his only reply was the creak of the cargo door, swaying with the ship. Ellis stepped into the cargo hold, glancing around.

"Gigondas? Is that you?" he shouted, but there was no reply. Ellis shook it off and closed the door. Kamina breathed a sigh of relief. Even with her sharp elven eyes, she could barely see in the dingy hold.

"Kaedin?" she whispered. The spirit phased into existence, his ethereal light illuminating their surroundings. Kamina found a small, hidden corner filled with spare sheets. She lay down, exhausted, while Kaedin perched by her side.

"What do we do now?" he asked.

"We will reveal ourselves to Callaghan when he can no longer turn back," she said. "We will help him find the Stone of Spirits, and save Talia." The mere mention of her name brought an uneasy silence between them.

"What if we cannot?" he said.

"We will not know unless we try." Exhausted from her efforts to board the *Arad Nor*, Kamina rolled over, hiding her face from Kaedin as she softly cried herself to sleep.

CHAPTER TWENTY-ONE

NIGHTMARES AND DISCOVERIES

KAMINA ADJUSTED TO THE GLISTENING SPACE OF HER DREAMS. She was her younger self again, perched on Talia's lap. Her sister... no, her mother fingered the page that showed colourful illustration of the Elementals rising into the skies and transforming into the two suns and two moons of Enara.

"The Elementals left the world to watch over us from the stars." Her elegant fingers flipped the page over. Here the figures of the four gods appeared as giants to the stick men, as well as elves, centaurs and many other races.

"Before they left, the gods bestowed their power upon their creations. They gave them magic." Kamina looked closer. She could just make out a small jewel being offered by each Elemental. "But the creatures misused the magic, and disappointed the goddsssss." Talia's voice deepened as she slithered her last syllable. Kamina stared at her mother's hand, sitting on top of her own. The flesh withered and decayed, flaking off onto the pages of the book. Kamina forced herself to look over her shoulder. It was no longer Talia's knee she sat upon, but an ætherghoul's. She could smell the acrid stench from the vile creature's rotten mouth.

"Ka...min...naaa" it growled, its ghastly, rotten teeth snapping in her face.

*

"Kamina! Kamina!" The ætherghoul was repeating her name, only it was not the ætherghoul, but Kaedin. "Stop screaming!" he insisted, trying in vain to clamp his ghostly hand over her mouth. She jolted out of her nightmare.

"Kaedin!" she exclaimed. The ghost placed his finger to his lips, indicating for her to be quiet "What is it?" she said, her voice hushed.

"I do not believe we are alone," he replied. No sooner had he whispered these words than they both heard a deep groan from within the cargo hold. a giant shape shifted behind a large box in the gloom. It lurched into the centre of the room, blocking their path to the exit.

"Kaedin," she said, as he stood up. "What are you doing?"

"It cannot hurt me," he assured her. The spirit wandered through the cargo towards the hulking mass. Kamina peered from behind her hiding space as he neared, his silver glow revealing exactly what the creature was.

It was Malenek's servant Gort, the man made of stone. Alerted by the spirit's luminescence, the rocky beast turned and caught sight of Kaedin.

"Ghoooosssst," it groaned, trying to grab at Kaedin with its ginormous hand. He was fixed to the spot in amazement, as granite fingers tried to grasp his intangible form. The spirit stepped back, and the creature followed. Kaedin glanced over at Kamina, urging her to use the diversion and escape. As the giant creature took one more lumbering step in the ghost's direction, Kamina abandoned her stowaway alcove and dashed for the door. She pulled at it, but the door was fixed shut. She yanked at the handle with all her might, but it would not budge. One of the crew must have locked it. The creature heard her commotion and turned its attentions away from Kaedin, stretching his stony hand towards her.

A key scraped the lock, and the door swung open.

"Gigondas, I thought the captain told you…" Roe started to say, entering the room. He laid eyes on a fearful young elf. "By the Elements!"

Kamina ran out of the cargo hold, bowling the crewman over. She heard him yell the captain's name as she rushed up to the deck. She no longer cared if Callaghan caught her. She had to warn him that Malenek had managed to sneak a spy on board.

"What in Risaar's blazes is going on?" roared Captain Pike, making his way to the steps below deck. He was startled as Kamina jumped up towards him and onto the deck in full view of the entire crew.

"It's an elf!" exclaimed Cobb.

"Kamina," said Callaghan's familiar voice. She ran past the crewmen towards him. "What are you doing here?"

"Below deck," she gasped, "in the hold… there is a creature… a man of stone… the one from the seeing spell… the one that was with Malenek."

Callaghan drew his sword. They heard the echo of something pounding along the corridor below deck. Kaedin dived out of the stairwell, soon followed by the stone beast, barely squeezing through the hole. The ranger readied Ascara to attack the stone man, but was surprised when Pike placed himself between his blade and the behemoth's rocky hide, his arms held out in defence.

"Step aside, captain," said Callaghan. "That thing is an ally of Malenek."

"I assure you, ranger, he is not the same creature you saw with the spirit army," urged Pike. "Gigondas here has been on the *Arad Nor* the entire time we have been docked in Calisto."

Callaghan looked closely at the creature Captain Pike had called Gigondas. While he shared many similarities with Malenek's bodyguard Gort, the ranger noticed subtle differences in their appearance. The creature himself was timid and afraid, with none of the confidence exuded by Gort in Mytor.

"How is this possible?" Callaghan asked, lowering Ascara.

"Gort is my brother," groaned Gigondas.

"They are twins," added Pike.

Peering out from behind Callaghan, Kamina gazed at Gigondas. Although she could not tell for sure, she thought that he was trying to smile at her. It looked like an uncomfortable position for the creature's face, an unpractised expression for him.

"I would ask that for the rest of our voyage, he stay away from me," said Callaghan. Kamina watched as sadness smouldered over Gigondas' stone face. She thought that, if it were possible, he would shed a tear. Instead he turned away from them, lumbering along the deck, descending into the gloom of the cargo hold.

"That was a bit cruel, don't you think?" said Captain Pike. "The only reason I volunteered my ship was to protect him."

"All I know is that his brother is in league with Malenek," said Callaghan. "Until I learn more I would prefer he keep his distance."

"Well underneath that stone skin of his, Gigondas is little more than a child, and I trust him with my life," stated Pike firmly. There was a general consensus amongst the gathered crew on this last point. "If you ask me, you're the exact opposite."

"And how is that?" asked Callaghan.

"You expect people to trust you because you're a Ranger of Ishkava," noted Pike, "but underneath, there's nothing but a heart of stone." With that stinging critique, Captain Pike followed Gigondas below deck, shouting at a bewildered Bosk to get back to work. "And if we make it through the Badlands alive," he warned his newest recruit, "you better not speak a word of this!"

The ranger reflected on Pike's words for a moment, before turning his attention to the stowaway and her spirit companion.

"You should not have come, Kamina" he said, chastising her.

"I had to help you find the stone," she murmured. "For Talia."

"Kamina, we have no idea what the Stone of Spirits does. There is very little chance the stone will save your sister," he said bluntly. "Do you not understand? You have put your life in jeopardy for nothing."

"She is not my sister!" snapped Kamina. "She is my mother!" The elven girl sulked off towards the stern of the ship, staring back across the ocean at the distant blur that was Amaros. She wanted to cry again, but her tears were all dried out from the day before.

"When did she find out about Talia?" Callaghan asked Kaedin.

"I told her after you left us in the library," he replied. "It seemed only right that she know."

"You were right to do so," said the ranger. Kaedin watched him follow Kamina to the stern of the ship, realising that Callaghan had knew the truth about Talia. The spirit started to wonder if the ranger had learned this knowledge recently as he had, or if he had been privy to it for a lot longer. The vague memory of Callaghan visiting Elgrin Forest when he was a child surfaced again. Could he have found out then?

"Will you take us back?" she asked guiltily, as Callaghan joined her by the railing, sharing the dazzling ocean view.

"No," said the ranger. "There is no time to turn back now. When we arrive in Zalestia, I will leave you in the care of Zahyr Zaleed Khan while I search for the stone."

"We could help," offered Kamina. "Kaedin and I."

"Of that I have no doubt, but believe me when I say you will be safer staying put." He placed a caring hand on her shoulder. "Now come, we shall find you a proper place to sleep, my young stowaway."

*

The ship's highly superstitious crew refused to sleep in the same room as a female, let alone an elven one. Captain Pike graciously gave up his private quarters to Kamina and Kaedin, although since the spirit never slept, he wandered the deck at night. He snooped on the sailors and, slightly mischievously, practised his abilities by misplacing their belongings.

Callaghan was also unable to sleep. He ascended to the deck, inhaling the fresh salty sea air, and saw the ghost gazing up at the stars. The sky was a clear black canvas, filled with bright twinkling lights.

"Beautiful, are they not?" said Callaghan.

"We rarely see them under the cover of Elgrin," revealed Kaedin, "unless we climb the tall trees at night."

"Very few people see them as clearly as this," replied the ranger.

"Is it Loria?" asked the ghostly elf.

"Heroshin scholars certainly think so. The Caspians believe they are other suns and moons created by the Elementals. The Zalestians believe they are the children of their gods, and their children's children, who used their powers to ascend up there, to watch us mortals down here."

"What do you believe?"

"I believe they are beautiful, and that is all I need," said Callaghan, adding, "I doubt we will ever truly have an answer to that question."

The spirit turned his attentions to the dark shimmering surface of the ocean. He wanted to broach the subject of Talia with the ranger away from Kamina. How had Callaghan known about their family plight? Kaedin wondered. He had vague memories of the ranger visiting Elgrin Forest when he was much younger, and guessed he had learned of it then. Even though they had shared their recent journey together, Kaedin felt that quizzing Callaghan about it would be crossing a line.

"Is there something on your mind, Kaedin?" asked the ranger.

"No," lied the spirit.

"In that case, I will try and rest. Good night." Callaghan descended the steps and quietly slipped past the snoring sailors in their quarters, leaving the ghost to his private thoughts.

*

The following morning, Kamina wandered onto the deck. The various crewmen, for she had counted seven now, not including the stone giant Gigondas, were below in the galley, chatting over Cook's breakfast. Only Captain Pike was on the deck, standing on the starboard side, eyeing the sea suspiciously.

"Thank you for the use of your bed," said Kamina, hoping to appease Pike. "It is very comfortable."

"I know," he groaned stiffly as he straightened his back, which was suffering from the tiny bunk he had chivalrously crammed himself into.

"What are you looking for?" she asked.

"You're an inquisitive little thing, aren't you? Cast your eyes out that way, tell me what you see." Kamina peered out in the direction Pike pointed at, but she failed to see anything other than the endless ocean.

"I don't see anything," she said.

"Keep watching." As time passed by, she suspected Pike of playing a practical joke. Then she saw what the old sailor had spied. A large fin protruded from the sea, a black triangle that disappeared in the blink of an eye. The dark outline of the creature it belonged to hung under the surface, as big as the *Arad Nor*.

"What is it?" she gasped.

"A shark," he replied with a bitter edge. "One of the deadliest predators to roam the waters, but also one of the most beautiful."

"What is it hunting?"

"Us." Kamina gulped as Pike continued. "It's been imitating our movements, you see, shadowing us. It thinks we're a big fish."

"Will it attack us?" she quizzed, worried.

"Not likely," he ventured. "It will tire, or find an easier prey. Young Toran spotted it. That boy has the eyes of an elf." The captain found Kamina looking at him funny. "Not literally, mind you. Just an expression us humans have. I best see what Ellis has in the way of food. Excuse me, Miss Kamina."

Captain Pike left her to keep an eye out for the oceanic predator. As the day wore on, and with the shark failing to re-emerge, Kamina's boredom ballooned. She offered to help the various crewmen with their dreary daily chores, but they all promptly refused. Toran Calder, the youngest and gangliest of the men, was so afraid of both her and Kaedin that he spent most of his time perched at the top of the mast. She resorted to sitting by the stern of the ship, keeping an eye out for sharks.

"Here," said Kaedin. Kamina turned just in time to catch a stick the spirit had managed to launch at her.

"Kaedin!"

"You should learn to defend yourself," he said.

"From sticks?" she asked sarcastically.

"No. Imagine it is a sword."

"We are not in the forest anymore, Kaedin," she said, dropping the stick in protest, "and I am not you."

"No, you are not. Swords cannot harm me, but given the dangers we may face, I thought… it does not matter."

The spirit sulked away in a sour mood that had gripped him since leaving Caspia. The sound of the stick rolling around on the deck started to annoy Kamina. She used her imagination to conjure up an army to fight with her mighty sword; a squad of faceless guards led my Lord Malenek. She wielded the weapon against the priest, in reality one of the ship's masts. She swung at him, slicing off one of his arms. Malenek collapsed, his helmet rolling away. He gazed up at her, his power-hungry face scarred with scorn. Kamina lifted the blade high above her head, preparing to deliver the killer blow, but the sword was stuck in the sky. She spun round to find Callaghan holding the sharp end of the pretend sword.

"I was just…" Kamina said, fumbling to make an excuse.

"You were attacking too low." He positioned the pointy end of the stick at his belt. "You imagine yourself to be the same height as your enemy, but in reality you are slightly smaller than the average man." He now brought the end of the imaginary sword up to his body, tapping the end against his chest, where his heart was located. "If you wish to slay your enemy, you will have to angle your attack upwards. But in all likelihood, your adversary will wear armour, which will require a significant force to penetrate. Instead, you should rely on your other advantages."

"What advantages?" she asked.

"A soldier may be strong," he elaborated, "but they are often slow. As an elf, you are naturally swift and agile, more so than a normal man, let alone one carrying the weight of armour and a sword."

To illustrate his point, Callaghan unsheathed Ascara and offered it to the elf. She took hold of the hilt in her dainty hands, but it weighed far more than she had anticipated. Kamina struggled to keep the blade aloft, accidently slicing into the deck as she dropped it. She panicked, making sure none of the crew had witnessed her damage their ship. Callaghan's rare smile put her at ease.

"Let us try again," he said. From watching the ranger wield the sword, Kamina had imagined Ascara to weigh far less. She tightened her grip again, and with considerable effort, managed to raise the sword into the air. The daylight of the twin suns bounced off the long blade, illuminating the symbols etched up one side. Kamina gazed along the full length of the magnificent weapon, and for a moment it was if the sword sang to her.

"How does it feel?" he asked. Kamina could not answer, nor did she get the chance. Bosk, forced to scrub the deck, had been spying on the pair with interest. When the ranger had gifted the elf his weapon, leaving himself unarmed, Malenek's spy decided to make his move. He withdrew a dagger concealed in his boot and casually made his way towards Callaghan, hiding the blade up his sleeve. When Bosk was close enough to strike at Callaghan, he flicked out the dagger, intending to ram it into the ranger's back.

A massive axe blade sliced through the deck from below. It cut a hole between Callaghan and Bosk, disarming the assassin of his dagger. Bosk toppled to the deck, clenching the cruel gash on his hand.

Callaghan's fleeting glance only saw the axe blade blast up through the deck. He pushed Kamina to safety, quickly relinquishing her of Ascara. He turned as Gigondas leapt up through the hole he had made with his mighty axe. The ranger prepared to attack, but the stone man shrank back, laying down his weapon.

"Stop," moaned the beast, dropping the axe to the deck. "Not me who attack you. Him." Gigondas thrust out a large stone finger, pointing at Bosk crawling away.

"Me?" Bosk cried. "It was you who attacked us!" By now the rest of the crew had heard the destructive blow and gathered around the damaged section of the deck.

"What in Risaar's blazes happened here!" exclaimed Pike.

"It was him, captain!" squealed Bosk. "The stone man cut through with his axe. He tried to kill the ranger."

"He lies" said Gigondas. "Gigondas saw from below. He had dagger. He try to kill ranger." They all scanned the ship's deck for the alleged blade, but found nothing.

"Captain," said the ranger, but Pike already knew what he was going to say.

"I know," he moaned. "Gigondas, I'm going to have to restrain you."

"You can't do this, captain" pleaded Oran Cobb. The staunch crew nodded behind him, in support of their friend. "If Gigondas says he saw something…"

"Don't question my orders! Come on, Gigondas, let's not make this any harder than it has to be." Gigondas lowered his head as he was led away by Pike, the crew protesting at his heels. They were more than a crew, they were family, and they trusted Gigondas more than the ranger or their new crewmate. They left Bosk bleeding upon the deck.

"You are hurt," said Callaghan as he helped Bosk up, blood trickling from his hand.

"It's just a scratch," shunned the spy, desperate to find his incriminating weapon. The insistent ranger guided him below deck to have his wound dressed.

With the drama over, Kamina picked up her stick before it fell into the newly created hole. Down below in the cargo hold, she glimpsed Pike tying Gigondas' hands behind his back.

"Did you see what happened?" she asked Kaedin.

"I did not," he replied. "Perhaps Callaghan was right, that the stone men are working together with Malenek."

"But he seems so... gentle," commented Kamina.

"Kamina, he is a giant made of stone!" exclaimed the spirit.

"And you are a ghost made of magic. Just because he is different does not mean we should be afraid of him," she said, recalling all too clearly how some of the citizens of Calisto had reacted to them.

Kamina continued to practise her sword skills with the stick, but she was put off by Gigondas' despondent groans. She too believed him, and besides, she did not trust Bosk Finney. Kamina decided to search the deck again, determined to find the dagger. Her sharp eyes found nothing, and she began to suspect that it had fallen overboard. A flap of the sails caused her to glance upwards. There, jutting out of the mast, was Bosk's dagger.

"Kaedin, look!" The spritely elf quickly climbed up the mast and plucked the blade from the wood. She dropped back down onto the deck, proud that she had proven Gigondas right.

"Give that to me child," said Bosk, standing behind her, his hand wrapped in fresh bandages. "It is very sharp. You might hurt yourself."

"No," she said. Kaedin quietly descended through the deck. Bosk cornered Kamina, lunging for her arm, wrestling for the dagger. Callaghan and the other crew rushed back onto the deck, spurred by the spirit's warning. Forced to act, Bosk snatched the dagger from Kamina's hands and held it to her throat.

"Back away!" he yelled.

"I knew it!" said Cobb.

"Bosk," addressed Callaghan, "trust me when I say you do not wish to harm that child."

"And why's that?" he rasped, edging towards the railing, trying to figure a way out of this scenario.

"Because she is bonded to a spirit!" replied Kaedin, having silently risen up behind Bosk. He thrust his hand into the saboteur's mind. Bosk's muscles loosened, dropping the dagger to the deck. Callaghan scooped it up, offering it to Pike as definitive proof of Gigondas' innocence.

Diving through Bosk's memories, Kaedin witnessed a flurry of recent events. He saw Bosk warning Malenek with a message attached to a herk, watched helplessly as he followed Darien Yore to a bar and then led him down a dark, foreboding alley. The spirit withdrew his hand from the traitor's bleak mind, leaving him to collapse against the railing.

"What did... what did you do to me?" he mumbled, as Oran Cobb and Uisnech Leith secured his arms, dragging him along the deck.

"He is a spy for Malenek," revealed Kaedin. "He sent a message to him before departing. He murdered your former crewman to take his place. His intentions were to kill Callaghan and sabotage the ship."

"Darien is dead?" said Pike, disheartened. The news struck the crew, who grieved for their former shipmate. Bosk regained his strength sapped by the mental encounter with the spirit. While the sailors were distracted by their sorrow, the traitor wrestled free. He broke Uisnech's nose with his elbow, and then kicked the feet out from under Oran Cobb. The remaining crew hounded him to the stern of the ship. With nowhere to run, Bosk clambered onto the railing.

"Wait!" cried Callaghan, but it was too late. The saboteur hurled himself overboard, plunging into the ocean. The crew gathered at the stern to see Bosk bobbing in the cold water.

"He's mad!" exclaimed Oran Cobb. "There is no way he can swim back to Amaros. Aquill will claim him."

"Or something else," said Pike, spying a large fin rising from the surface. The shark that had been following them broke through the water, its black beady eyes locked on Bosk. He screamed as the predator's razor sharp teeth penetrated his body. The shark dragged him back down into the depths of the ocean, leaving a red stain in the dark blue water.

"Well at least it gets the shark off our tails," said Pike sardonically. "Seems your enemies are one step ahead of you, ranger."

"You tried to warn me about Bosk in Calisto, captain," said Callaghan. "I should have listened to you."

"That's all good and well, but it's not me you should be apologising to." The captain wandered past the rest of the crew, barking orders. "Gigondas, get up here and fix that bloody big hole you've made!"

The newly freed Gigondas lumbered towards the hole, slinging his axe over his shoulder. He stared at the broken deck, scratching his stony head while trying to work out how to repair it.

"Gigondas," said Callaghan. The man of stone turned to face him. Even though he could easily flatten any man, he cowered back, afraid of the ranger.

"Did not mean to cause harm," he whimpered. "Gigondas sorry."

"No, Gigondas, it is I that should apologise to you. I judged you on the actions of your brother. Thank you for saving my life." Callaghan held out his hand. Gigondas stared at it for a while. The ranger urged him to take it. Gigondas gripped it, almost shaking Callaghan's arm out of its socket.

"Thank you," said the gentle giant. As he turned away, Callaghan caught sight of the axe slung over the stone man's shoulder. The blade was etched with markings and symbols similar to those that adorned Ascara. It appeared as if the original handle had been removed, replaced with a piece of driftwood.

"Gigondas, where did you get that axe?" he enquired.

"I..." started the creature, his back still turned, "Gigondas no talk about it." With that, he descended into the cargo hold, gazing up through the hole of the deck he had destroyed, planning his repairs.

"Would you like me to help you?" said the small elf, standing by his side.

"You no afraid of Gigondas?" he asked.

"No," replied Kamina, taking hold of one of his ginormous hands. "You saved Callaghan. You are a hero."

This time, Kamina was sure the stone giant was smiling.

*

By the time the spirit army reached Onassis, the town was nothing more than a borough of deserted buildings. The ghosts and ætherghouls searched thoroughly, but it was now obvious the inhabitants had been forewarned. Malenek eyed the elven ætherghoul suspiciously, her beautiful features erased by the transformation. In the far distance, he could just make out the green trees of Elgrin, no doubt where Jaelyn had died. The elves were proving to be a perpetual thorn in his side.

"Martyn," called out Malenek. Martyn Keyll emerged from the throng of spirits.

"My Lord."

"How much influence do you wield over these… men?" he inquired.

"Enough to direct them, although some have noticed they give in to their primal instincts over time." A squawk from the skies interrupted them. The leathery flapping of a herk descended upon them. It swooped down onto Malenek's outstretched arm. He removed his gauntlet and unwound the small message attached to the herk's claw. The words disappointed him. He let the creature go, but one of the ætherghouls snatched it from the air and devoured it whole.

"Not good news?" asked Gort.

"A message from one of our spies in Calisto," Malenek informed him. "Callaghan is alive, and has spread news of our spirit army. He has procured a ship, and is sailing to Zalestia as we speak. Bosk has snuck on board, but we must assume he will fail."

"What shall we do?" asked the stone giant.

"You will return to Mytor," ordered Malenek. "Inform Salamon it is as I feared. We have need of Xinder." There was a spasm of sorrow from the priest as he uttered the strange name.

"My Lord, I should remain with you," he protested. "You are weakened by the spirits."

"No, I must push forward," he insisted. "This task is yours, Gort. Make haste, and then join us in Gorran."

"Yes, my Lord." Gort bouldered out of Onassis, charging back to Mytor Castle, his large stride and mountainous legs faster than any horse's gallop.

"Martyn," said Malenek. "Send some of our forces into Elgrin Forest. Command them to trek across Legoria and through the Crymyr Pass into Caspia."

"And if they find anyone?" asked the spirit.

"Drag them to Calisto," decided Malenek. "You and the spirits can turn them when we regroup there."

"Yes, my Lord." The spirit bowed and drifted off to relay Malenek's orders. Soon a small rabble of ætherghouls howled away, heading towards the forest of the elves. Before he gloved his hand, Malenek stroked Shento's fine head. He looked at his own fingers, and could see they were thinner than before, paler, his skin translucent. Gort was right; the spirits were taking a severe toll on him.

"Do no fear my friend," he whispered to the horse, "we will rest soon." He slipped on his cold gauntlet, and stole one last glance at the deserted town. "Let us leave this barren place," he called out to his army. Malenek and his minions marched slowly out of Onassis, ascending the trail that ran along the border between Heroshin and Legoria, the same path Talia had ridden from Gorran. She had never considered she would return along it as an ætherghoul.

She had never considered she would return at all.

CHAPTER TWENTY-TWO
MEN OF STONE

LIKE KAMINA, CALLAGHAN FOUND HIMSELF WITH LITTLE TO DO ON the *Arad Nor*. He rested against one of the railings, staring out at sea, enjoying the warm sun on his face. Occasionally he watched Kamina help Gigondas with the repairs. The girl giggled every now and then, trying to teach the stone giant some elven words. Were they not sailing across the sea on a quest to save the world, Callaghan may have relished the scene more. Pike approached him, having spotted the ranger keeping a keen eye on Kamina, mistaking his expression for one of anxiety.

"He saved your life," said the captain. "The least you could do is trust him with the elf."

"I do, captain," assured Callaghan. "I was not watching out of protection, merely curiosity. You were right. Gigondas is little more than a child trapped inside that hulking body."

"Indeed he is," agreed Pike, shedding his hostility. "I doubt he's any older than the elf girl. Don't know for sure." He cut into an affel fruit with a small knife, offering Callaghan a piece.

"Thank you," said the ranger. The fruit had fermented during their time at sea. It proved bitter, but still edible.

"Not as ripe as it could be" said Pike, watching the ranger eat, "but needs to be used up."

"I feasted on far worse the last time I came to Zalestia." Before Pike could probe the ranger about that voyage, Callaghan continued to quiz him about Gigondas. "What do you know of his past?"

"Next to nothing. He keeps it guarded, even from me."

"Then how is it he came to be aboard the *Arad Nor*?" asked the ranger.

"Well, I suppose there's no harm in telling, we're all probably going to die in the Badlands anyway!" quipped the captain. "A few years ago, we were returning to Calisto, with a good catch as I recall. However, because we had sailed so far out, we returned late. Risaar and Aquill had both set, and the mists of Rundhale had spread east, curled around Caspia. Ygrain and Whirren were hidden behind horrendous clouds. In short, we were blind, but we could not delay, else our catch would rot."

"Darien thought he saw the beacons of Calisto, but we had misjudged our bearings, and it was not the beacons at all, but a fire in a cave far north. We would have smashed upon the rocks, if it had not been for Gigondas. We didn't know what to make of him at first, thought our eyes played tricks on us you see, mists and shadows and all that malarkey. We saw him on the rocks, this brutish beast. He waded into the water and grabbed the bow of the boat, and used his strength like a big stone anchor to slow us to a dead stop. Otherwise, we would have just been dead."

"And so you owed him a debt?" Callaghan filled in the rest for himself.

"We all do," insisted Pike. "But he was apologetic. You see, it had been his fire that we had mistaken for the beacon. Some of the men were afraid, but I could see he had a good soul, so I asked if we could offer him anything in return for saving our lives."

"And he asked to be part of your crew," guessed the ranger.

"Aye. He'd been living in that cave well over a decade, not alone neither, not to start with at least. I'll admit, I was wary about bringing him on board, the sheer weight of him, but he's proven to be a hard worker, and a good omen. Cheap as well, all he eats are rocks and the occasional shrub!"

"And everyone on board has kept him a secret?" asked the ranger, slightly surprised. Many of the sailors he knew would wax lyrical if liquor was involved.

"We all owe him our lives," explained Pike. "Our silence is a small price to pay. And all my men know I would spill their guts upon the ground if they spilled theirs."

"What of his brother?" asked Callaghan. "Gort?"

"From what I gather, and it ain't much, they were born far from Calisto. Gigondas is not sure where exactly. They were cared for by a guardian of some sort, who hid them in the cave, because of their appearance you see. But the guardian abandoned them, and the other one, this Gort you mention, was angry at being forsaken. He ventured out under the cover of darkness, and overheard tales told by travellers of creatures who lived underground, beneath the Tregorian Mountains."

"The Moltari," said Callaghan. "Oldwyn suggested Gort was a rogue golem Malenek had somehow captured."

"Well," continued the captain, "the older brother was convinced they might be of the same race, and decided to leave the cave. Gigondas refused to go with him, choosing to wait for the guardian's promised return. That was the last Gigondas saw of his brother."

"Until now," said the ranger.

"Aye, until now," repeated Pike. "But I know this for a fact. They are not Moltari, nor one of their golem soldiers."

"How can you be so sure?" asked Callaghan. In all his adventures, the ranger had yet to encounter the mysterious subterranean race. "No one to my knowledge has ever laid eyes on the Moltari, or if they have they have never lived to tell of it."

"My descendants came from Mytor," revealed Pike. "My great great great great great grandfather fought in the Mytorian Wars. He was there at the fall of Nimongrad. Can you imagine it? An entire city sinking into the ground?"

"I do not need to," said Callaghan. "I have ventured through the Region of the Damned, and saw the ruins of Nimongrad for myself."

"But it is forbidden!" hissed Pike, his voice low even this far from Amaros.

"As are many acts that I find necessary, but as I said, I saw no Moltari."

"Well my ancestors did. The stories have passed down my line. My grand pappy used to tell me tales as a nipper that left me afraid of the dark. He told me, during those wars, our ancestors had fallen with Nimongrad before clawing their way out. He saw the creatures the Moltari created to bring the city down. The golems. You see, that's what I thought Gigondas was too. When we first saw him, my crew ran away, but I was frozen stiff, thinking of those stories."

"Then what changed?" asked Callaghan.

"Gigondas spoke," explained Pike. "You see, my grand pappy said the golems ain't got no mouths." Callaghan mulled this over in his mind. If it were true, then why had Oldwyn told him otherwise?

"Captain," called out the stone man. "We finished."

"Is that so?" Pike shouted back, pacing over to inspect the sealed gap. As Callaghan watched the captain congratulate Gigondas and Kamina on a job well done, he was left with troubled thoughts as he sifted through Pike's tale. How had Gort found himself in Malenek's service, and more importantly, when? If Gort had travelled to Mytor seeking out the Moltari, it was possible he had heard of Malenek and sought council from the priest. But Callaghan and Malenek had been close friends during this period. If Malenek had kept this from him, what else had he hidden from the ranger? How long had Malenek's plan been maturing? Had he been nothing more than a pawn to the priest all along, nurturing him to use Ascara?

There was also the question of Gigondas' absent guardian, but Callaghan was beginning to piece together the puzzle of their identity.

"Gigondas," said Callaghan as he entered the cargo hold later that evening.

"I told you I do not wish to talk about it," groaned the giant.

"I am not here to ask about the axe, or your brother. I want to talk about your guardian, the person who watched over you."

"He said he would come back," grumbled Gigondas.

"Gigondas, was your guardian a man?" asked Callaghan.

"Yes, but..." The giant hesitated.

"But there was something different about him?" guessed Callaghan. Gigondas nodded. He brought his two stone hands together and formed a large 'O' on his forehead.

Oldwyn Blake, the cyclops mage.

"He did not abandon you, Gigondas," said the ranger. "He was wrongly imprisoned. He recently won his freedom, and the first thing he did was to try and find you. When we return to Calisto, I will see you reunited you with him."

"And Gort?" asked the stone man.

"Perhaps," he added, less positively. "Perhaps."

*

It was nightfall when Gort galloped over the stone arch that breached the abyss around Mytor Castle. It was deserted, save for a couple of guards and Salamon Silnor, whom Gort could hear singing with his slithering tongue.

"Salamon," beckoned Gort. The awful warbling was cut short.

"What has happened?" he asked, poking his head out of a doorway.

"We have taken Perhola," informed Gort, "but the ranger Callaghan is on a ship sailing towards Zalestia."

"Ah," he hissed with a certain glee. "Say no more. Come." Salamon took one of the torches from the bracket on the wall. Gort followed the man as they descended a stone staircase leading into the bowels of the castle, far deeper than it was tall. The stairs were less grooved the further down they travelled, until they finally reached a vast network of naturally formed caves. Gort could hear the crash of the sea as it echoed from the coast through the caverns.

"You go first," Salamon said, offering him the torch. Gort took hold of it and made his way into the gloom, followed closely by Salamon. Something moved ahead of them. Something big, bigger than Gort. The torchlight was too dim for such a vast space, but there was a shape in the darkness. A sudden flap of wind extinguished the flame.

"Now what?" groaned Gort.

"Just wait," replied Salamon in the dark.

A stream of fire blasted across the cave. Salamon hid behind Gort's stone body, protecting him from the heat. Gort shielded his eyes with one hand, while the torch disintegrated in the other. The blaze evaporated as quickly as it had struck. The rocks around them glowed orange with intense heat. In the incandescent light, Gort glimpsed the large, snarling teeth of the creature he had been sent to unleash.

CHAPTER TWENTY-THREE

RAIN OF FIRE

CALLAGHAN KNELT AT THE STERN OF THE SKIMMER, LIGHTING Ascara and offering his daily prayer to the Elementals as Risaar's dawn ushered in a new day.

"You better not set the ship on fire," said one of the crew, Irvine Burr, as he sidled up beside the ranger. "Captain Pike will sooner kill you than watch it burn."

"I will be careful," replied the ranger, smiling as he extinguished Ascara's flame.

"I hope you were praying for us, ranger. That ghost of yours is a bad omen. He's been as dour as a Gorran wench ever since he snuck on board." Burr indicated Kaedin, sat by himself on the side rail, gazing out at the sea. Callaghan had also made this observation, but had hoped Kaedin would approach him with his troubles.

"Do you still not wish to share your thoughts?" asked Callaghan as he approached the spirit. "You have been despondent ever since we left Calisto."

"The crew are afraid of me," sulked the ghost.

"They are men of superstition," said the ranger. "If the position was reversed, would you trust a human spirit in the company of elves?"

"I shall stay hidden to keep their superstitions at ease," he huffed, evaporating into the air.

"Kaedin, wait," begged Callaghan. "I know you are grieving for Talia. It could not have been easy to tell Kamina the truth..."

"I broke her heart," said Kaedin. "She trusted me and I broke her heart, and yet I feel nothing, except..."

"Kaedin," said asked. The spirit reappeared, his head hung low. "Except what?"

"I felt them," he confessed.

"Them?" asked Callaghan, concerned. "Who?"

"The other spirits," Kaedin finally admitted. "During Oldwyn's seeing spell, I could feel them all, as if... as if I was in a dark forest, and so were they, lurking in the shadows behind the trees, whispering to me."

"What did they say?" quizzed the ranger. He was unnerved by this news. If Kaedin could sense them, he thought, was the reverse also true? Could they be seeing through the spirit somehow?

"I could not understand them," he whispered. "But Callaghan, I have never been so scared in all my life."

"That is why you told Kamina the truth," realised the ranger.

"Kamina returned my soul after that mage stole my body from me," said Kaedin. "It is all I have left, and it felt as if they were trying to steal that away too."

"They will not succeed," he said, reassuring the spirit. "I promise." His words eased Kaedin's worried heart.

"I have always dreamed of being on an adventure with you," he confessed, staring back at the sea, "but this is not how I expected it to be."

"Life never is," replied Callaghan, leaving the elf to his own contemplations.

*

The ranger continued to mentor Kamina in the art of sword fighting, despite the choppy sea swaying them from side to side. He taught her some prerequisite skills, particularly how to defend herself. Just like Kaedin, he feared the young elf would have to do so in the near future. He granted her Ascara again, sparring with the wooden stick that was Kamina's imaginary sword. Callaghan was pleased to see Kaedin spectating by the side, joining in with the crew as they jeered and booed theatrically between their tasks. Gigondas also watched, having developed an affinity with the little elf.

"Keep your guard up," the ranger instructed, advancing on Kamina again. She shifted the sword to guard her face and repelled Callaghan back.

"This is senseless," she said with a defeated sigh.

"How so?" he asked.

"If you were attacked by someone with a stick, would you not simply set Ascara's blade aflame and burn it?"

"I suppose I would," grinned Callaghan, "if someone were foolish enough to attack me with a stick. Why don't you try it?"

"Try what?" she asked. Kaedin cocked his head up as Callaghan stepped over to Kamina and whispered in her ear.

"You know what. You must promise not to tell these words to another soul."

"I promise," she said quietly, excitement lining her quickened breath.

"Okay. Repeat after me," he instructed. "Ascentio. Risaar. Emanos."

"Ascentio. Risaar. Emanos," she whispered back.

"In the old language it means, I command Risaar to awaken. Or at least his elemental energy," explained Callaghan. "Try saying the words to Ascara."

Kamina brought Ascara's hilt before her lips, which she realised now were incredibly dry. She paused to wet them, and then whispered the words to the sword's red jewel. For a moment, she thought the symbols etched along the blade started to glow, but she may have imagined it. Ascara's fire did not emerge for her.

"What does it mean?" she asked, feeling a sense of disappointment from Callaghan. "What does it mean?" she asked, feeling a sense of disappointment from Callaghan. Kaedin hung his head, feigning frustration, but he was secretly pleased. If anyone other than Callaghan was to wield Ascara, thought the spirit, it should be him.

"It does not mean anything," said the ranger with a false smile. "Now, defend yourself." Kamina tensed her grip on Ascara, but they were interrupted by Toran Calder.

"The Badlands!" he yelled from the top of the mast. The entire crew, including Gigondas, gathered on the deck, all gazing along their current course. Thick black clouds of a storm stretched out as far as the eye could see. Sparks of lightning flashed here and there, the accompanying volleys of thunder audible even from this distance. As the *Arad Nor* sailed closer, the crew spotted typhoon funnels venting and colliding with the full might of Whirren. They stood still, staring out at the furore that hungrily devoured the horizon. Compared to this tremendous tempest, the *Arad Nor* was a mere pile of twigs foolishly floating in the ocean, waiting to be overwhelmed by the wrath of the Badlands.

"I wish to Ygrain I was back on land," whispered Oran Cobb, crossing himself. So great was the sight that it sobered the captain and his crew to their senses.

"Ranger, we cannot go through that!" insisted Irvine Burr. "We must go around!"

"No," replied Callaghan, resolute in his plan.

"Are you mad?" cried Uisnech Leith in his heavy Heroshin accent, who up until now had barely spoken to the ranger. "That there is certain death. It's suicide!"

"Amaros has ships that have not only made it through, but made it back," said Callaghan, holding steadfast in the face of the crew's fears. "Let us add the *Arad Nor* to their number."

"A handful compared to thousands lost to that watery graveyard," barked Leith.

"We must go around," repeated Burr.

"There is no time!" declared Callaghan. "This is what you signed up for. An army cuts across Amaros and will soon descend upon Calisto. If we go around, everyone we left behind will be dead before we even set foot on Zalestian soil."

"But we cannot survive that," said Leith despondently.

"We can," proclaimed the ranger, "and we must, not for our own sakes, but those of every man, woman and child on Amaros, in all of Enara. There are people in this world who are relying on us and they do not even know it." This sombre thought stirred the men from the fearful corners of their minds that they had receded into. Gigondas was the first to step forward.

"Ranger is right," he grunted. "No time. We go through."

"Aye, lad." agreed Captain Pike, finally intervening once his crew had vented their frustrations. "We all knew what we signed up for. If anyone wants off, Amaros is that way," he said, pointing past the stern to the ocean. "Happy swimming."

None of the men moved.

"Good," muttered the captain. "Gigondas, Leith, Burr, tighten up those sails. We want as much speed as possible going in there. Roe, Calder, get anything that isn't tied down secured in the cargo hold. Cobb, man the wheel."

"Where are you going, captain?" asked Cobb.

"I'm taking a leaf out of the ranger's book," he said. "It's been a while since I prayed to Whirren or Aquill. I think we might need them both on our side for this one."

"I suggest you two go below deck," Callaghan said to the elves, although they both knew it was an order.

"But we can help," insisted Kamina.

"Not this time," stated Callaghan firmly. "Besides, I need you to guard this." The ranger slipped the scabbard from his belt and handed his weapon over to Kamina. "Keep Ascara safe, I did not come all this way to lose her to a freak wave."

The *Arad Nor* screamed along at full speed, charging through the vicious waves that welcomed them into the Badlands. The crew gawked at the ominous black clouds that soon smothered their sails, listening as the thunder roared louder with every strike of lightning. The twin suns were low on the horizon, as though they were racing against them to reach their deaths.

"Brace yerselves!" roared Pike from the wheel. The thick torrent enveloped the *Arad Nor*, Pike unable to see very far ahead. The waves swelled up and the rain started to smack down upon the deck. The captain hastily turned hard to port to avoid a titanic typhoon bearing down upon them.

"Is that the best you bastards can do?" he yelled, as the steadfastness of his vessel was tested to the very last nail by the brutality of the Badlands. The ship creaked as waves tossed it around like a child's toy. The crew gripped whatever they could as the ship almost capsized. Bolts of lightning fired across the bow, one striking the centre mast, but the rain quickly extinguished any flames.

"I think they might have heard you!" screamed Cobb as he helped Pike with the wheel. The old friends laughed together in the face of fear and certain death. The waves quickly grew in size, the *Arad Nor* riding up and down the crests, struggling each time to scale over the watery peaks.

They battled through the Badlands for hours, although the eternal gloom slowed time to a crawl. Callaghan wondered if they should have waited for daylight before they breached the storm wall, but in retrospect realised it would have made little difference; this would always be a dark and violent tempest.

"Hold onto something!" he cried out to Gigondas as another wave rolled over them. The ship was almost completely vertical as it struggled up a sheer wall of water. The stone man slid down the deck, managing to catch the main mast with one of his giant hands. He soon lost his grip, plunging straight for Pike and Cobb hanging from the wheel at the stern. The ship righted itself just in time, and Gigondas crumpled on the deck before them.

"Get up, lad!" screamed the captain. "Someone fix that flapping sail!" Irvine Burr spotted the ropes slipping loose, gritting his teeth as he wrenched them tight.

"Captain!" hollered Leith. They all gazed up at the wave that was building up in front of them, at least ten times the size of the ship.

"May the gods have mercy..." pleaded Pike, but the wave was not to be their end. A large typhoon swept in from the starboard side, its swirling mass twisting the ship up into the air, above the monstrous wave.

Below deck, Kaedin and Kamina huddled together in the cargo hold. Crates and equipment clattered around them as the *Arad Nor* was wrenched up by the typhoons. Kaedin struggled to retain his connection with the ship, the space in constant flux. The ship swayed far to starboard, catching the spirit off guard.

"Kaedin!" cried Kamina as he dissolved through one of the walls. His comforting silvery glow re-appeared when the ship bobbed back the way, the hull groaning under the tenacity of the typhoon.

"I am here," he said.

"For how much longer?" she screamed over the sounds of the storm ravaging the ship. They crashed down with an abrupt splash. The ship cracked under the pressure, water spouting through gaps in the hull.

As if in answer to Kamina's question, there was a sudden, unexpected silence. They remained still, unsure if the precipitated calm was a trick of the Badlands, anticipating another violent jolted at any moment. Kamina picked herself up and carried Ascara to the upper deck. She emerged to find the storm had ceased. The disorientated crew helped each other up, staring back at the fierce storm they had just escaped. The ship skimmed through serene waters, as if they were back in Calisto's bay, protected by the crescent cliffs.

They were in a perfect circle of calm.

"The eye of the storm," said Callaghan as he stared upwards. He could make out muted stars hovering far above the funnel they found themselves in, the edge of Ygrain adding a green glow to the night sky.

"Leith, Burr, check the hull for any breaches," ordered Pike, sparing little time for stargazing. "The rest of you, lower the sails and make repairs!"

As the crew carried out the tasks they had been dealt, the captain joined the ranger at the bow of the *Arad Nor*. They gazed over the peaceful, calm waters to the opposite side of the channel, where the calmness ended and the wall of the storm ignited again.

"I don't know if my ship will survive another round like that," Pike confessed, with the wet grin of a man still glad to be alive. "I know my ship. She sounds bruised. We need to stop here for a while to look after her."

"As you see fit, captain. I have faith in your ability to steer us through whatever lies ahead." Pike mumbled something under his breath as he paced towards his quarters, an apology to the gods for his earlier blasphemy.

"Are we there?" asked Kamina as she climbed up onto the deck, with Ascara wrapped in her arms.

"No, we are only halfway through the Badlands," he replied. "We are at the core of the storm." Kamina gazed around them at the unexpected stillness, gawking at the stars above. The ocean was no longer a deep, dark blue. A spectrum of colours shimmered beneath the surface, like underwater clouds of glowing blues and greens.

"What is that?"

"I do not know," replied Callaghan, joining Kamina in her admiration.

"Sea creatures," said Roe, who had overheard the discussion. "Thousands of them. They give off a natural light. Taste funny though." They continued to watch the bioluminescence glimmer and ebb all around them.

"Will wonders never..." the ranger started to say. He was interrupted by the scream of Toran Calder. His foothold on the mast broke off and he plummeted to the deck. The young crewman managed to grasp one of the sail ropes and slow his descent. He dropped to the deck, howling in pain.

"Let me see," said Callaghan, kneeling by Toran. The friction from the rope had marked his arm and hand.

"Is he okay?" asked Roe.

"Nothing is broken, just a nasty rope burn. Could you bring me something to bandage it up, and some bohra seeds and an egg?"

"You'll be lucky if there's any eggs left after that," mumbled Roe as he ran down to the galley.

"The footing snapped," said Toran, shaking from the shock of the fall. "Must have been damaged in the storm."

Roe swiftly returned, holding an egg and bohra seeds in a bowl. "You are lucky, Toran," joked the cook. "Last one." Callaghan cracked the egg into the bowl and mixed it with the seeds. Roe handed him a natty looking shirt which Callaghan cut into strips and soaked in the solution, wrapping them around Toran's burn.

"It will sting at first," said the ranger, "but it will heal quicker." Toran winced as Callaghan applied the bandages. "There, that should see you through."

"Suck it up you big girl," teased Roe.

"This coming from the man who..." retorted Toran, but he was cut short by the sight of something behind Roe. A dark presence loomed in the gloomy squall they had just survived

"Toran, what is it?" Callaghan asked, staring at the Badlands behind them.

"I saw a shadow in the storm," he said, pointing with his good arm. The ranger followed the crewman's finger, but he could not distinguish anything amidst the clouds of black and grey.

"I do not see anything," the ranger started to say, but then a flash of lightning illuminated a shape lurking in the skies. They had only glimpsed it for an instant, but the intensity of the light had burned the shape into their retinas.

"What in the Elements was that?" murmured Roe.

"Kamina," said Callaghan, "I need Ascara back. Now."

*

Callaghan knocked on the door of the captain's private cabin. Pike soon appeared, clutching a bottle, reeking of Caspian rum.

"I thought we had time before we reached the storm again?" he slurred.

"We did, but I fear we are being followed," said the ranger.

"Who would be mad enough to follow us into the Badlands?" the captain crowed.

"Not who," warned Callaghan. "What."

"I do not have time for your riddles, ranger."

"Young Toran spotted a shape in the storm..." he started to explain.

"Have I ever told you that boy has the eyes of an elf?" said Pike, interrupting him. "Not literally mind you..."

"This is serious, captain," snapped Callaghan. "If Malenek is able to conjure spirits and has men of stone in his employ, who knows what other creatures he has kept hidden in the depths of Mytor."

"We are fishermen, ranger, not soldiers," replied Pike. "We have no weapons on board. Well, except for Gigondas. What can we do?"

"We need to continue on our course immediately," urged the ranger. "The storm will make it harder for whatever it is to find us."

"This ship won't survive in that squall without repairs," stated the captain.

"It will not survive here either," said Callaghan. Captain Pike begrudgingly left the bottle in his quarters. He ordered his men to stop the repairs and prepare to breach the other side of the raging tempest.

The *Arad Nor* broke through the curtains of torrential rain, and once again her crew faced certain death in the ferocious grip of the Badlands. They pressed on as the waves hurled the ship to one another, like men throwing a ball for sport.

"We're not going to make it!" bellowed Pike above the reaches of the storm. As if to add weight to his words, the central mast was suddenly enveloped in flames.

"It's the lightning!" yelled Leith.

"No," said Callaghan, almost to himself, his fingers gripping Ascara's handle. "It is something else." A large and sinister shadow rocketed through the torrential rain, cutting through the storm clouds. The heavy beat of disturbingly large wings pressed down upon the deck. For one brief moment, the crew forgot that they were in the centre of the Badlands as a larger danger loomed. Their fear-filled eyes failed to penetrate the gloom hiding the mysterious beast that stalked them.

A horrifying roar broke across the side of the bow, shaming the tirades of thunder that had terrified them until now. The crew stood tense as the *Arad Nor* creaked in the dark. Down below in the cargo hold, Kamina cuddled into her knees, frightened by a monstrous outcry. Kaedin stood nearby, eyeing the ceiling above.

"Something is wrong," he muttered.

"We are in the Badlands," said Kamina. "Of course something is wrong!"

"Something else!" he snapped back. Using his ghostly abilities, Kaedin climbed up the wall and popped his head through the ceiling out onto the deck. A stream of fire snarled out of the dark, setting the deck ablaze. Kaedin tumbled back down into the hold.

"What is happening?" quizzed Kamina.

"Something bad," replied the ghost.

Captain Pike co-ordinated the crew to extinguish the lethal inferno that plagued his ship. The eternal rain did nothing to dampen the demonic fire. Uisnech Leith tackled the flames with a wet sack, but the fiery tongues lashed his clothing, setting his arm alight. Callaghan ran to help them man, but a vicious wave threw the boat sideways, knocking the ranger off his feet. He looked up to see a desperate Leith leap off the ship and into the seas. The deck began to give way, burning beams falling into the hold below. Kamina screamed out above the roar of fire and rain.

"Kamina, get out of there!" yelled Callaghan. She crawled out of the cargo hold and into the corridor, Kaedin not far behind. They climbed up onto the deck, watching helplessly as the crew tried in vain to douse the fires that consumed their vessel. Gigondas scanned the skies, unaffected by the flames. He tensed his hands around the makeshift handle of his mighty axe as their unseen tormentor shrieked towards them, piercing through the chaos. The large, scaly underbelly of the creature soared over the *Arad Nor* and snatched Gigondas in its claws.

"Gigondas!" cried Kamina above the raging tempest. The only reply was the resounding clang of his giant axe as it clattered upon the deck.

"What in the name of Risaar's fiery beard was that?" beseeched Pike.

"A dragon!" responded Callaghan, as they continued to fight the flames.

"They're extinct!" yelled Oran Cobb.

"So will we be if it attacks again!" said the captain. Callaghan weighed Ascara in his hand, wondering if he could fight fire with fire. Gigondas' giant axe caught his eye, gleaming in the flames. Callaghan fought his way through the inferno and claimed it as his own. The handle was slightly scorched, but the blade was magnificent and sharp.

This was a weapon that could slay a dragon.

Kamina stared after Callaghan, guessing what he planned to do. He clambered over to her, once again offering the elf his sword.

"Keep Ascara safe," he said, "and she will do the same for you."

"No, I cannot," Kamina stammered, soaked and shivering.

"You must get to Zalestia and find the Stone of Spirits. This is your mission now."

"I cannot do this without you," she wailed.

"You can, and you must. Both of you," he said adamantly, glancing at Kaedin.

The dragon screeched close by, preparing for another pass.

"Callaghan!" she screamed, but he had already turned his back to her, studying the squalid skies as Gigondas had done. His muscles tensed, ready to react as soon as it was in his sights. He spotted the shadow off the starboard side. The ranger pounded along the deck, building up momentum as he raised the axe. A ball of fire shot out from beyond the side of the ship. The ranger screamed a battle cry as he bound over the flames and onto the side railing, propelling himself and the axe to meet the dragon.

And just like that, Callaghan Tor, the Ranger Elite, was gone.

Kamina stared at the side of the burning boat where he had leapt to his doom, distraught, unable to breathe. The sounds of the crew yelling as the ship broke apart were dulled by despair. She did not register Kaedin running after the ranger, pausing at the edge, staring into oblivion.

The ship's hull groaned and split apart right under Kamina's feet. She fell through the floor, clawing at the edge of the deck. The elf fought to keep hold, but splinters of wood jabbed into her hands.

"Kaedin!" she screamed. The spirit returned to her. He tried to pull her up, but he could not concentrate in the chaos. Kamina's bloody fingernails lost their grip on the wet wood. Kaedin grasped at her with his ghostly hands, but he could not focus his energy long enough to keep hold. Her fingers slipped, and gravity yanked her down. She would have plummeted into the wild waters below were it not for Captain Pike. The old sailor seized her arm, wrenching her back from the brink of the broken hull.

"Thank you," she wheezed.

"Don't thank me just yet," he said. "We need to get you off this boat before that creature comes back."

"What about the rest of the crew?" she begged, but Pike did not answer. He hobbled along what was left of the deck, striving up a steep incline. The lower half of the ship was sinking, dragging both parts down under the surface. The captain cobbled together some barrels with a length of rope, tying the end around Kamina's waist, knotting Ascara as well.

"The barrels will keep you afloat," he instructed.

"But..."

"But nothing!" Pike replied, tying off the rope. "If you make it out of the Badlands, get to Zalestia and do what the ranger told you do to." He knelt down beside her. "Do not let the death of my men be in vain."

"Come with us," she implored.

"No," he said, rising to his feet. "A captain stays with his ship. Rules of the sea." The dragon roared again, circling nearby, signalling another attack.

"Go, now!" ordered Pike, helping her onto the railing. The captain launched the barrels over the side. Kamina took a deep breath and dived into the dark water. Kaedin stood beside the captain, in awe of him. The man turned to look him in the eye, and offered a farewell nod. The ethereal elf nodded a solemn reply, and then followed Kamina into the seas.

Kamina opened her eyes in almost complete darkness, save for the glow of the fire that ravaged the *Arad Nor* above. Through the watery gloom, she could see part of the hull, hidden underneath the water, dragging the ship down to a watery grave. The bodies of the dead crew floated down with it, like statues sinking into an empty void.

Kaedin slipped through the surface of the sea, his luminescence strangely beautiful underwater, like the rain in Calisto. He guided her back to the surface, the ghost finding it easier to swim than Kamina. She struggled against the current, trying to kick upwards, but it was useless. She grasped the rope and pulled herself up through to the surface, spluttering seawater as she gasped for air. Kamina locked her arms around one of the barrels bobbing in front of her, pressing her face against it as her panting slowed. Kaedin materialised on top of them, and managed to fish her out of the water. She lay face down, exhausted, her body seizing as the chill of the ocean caught up with her. She suddenly remembered Ascara, her hands clutching at its hilt, making sure the sword was still tied tight to her belt.

The savage roar of the dragon rumbled over the howling winds and heavy patter of rain. Its silhouette shot by the flames that engulfed the last section of the ship still above water. The creature released one last volley of fire. The stores of food and alcohol finally ignited.

The *Arad Nor* exploded, ripped apart from the inside.

The force blasted Kamina back into the water. Parts of the flaming hull rained down around them, but the fires were soon extinguished in the storm. Kamina clasped at the barrels again, salvaging a charred plank of wood to use as a paddle. Without the ship's fiery beacon, Kaedin was her only source of light, save for the violent flashes of lightning. The spirit tried to help her back up, but another snarl reverberated through the rage of the storm. The dragon swooped down again, circling the wreckage. Kamina slipped back into the water, hiding behind the barrels. The ghost glanced around, wondering what the dragon was looking for, before he saw his own shimmering hand.

"It can see me," he realised.

"Kaedin, do not turn invisible," pleaded Kamina. "Do not leave me alone."

"I will be right here." Kaedin's glow faded, and Kamina was left in darkness. Once or twice she thought she heard the beat of wings above her, but the dragon never appeared. They were all alone, bobbing with the barrels, a plaything for the wicked waves.

Bolts of lightning ripped across the sky. The brief flash revealed an object floating nearby. Kamina feared it was a shark, but another snap of light illuminated a piece of flotsam from the *Arad Nor*, larger than the barrels she clung to. She sank into the water while holding the rope, splashing her little legs until she reach the debris. With Kaedin's help she forced the barrels under the hull fragment, combining them into a sturdy makeshift raft. She dived underwater to tie off the ropes, but a wave thrust the raft toward her. One of the barrels cracked her in the side of the head. Her world flashed white, and then dark. She struggled through the darkness back to the raft, as the warmth of the blood trickled down her face.

"Kaedin," she whimpered, "I can..." Her words trailed off as her consciousness waned. With several attempts, Kaedin eventually yanked her out of the water. She collapsed on the last remnants of the *Arad Nor*, while he stroked her blood-stained hair with his odd touch.

"Sleep," said Kaedin. "I will make sure you do not fall over."

"No, we... we need to get to... Zalestia," she muttered, her words garbled as she fought to stay awake.

"We will," he assured her. "We will."

Kamina lost consciousness, as their crude lifeboat was carried along by the callous sea.

CHAPTER TWENTY-FOUR
THE LOST CHILDREN

As Kamina and Kaedin drifted through the Badlands on the sliver of a hope that was their makeshift raft, a pair of human children entered the elves' home of Elgrin Forest. Ponyo and Kiki Hyaegan, the only survivors of the spirits' assault on Perhola, had heeded Talia Elloeth's words and ridden across Legoria under the cover of night. On their way, the siblings had spotted the human township of Onassis, but from the distance it appeared deserted, and so they had continued their trek to Elgrin. When they finally crossed the threshold into the forest, Plagacia was in urgent need of rest. The children, hungry and afraid, guided the mare to a babbling brook, where the grateful horse lapped at the flowing water.

"There you go," said Kiki soothingly, stroking Plagacia's white coat, curiously fingering the spots of grey. Her elder brother Ponyo stared at the endless rows of enormous trees in the opposite direction.

"We will get lost in these woods," he said. "We should return to the road and ride to Gorran."

"The elf said to come here," Kiki reminded him.

"Maybe she was..." Ponyo protested, but he was cut short by a sharp snap. He gasped, scanning the nearby trees, but seeing nothing.

"What is it?" whispered Kiki. Plagacia also sensed something, snorting softly as she backed away from the brook.

"I think we are being watched," he replied.

The horse suddenly reared up on its hind legs, neighing a warning before she galloped off into the forest. The children screamed as an ætherghoul appeared on the other side of the water, snarling at them with a ghastly tongue. It rushed through the flowing stream and loomed over Kiki. She trembled with fear as it hissed at her.

An arrow pinged through the trees, hitting its target dead centre in the chest. The ætherghoul plunged into the stream. The children turned to see a band of elves emerge from the forest, led by Endo Eredu.

"This is our territory, upon which you are infringing," he stated. Ponyo did not know who he was more afraid of, the ætherghoul or this angry elf.

"Please sir, master elf sir, we were told to come here," pleaded his sister. "By one of your kind."

"By an elf?" Endo asked, although he suspected who it might be.

"Talia Elloeth," Ponyo blurted out, confirming his suspicions.

"And what is that you have brought with you?" asked another elf, Tealk Ennor.

"A demon," said Ponyo, eyeing the elf's sword. "It cannot be killed."

"Maybe not by a man," Endo began to boast. The ætherghoul made a timely snarl, rising up from the water. Endo quickly loaded another arrow from his quiver and shot the human depravity again, this time through the throat. Thick black blood poured out what should have been a mortal wound, but the creature staggered forward, determined beyond death. The human children darted behind the elves. Endo fired another arrow, and another, but the ætherghoul defied his intent and continued to march towards them.

"I told you!" whimpered Ponyo. "It cannot be killed."

"We shall see," said Endo. "Tealk, your tree blade." The slender elf tossed Endo his weapon; a short sword with one sharp edge, the other serrated. Endo caught the handle as the ætherghoul pounced towards him. He swiftly pirouetted out of the ætherghoul's reach, managing to slice across its chest with the blade. The body thudded down upon the forest floor and lay still.

"See," said Endo to the human child, but Ponyo's eyes remained fixed on the ætherghoul. It groaned as it tried to pick itself up, its inner organs, black and decayed, oozing out of its body. Before the undead beast could find its balance, Endo took a running swing and lobbed the ætherghoul's head clean off. The body convulsed and then exploded in a cloud of ash. They witnessed the glowing soul, freed from the prison of its rotting body, disperse in a brief shimmer of radiant silver light.

Without boast or celebration, a confused Endo cleaned the blade and returned it to Tealk. "Now, little humans," he said, kneeling down next to Ponyo and Kiki, "you will tell us everything you know."

The children told Endo and his elves of the attack on Perhola by the spirits, how they had watched their parents and friends dragged away, only to be turned into the creatures like the thing that had pursued them. They told the brave story of Talia Elloeth, who had sent them to Elgrin Forest not only to be saved, but to warn the elves.

"Please master elf," said Kiki at the end of their tale, "there are more of them coming."

"A lot more," added Ponyo.

The elves pricked their ears, and in the distance, just beyond Elgrin's borders, they could hear heavy, clumsy feet ploughing through the grass. Without further delay, Endo picked up Ponyo and slung him on his back, while Tealk did the same with his sister. The band of elves and humans raced through the forest, the trees rushing past them. As they hurried to warn the elven settlements, Endo carried with him a heavy heart. Talia was almost certainly dead, or worse, one of the spirits' undead slaves, the horrific *gwann'gul* of legend brought to life. He thought of his last conversation with her and felt ashamed. He had been wrong. There could be no justification for this abhorrence.

PART TWO

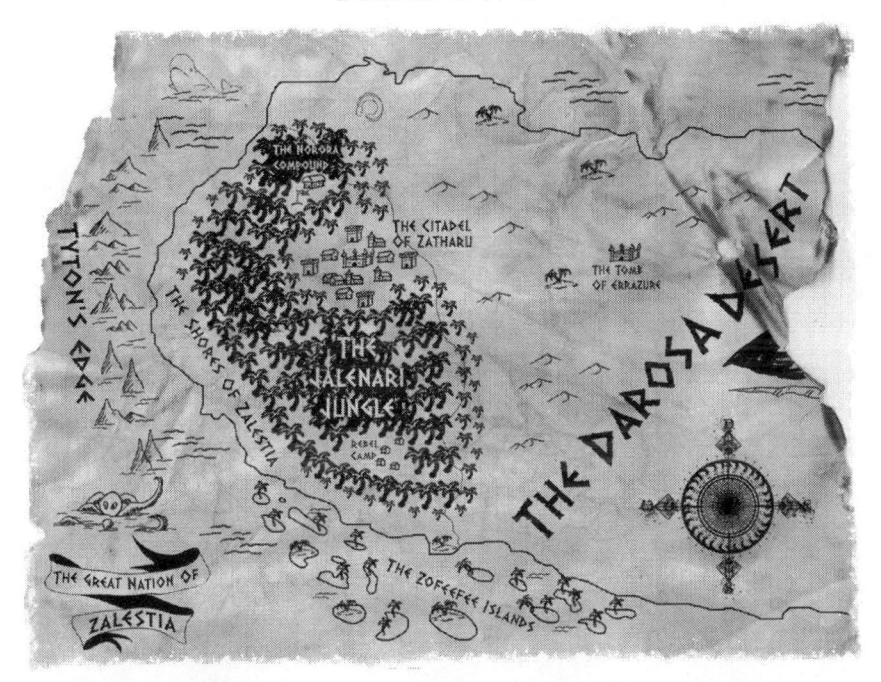

In the beginning there was Gianna. On the first day, she created the world, Emdara.

On the second day, she met Egaros, who kept her world safe by forming the sky. They were the mother and the father.

On the third day, together they sculpted the land and sea.

On the fourth day, she mothered his children, who populated the lands.

On the fifth day, her eldest child, Azik, betrayed her love, and slaughtered his father, scarring the soil.

On the six day, Gianna built Haegor, where the Betrayer was cast down, to be followed by any who harmed her creations.

On the seventh day, she created Yannah, her resting place to watch over the world, where those faithful to her love would join her in the hereafter.

Excerpt from the Xe'rath (as translated by Jada Zaleed Zhan), the religious tablets of the eastern continent of Zalestia.

CHAPTER TWENTY-FIVE

THE SHORES OF ZALESTIA

KAMINA'S GREEN EYES FLUTTERED OPEN, FILLED WITH THE SIGHT of a clear blue sky, the harsh dual heat of Risaar and Aquill beating down upon her. She sat up to find Kaedin perched on the edge of the raft, his ghostly feet dangling in the calm water. Far behind them, she could still make out the massive grey clouds of the Badlands. The stormy weather had spat them out far from its reach. She collected her thoughts, admiring the vast splendour of the open sea, before the horror of their reality overwhelmed her.

"Did anyone else...?" she started to ask, but Kaedin just shook his head. Suddenly the sea did not seem so vast and beautiful as it was endless and forsaken, a watery grave for Callaghan and the brave crew of the *Arad Nor*.

"What do we do now?" she asked the spirit.

"We do what Captain Pike and Callaghan told us to do," he replied solemnly, his attentions still upon his ghostly toes wiggling beneath the surface. Kamina rose to her feet, Ascara still at her side, tied to the rope. She slid the sword from the sheath ever so slightly, just enough to glimpse the blade. It felt wrong, without the ranger there, to even touch Ascara. She quickly hid the blade back within its scabbard.

"You should have saved him," she said, still half in shock. "He would know what to do."

"I am not bonded to Callaghan," Kaedin retorted. "And even if I were, the dragon took him from us. What was I to do?"

"Sorry," she said wistfully. Kamina gripped Ascara's handle and whispered a small elven prayer for Callaghan, just as the ranger had done to the Elementals each morning. "May he find peace in Loria."

As if in reply, something struck the barrels. Kamina jumped, only to realise it was a fragment of the sail, caught up in the ropes with some wood that had shattered from the mast.

"Kaedin, I need you to help me," she urged, fishing the sail out from the water.

"I am helping you." His ghostly feet still glowed under the surface. His hands suddenly lurched into the water, and without a splash he caught a large fish that had been attracted to his luminescence. He tossed it to Kamina, the sorry-looking creature flapping at her feet as it suffocated. "You need sustenance."

"I will eat when we are moving," she replied, focused on the floating rag. They worked together, recalling how Link Raliss had constructed his temporary sail aboard the *Tepona*. Their crooked effort quickly caught the wind, propelling them further away from the Badlands to whatever lay ahead.

Once they were under way, Kamina used Ascara to slice open the fish, cutting pieces small pieces and feeding them reluctantly into her mouth. Although she consumed it raw, it was warm. The twin suns were much stronger here than in Amaros, and had almost baked the meat. However, the heat did nothing to counter the fishy, acidic taste.

"This is disgusting," she mumbled, resisting the urge to spit it out.

"You must keep your strength up, for both our sakes," said the spirit, now acutely aware of his reliance on Kamina's life energy for his own existence. "Have you noticed you are eating more since... since it happened?" Kamina shook her head, her mouth full as she tried to swallow. "Then maybe you are just becoming a fat wood hog," he said jokingly.

"And perhaps being a ghost will be good for your gluttonous appetite," she replied, swallowing more of the fish.

"What I would not give to be able to taste a crumb of grandmother's fruit bread," he said. Although Kaedin was unable to actually salivate, Kamina's mouth grew taut at the mere thought of elven food. She closed her eyes, recalling the sweet smell of Lashara's kitchen while sucking in the salty, bitter stench of the sea.

When she opened her eyes again, her mouth dropped in astonishment. Far in the distance, on the edge of the horizon, was the faint blur of land.

"Can you see it?" she asked, not wishing to raise her hopes in case her imagination was playing tricks.

"I see it," he said. "I see it!"

Thinking of Captain Pike barking at his crew, Kamina tightened the sail as much as the rope would allow. She used the piece of charred wood as a rudimentary rudder to steer them straight toward the landmass. The raft coasted over the surface of the sea, a strong breeze blowing them onwards. Soon they could see it more clearly, and immediately they knew the unfamiliar landscape was Zalestia. A reef of razor-sharp rocks rose out up before the shore, stretching along the entire coastline.

"Careful," advised Kaedin. Kamina scowled at him as she loosened the sail, reducing their speed in order to manoeuvre through the reef. The raft nudged the rocks once or twice, cracking the driftwood before it recoiled. Underneath the barrels groaned as they scraped along the reefs that lay hidden under the surface.

"We will not make it," said Kamina, as the current careered them towards a looming rock. She snatched Ascara before the sword slid overboard, tying it tightly to her side.

The current unravelled the vessel beneath her feet, hurling it towards a sharp outcrop. Kamina managed to balance on what little was left. Her efforts to stay above the treacherous water caused her to lose focus of the ridge of rocks ahead. She caught sight of it through the blinding spray, a sharp formation eroded by the waves over time into a deadly pinnacle.

"Jump!" yelled Kaedin. Kamina launched herself off the raft moments before it was torn asunder. It exploded against the rocks jutting out from the water. She resurfaced, gasping for air. She swam hard, spotting the near shore through bloodshot eyes. The undertow sucked her back towards the row of rocks that had blighted the raft. The little elf fought ferociously against the current. Using the last of her strength, she managed to kick free of its clutches, splashing her way along with the waves.

Kamina staggered up from the foamy surf, haggard after her strenuous swim to shore. She fell face-first onto the wet sand, panting for air. Kaedin's ghostly boots appeared next to her, the spirit's soft step not making any prints, barely disturbing the grains of sand. He gazed in awe at the beach, not at its beauty, but at its destruction. The trees nearest the beach were scorched with fire, hacked down by swords and axes. Further along, he could see the rotten wreckage of some Amarosian ships and abandoned Zalestian barricades.

Kamina was also disenchanted by her surroundings. When she managed to rise on her wobbly legs, she stood on sand that did not sparkle or shimmer like it had in her dreams. It was a nightmare, a leftover wasteland of war. A terrifying screech emanated deep from within the jungle, severing the pair from their pensive state.

"What do we do now?" asked Kaedin, peering into the thick, dense foliage that lay before them. Kamina gripped Ascara, preparing for anything this new continent could throw at them.

"We find the Stone of Spirits," she stated, taking her first steps into the jungles of Zalestia.

*

Kamina cautiously chopped through the thick vines and oversized leaves, fighting her way through the foreign jungle. She was enamoured by the wonderful sights and bright colours of exotic plants and strange fruits, but she remained cautious to every rustle within the trees, and every loud, bizarre bird call overhead. As an elf she had been raised to protect the trees of Elgrin, to cultivate them and live symbiotically, but here it was impossible to move without cutting through. The trees were different here; tougher, more resilient.

"I cannot hear them," she muttered to herself.

"Hear who?" Kaedin asked, the dense leaves distorting his ghostly form.

"The trees," she said. "I cannot hear them sing like those in Elgrin."

"I have not heard them sing since I was turned into a spirit," he confessed. Kamina felt pity for him, even remorse for having accidentally brought him back from the dead, half whole. She shrugged off these emotions; there was no time for such regrets.

Kamina swung round sharply as a rabble of animals crashed through the jungle towards them. She raised Ascara, her hands shaking with trepidation. A flock of small lizards, no taller than Kamina's knee, filed out of the undergrowth. They ignored the elf and the spirit, streaming straight through the jungle. Kamina lowered her sword. A smaller, clumsier specimen chased after them from the rear, managing to stun itself by slamming into Kamina's leg, falling backwards. Kamina smiled at the little lizard, almost cute in its own way. With Ascara still in one hand, she bent down and picked up the dazed animal. It cocked its head towards her, scrutinising her face with pale yellow eyes, waving a forked purple tongue in her direction.

"I think he likes you," said Kaedin with a smile.

The small lizard's body tensed up, sensing danger. It hissed in the direction it had escaped from. Something a lot bigger than either it or an elf roared from the jungle. The small lizard leapt down from Kamina's hand and sped away to re-join its pack. The ground shuddered again. Kamina's heart beat faster as the quakes grew stronger.

"Kamina, run," whispered Kaedin, already edging back to follow their tiny lizard friend in retreat. Kamina's legs would not budge. Her tight grip on Ascara's handle caused her hands to sweat. But she was not scared.

"Kamina!" he hissed again.

She wanted to see it.

When she finally did, she wished she had not.

It was a giant lizard, ten times the size of her if not more. It reminded her of the old tales of ancient creatures, the dragons, but without wings and, hopefully, the ability to breathe fire. Only the dragons were real, she knew now. Monsters existed, and the one in front of her brandished long, flesh-chomping teeth. It smashed through the trees and let out a reverberating roar. Kamina snapped from her astonishment. She fled through the jungle, following the small pack of lizards. She held Ascara out in front of her, slicing through the dense foliage. Kamina tried to tail Kaedin as he navigated her through the maze of branches and vines.

"No, this way!" he screamed, but she could barely see him within the wild jungle. "Here!" She followed his voice, eventually catching up to him. They were joined by other small animals running for their lives. Kamina ducked as something akin to a small horse bounded over her head. She glanced back to see the ginormous beast breaking through the trees, showing off its strong jaw and sharp teeth as it snarled in anger.

They stumbled into a large clearing where the suns managed to penetrate the jungle canopy. Kaedin darted right through and into the shade of the trees once more, but Kamina stopped in the light.

"What are you doing?" he barked at her.

"We cannot keep running," she argued defiantly, catching her breath. She turned and prepared Ascara, ready to attack the colossal creature as soon as its massive clawed foot thudded into the clearing. The ground juddered as the behemoth boomed towards them, shaking Kamina to her spine. Her teeth rattled inside her mouth, filled with the bitter taste of adrenalin.

The gargantuan lizard burst through the trees and into the sunlight. Kamina tensed herself, ready to attack its legs, but something was wrong. A flurry of whizzing sounds zipped through the air. The creature let out an excruciating howl, followed by one last mortal groan. It staggered slightly, before crashing down in the clearing, its head falling in front of Kamina. It looked at her with its large, yellowish-green eyes, filled with sadness and pain. Her fear melted into sympathy for the beast, as she reached out and touched its cold, leathery skin. The light in its strange eyes faded and disappeared as they closed forever.

A swarm of arrows and spears protruding from the beast's back. She heard more sounds, but these were man-made; the hoots and yells of victory. A party of boisterous Zalestian hunters entered the clearing, riding on the backs of other exotic creatures the way an Amarosian would a horse. These beasts were bulkier, their hides course and grey, with large horns jutting up from their snouts.

The men that rode them were also unusual to her eyes. Although she was aware of their darker complexion, Kamina was still amazed by the sight of their brown skin, as if they had emerged from the finest soil. They wore little clothing in the sweltering jungle climate, only loincloths or skirts fashioned from animal skin, their toned bodies glistening with sweat. They surrounded the clearing, and now all eyes shifted from their hunted prey to her. Kamina thought to run in Kaedin's direction, but found that she had been outflanked, and that Kaedin had made himself invisible to the newcomers.

"Kaedin?" she whispered, but he did not answer.

The pack leader leapt from their animal, performing a mid-air flip and rolling onto the jungle floor. A colourful spear blurred with them, coming into sharp focus when the end was pointed at Kamina. She was surprised to discover her challenger was a young woman, a beautiful one at that; her long black hair blowing in the breeze, her athletic body barely hidden by straps of animal fur. The woman shouted at Kamina in her native Zalestian tongue. While the elf could not understand the words, she grasped the angry sentiment. The Zalestian warrior repeated her forceful, foreign sounds, jabbing the spear at Kamina.

"I wish to speak with Zahyr Zaleed Khan!" Kamina finally blurted out. The woman laughed while the men surrounding them howled in some sort of chant, as if expecting a duel. Kamina glanced around, counting them, making herself aware of her enemy, just as Callaghan had taught her.

"You ins no positions to make demands," replied the woman in flawed Amarosian. She thrust the spear at Kamina. The elf narrowly dodged the tip, acting on instinct. She raised Ascara's heavy weight and sliced through the spear, chopping it in two. The woman dropped the useless shafts and reached for a pair of large curved daggers hanging from the back of her belt. Kamina readied herself for the next attack, but it did not come. The men were silenced by a wave of the woman's hand. Kamina realised she was staring intently at Ascara's jewel, shining in the twin suns.

"Where dids you gets this sword?" she asked.

"It was given to me," Kamina replied.

"Who? Who dids gives this to yous?"

"I will speak only to Zahyr Zaleed Khan," said Kamina bravely, hoping to use the woman's sudden interest in Ascara to bargain her way out of this tense situation.

"You will speaks to me or you will die now," snapped the jungle warrior, brandishing her twin blades.

"No," echoed a voice, "you will put down your weapons, or I will kill you and your men."

"Who speaks to me is such ways?" she demanded, her startled eyes quickly glancing in all directions.

"I did," replied Kaedin, materialising between Kamina and her antagonist. The surrounding men crowed in fear, cowering behind the grey creatures they rode. Kamina picked out a Zalestian word being repeated over and over.

"Firentazme! Firentazme!"

The young woman attacked, the long curves of her daggers slicing through Kaedin repeatedly, but ultimately in vain. The warrior staggered backwards, mystified when she saw that the spirit was unharmed.

"What sorts of magics is this?" she quizzed.

"I will speak only with the Khan," said Kamina, feeling much bolder with her ghostly brother beside her. The young woman scrutinised the elves with her large brown eyes.

"Then I will takes you to him," she conceded. Her temperament softened as she replaced he knives in their holders.

"You have the ear of the Khan?" asked Kamina.

"I should hopes so," replied the young woman. "I am daughter."

"You are Princess Jazintha?" The jungle warrior was the furthest idea of what Kamina had imagined Zalestian royalty to look like.

"No Princess. Zhar-ie," corrected Jazintha, emphasising her title. "Much betters than Amarosians Princess. How do yous knows my name?"

"The Ishkava Ranger Callaghan Tor told us about you," admitted Kamina, still unsure whether to trust Jazintha.

"Callaghan," muttered the zharie. Jazintha's hard-hearted veil slipped for a second, revealing a tender spot for the ranger. She quickly recovered, flashing a beautiful yet narcissistic smile. "So he talks of me, your warrior man. I am famous evens in Amaros!" She translated this into Zalestian for her men, who laughed with her. "What are your names? What are yous of?"

"I am Kamina Elloeth, of the elves of Elgrin Forest."

"Kamina?" asked the zharie, as if the name conjured up some sense of recognition.

"Yes, and this is my… this is Kaedin." The ghost nodded at her but Jazintha only grunted as she turned her back to the spirit. She fed her men orders in her native tongue, but the men shook their heads disobediently, pointing at Kaedin, repeated the word Kamina had identified before.

"Firentazme."

Jazintha shouted at them angrily, and then addressed Kamina in her distinct form of Amarosian. "You, you wills ride with me. The firentazme can walks." Kamina slung Ascara over her back, and cautiously followed the zharie to her animal. The young woman elegantly flipped onto its tough hide, grabbing the reigns. The creature's head swivelled round, staring at the small elf with dark eyes that were buried in a layer of wrinkled, grey skin. Kamina gently patted the animal.

"What is it?" she asked.

"This is Zane, he is rhenzo. Very loyals, but also is dangerous, yes?" The strange creature snorted suddenly, causing Kamina to jump back in fright. Jazintha laughed at her without hesitation or shame. "He will not hurts you," she said, adding, "unless I commands him to. Now, if you are done admiring our animals, we will leaves."

Kaedin tried to frighten the rhenzo as he had the horses in Tilden, but Zane did not seem to mind the spirit, or even acknowledge him. Kamina clambered on board Zane's back behind the jungle zharie, who watched the elf's inelegant effort with a smirk. Behind them, the other men wrapped the dead reptilian monster in vines, tying them to a herd of rhenzos. They soon set off, Kamina and her warrior princess leading the way, Kaedin pacing by their side, as the men proudly dragged their kill through the jungle.

CHAPTER TWENTY-SIX

THE CITADEL OF ZATHARU

Little was said on the languid journey through the dense Jalenari jungle. Kamina sensed her uneasy companion wished to ride ahead in order to present the elves to her father, but Jazintha would not leave her men to drag their slayed conquest alone.

"You are not of mens," said Jazintha, breaking the silence.

"No, I am elf kind," explained Kamina, "from the forest of Elgrin."

"And this one? Kaedin? What is hims?"

"Complicated," replied Kamina eventually.

"How dids he becomes... firentazme?" asked Jazintha.

"That is also complicated," Kamina said, not wishing to explain about the spirit until she had an audience with the Khan himself. Jazintha seemed to understand this, and stopped asking questions.

They paused for a moment on a ridge so that the men could tighten the vines around the rhenzos' horns. The view from the vantage point was breathtaking, the exotic jungle stretching out like a sea of green. Flocks of colourful birds soared above the canopy, watched by other animals hanging from the treetops. In the near distance, a large island of buildings rose up from the ocean of trees, separated by a giant wall that stretched around the entire perimeter of the citadel.

"Zatharu," announced the zharie, answering Kamina's eager gaze. It was a sprawl of architecture unlike anything the elves had recently glimpsed in Calisto. Zatharu appeared to be ten times the size of the Amarosian seaport, if not more. From this distance the buildings nearest the outer wall looked as though they had been hastily stacked on top of one another in a jumbled mess. Those nearer the centre appeared far grander, with many large pyramid structures of note on the gentle slope of the hill the citadel was centred around. Amassed on the central peak, lording over all of Zatharu, was the palace of Zahyr Zaleed Khan. It was decorated by glittering golden domes, held up by pillars and walls of the purest white, blinding in the light of the twin suns. The palace shared the crest with a taller, less attractive edifice, constructed from the ancient stone of the hill itself, graced by thin clouds as it spiralled up into the sky.

"It is incredible," said Kamina, unable to hide her expression of awe.

The troop of rhenzos descended along the trail that zigzagged down the ridge. They met a well-beaten path that cut through the jungle, all the way to the impenetrable walls of Zatharu that protected its citizens from the savage wildlife roaming beyond. A spotter shouted down to the sentries that manned the gate. They heaved at a mechanism that slowly dragged the stone slabs apart.

Jazintha led her pack through, her head held high, proud of her trophy prize. Swarms of Zalestians surrounded them, offering praise to the zharie, marvelling at the monster her men hauled through the gates. Kamina noticed Jazintha scanning the masses in anticipation of spotting someone in particular, but whoever it was had chosen not to greet them.

The citizens' astonishment quickly soured into apprehension as they caught sight of Kaedin. Like Kamina, the spirit had been so in awe of Zatharu that he had forgotten to cloak himself. Jazintha offered soothing words to them in her native tongue, which were lost on the elves, but they understood the sentiment from her lenitive body language. The crowd quietened a little, still showing signs of trepidation as Kaedin traipsed by. However, he did not deter the poorest of the population from begging to the citadel's most celebrated daughter. Many of them clambered near Zane, their hands shaped in bowls, imitating food. The zharie reached into one of the supply sacks that hung from her saddle and threw them whatever she had not eaten during the hunt. The beggars' hands fought in the air to catch even a scrap. Kamina heard Jazintha mumble an apology of some kind to them, but it was lost amidst the clashing of human scavengers.

"I tires of this," muttered the zharie, their path to the palace blocked by more people wishing to see either the dead lizard or the dead elf. "I hope your firentazme can keeps up." She yelled an order to Zane, jabbing her heels into his grey hide. The rhenzo rifled unforgivingly through the crowds, who were quick to leap out the way or else end up as a bloody afterthought on his sharp horn. Kaedin gave chase, cloaking himself to avoid any further hysteria.

Zane galloped up the hill, passing another fortified wall that surrounded the upper level of the city. Masses of Zalestians still swarmed the streets, parting like water around the rhenzo's bulk when he approached. The buildings beyond this inner wall were more distinguished and majestic in their design and décor. The people here were not draped in dirty rags, but dressed in fine coloured silks that dazzled Kamina's eyes.

Further towards the central peak, they passed a large structure with an open courtyard. Kamina mistook it for a school, until she realised the children within the compound, younger than herself, were practising military formations, brandishing a wealth of weaponry.

"The new armies of Zalestia," Jazintha explained when Kamina pointed. "My father has decreed every Zalestian womans must bless him with ten childrens for the wars."

"But they are so young," said Kamina, horrified. "And there are girls?"

"You is a girl," Jazintha pointed out.

"But I..." Kamina started to protest. She was about to say she did not have a choice, but she had made her choice in Calisto. "How do they fight if they have to mother all these children?" she eventually asked.

"A Zalestian womens manages. No lazy like Amaros cows. Father has specials troop. Hazzarin. Only female. Special trained. As quiet as firentazme, but deadlier. All womens aspire to be them."

"Are you one?" Kamina inquired, only to be met with more ridiculing laughter.

"I am zharie. Must be seen. Hazzarin, never seen."

They followed the path that wrapped around the upper echelons of the citadel, picking up pace until they arrived at the palace. Jazintha guided the rhenzo to a small paddock, where a few of Zane's companions roamed. She whispered some tender sounding words into the creature's twitching ear after they dismounted. It reminded Kamina of the little messages of comfort she used to whisper to Eshtel.

She wondered if he had ever understood her.

Zane was led away by Ozbie Zaul, the heavily-scarred paddock master, while Kamina followed Jazintha through the exotic gardens to the grand front entrance.

"Kaedin?" whispered Kamina.

"I am here," he whispered. "Barely. The rhenzo was fast."

Four ceremonial guards, known as zat-ash-ra, stood to attention at the entrance of the palace. They wore a distinguished, official cream uniform with bulbous helmets. As one they saluted their zharie, but froze as they spotted Kamina, Ascara's hilt jutting out behind her shoulder. Jazintha intervened as they reached for the scimitars hanging from their belts. The elves listened to the heated exchange of incomprehensible Zalestian words, but from their actions, it appeared the za-tash-ra were winning. Jazintha melodramatically threw her hands up in the air, and turned back to Kamina.

"They says before you enters palace and be grants audiences with Khan, you must gives up sword," explained the zharie.

"That was not what we agreed," said Kamina.

"These are za-tash-ra, mens loyal to my father. If you gives me sword they will allows us enter." Kamina glanced between the guards and began to suspect that Jazintha, who up until this moment had been denied nothing, was lying in order to claim the sword for herself.

"Did they say that, or did you?" she asked.

"It is ways it must be," asserted Jazintha. "No-one enters with weapon. You are stranger to me. You could be hazzarin sent by Amarosian heathens."

"We are not... hazzarin. The elves have nothing to do with the war."

"Yet you carries stolen sword!" exclaimed Jazintha.

"We did not steal Ascara," maintained Kamina. "It was gifted to us. To me."

"Ranger would nots gives his sword to child. The only reasons you breathe in Zalestia is that you holds his sword."

"I thought I was the reason," said Kaedin, standing beside her, invisible to her eyes.

"You cannots harm me!" she threatened. The za-tash-ra shifted slightly, uneasy that their zharie was conversing with thin air. "You are but a firentazme, echoes of what was. You are already deads, but you are just too stupids to believes it." Jazintha suddenly felt a cold sensation run all the way down her spine as Kaedin placed his ethereal hand on her arm.

"If we wanted to kill your father, we would not need a blade," said Kaedin. "I could simply reach into his body and stop his heart."

"Kaedin," hissed Kamina, her expression urging him not to pursue these dispiriting negotiating tactics any further. He released his ghostly grip on Jazintha's arm, leaving a cold, discoloured handprint on her skin. She rubbed at it, warming her skin until it had returned to a healthy shade of brown.

"Fine, you keeps stolen sword. And you," she spat at the invisible elf, "you keeps your hands to yourself." The failed ruse over, Jazintha barked a simple command, and the za-tash-ra stepped aside to allow the angry zharie and her companions entry into the heart of Zalestia. Once the zharie was out of sight, the za-tash-ra shrugged their shoulders at one another.

The entrance hall of the palace was large and airy. Wide diamond-shaped windows diffused the light over the white marble floor. The walls were draped with expensive tapestries of purples, blacks, scarlet and gold. On either side was an elegant fountain, where a few visitors to the palace sat and cooled. Two angular staircases jutted around the large ground floor entrance, meeting at a balcony above that led to the upper levels. At the bottom of each lay a large sabre-toothed cat, their golden fur decorated with distinctive black stripes. Jazintha fearlessly stroked one, the beast purring tenderly at her touch.

A scant looking servant girl appeared carrying a tray of tropical refreshments. As she approached the zharie, she felt herself shiver uncontrollably, dropping the platter. The servant girl let out a sharp scream as the food clattered upon the floor. Still tingling with humiliation at her failed attempt to secure the sword, Jazintha unleashed her fury on the girl, screaming at her in Zalestian.

"Kaedin? What did you do?" asked Kamina quietly.

"It was not my fault," he said. "I did not see her. She walked right through me."

Other attendants emerged, curious to see what had happened, although none were brave enough to rescue their fellow servant from Jazintha's verbal mauling. The wildcats padded over to the fallen food, lapping it up from the floor.

"Jazintha, it was Kaedin's fault," said Kamina. "She felt him as she walked through him." The zharie felt a pang of shame for her sharp remonstration of the servant, now cowering before her, hiding her face in her hands.

"Come," she said, leading the elves away from the humiliated servant girl. Kamina glanced back to see the girl being spirited away by her fellow servants.

From the balcony they walked along a triangular hallway. Any servants they met stopped to bow before the zharie as she graced past them. Jazintha turned into one of the rooms, leading them through a series of silk curtains into her private chambers, though it could easily have belonged to a man. Although the marble was touched with light reds and rose pinks, the room was decorated with trophies from Jazintha's triumphs as a hunter and warrior. Kamina was startled by a savage looking lizard, until she realised it was dead, and merely stuffed. Their host hooted a mocking chuckle.

"Make yourself at homes," she called out, disappearing behind a decorative folding screen. "We will have foods brought, helps yourself." Kamina felt slightly embarrassed as she watched Jazintha's clothes thrown over the dressing screen. She realised she had no idea where Kaedin was.

"Kaedin?" He did not answer. "You better not be spying."

"As if I would," he said, standing beside her. She could tell he was grinning at the possibility.

Two light-footed servant girls entered with a tray of succulent sliced fruits and freshly squeezed juice. Kamina was ravenous at the sight of the food, but waited until the servants had disappeared before devouring it, tantalising her tongue with unusual tastes. She washed it down with the sickly-sweet juice. With her thirst and hunger satisfied, Kamina wandered the room, despairing at the dead animals, but admiring some of the sculptures and vases on display. Beyond these, there were three pools built into the marble floor. The first two were filled with water, while the third was brimming with bubbling mud. Kamina leaned in closer, inspecting a large bubble as it expanded. It popped in her face. Gobs of dirt landed on the elf's cheeks, repulsed by the disgusting odour infesting her nostrils. She jumped back, wiping the mud off her face. Jazintha laughed behind her, now wrapped in an elegant white robe.

"You shoulds bathe in it," she joked. "It may adds some colour to chalky whites skin of yours."

"When will we see the Khan?" asked Kamina.

"He is awares of your presence, but my father is man of very busy. Besides, you cannot appears likes this before him." Kamina glanced down at herself; her Elgrin green clothes were ripped, muddied, burnt and bloodied. With two sharp claps of Jazintha's hands, the pair of servant girls reappeared. Kamina could not tell if they were twins, or if all the servants in the palace were forced to adopt the same facade. Jazintha issued them a command, and the duo approached Kamina.

"What are they doing?" asked the elf.

"It is surprise," said the zharie with a smile. "Allow thems to do job." Kamina stood relatively still as the two girls moved her limbs, marking her measurements with string. One of the servant girls, Zofi Fazar, addressed Kamina in her native tongue, while her sister Rozi continued to measure, but the elf was at a loss.

"Colourings?" translated Jazintha.

"Green," replied Kamina. She had always worn the colour of Elgrin.

After a brief exchange with Zofi, Jazintha asked "What shade?"

"I... do not know," answered Kamina.

Jazintha said something to the servant sisters, who both bowed and promptly departed. "They will makes something to matches your eyes," she explained. "Now, you must be cleans and beautifuls for the Khan. Come."

Jazintha invited her over to the mud bath. Large bubbles oozed out of slowly, the stench reminding Kamina of the swampland where they had encountered the Ogarii.

"Do nots be shy," teased the zharie as she shed her robe and stepped into the shallow mud bath. Kamina followed gingerly, shirking off her ripped rags and tiptoeing into the warm mud. Despite the smell, the elf found it remarkably relaxing. After a short while, Jazintha rose up, caked in mud, and made her way to the middle pool. She waded in one side and out of the other, leaving a trail of mud in her wake. She stepped into the third pool, steam rising off its surface, and sat down in the warm water.

"Do nots stay in mud too long," she shouted to Kamina. "Very bads." The elf followed in the zharie's footsteps, eventually splashing into a seat in the third pool, the water unbearably hot. Kamina's body acclimatised as the two servants appeared again, pouring perfumed oils and liquid into the pool that caused the water to foam up. They sprinkled bright flower petals over the foamy surface, leaving the zharie and her guest to relax. Jazintha picked up a ladle that lay by the pool. She dipped it into the water and carefully poured it over her hair, avoiding her face. Seeing no ladle by her side, Kamina submerged her head under the water, but sharply burst back up, the solution stinging her eyes.

"Do not rubs it," she heard Jazintha say. "It wills pass soon." When she could open her eyes without pain, Kamina once again relaxed, smoothing her wet hair back as Jazintha had, fully revealing her elven features; her pointed ears, her porcelain face and her sparking green eyes.

"The ranger said elves were beautiful," said Jazintha. "He was rights."

"Callaghan said that?" asked Kamina, slightly surprised that any human would offer a compliment about her race, even a ranger.

"I did nots believe him," continued Jazintha. "The Zalestian zeetoo, the soldiers, I have heards them talk sometimes of Amarosian cows. They say they are poor and pale compares to Zalestian colour."

"I heard the men of Tilden talk of a princess," said Kamina, "a zharie of Hylan, Princess Fyora Aregya Arthadian. They say she had skin as white as purest snow, hair as red as Risaar's fire, and eyes as blue as the clearest sky. How is that for colour?"

Jazintha sneered at the elf's riposte, turning her attentions to Kaedin, who was visible now that the servants had left. The spirit was oblivious to the bathing girls' verbal spat, staring out of the open balcony at the marvel of Zatharu below.

"What say you, firentazme?" she asked "You are male. Who is more attractives? Me, or your Amarosian princesses?" Kaedin's thoughts were drawn to memories of Nyssa, but before he could share them, he heard someone sneak into the room. On instinct, he vanished into thin air.

Kamina spotted the culprit first; a young boy spying on them from behind a vase sat on a pedestal, his curious eyes catching Kamina's.

"Hello," she said.

"Raztan, my brother, but we calls him Zutee. What is it, little kharie?" teased Jazintha. "Did you come to spies on naked elf? You seems to have colour on your cheeks now," said Jazintha as Kamina blushed.

"Father is ready to see you," said her inquisitive brother. "He will not be pleased that you have an Amarosian with you."

"Get out of my chambers!" yelled Jazintha, startling Zutee. In his rush to escape he knocked the pedestal forward. The vase tipped over and tumbled to the floor. Against all laws of gravity, it suddenly stopped in mid-air. Kaedin appeared now, holding the vase in his ghostly hands, shocking Zutee. He flashed a cocky grin at the young kharie, but his ostentation was short-lived. The twin servants promptly returned after hearing Jazintha's screams. Kaedin cloaked himself, losing his tangible grip on the vase. It dropped from his invisible hands and smashed into pieces.

"Stay there, Zutee!" Jazintha commanded. "You will come with us and explain to father why you broke his vase."

"But it was... it was..." protested Zutee, but in vain. Zofi and Rozi brought soft, thick robes to the zharie and her guest. Kamina followed Jazintha's lead and stepped out of the bath, Rozi wrapping her up tight.

"We will prepare to meet the Khan," Jazintha said, leading her to a seat. The servant girls sat opposite them, armed with a box of beautification; a palette of a thousand shades which the twins painted upon Jazintha and Kamina's faces. When they were finished, they held a mirror up for Jazintha, and then Kamina. The zharie made little attempt to mask her amusement. Kamina could also hear Kaedin sniggering somewhere nearby.

"What is so funny?" fumed Kamina.

"Come, my painted elf," said Jazintha. "The Khan awaits."

CHAPTER TWENTY-SEVEN
THE RELICS OF ZOREN

K AMINA FOLLOWED JAZINTHA AND TWO ZA-TASH-RA BACK ALONG the corridor to the lobby, her face caked in colourful make-up. She wore an emerald green outfit crafted from Zalestian silk, hastily stitched together by the Zofar sisters. The zharie dragged along her misbehaving brother, whose head cocked around as he looked for signs of Kaedin's spirit. Once or twice he was sure he saw something, as if the air was rippling and contorting in the shape of an elf.

They descended down into an airy chamber filled with columns. Each one took on the form of a Zalestian god; some appeared human, while others were carved in the forms of animals or demons. The walls were etched with scenes from the country's myths and legends, broken only by a series of small diamond-shaped windows. Kamina gazed up at the ceiling and discovered a colourful collage that seemed to stretch forever, a clever trick of the eye employed by the artist. It reminded her of the council chambers in Calisto, although she imagined the councillors and citizens there would contest the beauty of this piece as little more than blasphemy.

They eventually reached the opposite end, sweeping through a triangular archway into a long throne room. The imposing ruby red walls were offset by the dazzling gold ornaments and silk tapestries. At the far end was a raised platform, upon which rest the throne of Zatharu. The ceremonial seat was a fusion of stone and gold, swathed with crimson cushions, while the armrests were decorated by oversized ivory rhenzo horns arcing out to the sides.

Zahyr Zaleed Khan sprawled over the throne, his bulky frame draped in the finest golden silks. His thick neck was swathed with jewellery, while nearly all of his fingers were embellished with glittering rings. His black, dreadlocked hair overflowed from a golden crown band, encrusted with rare stones and jewels, with pieces of ivory and bone jutting out around the top.

"I see the rumours floating around my palace are true," he bellowed in heavily accented Amarosian, as the za-tash-ra led the party inside. "Our enemies invade our shores, and yet my daughter decides to take them in like another of her pets." An older soldier with a shaved head stood near the throne platform, smirking as Zahyr spoke. The movement caused his black goatee beard to rise, highlighting the curl of a scar the beard failed to hide.

"Father..." started Zutee, but his older sister shoved him behind her, silencing him. Kamina caught a flash of movement in the corner of her eye.

There were other soldiers in here besides the za-tash-ra. These were the Khan's private guards, the skado, who managed to blend into their surroundings and shirk off any undue attentions. Their robes covered everything but their eyes, and Kamina could not tell if they were men or women, merely shadows.

"There had better be an explanation why you did not slaughter this… thing on sight," warned Zahyr, snapping Kamina's attentions back to the Khan.

"Father," said Jazintha, bowing before him, "I presents you Kamina Elloeth, elf kind of Amaros." The zharie glared behind her at Kamina, until she took the hint and also bowed. "She carries with hers the sword of Ishkava Ranger Callaghan Tor, but she insisting on telling you story first."

"Show me the sword," ordered the Khan. Kamina very slowly removed Ascara from her scabbard, all too aware of the eyes of the various skado upon her. "Bring it to me," he commanded. She stepped towards the throne, but found her way blocked by the bald soldier, Armin Zool, Mazban of the armies of Zatharu. Kamina begrudgingly gave it up to the stranger, who swiftly ascended the steps to the throne and presented the blade of Risaar to Zahyr. He weighed the weapon in his hand, and found it perfectly balanced, enjoying the texture of the handle in his grip.

"Father…" tried Zutee again.

"Silence, Raztan!" The young prince knew to be quiet when his father used his real name, which he shared with Zahyr's slain brother. "How did you come to possess such a weapon?"

"It was given to me by Callaghan," she replied. "He asked me to seek you out in the hope that you would help me."

"And why would I help a thief?" quizzed Zahyr, rising from his throne.

"I am not a thief," said Kamina weakly, unsure of the dark turn the conversation was taking.

"Father," said Jazintha in protest, but he silenced her with a wave of his mighty hand. He descended the steps, joining them on the floor, his fingers wrapped tighter around Ascara's handle.

"The ranger would not give his prized sword to a child, let alone an elven one." Kamina's face betrayed her surprise. "Oh I know what you are," continued Zahyr. "Callaghan and I talked at length about his country's history. So why would an elf wander beyond her precious forest, over her pathetic country, and across the great ocean? Were you banished for stealing the sword? Or did you flee Amaros to escape the ranger's wrath?" Zahyr held Ascara's hilt in his hands, her blade intimidatingly close to Kamina.

"We had no choice," Kamina said.

"We?" said Zahyr.

"We, said Kaedin, choosing now to appear beside her. Zutee and Armin Zool both gasped, but Zahyr was unimpressed.

"News of your existence also reached my ears, firentazme," said the Khan.

"I assume there is a good reason why you did not mention this phantom to me sooner, Jazintha?"

"I tried to tell you!" exclaimed Zutee.

"I know, my son. Skado, seize them both. They will be executed as enemies of the great nation of Zalestia!" The shadowy guards surrounded the pair, ready to attack. Kaedin poised himself to retaliate, even if that meant turning them into ætherghouls.

"Kaedin, no," hissed Kamina. She had not travelled halfway across Enara, having lost so many friends along the way, only to fail through diplomacy. She remembered the story that the teacher had told them, how the war had begun through violence and pride. Not wishing to let history repeat itself, Kamina addressed the situation with humility. "Please, Zaleed Khan!" begged the young elf. "Let us explain."

"Skado," he commanded again. His men were fearful of the firentazme, but even more afraid of the Khan's wrath. They edged towards the elves with their scimitars raised. Kamina desperately decided she had to reveal everything to the ruler, or else they would end up doing Malenek's work for them by unleashing the ætherghouls on Zalestia.

"Please, we were sent here by Callaghan to find the Stone of Spirits. It is hidden in the tomb of Errazure!"

"Wait!" ordered Zahyr. His men stepped back, weapons still raised. "What do you know of Errazure's tomb?"

"Call off your men and I will explain everything," she said.

"Why should I believe you?" he asked.

"Father, the firentazme could kill us all," said Jazintha, "but he has not, even when you threaten them." Zahyr eyed Kaedin with disdain and fear, but nodded. His guards stood at ease.

"Now, elf child, tell me everything you know of Errazure."

Kamina told Zahyr everything, from Lord Malenek's creation of the spirit army to the death of Jaelyn at her hands. However, she was vigilant enough to omit exactly how the spirits had been brought forth from beyond the grave.

"Jaelyn is dead? At your hand?" inquired Zahyr, almost impressed. Kamina nodded in reply. "And he was a practitioner of magics?"

"Yes. He used his powers to trick his way into becoming the ranger's chosen apprentice. Callaghan overheard him conspiring with Lord Malenek, saying the only thing that could stop them was the Stone of Spirits, which was hidden in the tomb of Errazure, somewhere in the deserts of Zalestia."

"Then where is Callaghan? Why has he sent a child to tell me this?"

"Callaghan is dead," Kaedin said eventually, after it became evident Kamina could not bring herself to utter the words. "Our ship was attacked in the Badlands, and Callaghan perished along with the crew."

"And you say Malenek has an army of these vengeance spirits at his command?" asked Zahyr. "What makes them so dangerous if all they can do is walk through walls? Excellent spies yes, but soldiers, no."

"That is not all we can do. We can reach inside a man, see his thoughts, or snap his soul from his body, a prisoner of the flesh."

"Interesting," said Zahyr, more intrigued than apprehensive. Jazintha, still in shock from the news of Callaghan's death, eyed the spirit warily.

"No, it is not. There are consequences," added Kaedin. "The soul is trapped, unable to escape to the afterlife, but the body turns into a monster." Zahyr contemplated Kaedin's words, glancing down at Ascara.

"Show me," he demanded finally, signalling two of his skado, who fled the throne room. They returned moments later, dragging a scraggly prisoner with them, his hands bound in a mass of sharp, metal chains. They rattled as he wrestled in vain to break free from his captors.

"I... I cannot," said Kaedin, as it dawned on the spirit what the Khan expected him to do.

"And yet you claim otherwise," stated Zahyr.

"The monsters, the ætherghouls, they are dangerous," said Kamina.

"I have a room full of skado, my finest soldiers! If you want my help in finding the stone of which you speak, you will show me that this threat is real." Kaedin looked down at the prisoner, whimpering and pleading with his eyes. "Do not pity this man," said Zahyr. "He is a criminal, a miscreant. He will die regardless, whether you do this or not."

"It is a fate no man deserves," said Kaedin, recalling the face of Slavek Isten, the marauder he had accidenty transformed.

"As you wish," said Zahyr, raising Ascara up to decapitate the man.

"Wait!" said the spirit. He considered other options, but there was none. Kaedin stepped towards the prisoner, trembling in his ghostly presence.

"Kaedin, no," begged Kamina, but she knew there was no other choice.

"Tell your men to be ready," warned the spirit, turning to the forsaken captive. "I am so sorry," he whispered to the man, who did not understand the words. All he could see was the desperation in the whites of the man's eyes. Kaedin could not face him, looking away as his hand crept towards the criminal and softly slipped his fingers through his skin.

Zahyr gawked in astonishment as the man convulsed and shivered. With one wrench of Kaedin's arm, he snapped the soul from the man's body, trapping it inside. The prisoner collapsed in a fit, his dying screams mutating into morbid moans as the colour drained from his skin and his eyes turned a ghostly shade of white. Kaedin and Kamina retreated, as did most of the skado, while Zahyr watched the transformation in fascinated horror.

The Zalestian ætherghoul rose up, snarling and lashing out. It wrenched itself free from the metal bonds that had so easily restrained the prisoner. The Khan shouted commands at the skado, but they were petrified by the ætherghoul's screams. Zahyr barked again, backing away. His men complied, attacking the abomination with spears and scimitars, cutting into the flesh, but not enough to stop the creature. The ætherghoul snapped a spear out of its body, and leapt onto one of the skado, chewing off his face.

Zahyr screamed angrily in Zalestian, arcing Ascara down upon the creature. He attempted to decapitate the ætherghoul, but the blade wedged halfway through its spine. It clawed at Zahyr as he tried to free the sword. Armin Zool swiftly came to his Khan's aide, finishing what Zahyr had started with a handcrafted scimitar. The ætherghoul's head rolled away as the body crumpled to the ground. They heard the volatile shriek of the soul as it was freed from its short-lived prison, before it exploded in a cloud of ash. Those who had witnessed the event struggled to catch their breath. Jazintha knelt down to comfort Zutee, who cried in her arms.

"You say there is an army of those…?" Zahyr eventually asked. Both Kamina and Kaedin nodded, still traumatised by the ætherghoul's transformation. Kamina stared at her brother, disappointed that he could deliberately create one, while the ghost himself was overcome with remorse.

"Come with me," said the Khan. Accompanied by Mazban Zool and the skado, they were led out of the palace towards the structure that shared its peak, an ugly spire shaped from the mountain rock.

"This is the Tower of Zoren," explained Zahyr, as they entered through the natural cave doorway. "He was the first of my people. He carved this tower from the mountain itself, founding the great Zatharu." They passed through a smoothed tunnel into a single, giant chamber, one which stretched all the way up to the very top of the building. Platforms jutted out from the walls, held up by stalactites. In the centre of the room was a statue of Zoren himself, posed to look like a thinker and philosopher, a saviour and prophet. "He is my ancestor, descendant of the gods, founder of our civilisation. It was he who first heard the words of our Mother Goddess Gianna."

Zahyr led them up a spiral stone staircase that wrapped around the interior wall all the way to the top. They passed several women wearing similar robes of black and purple. "This was once home to the shamen, occultists, practitioners of magic, but after their banishment, the Zorento, the Sisters of Zoren, took over."

"They are priestesses?" asked Kamina.

"They communes with the gods and spreads their will from the Zirkesh," said Jazintha, making a triangle symbol with her hand. Kamina realised that the pyramid structures they had seen as they arrived were the Zalestian houses of worship.

"Why were the shamen banished?" asked Kaedin.

"You will soon see," replied Zahyr. As they neared the top, the Khan led them out onto a stone platform, held up by three giant stalactites. Several stumpy stalagmites rose up from the floor of the floating terrace, smoothed by hand in order to hold something in place.

"What do you see?" he asked them.

"Nothing," answered Kamina, wondering whether it was a trick question.

"Exactly. You asked me why the shamen were banished, little one. It was because they aided the Amarosians who first came to Zalestia, those who insulted our ways and massacred my people. The shamen helped them escape."

"Malenek," Kaedin whispered to Kamina.

"They were banished by my mother, Jada Zaleed Zhan, but before they were tossed out into the desert wastes of Darosa, they stole from us, hence why you see nothing."

"What did they steal?" Kamina asked. "What lay here?"

"This is where the shamen would worship the seven stone tablets of the Xe'rath. Each stone was etched by Zoren himself with the sacred words Gianna blessed upon his ears," said Zahyr, stalking around the seven outer stalagmites. "He carved them with our most precious treasure, the Jewel of Gianna, which the Mother Goddess imbued with her powers." The Khan's fingers graced the central column where the jewel had once rest. "I used to come here as a boy and watch it light the room as if it were alive. It was nothing short of exquisite, and I would do anything to have it returned."

"What does this have to do with the Stone of Spirits?" asked Kamina.

"The seventh stone, the Xe'rath zo Yann," said Zahyr, indicating one of the empty stalagmites, "roughly translates as the Stone of the Afterlife."

"The Stone of Spirits," said Kamina. "So Errazure, he was one of these shamen?" Zahyr clenched his fist, as the conversation dredged up some raw, bitter memories.

"Not one of. Errazure Ecko was the head shaman," said Mazban Zool, speaking only when it became evident the Khan would not. "After he and his disciples disappeared into the Darosa Desert, they were never seen nor heard from again."

"And the stones?" inquired Kaedin.

"I do not care for the slabs," said Zahyr, "but I have had my men scouring the desert for the Jewel of Gianna ever since I became Khan. Its loss was greatly felt in my family. I had hoped that its restoration would lead us to victory in our war with the Amarosians. But in all that time, not a trace of it has been found, although many have been lost to the gruzalugs, or worse, the firentazme."

"Your men called Kaedin that," said Kamina. "What is a firentazme?"

"Phantoms of the desert, clouds of sand that move like men," said Zahyr. "Their very touch drives a man mad."

"Ghosts of the desert," whispered the spirit.

"And gruzalugs?" asked Kamina.

"Snakes of the sands. Very large. I am afraid Callaghan has sent you on a *zamovrazda*; a mission of no return," declared Zahyr. "The only thing you will find in the Darosa Desert is your death."

"We have to try," said Kamina, remembering Callaghan's last words to them. "The lives of everyone in this world depend upon it."

"I admire your tenacity, young elf," said Zahyr. "If you are adamant about this suicidal trek into the desert, I will aid you with supplies and a lalaca. In exchange, I would ask that you bring me back the Jewel of Gianna, and I will allow you to keep the Xe'rath zo Yann."

"Agreed," said Kamina.

"I cannot give you any of my men though," warned Zahyr. "I have little to spare, and there are those who would rather be stoned to death than face the firentazme."

"Thank you, Zaleed Khan," said Kamina, attempting to bow. "I ask only one more thing?"

"Which is?"

"The return of Ascara."

"This I cannot grant you," he said, placing the sword on the stalagmite previously occupied by the Jewel of Gianna.

"Callaghan gave her the sword to protect, not you," urged Kaedin.

"The desert has already swallowed up one priceless jewel. I could not forgive myself if I were responsible for the loss of another. I will give you whatever weapons you can carry, but not this one. Now, you must be tired. I suggest you rest in the palace for the night and enjoy my hospitality. You can begin your journey at dawn, if common sense has still not taken hold of you."

They followed Zahyr back down the steps of the tower, Kamina eyeing Ascara before she left. As they descended, Jazintha pulled her back from the troop, pausing in a nook within the wall so they could speak in private.

"Is it trues what you saids?" she asked. "Is Callaghan really dead?"

"He died trying to defeat a dragon," the young elf said. Kamina could see the sadness well up in Jazintha's eyes, but the brave zharie quickly fought back any tears.

"He was a fine warrior, even for Amarosians," she said. "Comes, we will find you somewheres to sleep."

The little elf was already asleep by the time the twin suns began to set, exhausted from her arrival in Zalestia. She had been granted the use of a guest room near Jazintha's own chambers. The zharie knelt by her window and lit a triangular candle, mirroring the large pyramid of the goddess Gianna that she could glimpse in the city below. In the candlelight, she shed a single tear, and whispered a prayer for the fallen ranger who had captured her heart.

CHAPTER TWENTY-EIGHT
THE RANGER'S FATE

As Jazintha's candle mourning the loss of Callaghan was extinguished by a cruel morning breeze, the ranger regained consciousness upon a strange shore. His body ached beyond agony. His burnt clothes stuck to his bloodied skin, while the twin suns frazzled his eyes. His fingers twitched in the wet sand, trying to discern by touch if the grains were real, or if he had finally passed over into the warmth of Illyria.

Gentle waves lapped over his legs, slowly awakening his senses. Over the serene repetition of the surf, he heard several loud splashes further away. With considerable effort he leveraged himself up and looked out over the ocean. A giant shark reared its frightful body out of the water, basking in the air before splashing back down below the surface. The cold-blooded killing machine repeated the gesture a handful of times, as if in frustration from losing the ranger as a meal. Its black fin glided back into deeper waters to hunt for its next prey. Callaghan wondered just how close he had come to a grisly fate being gnashed in its jaws. Instead he had been deposited here, with no idea how. The last moments upon the *Arad Nor* were a vague blur. He remembered the scaly, horned face of the dragon cast in shadow. There were flashes of fire, and blood, and then water, and finally darkness.

Forcing himself to his feet, he staggered slightly while surveying his surroundings. The shallow sea was clustered with islands shaped like trees, with thick rocky trunks that burst into an island of life above. It was as if someone had taken the idea of islands as the Amarosian knew, and turned them upside down. He had not witnessed these marvels of nature on his previous voyage. From his limited knowledge of Zalestia, he assumed they were the Zofeefee Islands located south of the main continent. In the near distance, he saw a shape jutting out of the water. At first he thought it was a lone rock, but as he staggered closer, he recognised the hull of an Amarosian warship. The crustacean-covered corpse served as a lasting reminder of a failed mission in a relentless war.

The ranger realised he was inside rebel territory, far from Zatharu. The native Jalenari had shared what could best be described as an uneasy alliance with the Amarosian forces, although in truth it had been a strategy of dual ignorance, neither side opposing the other in their separate wars on Zatharu. However, the decision by the Alliance to retreat from Zalestia had sullied this stalemate, with bitterness turning to bloodshed. Callaghan had not helped the situation by stealing Jazintha back from her Jalenari kidnappers, during which he had been forced to take the lives of two men. He had to reach Zatharu as quickly as possible and avoid the rebels at all cost, but his most immediate concern was survival.

Callaghan clumsily crashed through the jungle, clutching his torso in anguish as he fought through the shade of the thick trees. He could hear animals calling to one another, rummaging around, scrambling up the surrounding trunks and branches, wary of his presence. He ignored them, focusing on the faint trickle of a small stream. He eventually found the source, collapsing to his knees as he drank the water from his cupped hands. He swallowed too fast, coughing it up. He sipped slower, offering Aquill a prayer in between. As he finished, he glanced at the rippling surface of the water and saw Kamina's reflection. He quickly spun round, but all he saw was the shade of the jungle. Callaghan rubbed his eyes, beginning to wonder if his lack of nourishment had made him delusional, worrying about the innocent elf he had brought on this reckless quest.

He spotted something in the direction his hallucination had appeared. Three Jalenari warriors, their bodies marked by tattoos and paint, cut their way through the foliage towards him. Callaghan slowly crawled backwards along the river until he came to a small overhang. He crept under it, and lay down in the stream of water while listening for the men. Their feet stomped above him, the tip of a spear hanging over the small brook. The ranger tried to interpret their words, but their accent was different from that he had learned in the citadel.

"I was sure I heard something," growled one.

"Probably just a lizosaur," said another.

Callaghan kept perfectly still, even when a large, poisonous insect scuttled along the ceiling of the overhang and onto his body. When it reached his hand, he batted it into the water, causing a small splash. The men were suddenly silent. The ranger realised the bloodstains from his clothes were washing off into the water, causing faint swirls of red to appear on the crystal clear surface.

Eventually they stalked off in another direction. Callaghan waited until he could no longer hear the crunch of the ground under their feet. He emerged from his hiding place, only to have the handle of a spear slammed into his face. Callaghan crashed into the water, but before he could pick himself up, the sharp end of the spear prodded his chest, forcing him to stay down. The Jalanari holding the weapon made a quick succession of whistles. His two companions soon returned, having left as a ruse to lure the ranger out. Callaghan's hand felt around the bottom of the stream for a rock to use as a weapon. He found one half buried in the riverbed, and wedged it out with his fingers.

"Look what I found," said the brutish spear holder, the largest of the three. "He's Amarosian."

"Not just any Amarosian," stated the second. From the taciturn stance of the man, Callaghan assumed the speaker was their leader. "This is Zahyr's white dog, the one that rescued the zharie." This new knowledge caused the brute to erupt with anger. He tossed his spear aside and grabbed Callaghan by the throat, hoisting him into the air. The ranger's feet dangled above the ground as he was slowly choked to death.

"You killed my brother!" his attacker grunted through gritted teeth.

"Xiljin, enough," commanded the second man. With his adversary distracted, Callaghan cracked the rock against his head. Xiljin staggered backwards, dropping the ranger. Callaghan clawed his way up the riverbank and tore through the jungle. The trio of Jalanari rebels gave chase. Xiljin recovered from his blow and hulked towards Callaghan, quickly gaining on the injured, exhausted ranger. Eventually the rebel brute thrust himself at Callaghan, crushing him between his own weight and a tree. The ranger drooped down to the jungle floor, where Xiljin pounded at him with fists of rage.

"Where is your fire sword now, white man?" he sneered, unleashing his bare knuckles upon Callaghan's face. The ranger could feel blood dripping from his nose and mouth, his vision blurred. He struggled to remain conscious.

"Do not kill him!" said the third rebel in protest, finally finding his voice, but their leader did nothing. "Hazkeer?" he continued to beg.

"Stop," ordered Hazkeer, their leader.

"I want my revenge!" snarled Xiljin.

"You shall have it my friend, in the arena. Ajarone, since you wish to delay this man's death, you can bind him and carry him back to the camp," Hazkeer said to the third man. As Callaghan felt his arms tied together with rope, he submitted to his shattered body and blacked out.

CHAPTER TWENTY-NINE
THE DAROSA DESERT

AFTER A TROUBLED NIGHT'S SLEEP, KAMINA WOKE BEFORE DAWN. She joined Kaedin to watch the sunrise, the spirit cursed to be forever awake. Risaar's reddish light hit the peaks of the palace before spreading over the citadel below, drawing away the shadow as if it were a blanket of silk. The dawn chorus of morning prayers sang out from the zirkesh nearby, the beautiful hymns of the Zorento sisterhood calling out to those who still slumbered.

The elves joined Jazintha for a breakfast feast of fruits, breads, and meats. Kamina filled her belly with them all in preparation for her quest. After her previous day's erratic behaviour, the zharie was being surprisingly helpful. She had dug out a map of the Darosa Desert region, although much of it remained unfinished, the artist having filled those large spaces with depictions of gods and monsters.

"It is said the deserts was once beautiful lands of endless jungle," recalled Jazintha, "until Azik, the God of Joy, betrayed the Mother Goddess and kills his father, Egoras. Azik burned the jungles until it was justs sands, endless sands, and turned the mens into firentazme. Gianna led an army against hims, and defeats him before he could burns it all. She could not kills her child, so she banished Azik to Haegor, where bad mens go after they is passing. Some says the entrance to Haegor is somewhere in Darosa, where Egoras perished."

"What are the firentazme?" asked Kaedin. "You said they were like me?"

"Yes. Same same, but differents. Hards to say." Jazintha struggled with her Amarosian, eventually settling on, "You see them, but not. Like dust." Kamina finished her breakfast, wrapping some of the food up in a tablecloth. "Come," said the zharie, "we will finds you a strong lalaca."

They wandered beyond the sleeping rhenzos in the paddock to a large stable. Held within its walls was a harem of lalacas, an animal that even Kamina considered ugly, like a deformed, hunchbacked horse, constantly chewing on its gums.

"Her name is Yaza," said Jazintha as she led the creature out of its stall.

"What in the name of the Elementals is that?" commented Kaedin.

"She is a lalaca," said Jazintha. "Not fast like rhenzos, but betters for desert trekking. Survivors." Like the horses in Tilden, Yaza caught a sense of Kaedin and backed away, baring a set of flat, yellowed teeth.

"Perhaps you should stay away from her," suggested Kamina.

"With pleasure," he murmured, withdrawing from the stables.

Jazintha helped Kamina up onto the tall animal. She also slung some supply bags over Yaza's back. "You must ration your foods and waterings," she warned the elf. "It not last long otherwise. Follows, I will leads you to the eastern gate."

The zharie left the stables and leapt upon an awaiting Zane. The rhenzo trotted off at a slow enough gallop for the lalaca to keep up. Zahyr Zaleed Khan greeted them at the entrance to the palace, his servants preparing his personal carriage, a britzka, pulled by two rhenzos.

"I wanted to wish you good luck, little elf," said the Khan. "I would accompany you to the gate, but I must join the Zorento at the Great Zirkesh of Gianna. Your presence here has caused concern among my subjects," he explained, eyeing Kaedin, who kept back from Yaza so as not to spook her. "I will appease them while you slip into the desert. I also wanted to give you this." He handed her a small Zalestian scimitar. "It is not Ascara, but it is a fine blade."

"Thank you, Zahyr Zaleed Khan," said Kamina, attempting the Zalestian salute. He smiled at her efforts, but it was a fleeting grin, wiped away by a heated look from Jazintha. They pressed forward, leaving Zahyr Zaleed Khan as he clambered into his britzka.

Kamina and Kaedin followed Jazintha down from the palace and through the streets of Zatharu. Many market stalls were being set up by the vendors, who paused to stare at the strange creatures from Amaros. They passed by a pyramid zirkesh, smaller than the central one dedicated to Gianna, belonging to one of the other gods. Some of the more stringent citizens had already gathered outside to attend morning prayer. Beyond that patches of farmland prevailed; even in the searing heat, the Zalestians managed to grow giant, juicy vegetables.

Eventually they reached the double walls that marked the edge of the citadel, watched over by the soldiers in an adjacent zeetoo barracks. All the men and women were standing at attention for the zharie. A high-ranking zaydani barked an order at a group of malnourished soldiers. As Kamina approached on the lalaca, they started to work a wheel. The portcullis of the first wall rattled as it was raised, clanging to a halt. The zeetoo moved past the inner wall and unbarred the heavy stone doors blocking the outer wall. The zeetoo pulled these doors apart, shaking the sand from their surface. Kamina peered through the open doorways into the barren waste of the desert beyond. The first glimpse of the Darosa Desert dried her mouth immediately, the exact opposite of the lush, glistening ocean she had sailed to get here.

"According to father," said Jazintha, manoeuvring Zane alongside Yaza, "Errazure left this gates and continued east, but the deserts is very large, very large indeed. My father hads men search for the Jewel of Gianna, but firentazme scares them away. I do not thinks it wishes to be found." As the elf met the zharie's eyes, she saw they were laced with trepidation. "Good lucks,

Kamina Elloeth. I fears you will needs it." Kamina nodded, sharing her anxiety. The day before they had faced each other in a brief duel in the jungle. Now it was almost as if they were friends.

"Thank you, Jazintha Zaleed Zharie," said Kamina, attempting to bow, which was impossible on the lalaca. Both smiled at the effort, breaking the awkward goodbye.

"There is no shames in returning empty hands," added Jazintha.

"It is not a matter of pride," said Kamina. "I know you do not believe it, but the fate of Enara, of both your home and mine, depends on our success." Kamina nudged Yaza with her feet. The lalaca slowly wandered beyond the safety of the walls, into the blustery breeze of the Darosa Desert.

"You better look after her, firentazme!" Jazintha yelled at Kaedin as the doors closed and the portcullis dropped. He nodded, and then walked straight through the metal and stone, causing the zeetoo to gasp.

As the day stretched on and hours wilted by, the concentrated heat from Risaar and Aquill seared Kamina's skin. She wrapped a green scarf around her head to offer some shade, but even under the thin silk she felt as though her skin was melting. Yaza, on the other hand, did not seem to notice the heat, plodding onwards at a slow but steady pace.

"What I would not give to be bathing in the stream in Elgrin Forest," she said to Kaedin as she sucked on a skin of water.

"You did not mention Talia once to the Khan," said Kaedin. Ferocity laced his words, the thought having been swirling in his mind since the prior evening.

"I thought it best not to," she replied. "They would not have cared about a personal quest. They needed to know the world was in danger."

"It is not the world you are trying to save," he muttered. "You do this for your own selfish reasons."

"Selfish? I do this to save my mother! Your sister! What is wrong with you?" she demanded.

"Nothing," he grumbled.

"You are not the one that has to suffer this intense heat, sand in your eyes, and a constant thirst…"

"I would give anything to feel the heat of the sun again!" he fired back.

"And I am trying to make that happen, so that you can fulfil your destiny and become a great and mighty ranger!" snapped Kamina, the wind wailing around them.

"And what if the Stone of Spirits cannot restore me?" he posed. "Or Talia? What if we can never be what we were before? What if saving the world means she has to die?"

"You mean what if saving the world means the spirits have to die?"

"Yes!" he admitted.

"Now who is being selfish?" she retorted.

"I am trying to prepare you for the fact that we may never see Talia again," he reasoned after regaining his temper. "That you may never see me again. That it will be your choice, and yours alone, to make."

"You think I do not know that?" she said rhetorically. "You think I am not old enough to know what the consequences might be?" Kaedin stopped listening, as the ground started to shake. "I wish our positions were reversed," continued Kamina, "so that you could feel the weight of Enara upon your shoulders!"

"Kamina, quiet!" She too now felt the quaking of the ground. Yaza started to struggle against her directions. The elf tried to calm her with soothing words in a tongue the animal did not recognise or understand. The shuddering stopped, replaced by a rushing whoosh, but there was nothing around them to cause the sound, except for the sand of an empty desert.

"What was that?" Kamina asked.

Suddenly a fiendish beast burst from the ground. Through the cloud of sand Kamina caught sight of what looked like a snake, but larger and more ferocious, with a ghastly series of intricate mouths and hard plates for skin. It dived back into the sand, quickly wriggling down under the surface.

"What in the name of Ygrain was that?" whispered Kaedin.

"I do not..." started Kamina, but the creature launched out of the sand again, catching Yaza in its mouth. The blow knocked Kamina from the saddle. She landed on the sand with a thud. She turned to hear the horrible cry of the lalaca as she was dragged deep underground by the snake-like menace. She bleated her last breath, her legs flailing as she was viciously wrenched under the surface. Kamina leapt to her feet, dusting the sand from her robes. Kaedin joined her, standing back-to-back, anticipating another attack from the desert menace.

"Where is your sword?" he hissed.

"It was with Yaza," she replied in a hushed tone.

"Hopefully that thing will swallow it and cut itself open," he said, scanning the desert floor. They could see the top layer of sand shift as the mysterious creature circled them. It broke through the ground again. Kamina sprinted away from the clutches of its jaws, striding up a nearby dune, Kaedin following her. He saw the sand moving behind them, the snake swimming through the ground below faster than they could run above. It surged out of the sand, its wide jaws ready to devour the little elf. Kaedin stepped in front of her, but there was little protection he could offer.

The sound of another animal drew near. Jazintha, riding fast on Zane, screamed a war cry at the snake as they bound over the dune. The rhenzo launched himself into the air with his muscular little legs and impaled the beast with his horn. The creature writhed about on the sandy surface. Jazintha quickly leapt from Zane, stabbing her twin blades deep where the rhenzo's horn had punctured the armoured skin. She sliced it open, causing a foul stench as its oozing guts spilled out onto the baking sand.

"I may have forgots to warn you fully about gruzalugs," said Jazintha as she caught her breath.

"Forgot?" shouted Kaedin. "How do you forget that?"

"That?" said Jazintha dismissively, cleaning her blades of the gruzalug's innards. "That was baby. They usually keeps to northern deserts, pick off animals that wander from jungle."

"Your father said they were snakes!" he yelled.

"Very large snakes," she said calmly, echoing the Khan.

"It ate Yaza!" exclaimed Kamina.

"Larger dangers lie aheads," said the zharie. "If you cannots handles baby gruzalug, you should turn backs now."

Kamina glanced at the corpse of the creature, its rancid organs cooking in the twin suns. "No, we keep going," she said with an assertive tone. "But we have no weapons or water."

"Then I will joins you, to protects you," said Jazintha. "If Callaghan believed in plans so much that he was willing to dies for it, then I owes him that." She glanced back towards Zatharu. "Ah, refreshments."

Zofi and Rozi had followed their zharie on the back of another lalaca, a larger male. The twins stopped, and exchanged words with Jazintha in their native tongue.

"Zharie, you risk certain death by following these Amarosian fools," pleaded Zofi. The servant knew the zharie was likely to scold her for talking out of turn, but instead Jazintha smiled.

"I suspect the desert holds a kinder fate for me than at home with my father," she said with a sly grin.

*

On the balcony of the throne room overlooking his vast citadel, Zahyr Zaleed Khan gazed beyond Zatharu to the jungles of the north. Armin Zool was stood behind him, awaiting the wise words of his Khan.

"Will they be ready?" asked Zahyr, trying to resolve some inner turmoil.

"The latest tests have proven more successful," offered the mazban, "but they have also illuminated other problems."

"Then drag the inventor from his hole and have him fix it!" barked Zahyr. "If what the elves said is true, then now is the perfect time to strike."

"Zaleed Khan!" cried a za-tash-ra from within the room. Zahyr broke his stare from Zool to attend to this new call.

"I was not to be interrupted!" he bellowed at a pair of za-tash-ra, but his tone softened when he saw that Zutee was in their custody.

"Yes, Great Khan, but we found your son in the Tower Of Zoren."

"He is my son!" snapped Zahyr, ready to execute the man himself. "He may go where he pleases!"

"He was in the Cradle of the Xe'rath," replied the guard quickly. Not even Zahyr could ignore the severity of this claim.

"Is this true, Raztan?" asked the Khan.

"Yes, but..."

"Take him away," said Zahyr, turning his back on his son. "I will deal with this later."

"But father, it is gone!"

"Wait! What is gone?" he asked, although Zahyr already knew what the answer would be.

"The ranger's sword," replied Zutee. Zahyr's hands tensed up into fists.

"That... Where is my daughter?" The first za-tash-ra to catch the Khan's glare opened his mouth to respond, but without an adequate answer, no words came forth.

"We... we do not know, your majesty," stuttered the second za-tash-ra. The Khan tightened his fist and cracked the guard in the face, sending him sprawling across the marble of the throne room.

"What about you," growled Zahyr, looming over the remaining za-tash-ra.

"I believe the zharie travelled to the eastern gate, Great Khan, to bid farewell to the Amarosians. I do not believe she has returned."

"Nor will she, if she has any sense."

"Should I send some men after her?" asked Armin Zool, stepping in from the balcony. Zutee peered at him from behind his father, fearful of the dark aura the mazban exuded.

"No, there is no use. They will be deep within Darosa by now. We will deal with Jazintha when she returns. Focus on the task at hand. Once the contraption is ready, we shall use that to find them."

"Is that wise, my Khan?" questioned Zool.

"When we reach Amaros," declared Zahyr, "I want whatever worthless scum that has managed to survive the spirit army to see that sword in my hand. Is that understood, Mazban Zool?"

"Yes, my Khan." With a salute, Zool quickly marched away, leaving Zahyr to contemplate his only daughter's latest rebellious act.

*

Jazintha exchanged animals with her servants, Zane unable to stand the intense desert heat for very long. She kissed his grey face goodbye, and then mounted the male lalaca named Broza, helping Kamina clamber up beside her.

"I brought you a sword so you can better defend yourself," said Jazintha, nodding towards one of the saddlebags hanging down Broza's side. Kamina reached in and felt the familiar hilt of Ascara. She drew Callaghan's blade into the harsh light, the centre jewel sparkling at her, more alive now in the hot desert suns.

"You stole it," she said, slightly enamoured by the act.

"If Callaghan wished for you to haves it, my father should nots have any says in the matter," stated Jazintha with a shrewd smile.

"But I thought you wanted it for yourself?" quizzed Kamina.

"I only wished to keeps it from my father's graspings," revealed the zharie.

"You have a great respect for Callaghan, to place him above your father," said Kamina, returning Ascara to the bag.

"I do not see, what dids Callaghan say, eyes to eyes with the Khan on certain issues."

They journeyed on slowly, the lalaca trekking over the endless desert dunes. They came across a small oasis, and allowed Broza to drink while they refilled their own water supply. In the distance Kamina could see wild lalaca with shaggy hair. They wandered away, wary of their presence.

They rode for hours, every now and then passing by the remains of failed explorations that the sand had yet to cover; a post, a wheel, a rhenzo's skeleton. The temperature began to cool as the suns started to fade. As dusk descended over the Darosa Desert, something started to spook Broza.

"Kaedin, move further away from the lalaca," said Kamina. She glanced around, and found he was already quite far from the creature.

"Any further and I'll start fading," he shouted back.

"It is not him," said Jazintha with some urgency. "It is the firentazme." They scanned the desert, but saw nothing out of the ordinary.

Broza suddenly bucked hard, throwing Kamina off. She rolled down a steep sand dune. Jazintha tried to regain control of the lalaca, but he danced around in a frenzy. She hastily dismounted as Broza slid down the slope of the dune. He flipped over, landing awkwardly near Kamina. One of his gangly legs cracked while trying to stand. The male lalalca shrieked in pain. Jazintha did not have time to worry about him though, still scanning the sands for signs of the firentazme that had agitated the lalaca. She spotted it, a cloud of sand, dancing in its own tight wind, almost the shape of a man, descending upon the fallen elf.

"Kamina!" yelled Jazintha. She dashed down the slope, but she was too far away to reach her in time. Even if she did, Jazintha was unsure how to fight the firentazme.

Kamina turned to find the vague form of a person looming above her. It was as if the creature was invisible, shown only in the sand that swirled around them. It reached out its arm towards her, more a cloud of sand than a limb, as a rasping windy sound escaped its mouth.

"Get your hands away from her!" growled Kaedin, launching a ghostly fist at its obscured sandy face. The thing released a high-pitched shriek that forced Kamina to cover her ears. Jazintha was also struck by the same sound, falling to the sand, struggling to focus as the screeching pierced her brain. Kaedin glared at the firentazme, his hand stuck in what looked like its head. The phantom's shrieks stopped abruptly, replaced by an ominous silence. The firentazme shook and then exploded in a burst of sand. Kaedin stared at his hand, wondering what had just happened.

His thoughts were interrupted by awful wails of pain from the lalaca. The trio made their way to where Broza lay, unable to stand on his fractured front leg despite his best efforts. He reminded her of Eshtel, wounded by the riverbank.

"Can we heal him?" asked Kamina. Jazintha withdrew one of her daggers in reply.

"I am sorry," she whispered, plunging the steel straight into Broza's heart, granting the animal a quick death.

"You did not have to do that!" screamed Kamina.

"He woulds not have survived," insisted the zharie solemnly. "Better now than days of agony. We will make sure his trek was not in vain." Jazintha squinted into the sky, Risaar and Aquill low on the horizon. "We will camp here," she told them. "The firentazme should not bother us with Kaedin protecting us. Build a fire."

"With what?" asked Kamina.

"Whatever you can find," Jazintha replied, as she started to skin the lalaca.

The pink haze of dusk was blotted out by the dark twilight. Kamina managed to construct a fire from some wood Kaedin had located with the aid of his ghostly glow. It had been the shield of a Zalestian soldier, his bony hand still clutching the handle.

"I wonder who he was?" asked Kamina after she had broken the sword from his grasp.

"Another spirit," murmured Kaedin, traipsing back to Jazintha. As Kamina finished the fire, the zharie started to cut succulent slices of meat from the lalaca's bones. Realising she had no way to light the fire, the elf's eyes fell upon Ascara, the magic within the jewel glowing a deep red in the darkness of the desert night. Kamina made sure Jazintha was not within range of her voice, before she whispered the incantation.

"Acsentio Risaar Emanos."

Nothing happened. Not even a spark.

Kamina tried again.

"Acsentio Risaar Emanos," she repeated, louder and more forceful, but the result was disappointingly the same. Jazintha spotted Kamina, and guessed what she was attempting to do.

"Only ranger can commands Ascara's flame," she said, chuckling to herself as she cut a handful of Broza's short hair.

"Then how are we meant to start the fire?" blurted Kamina.

"Like this," said the zharie. She took a flat piece of wood and cut out a small divot, into which she placed the lalaca hair. She then fit a smaller stick into the divot perpendicular to the first, the hair caught underneath. She rolled it rapidly in her hands until a tiny track of smoke trailed off. With little effort, Jazintha manage to call forth a small spark of fire. She carefully positioned the wood under the pile Kamina had built, billowing the flame with her breath.

They were soon warming themselves by a healthy fire. Once it was hot enough, Jazintha balanced Ascara across some of the white hot embers separated from the flames, and lay the lalaca meat upon the weapon. She sat in the sand as they listened to the meat slowly sizzle.

"I doubt Callaghan would have approved of using Ascara like this," said Kamina.

"It was he who show me hows when he was lasts in Zalestia," she revealed. "Her blade is immunes to fire." Jazintha continued to cook, occasionally turning the meat over. Kamina's stomach growled now she could see the strips of half-cooked lalaca meat, crackling and spluttering in the heat.

"How did you come to meet him?" inquired Kamina, trying to stave off the thoughts of hunger.

"I had been taken, kidnaps by Jalenari rebels of the south. Savages!" she hissed. "As fates would haves it, Callaghan had journeys to Zalestia in search of apprentice. The Khan would have imprisons him, or executed him, but Ishkava Rangers are famous even here, some have foughts against the Zalestian armies, foughts well. My father made a deal with Callaghan. He could have a Zalestian as apprentice if he rescues me."

Jazintha rose up and brandished her daggers. "He stormed rebels' camp, stole me froms their clutchings, killing any who gots in his path!" The zharie acted out the scene, swishing her daggers through the air. "We spent days in jungles, avoids the rebels that hunted us, setting traps together." Jazintha hung on the last word longer than the rest, and it was clear to Kamina that while he had freed her from the rebels, Callaghan had captured the heart of the zharie.

"When we returns to Zatharu," continued Jazintha, "my father held contests to finds the bravest Zalestian that would be the ranger's apprentice."

"And he chose Jaelyn," added Kamina.

"Jaelyn was worthy warrior," said Jazintha, "although it is clear nows that he deceived us with poisonous magics." Kamina wondered what Jaelyn had found in the desert, what had driven him to seek out an elf on the other side of Enara. She remembered his face as she had buried the tree axe in his chest, how he had fallen next to Kaedin's body. Kamina turned to her spirit for comfort.

"Kaedin?" she asked. Kaedin was consumed by his own thoughts, fixated upon the flames of the fire dancing in the twilight.

"Yes?" he said, turning to her as if in a trance.

"When you touched the mind of the firentazme, did you see anything?"

"Fire," he muttered in reply. "And death. That was all." Kamina wished to find out more, but from Kaedin's morose expression it was clear that whatever he had witnessed had frightened him. She left him to reflect on the flashes of thoughts stolen from the firentazme.

Kaedin continued to stare into the flames while his corporeal companions satisfied their stomachs, devouring the cooked lalaca meat. He grew bored, scouting around the camp for more firentazme as the girls curled up to sleep beside the dying fire. Kamina's bright green eyes watched the last of the embers fade into the darkness. She squeezed her body up in a ball, shivering in the deep chill of the desert, unable to comprehend how one place could be so hot during the day and yet so cold at night.

"Are you colds?" asked Jazintha, wrapped in the lalaca skin she had cut earlier. Kamina nodded. "Come and share this with me," she said, indicating the skin. "It stinks, but you wills be warms at least."

"I am fine," lied Kamina, turning to face the other way. She heard Jazintha move, and was surprised when the zharie nestled up beside her, draping the lalaca skin over them both.

"Do nots be embarrassed," whispered Jazintha. "The desert can be a cold place at nights. It is betters if we share warmth, and keeps us from Death's reach." Jazintha wrapped her arms around the little elf, embracing her in a friendly hug. Given all that had occurred recently, Kamina welcomed the affection, but even still, she kept Ascara clutched tight to her chest.

CHAPTER THIRTY
THE KINDNESS OF REBELS

CALLAGHAN AWOKE IN THE DEAD OF NIGHT INSIDE A SMALL HUT. A flimsy piece of canvas hung from the entrance like a makeshift door, flapping in the breeze. He was lying on a hard wooden bed, his torso naked, his wounds cleaned and dressed. He could smell a strange ointment that had been rubbed over his burnt skin. The ranger tried to move, but found his wrists restrained by rope. He tensed his arms and tried to break the bonds with sheer might, but they were unyielding, his strength not yet recovered. His clattering caused one of the trio that had captured him, the one named Ajarone, to check up on him.

"I see you are finally awake," said the Zalestian, carrying a pot of water. "You have slept all day. Do not move around so much, you will reopen the wounds." Ajarone dipped a ladle into the water, and brought it to Callaghan's parched lips.

"Thank you," he murmured.

"Do not thank me just yet," replied the rebel. "I was ordered to keep you alive until Hazkeer decides what to do with you."

"Hazkeer is your leader?" Callaghan asked.

"He speaks for all of us, so in the way you mean, yes."

"What other way would I mean?" inquired the ranger.

"That he is our ruler," replied Ajarone, "like your friend Zahyr, speaking to us, but never for us."

"I would ask you to send word to the Khan about my capture, but I believe I would be wasting my breath."

"You would be correct." Ajarone smiled, not from happiness, but from the ridiculousness of the ranger's request. His expression stiffened as he continued. "Zahyr Zaleed betrays our people, proclaiming himself a direct descendant of the gods while forcing his subjects to breed in order to replenish his armies."

"You do not believe in the war?" asked Callaghan, his throat dry.

"The jungle tribes had it thrust upon them," explained Ajarone, feeding him more water. "Either Zahyr's men hunted us down and forced us to fight for him, or your kind invaded our shores and cut us down without distinction, without questioning our beliefs and seeing they are different to those of the citadel."

"You speak Amarosian well," noted Callaghan. "Did the Amarosian army help you?"

"They used us while they helped themselves," rebutted Ajarone. "They could never have hoped to defeat Zaleed Khan while also fighting us."

"Nor you with them," said Callaghan.

"This may be true," conceded the Zalestian, "but when we needed them most, they abandoned us. Now we are worse off than before."

"Is that what you believe in then? Defeat?" challenged Callaghan. "Is that what sets you apart from Zatharu?"

"Better that than a thousand false gods. You have been there, yes?" Callaghan nodded. "Then you have seen the statues and murals and temples devoted to the deities. They are nothing but a creation of man. Gods, myths, legends, little more than a means to control us through fear of retribution."

"You have not yet answered my question," said the ranger.

"There are no gods, no Yannah or Haegor. Only life. Only now. We believe that one force connects all living things, a fusion of good and bad energies. Mana. If you are kind to people, you will receive good mana in return, but if you are evil to them, bad mana will be your undoing."

"This is similar to the beliefs of the Ishkava Rangers," said Callaghan.

"Then why did you kill two of our men when you raided our camp to save the zharie?" asked Ajarone, annoyed that Callaghan would dare try and forge a spiritual bond between them.

"Why did your people kidnap a helpless young woman?"

"Jazintha Zaleed is many things, but helpless is definitely not one of them."

"Agreed," said Callaghan, "but that still does not justify her kidnapping."

"I admit the decision was a mistake, but her father has stolen thousands of our wives and daughters for use as servants and slaves. We were presented with an opportunity to do the same, so he may share our pain. We were ready for a full reprisal, expecting him to send his entire army. Instead, he sent only you." Ajarone locked eyes with the ranger, who refused to look away.

Their staring match was broken by angry shouts from outside. Ajarone left the ranger to investigate. Through the slit of the canvas flap, Callaghan spied Ajarone arguing with Hazkeer and Xiljin, among others. From his posture, Callaghan believed Ajarone was defending him, but Xiljin was a mountain of fury, poking his angry face into Ajarone's. Hazkeer sided with Xiljin, who barged past Ajarone and into the hut, brandishing a large knife. Callaghan struggled, but with his arms tied up and his legs bound together, there was little he could do to defend himself.

"That's right," sneered Xiljin, "squirm like a coward." The rebel's tattooed arm lunged at Callaghan, grabbing the ranger's head and slamming it against the wall. Xiljin cut the ropes and thrust him down onto the hard floor. The rebel wrapped the rope around the ranger's neck, and then used it as a leash to drag him out into their camp. Callaghan could see little beyond the blur of the ground passing beneath him. The rebels chanted as the flames of torches licked his bare torso. He glanced up to see some sort of framework beyond Xiljin's bulk. As they neared the ranger realised it was a large, dome-shaped cage, possibly for keeping untamed lizosaurs or their winged counterparts, pterazachs. Xiljin dragged him inside and locked the gate, leaving him in the dirt. Callaghan picked himself up, but a foot kicked him back down.

Xiljin had locked himself inside with the ranger.

Howls of laughter erupted from all sides, as the rest of the rebels gathered around the perimeter of the cage.

"Stay down," snarled Xiljin. The crowd quietened as Hazkeer prepared to address them.

"A short time ago, two of our own were lost to this Amarosian…"

"Zahyr's mistress!" interrupted a joker, igniting more laughter.

"But the Mana has returned him to us, so that one of us may seek our revenge. Xiljin lost his brother Jamus to the ranger's blade, and now he will have his revenge."

On cue, a single scimitar was tossed into the centre of the cage. Xiljin quickly claimed the weapon for himself. Callaghan loosened his bindings and scrambled to the other side of the cage so he could speak to Hazkeer.

"You must stop this," urged Callaghan.

"Do you have any last words, ranger?" asked Hazkeer.

"I am on a mission that affects the lives of each and every one of you, and if you do not grant me my release, you are all in danger from a force far greater than the Khan's army." The mention of their enemy's name was met with boos and hisses from the crowd.

"Then you must defeat the man you face to win your freedom," shouted Hazkeer, with a nod to Xiljin. The armed rebel attacked the ranger. Callaghan dodged the fury-driven blade. Xiljin swung back with the hilt, catching the ranger in the face. Callaghan tasted the sandy soil as he stumbled to the ground. He glanced up to see the blade slicing down towards him. He rolled out of the way, the sword sweeping the air by his side.

Callaghan felt the discarded rope bindings by his hands. He gathered them up and wrapped the rough rope around his knuckles. Xiljin slashed at the air again and again, Callaghan jumping backwards to avoid the scimitar. The ranger knew that this would not last long, that Xiljin would eventually land a lucky blow or a fatal strike unless he managed to disarm him.

The ranger retreated until his back was against the cage. Xiljin brought the full weight of the sword down upon him. He did not manage to dodge it entirely, the blade grazing his arm before it struck the wood. Callaghan dashed a few paces, leapt onto the cage and jumped towards Xiljin. The ranger turned in mid-air, timing it so his foot thrust forward into the rebel's face. The brute howled as the blow caused him to stagger backwards. Callaghan landed on his feet and sprung up again, delivering his knee directly into Xiljin's jaw, jamming his tongue between his teeth. The rebel cried out in pain, but Callaghan's rope-hardened knuckles connected with his opponent's jaw, spraying blood and teeth upon the crowd. The jolt caused Xiljin's hand to spasm, dropping the sword. Callaghan swooped low and gathered it up. The giant Zalestian teetered back but still he did not fall. The ranger lashed out, his feet slamming into the side of Xiljin's shin until the gargantuan rebel fell to his knees.

Callaghan rose up with the scimitar in his hand. Blood flowed down his arm, trickling off his fingers into the dry sand. He circled around Xiljin until he was facing his opponent. Callaghan had the upper hand, the sword hovering by the rebel's thick neck. The spectators were silent now, fearful that they would lose another of their warriors. Before the rebel could climb to his feet, Callaghan slammed the butt of the sword into Xiljin's throat. He fell backwards, writhing on the ground, gasping for air. He was defeated, but alive, his pride receiving the greatest blow.

"I have spared your man!" announced Callaghan. "Now free me."

"I admire your mercy, Amarosian," said Hazkeer, "but our beliefs require the balance of energies to be readdressed. Xiljin's thirst for vengeance will not be sated. Either he dies, or you do."

As his rebel leader made the elongated response, Xiljin managed to recover. He clambered up the frame of the cage for support, and saw that a beam was broken, cut by his sword moments ago. He broke off the jagged piece of wood and crept up behind Callaghan, ready to bury it in his back.

"Ranger! Behind you!" screamed a voice from the crowd. Callaghan turned quickly, the scimitar leading. It sliced through Xiljin's torso, his hands holding the wooden shiv above his head, ready to thrust it down into the ranger. Xiljin's blood sprayed out of his body, seeping into the sandy soil of the arena floor. His last thoughts were of the failure he had brought down upon his brother's name, before his dead body collapsed into the dirt.

"Who warned the Amarosian?" yelled Hazkeer. The crowd parted, revealing Ajarone, isolated from the masses. Hazkeer stared him down, but Ajarone met his gaze.

"You betray a brother for this murderer?" barked Hazkeer, marching around the cage to where he stood.

"You distracted him so Xiljin could stab him in the back like a coward," retorted Ajarone. "There is no honour in that." The leader could sense the crowd swayed by Ajarone's words.

"Hazkeer!" interrupted Callaghan from the other side of the cage's door, weary from the fight. "You have your balance, now release me." Begrudgingly, Hazkeer conceded, nodding to one of the rebels near the gate to unlock the cage. He hesitated as the crowd erupted in a hail of slanderous howls.

"Release him," urged Hazkeer. The rebel followed his orders rather than relenting to mob rule. Callaghan staggered out clutching the bleeding gash on his arm. However, his senses were sharp enough to see Hazkeer signal two rebels behind him. They approached carrying more rope bindings. Callaghan knocked one down, and then grabbed the other, forcing the scimitar under his throat. The callous crowd erupted again, baying for blood, but no-one dared approach the ranger after his impressive display in the arena.

"You promised me my freedom," said Callaghan.

"More than one person lost their life when you removed Jazintha Zaleed from our camp. Tomorrow you will fight another who seeks revenge."

"I do not have time for your games," said the ranger. "I shall fight him now."

"He is not here," replied Hazkeer, "but the man you hold under your blade is innocent. I promise you, if you win tomorrow, you will be free to walk out of our camp and back to your precious Khan."

Callaghan knew he could not hope to take on all the rebels, especially with blood seeping steadily from the wound on his arm. He threw the scimitar down and allowed his wrists to be bound by rope once more. As he was led away, Hazkeer issued a deathly stare at Ajarone.

"You can lick the Amarosian's wounds again, since you care so much for him." Ajarone followed Callaghan, mocked by the mob as he walked away. Someone hurled a rock, striking Ajarone in the face. He fell as more laughter spewed from the brazen rebels.

"Enough," commanded Hazkeer. No more violence befell Ajarone, but nor did anyone stop to help him to his feet. He picked himself up and limped back to the hut where Callaghan was being kept prisoner.

The din of the crowd withered from the shouts of the cage match to the occasional footstep of the guard on night patrol. Ajarone was still awake, tending to Callaghan's wounds. The pacifist rebel had suffered some cuts and bruises of his own, visible to the ranger even now in the dim glow of the torch embers.

"Thank you," said the ranger.

"No thanks are necessary," replied Ajarone. "Every man deserves a fair fight."

"It seems your beliefs may have caused you some undue suffering," noted Callaghan, eyeing the blemish on his face. Ajarone merely nodded as he finished dressing the wound on the ranger's arm.

"There, that should keep it clean for now." He rose gingerly to his feet, limping towards the exit.

"Even if I win tomorrow, Hazkeer will not grant me my freedom, will he?" asked Callaghan. Ajarone paused before the doorway.

"No," he answered, unable to face the ranger. "I told you Hazkeer is not like Zaleed Khan, but power corrupts even the most noble of men."

"Ajarone, you must help me escape."

"Because you claim to be on some quest? Tell me what it is, and I will consider it."

Callaghan was left with no option but to divulge his mission. "There is a man in Amaros who has created an army of ghosts. With them he plans to cleanse the world in his image, but I believe he is a pawn in a much larger plan."

"If this is true, then why would you journey to Zalestia?" quizzed Ajarone. "Why not stay and fight?"

"They cannot be fought with sword or spear, but I overheard the conspirators mention an object, the Stone of Spirits." A hint of recognition flashed over Ajarone's face as Callaghan mentioned the artefact. "I have reason to believe it is hidden somewhere in the Darosa Desert, in Errazure's Tomb. I see from your expression that you have heard of it."

"Yes, but not for many, many years," said Ajarone, sitting down as the distant memories struck him. "What you seek… it cannot be found."

"I must try," urged Callaghan. "Please, release me, and tell me all you know about the stone."

"If I free you, then I am as good as dead," said Ajarone.

"Then come with me."

"To Zatharu?" mocked the rebel. "The Khan would have me executed as soon as he lays eyes on me."

"I will protect you," promised the ranger. Ajarone weighed everything up in his mind. Hazkeer would have the ranger executed, not because it was justified, but to appease the mob. If the ranger's tale was true, and the mention of the Stone of Spirits made Ajarone believe it was, then he could not allow Hazkeer to throw Callaghan back into the cage. The rebel removed a small dagger from his belt. It wavered in the air, his hand shaking as his mind deliberated his next decision.

He cut Callaghan free.

It would be hours before their absence was noticed, along with two lizosaurs. When Hazkeer was finally informed, he ordered every spare rebel under his command to pursue the pair into the darkness of the jungle.

CHAPTER THIRTY-ONE

THE GHOST TOWN OF GORRAN

As the suns heralded a new day in Amaros, the marauders peered over the small, strategic hill they had paused on, gazing down at Gorran. There was no movement beyond the flapping of the flags, which had remained aloft all through the night. Vangar sensed something was amiss. The uneasy feeling had been gnawing at him ever since their encounter with the ranger, the elf, and her ghostly companion. As they descended the hill and wandered through Gorran's unguarded gates, he was now sure of it, the pit of his empty stomach filled with fear.

The other marauders entered the seemingly abandoned town, shouting with delight when they discovered it was devoid of life. Now that the ranger had been proven right, Vangar was even more on edge than he had been during their trek to the city. He spotted someone approaching from the south; their young scout, Terris Todd, galloping back from his mission. He was barely a man, thought Vangar, as he watched Terris approach from the gates. He was too young to be one of them, his small frame not built for combat, of which he had seen little, and yet at the same time, all too much.

"Well?" Vangar hollered to Terris as the horse galloped up to the gates.

"People are trekking to Calisto in their thousands," revealed the scout.

"Guess we didn't need to travel so stealthily after all," Vangar muttered to himself, wandering through the forsaken streets. The more morally questionable marauders began looting the nearby buildings.

"They've left everything!" he heard Maulin exclaim from a nearby house, followed by the jangling of jewellery and the smash of more on the ground.

"Two Hooks can't hold onto anything for long!" he heard someone jest.

"Do you need a hand?" joked another. Maulin sneered as he came spilling out of the doorway, trying to loop a long golden chain around his neck.

An arrow pierced the ground near Vangar's feet. His sword was raised before the trinkets Maulin dropped hit the flagstones. They glanced up to see Ariel Atari perched on the roof of the building opposite, bow in one hand, the other pointing to the north. Vangar quickly climbed up the steps to join the archer, leaving Maulin to scrape the ground with his hooks in a vain attempt to reacquire a lost golden ring.

"This had better be worth it, Ariel" Vangar huffed as he reached the roof. He gazed north to where the archer pointed, and suddenly forgot he was out of breath. On the distant horizon he glimpsed Malenek's army marching towards them. The spirits' eerie glow illuminated the thousands upon thousands of ætherghouls that scurried and scuttled ahead.

"Retreat!" he shouted. The marauders rounded on his call, abandoning the buildings they were busy pillaging. Maulin had just managed to hook the ring on one of his metal claws when the retreat was sounded, startling him. He cursed the gods as the ring fell back upon the cobblestones, prancing away down the street. Maulin ran after it, desperate to claim it as his own.

"What is happening?" asked Creevy Keel.

"The ranger was right. We must retreat to Calisto," bellowed Vangar from the roof, as Ariel swiftly slid down the side of the building. "Malenek marches upon Gorran."

"But some of us have prices on our heads," said Maulin, having lost the ring. A few others nodded in consternation. Vangar climbed down to join them on the ground.

"If we do not retreat you may not have a head to speak of!" snapped Vangar. "Stay here and face the spirit army if you wish, but if there is any way of stopping them, it will be in Calisto, and so will I. Leave anything you have found here, I fear it may be cursed." With that, Vangar hastily retreated from Gorran with his faithful friend Ariel Atari by his side. Most of the marauders followed them, but Maulin gazed down at the golden ring. Ghosts and rangers were not his concern, imagining the luxurious life that should have been his.

"What do we do?" asked one of the handful who had remained.

"Hide," hissed Maulin. "They will think this place deserted and pass by, leaving us to the spoils." They wore greedy sneers as they searched for somewhere to hole up as the spirits approached.

Malenek and his army of ætherghouls soon marched through the gates of Gorran. The spirits swept through the walls, searching the town for those stupid enough to have stayed behind.

Maulin managed to peer out of the pile of manure he had dived into, the horrid stench warding off the ætherghouls, while the spirits overlooked it completely. One by one he heard the terrifying screams of his fellow marauders as they were uncovered. He was forced to listen to their sickening cries as the spirits snapped their souls from inside, giving way to the morbid moans of creatures that were once men he knew.

"Lord Malenek! Lord Malenek!" cried an old voice. Malenek turned to find Priest Engel Larson being dragged through the streets by the elven ætherghoul. The old man was dumped before Shento, sobbing as he prayed to the Elementals. He looked up and found Malenek, almost unrecognisable in his suit of armour, until he removed his helmet. Larson blubbered and begged his fellow priest, pawing at the horse's hooves. For a brief moment, Balen Malenek thought of his days following the start of the war, of spurning his life as a soldier, his father's dream, and following his own. He remembered how proud he had felt to gain the title of priest, only to have it quickly sour, as sanctimonious religious leaders pushed them further into conflict. It had been their blind beliefs, their inherent inability to accept change, or even the idea that there may be more than the sacred Orico, that had led him to this.

"Martyn," uttered Malenek. The spirit stepped forth and ripped Engel's soul from his frail body, transforming him into a grunting ætherghoul. "Make sure he was the last." The spirits streamed away to search every last corner of Gorran, the ætherghouls following. From the stables, Maulin could see Malenek, left alone except for a handful of his minions. There was a clear run between himself and the former priest. The marauder watched Malenek visibly grow weaker, slumped on his horse as the spirits drifted further from him. Although he wore armour, he had removed his helmet. All Maulin had to do was reach him before his henchmen had time to react, and slice open Malenek's throat with his hooked hands.

He could end this, thought the marauder. He would no longer need to steal. Gifts would be showered upon him. Vangar would never be able to label him a coward again. He would be a hero.

The Spirit Killer.

Maulin liked the sound of that.

While the marauder was deluded by dreams of selfish heroism, Malenek assessed his once steadfast opinion that the spirits were the necessary tool to rid Enara of the evils of men. He looked down upon the ætherghouls from his saddle, focusing on the elven one. He was saddened by their necessity, but also disgusted by them, their foul, deathly odour and their primitive, vicious snarls. However, they were his creation, his actions personified. As the fatigue from the spirits' bond gripped his body, he found that the true target of his loathing lay within himself.

With Malenek drained and distracted, Maulin decided to make his move while he still held the element of surprise. He burst out of the pile of manure and padded towards the priest.

Malenek was alerted to the threat when the elven ætherghoul growled. He glanced around to see a marauder with two hooked hands running towards him. The man pounced into the air, ready to strike. Malenek raised his gauntlets to defend himself. He managed to grab the marauder's arms, the metal hooks scraping against his head. The force hurled them both off the horse, tumbling down onto the street. When they stopped, the marauder was on top of the helpless priest. He flashed Malenek a lecherous smile as he jabbed his sharp hook towards the priest's larynx.

A sudden shadow loomed over Maulin. A hand of stone grabbed his arm and tossed him into the air as if he were a dead tree branch. Maulin smacked against the wall of a building, crashing down upon a cart. He glanced up from the wreckage, his vision blurred by dust and blood, catching sight of a large rock monster thundering towards him. The thing's hand scooped down and grabbed him, flattening his body against the wall.

"Please don't..." whined Maulin.

"Gort, do not kill him," said Malenek, staggering up behind him. The stone giant released Maulin, his crushed body slumping down onto the ground.

"Thank you, my Lord," he wheezed.

"Let the spirits have him," added Malenek. Any doubts about his plan evaporated immediately thanks to this wretch of a man.

"No, no, please, no!" whined Maulin, but he was soon silenced. A spirit slipped through the wall behind him and reached into his back, snapping his soul from his broken body, trapping it there. The marauder's menacing hooks clanked against the cobblestones as his ætherghoul shrieked into existence.

"Are you hurt, my Lord?" asked Gort. Malenek allowed himself to use the stone giant to lean upon, his strength slowly returning as the spirits regrouped.

"Your timing is impeccable, Gort. I…" Malenek felt faint, swaying slightly, steadied by Gort's arm. "I am fine," he insisted. "It is the link to the spirits. We must march on to Calisto."

"No, we must stop so that you can rest, and eat," replied the stone giant, in a voice that even Malenek would not argue with. He merely nodded. Gort helped him inside a small house, onto a simple bed of straw. "Rest, my Lord. I will find you some food."

"Gort," whispered Malenek.

"Yes, my Lord?" he replied, hunched in the doorway.

"Thank you," said Malenek humbly. Gort nodded, bending low to leave the house. He passed through the spirit army standing guard outside, while the ætherghouls tore the town of Gorran apart. Gort watched the destructive creatures, a glum, sad sigh rumbling from the stone man's heavy heart.

CHAPTER THIRTY-TWO
THE DESERT STORM

KAMINA WOKE WITH A START FROM A NIGHTMARE, ONLY TO realise she was currently living one, camped in the middle of the dry Darosa Desert. Something moved behind her. Kamina clutched Ascara and pointed it at an unflustered Jazintha.

"Good mornings," said the zharie, performing some form of meditation, a slow, purposeful dance. "How dids you sleep?"

"Not well," replied Kamina, lowering the sword.

"You talks in your dreams," she said, grinning her trademark knowing smile, which Kamina was already starting to resent.

"I do not," she retorted, rising up and shaking the sand from her clothing. She scanned the campsite for Kaedin, eventually spotting him on the peak of the nearest dune.

"Then who is Talia?" asked Jazintha.

"She is my... she is my mother," muttered Kamina, walking away, unsure of herself.

"I did not mean to offend," Jazintha called out, pausing in her exercise, but Kamina was already scaling up the sand dune to join the spirit. There was stern concentration in his eyes, as he stared out across the unending desert.

"What is it?" asked Kamina, her acute gaze unable to see anything out of the ordinary.

"The firentazme the Zalestians spoke of, they are watching us."

"I do not see them." She followed Kaedin's pointed finger, her eyes resting on an unassuming area of sand. A small cloud of dust move against the general breeze, shaped vaguely like a man.

"They are afraid," stated Jazintha confidently as she regrouped with the elves on the dune. "Of you," she added, answering Kaedin's question before it was asked. "As far as I knows, he is the only... person to defeats one. Now come." Jazintha descended the dune, heading east.

"Kaedin," said Kamina timidly, stopping him before he could follow Jazintha.

"What?"

"Do I talk in my sleep?" she asked.

"Well..." started Kaedin, his expression betraying what was going to be a gentle lie.

"Why did you not tell me?!" interrupted Kamina.

"We are trying to save the world," he replied, sauntering after Jazintha. "Your dreams are not important."

They traipsed further into the heart of the desert, filtered out in single file. Kaedin lead the way, keeping an eye out for any more firentazme. Jazintha followed him, while Kamina lagged behind. They marched all day and into the evening with little conversation, until Jazintha suggested they make camp. After a small evening meal of rations, Kamina and Jazintha once again shared their warmth in the cold desert night.

"Your mother, Talia, where is she now? asked Jazintha. "In Amaros?"

"No," uttered Kamina. "She…" Kamina could not continue, because she was not yet certain of Talia's fate.

"I am sorry," said Jazintha, placing a hand on Kamina's shoulder. "My mother also moved ons to Yannah when I was young."

"Yannah?" asked the elf.

"The life after this one, where Gianna watches over us all," she answered. A confused look crossed Kamina's face. "What puzzles you?"

"If Malenek is successful and brings the afterlife to Enara, you may see her again," said Kamina. "Why would you wish to help us stop him?"

"Because what you claims is impossible," said Jazintha, "and even if it were true, you fails to look at it from the views of those who are already deads."

"What do you mean?" asked the elf.

"You talks about this Malenek drawings the afterlife to us, how it will affects us. How do you think it will affects those who has already earns their life in the world beyonds this one?"

"I do not know," admitted Kamina, never having considered those in Loria, like Sharla and Kaman.

"Besides, you assumes the afterlife of Amaros is the same as Zalestia, when our gods are not, our skins is not. We are not evens of the same race. Do you thinks all our spirits end up mixed together in one place, like a… stew?"

"A stew of spirits," said Kamina, smiling.

"Sounds gruesome," grinned Jazintha, as they giggled themselves to sleep.

The next morning, after another rough night's sleep in the sand, Kamina emerged over a small dune to see that Jazintha had discovered a tiny oasis of water, flagged by a dying tree. She collapsed beside the puddle and drank from her burnt cupped hands while Jazintha filled her empty skins.

"Spirit, scout aheads while we replenish our waters supplies," commanded the zharie.

"I would rather stay here," said Kaedin, unhappy with the way Jazintha was bossing him around.

"You no needs rehydration," she retorted. He glanced down at Kamina, who was wiping the wet sand from her lips. She nodded for him to follow Jazintha's request. He wandered off, climbing yet another dune.

"Do not drinks so fast," Jazintha advised, "Your body wills only be wishing for more." Kamina stopped drinking for a moment to store some of the water in a skin for later, air bubbles gurgling as she did. Kamina laughed at the sound, but Jazintha frowned, avoiding her gaze.

"Jazintha, is something wrong?" she asked.

"If we do not finds anything today, we should go backs to Zatharu."

"We cannot turn back," said Kamina. "Not now."

"If we do nots, we may never return," warned the zharie. Before they could continue the debate, Kaedin rushed back over the sand dune. The spirit was shouting and waving his arms in alarm, but he was too far away to make out the words.

"What is it?" shouted Kamina.

"Storm!" he cried, but his scream was lost in the howl of the huge sandstorm that was bearing down upon them at speed. Jazintha moved quickly, unfurling the lalaca skin and fastening it to the dead tree, creating a small tent.

"Get in!" she screamed to Kamina, who hastily joined the zharie. They cocooned themselves in the skin just as the fury of the storm slammed into them. The pair huddled together as the wind bawled all around them, threatening to tear apart their shelter and submerge them in sand.

"Orora is very angry!" yelled Jazintha over the noise.

"Who?" replied Kamina.

"The Goddess of the Wind!"

"In Amaros, the God of Air is Whirren."

"That is a stupid name!" barked Jazintha.

Whether in reply to Jazintha's remark, or just a coincidence, the dying tree was uprooted by the prevailing storm. The two girls dived out of the way as it crashed down. The lalaca skin was sucked up into the sky, while the tree was hurled through the sand-filled air, colliding with Kamina. She fell to the floor, trying to open her eyes against the ferocity of the storm, but they were struck by sharp specks of sand. She tried calling out to Kaedin or Jazintha, but even if the sand had not filled her throat, her voice carried no weight against the rush of the erosive wind. She heard Kaedin somewhere nearby, invisible in the swirling fog of sand.

"Kamina!" he yelled. "Dig down!"

She pushed the sand around her away, creating a small hollow to lie in. It offered some protection to her, but the storm coated her in layers of sand. Kamina was pinned down in the shallow grace, slowly being buried alive.

The blistering calm of the desert returned. The storm had passed as abruptly as it had descended upon them, leaving a void of sound in place of the wind's vehement vortex. Kamina crawled out of her sandy sepulchre, hawking the grit out of her mouth. She dusted herself down, making sure Ascara had not been lost to Whirren, or Orora's, wrath.

"Kaedin!" she screamed as she searched for the others. "Jazintha!"

"Down here," came a reply. She gazed down to find Kaedin standing in a sinkhole that had opened up during the storm. Jazintha lay at his feet, unconscious. Kamina climbed down and pulled the zharie up to the surface.

"Is she all right?" asked Kaedin.

"She appears to be," said Kamina, as Jazintha stirred softly.

"I wonder what caused that?" said Kaedin, indicating the cavity, but Kamina had already guessed. Before she could act on her realisation, an adult gruzalug surged through the desert floor, its giant body arcing through the air before plunging back down into the sand.

"You just had to ask," groaned Kamina. "Jazintha, wake up," she urged, kneeling over the zharie, but she was still out cold.

The gruzalug broke through the surface as it launched another attack. Kamina grabbed Jazintha's limp body and dragged her across the desert, diving out of the way of the descending monster.

"Kaedin!" Kamina screamed, unable to see him. She jumped as a hand gripped her arm. It was Jazintha, regaining consciousness. She urged Kamina closer to her mouth.

"You must be quiets," she whispered. "The gruzalugs hunts by sounds." Kaedin appeared beside them, his spirit feet silent upon the sand. Kamina ushered him not to speak as she lay the woozy zharie down gently.

"Protect her," Kamina whispered, drawing Ascara.

"How am I meant to do that?" he asked in hushed tones, but Kamina was running away. "Where are you going?"

"To lead it away," she cried back, bounding across the desert surface as loudly as possible. Soon the gruzalug sprang up from the sand in pursuit of the spritely elf. Kamina ran as fast as she possibly could, but the gruzalug was quickly gaining ground on her, swimming through sand like the deadly shark in the ocean.

She stopped abruptly, hoping the creature's momentum would propel it far ahead of her. The shift in the top layer of sand rushed by her and into the distance, until she could no longer see it. She let out a sigh of relief, and turned back to Kaedin and Jazintha.

"I think it is…" she started to shout, but the gruzalug shot up beside her, knocking her down. Ascara fell out of her hand. The giant snake disappeared under the surface once again, as Kamina grasped for the sword.

"Kamina!" screamed Kaedin, but his warning was unnecessary. As she scrambled to reach Ascara, the gruzalug erupted from the sand and soared high into the air. It descended upon her, its gnarled nightmarish mouths open wide. He watched in horror as Kamina was consumed by the creature as it crashed back down through the sand.

"No," he gasped. "No!"

"Silence!" said Jazintha, regaining her strength. "She is dead, and we wills be too if the gruzalug returns." The pair stared across the flat of the desert.

"She cannot be dead," Kaedin whispered. "I am still here, which means she is still alive."

A loud groan echoed below their feet. The giant gruzalug surfaced, but with none of the ferociousness it had displayed earlier. It slumped over onto the sand, gnarling and rumbling in distress. It wheezed its final breath and lay still upon the ground. Jazintha and Kaedin edged cautiously towards the monstrous corpse. They could hear a constant thumping sound. Jazintha stopped in her tracks.

"It is still alive, I can hear its heart beat."

"That is not its heart," he said.

Ascara's blade jabbed through the tough skin and sliced across its belly. Kamina clutched the sides of the incision and squeezed out of the gruzalug, covered from head to toe in the creature's gungy innards. The elf coughed and spluttered as she wiped the slime from her eyes, until she could finally see Kaedin's wide smile.

"That was unbelievable!" he exclaimed, beaming proudly. Kamina turned from them and vomited.

"Sorry," she mumbled.

"Do not apologise," said the zharie, offered her the last of their water. Kamina guzzled it, rinsing away the foul taste. "You protects me by facing off against a gruzalug and survives. You truly are a warrior." Kaedin nodded, in agreement.

"I am not warrior," said Kamina, catching her breath. "Just an elf." Jazintha laughed, forcing a grin from the gunk-covered girl.

Their celebrations were cut short by the sound of a solitary clap echoing across the desert. A nomadic figure was poised on the dune above them, silhouetted by the twin suns. He was wrapped in black rags that flapped in the desert breeze.

"A warrior is definitely what you are," he said, striding down the sand dune towards them. Kamina raised Ascara, wary of this newcomer, as was Jazintha, who reached for her daggers.

"Who is you?" asked the zharie.

"And how do you speak Amarosian?" asked Kamina.

"Please," he said, his hands raised. "I come in peace." The stranger disregarded their hostility towards him, his gaze fixed intently on Kaedin. He reached out his bony hand and moved it through the spirit's body.

"You are a spirit of vengeance!" he exclaimed.

"You know of the spirits?" she asked. Who was this desert nomad? Kamina thought. And more importantly, was he a friend or foe? She exchanged a quick look with Jazintha, who shared her trepidations.

"Only from legend," he replied. "Please, come, you need water." He urged them to follow as he retraced his footsteps back up the dune. With little choice, the trio followed the stranger. As they mounted the sandy peak, they were met with a curious sight. The nomad was leading them towards a small palace in the distance, modelled on Jazintha's home in Zatharu.

It seemed to be made entirely of sand.

CHAPTER THIRTY-THREE
THE JALENARI JUNGLE

Callaghan and Ajarone rode their stolen lizosaurs until dawn, through the eerie gases given off by the rich jalaaroca minerals and ores found scattered throughout the jungle. The Zalestian navigated their path across the territory of the ferocious jaxosaurus, deep in the jungle valleys.

"The rebels will not dare follow!" Ajarone had said. And with good reason, Callaghan later thought, as a hungry jaxosaurus pounded after them, its teeth snapping through trees as it tried to snack on their bones. The lizosaurs' quick legs were fast enough to carry their human riders to safety. However, the trek through the huge predator's domain had taxed their energy. Ajarone had suggested to Callaghan that they cut them loose.

"The rebels will follow their tracks," he explained. Seeing the sense in the plan, Callaghan watched the lizosaurs slink off into the foliage, while he and Ajarone hiked in the opposite direction.

For hours the two men fought their way through the jungle gloom, with only a few rays of light managing to penetrate the thick canopy above. Squawks and squeals from the bounty of wildlife surrounding them kept the ranger on edge. Ajarone paused, eyeing some fruit hanging from a nearby tree.

"Stop here," he said, climbing the branches to retrieve the fruit.

"We must keep going," said Callaghan, but his body was still weak, stifled by the torrent of adversity that had plagued him over the last few days. Ajarone admired the stubborn man who had been drowned, burned, and beaten, yet refused to allow himself the luxury of a seat. He returned to the ground, breaking the hard fruit on a rock and offering the ranger half. Callaghan tore at its skin with his hands, drinking its sweet juices before gnawing at the tender fruit within. They continued to traipse through the jungle while they ate.

"You are a brave man to journey to Zalestia a second time," said Ajarone. "From what I have heard, it is a perilous voyage. Why would anyone undertake such a thing?"

"On my first visit I came to find a Zalestian willing to become my apprentice," explained Callaghan. "I had hoped he would become a symbol of peace between our two lands."

"Where is he now, this apprentice?" asked Ajarone, nibbling on the fruit.

"Dead," said Callaghan curtly.

"I am sorry," replied the rebel.

"Do not be. Jaelyn Zsatt does not deserve your sympathy. The man deceived me. He was a mage, a shaman to you, part of the plot to raise the spirit army. It was from his traitorous tongue that I learned of the Stone of Spirits."

"Hidden in Errazure's tomb," recalled Ajarone. "If the stone is what I think it is, I know where it was long ago.

"Where?"

"In the upper echelons of the Tower Of Zoren, before Errazure and his men stole it into the desert."

"Who is Errazure?" asked Callaghan. "How is it I have never heard of him before?"

"If the Khan were to speak of him, it would only be to slander his name, and label him as a villain and a thief, but Errazure Ecko was once the most trusted shamen of Jada Zaleed Zhan," explained Ajarone. "That is why his name would not have come up in conversation with Zahyr Zaleed or his daughter. During the massacre which started this long and bloody war, Errazure and his disciples helped those Amarosians still alive escape to their ships in an act of mercy. Jada, grieving the loss of her son Qeuzz, unleashed her anger on the shamen. They tried to reason with her, but she blindly banished them into the desert. It was a decision that would haunt her until her death. The shamen had predicted the war would be long and claim many lives. They blamed the arrogant Zaleeds for igniting it, and when Jada ordered their banishment, they took her most prized possession with them."

"The Jewel of Gianna," said Callaghan.

"Indeed," confirmed Ajarone. "They took it along with seven stone slabs, upon which Zoren carved the original version of the Xe'rath, the commandments of Mother Gianna, using her jewel."

"And you think one of the pages of the Xe'rath is the Stone of Spirits?" asked the ranger.

"It is very possible, especially if it is buried with Errazure as your dead apprentice claimed. The seventh stone is said to focus on Yannah, the afterlife. There have been many translations and interpretations by different Khans and Zhans over the ages, but the seventh was always the most elusive."

"It could relate to the spirits and how to stop them," muttered Callaghan. "What became of them? These shamen?"

"They vanished into the hot winds of the Darosa Desert. Jada Zhan sent legions of men to scour the sands, but they found nothing. That is not entirely accurate. The firentazme found them."

"The desert phantoms. Zahyr spoke of them," recalled Callaghan. "I thought he was mocking me."

"No, they are very real," warned Ajarone. "No-one knows for sure who or what they are. Some say they are followers of Azik, trapped in Darosa for all eternity, unable to re-join their master in Haegor. Those they did not kill with their penance touch were driven mad by their whispers carried on the winds. Jada Zhan declared the Darosa Desert off limits, something Zahyr later overruled."

"But someone must have found the stone," said Callaghan, "otherwise Jaelyn would not have known of it."

"Years later," continued Ajarone, "when Jada was on her deathbed, there was an uprising, formed by many of those who had been sent out in search of the shamen. Some say the firentazme were still whispering to them from beyond the walls of Zatharu, but there were others who joined, unhappy with the toll of the war, who saw an opportunity in Jada's weakness. Zahyr, preparing for the mantle of Khan, cut off the dissenters before they could act. He rounded them up and cast them into the desert, telling them they could join Errazure and his shamen in their sandy graves. The members of this failed insurrection later became known as the Stone Sect."

"What has this to do with Jaelyn?" asked Callaghan.

"One of the men who escaped was named Faizon Zsatt," revealed Ajarone. "He had a young son, although I did not know his name."

"It must have been Jaelyn," assumed the ranger. "They must have found the Stone Sect, and the Jewel of Gianna. It is the only way to explain Jaelyn's powers. But how do you know all this?"

"I was one of those cast out by Zahyr," admitted Ajarone. "While the purists headed east into the desert, myself and many others journeyed south back into the jungle, eventually joining the Jalenari rebels." His confession chilled the mood between them in the humid jungle. Callaghan did not wish to alarm Ajarone, so kept walking, while he scanned his surroundings for a suitable weapon.

"Then why did you not enter the desert?" he asked cautiously, as his eyes caught sight of a small branch. Callaghan ducked down and swiftly picked it up. Ajarone, sensing the tension, turned just as the ranger cracked the branch over his head. Ajarone fell to the jungle floor, blood trickling down his face.

"Ranger, stop. We do not have time for this. We must go!" pleaded Ajarone.

"And walk into a trap," said Callaghan, ready to strike again. "You knew Faizon Zsatt."

"Only by name," conceded the rebel. "I am trying to help you. Please." Callaghan was unsure whether Ajarone was telling the truth or not, but his hand was forced as the other rebels careered through the jungle towards them. "You must trust me," insisted the rebel.

The ranger, deciding it was worth the risk, helped Ajarone up. They ran through the jungle, evading the pursuing rebels. Angry shouts in Zalestian echoed behind them, followed by a volley of spears. As they broke out of the canopy at the top of a small cliff, one of the spears caught Ajarone in the leg, knocking him into Callaghan. They tumbled down the side, grasping at hanging vines. Callaghan managed to slow his descent, but Ajarone's weight pulled him down, and they both landed hard.

"Are you hurt?" asked the ranger. The rebel groaned, a thin spear embedded deep in his leg. The Zalestian grit his teeth as he plucked it out, blood oozing from the wound. Callaghan gathered a strip of vine and wrapped it above the gash, tying it tight.

"Thank you for trusting me," said Ajarone.

"Can you walk?" he asked, not entirely hopeful. Ajarone surprised him by lifting himself up, using the spear as support.

"Yes," he grumbled, "but not fast enough to evade them. I will lead them this way. When it is clear, head in that direction," he instructed, pointing the way. "It will take you straight to Zatharu."

"But they will kill you," said Callaghan.

"We must all die someday, Ranger of Ishkava," stated Ajarone. "Let my death be when I decide."

"I am sorry I doubted you, Ajarone," said Callaghan.

"Just find the stone," said the rebel, limping away. Callaghan sank back into the dark of the jungle, and waited until it was clear.

*

Ajarone staggered through the thick jungle, Hazkeer hot on his heels, mounted on top of a muzzled xanzasaur, a beast twice the size of the lizosaurs he and the ranger had liberated. The chase stopped abruptly when Ajarone skidded to a halt on a high outcrop. Hazkeer and his xanzasaur emerged, blocking the only exit. The Jalenari leader climbed down from the hungry beast.

"Look at you," smirked Hazkeer. "A worthless traitor, helping our enemies."

"The ranger is a better man than you will ever be," retorted Ajarone, raising the spear to defend himself, but struggling to stand without its support.

"Take your best shot," boasted Hazkeer, his arms open wide. "I will not even move." Ajarone hurled the spear, but it soared well over Hazkeer. The effort caused him to fall.

"Unlike you," said Hazkeer, "I will not miss."

*

A mortal scream echoed out across the jungle. The ranger closed his eyes and offered a silent prayer for the man who had freed him. He shot off through the jungle as fast as his weary legs would carry him, propelled by the thought that he could not allow Ajarone's sacrifice to be in vain.

It was not long before he found himself at a ridge overlooking the treetops of the jungle, and in the far distance, the magnificent citadel of Zatharu. Although still a day away on foot, it was a welcome sight. His jubilation was shattered by a shriek from the sky. Two Jalenari rebels were circling above him on a pair of pterazachs, winged reptiles similar in size to the lizosaurs. They spotted him on the ridge and swooped down. The ranger started to run but one of the pterazachs caught him in its claws. The rebel riding the creature laughed through his red-painted face as Callaghan wrestled from its grip. The pterazach let go, but they had soared higher into the sky, forcing Callaghan to cling on to the sharp claws or else fall to his death. The rebel pilot tried prodding at him with a spear, but the ranger managed to wrench it from his grip and thrust it back, plunging it into his side. Callaghan kept a hold of the spear as the rebel slid from his saddle, the weight leveraging him onto the beast's back. The rebel plummeted down to his doom, while Callaghan took the reins of his pterazach.

Unlike the lizosaur, the pterazach was difficult to manoeuvre. Callaghan struggled with the straps as the flying lizard careered into the jungle canopy. The ranger was smacked and clobbered by leaves and branches. The lizard ignored his rider, soaring back into the clear sky. The ranger slowly steered the pterazach towards Zatharu, although the creature opposed his commands, wary of the citadel.

While he tried to work out how he was going to land, the second pterazach pilot dived down, attacking him. The two pterazachs tussled in the sky, clawing at one another. Callaghan hugged the creature tight as it spun wildly to defend itself. The rebel whooped with delight as his pterazach snapped at Callaghan with its large triangular beak. Both man and beast were painted with red and yellow war paint. It was a losing battle, with Callaghan unable to defend himself or control his flying lizard. The rebel pterazach sliced open its rival's hide, delivering a fatal blow. His attacker pulled away, content with watching Callaghan fall to his death. With Zatharu not far, the ranger grasped the spikes that protruded from the pterazach's wing joints, forcing the dying creature to glide towards the citadel.

Far below on the outer wall, the zeetoo on guard had spotted the aerial assault, and were pointing at the pterazach that was now fluttering towards them. They aimed spears and arrows, but the pterazach was approaching too fast for them to hit their target. Callaghan flattened himself against the lizard's skin as it swooped towards the wall, its beak crashing into one of the towers, sending it into a spin. They tumbled over the wall, crashing into the shanties on the outskirts of the citadel.

Callaghan dizzily climbed off the dead pterazach, collapsing to the ground to catch his breath, despite several scimitars being thrust in his direction. A cavalry of rhenzos had arrived, their riders heavily armed, assuming this to be the start of an impending attack.

"I seek an audience with Zahyr Zaleed Khan," the ranger managed to say. The contingent of zeetoo were unsure what to make of the man. Before a decision could be made, a luxurious britzka blistered through the city towards them. One by one the Zalestians dropped to the ground as Zahyr emerged from the carriage.

"What is going on here!" boomed the Khan's voice. "Why were the warning bells rang?" He stopped in his tracks when he saw Callaghan in the centre of the kneeling zeetoo. "Ranger? Is it really you?" asked Zahyr.

"It is, Zaleed Khan," he said, performing a small, painful salute. The crowd parted as Callaghan staggered past them to join the Khan.

"I was told you were dead," uttered Zahyr, an astounded smile beaming on his face as he patted him on the shoulders. "You have looked better."

"You spoke with Kamina?" he asked, wincing in pain. "She made it here?"

"She and her ghostly companion," said the Khan. "They told me the most fantastic tale when they were guests at the palace."

Kamina was alive, thought the ranger. She had made it here alive. Callaghan's elation at this news finally allowed him the luxury of relief, unburdening himself of the tension that he carried. The distress of his injuries caused him to falter. Zahyr caught his slumping body before he hit the ground. The Khan and a pair of zeetoo helped him inside the britzka, which soon jolted towards the palace.

"Zahyr, where are they elves now," asked the ranger as the britzka began to move. The Khan hesitated. "Zahyr, what happened to them?"

"They marched into the Darosa Desert on some fool's errand!" he admitted. "They said they were looking for Errazure's tomb."

"How many of your men did you send with them?"

"None."

"Why did you not aid them in their quest?" demanded the ranger. "I sent them to you for help, to return the favour you owed me."

"As I said, they came to me with a tale so fantastic it was hard to believe. They told me you were dead, which clearly is not so. They were liars." Callaghan's heart sank. He had brought them to this place, and now he would be responsible for their deaths in the desert wastes.

"It was not a lie," said the ranger. "I am unsure how I survived the seas, but they have surely died in the desert."

"Do not give up hope in them just yet, ranger," said Zahyr. "My stubborn daughter saw fit to join them on their quest."

"If Jazintha is with them, they may stand a chance," said Callaghan, feeling the rush of hope return to his heart. "The elves are not used to the desert, but a Zalestian will know how to survive. We must..."

"I already sent a scouting party out after them," interrupted Zahyr, "but they returned this morning, unable to find any sign of them."

"Then I will go," urged the ranger. "Take me to the east gate."

"No, it is *zamovrazda*, especially in your condition," noted the Khan, indicating Callaghan's dishevelled state. "Look at you. You can barely walk."

"They are my responsibility!" exclaimed the ranger. "The girl is... this all started because I brought Jaelyn Zsatt back to Amaros."

"The elf told me he was a traitor," said the Khan. "A mage."

"Not just a mage. A member of the Stone Sect," he added accusingly.

"I see you have been listening to the rebels spinning their yarns," said Zahyr.

"It was more than you told me," said Callaghan. "You seemed to have left a lot out during our past discussions."

"Just as I am certain you omitted details from the tales of Amaros you shared with me," said the Khan. "And I am sure your reasoning was the same as mine. I did not need to know."

"A former member of the Stone Sect managed to tell me all he knew," revealed Callaghan. "Jaelyn's father was a man named Faizon Zsatt, who escaped into the desert with his son."

"Then they must have found Errazure's Tomb..." whispered Zahyr, scared at the thought. "And if they found it, it is possible Jazintha will find it as well."

"Which is why I must go after them," urged the ranger.

"You will not find them alone in Darosa's wastes," scoffed Zahyr. "Besides, they have a three day start on you."

"Do you have a better idea?" he asked. The Khan flashed him a wide toothy smile, exposing his replacement gold teeth.

"As a matter of fact, I do. Skado, take us to the north gate. Quickly!"

CHAPTER THIRTY-FOUR
THE TOMB OF ERRAZURE

THE UNLIKELY TRIO OF ELF, SPIRIT AND ZHARIE FOLLOWED THE mysterious nomad as he led them through the mouth of the castle made entirely of sand. They were taken aback by the sheer size and scale of the structure. It was remarkably similar in design and décor to the Khan's palace in Zatharu, right down to the most intimate detail. Kamina glanced up the ceiling to find a replica of the mural seen in Jazintha's home. The zharie herself ran her fingers along the wall, which while appearing to be as a solid as stone, disintegrated into grains under her fingernails. The chunk of missing wall was quickly filled by the surrounding sand, as if she had never scratched it.

"What is this place?" she whispered to herself.

"This is the Tomb of Errazure," said the nomad. He removed the hood of his tattered robes to reveal a haggard Zalestian face, crowned by a head of short silver hair. "Please follow me, you must be parched."

They followed him as he descended down into another room, where the throne of Zatharu would have been found. There were no windows here, but balls of silver flame hovered eerily in torch holders made of sand, like everything else in the castle. In the centre stood a fountain carved from the dry grains into an effigy of the beautiful Gianna, yet the crystal clear water did not turn the sand to mud. It was surrounded by seven pedestals, each presenting a stone tablet suspended in a thick slab of glass. The nomad stalked past the stones and collected a glass goblet from the base of the fountain. He filled it with water and offered it to Kamina. Her thirst was great, but Jazintha stopped her from raising it to her lips, snatching it from the elf's hand and tossing it to the floor.

"Do not drinks that," warned the zharie. "He cannot be trusted. He is a member of the Stone Sect."

"I am not of the Stone Sect," assured the man.

"And yets the seven stone pages of the Xe'rath surrounds us." Kamina peered at the glass case upon the nearest pedestal. The ancient stone tablets inside each one were etched with Zalestian symbols. "Explain yourself."

"I am Errazure Ecko, the last of the shamen the Stone Sect set out to find, and find me they did." Upon hearing the name of the man who had betrayed her family, from his own lips no less, Jazintha unsheathed her twin daggers.

"But you said that this was Errazure's tomb," recalled Kamina, trying to diffuse the situation, although she realised this may impossible.

"It is my tomb," explained Errazure. "I can never leave this place, or stray too far from it. It is my final resting place, my sanctuary."

"This is impossible," said Jazintha. "The traitor would be deads with age by now."

"And I would have been, were it not for the love of the blessed Mother Goddess Gianna."

"You lie!" roared the zharie. "Gianna would not keeps a treacherous thief alive. I should strike you downs where you stand."

"If you must," said Errazure, amused by Jazintha's anger, "but then your friends would not find the answers to the questions that led them here from Amaros. Put your daggers away and I will explain." Jazintha was reluctant to do so, until Kamina laid a friendly hand on her shoulder.

"Let him speak," said the elf. "There is much we need to know." The zharie saw reason through her rage and replaced the blades back in her belt.

"I will allows him to talk, but all he will tells us is lies," she warned. "Gianna would never saves the likes of him."

"Unlike you, my dear zharie, I do not question the will of the gods." Jazintha was slightly shocked, as she had been careful not to reveal her title. "Oh yes, I know who you are, and why you came here. You blame the gods for your family's bad fortune, whereas I only thank them through prayer, which is how Gianna found me all those years ago, on my knees, praying for a miracle." Errazure side-stepped Jazintha so he could address the elves. "My shamen and I escaped into the desert, each carrying a page of the Xe'rath. We were pushed deeper into Darosa by Jada's pursuing forces. One by one, the other shaman met their deaths, until it was left to me to drag the seven stones across the endless dunes, away from the Zaleeds." Errazure walked around the pedestals, gracing one of the glass cases with a long, bony finger. "I had stumbled so far I could see nothing but sand and sky. When I was within death's grip, I was certain our sacrifice had been worthwhile, if only to remove the Jewel of Gianna from a ruling family rich in every way except that which truly matters, namely wisdom and benevolence."

"What is that supposed to means?" snapped Jazintha.

"It means it has always been too easy for rulers to incite man to war," said Errazure. "The war between our two continents was started by the arrogance of a young prince, your uncle, who believed himself better than everyone. It was started out of conceited pride, where modesty would have prevailed."

"You dares disrespects the names of my family?" snarled Jazintha. "Enough. Give me the jewel, and gives them the Stone of Spirits."

"I bore witness to the beginning of this war. Did you, young zharie? Or have you believed every word your father has fed you with your silver spoon?" Jazintha remained silent, teeming with anger, as the shaman continued. "You asked me how I survived. It was because I was brave enough to free the jewel from the clutches of your family. This is why Gianna chose me."

Errazure reached into the spout of the fountain, and from the bust of the Mother Goddess he revealed the fabled Jewel of Gianna. It glowed brightly from within, swirling strands of silver and cream. Kamina, Kaedin and Jazintha were all enthralled by the jewel's magical energy dancing inside, as though it were alive.

"She found me dying in the desert, and cried for my pain. Her tears revived my wearied body. I asked her why she cried, and with the most beautiful voice I have ever heard, she replied that she grieved the wasted gift of life squandered by so many of her subjects, extinguished with such thoughtless disregard. She could foresee the endless war and the lives that would perish as a consequence. She said I had been chosen to carry out her plan, a plan that would end it all, all the killing, all the suffering, forever."

"This is lies upon lies," declared Jazintha. "I have heards enough." She withdrew one of her daggers and held it to the nape of Errazure's wrinkled neck. "Give me the jewel." She was surprised when Errazure handed it to her without protest.

"Jazintha, we need the Stone of Spirits," Kamina reminded her. "Which one is it?" The zharie glanced between the stone tablets, but she was not familiar with the Xe'rath.

"I do nots know," she admitted. "We will takes them all."

"You cannot carry all of them," said Kaedin.

"Shows us which one of these is the Xe'rath zo Yann?" demanded Jazintha, grabbing Errazure and pushing him to the pedestals. The shaman slowly wandered around them.

"I cannot remember," he said. "No wait, it is this one." His aged hands rest upon one of the glass cases. Before Kamina could reach it, the old Zalestian sneered, shoving the glass case from its plinth. It tumbled to the floor, striking a rock in the sand. Both the stone tablet and the glass protecting it smashed into pieces. Kamina fell to her knees, cutting her hands as she fished out pieces of the Xe'rath from the glass. The fragments of stone crumbled to dust between her fingers. Her breath caught in her throat as tears welled up in her eyes.

The Stone of Spirits was destroyed.

She had failed. Everyone who had relied on her - Callaghan, Talia, and even Kaedin - she had failed them. The same anger that had gripped her when Kaedin was murdered strangled her heart. Kamina withdrew Ascara and pointed the sword at Errazure, who raised his arms in mock defeat. She forced him against a wall until the tip of the sword touched his chest. With one thrust she could puncture his body and skewered his ancient heart.

"Why did you do that?" she screamed. "Why did you destroy the Stone of Spirits?" The trio were puzzled when Errazure started to laugh.

"My dear child," he said sardonically, "the Stone of Spirits is not a page of the Xe'rath. The Stone of Spirits is the Jewel of Gianna."

"No, he is lying!" said Jazintha as Kamina glanced at her. "It cannots be."

"I promise you it is true," claimed Errazure. "Look within, look at its power, and then look at your friend." The ethereal energy that held Kaedin's form together was very similar to that swirling within the jewel.

"Jazintha, we need that stone to save Enara," said Kamina.

"No, it belongs to my family," claimed the zharie. "We needs it. My father needs it." Kamina turned her sword from Errazure to Jazintha. The zharie met the elf's stance, her dagger pointing at Kamina while she held the Jewel of Gianna away from them in her other hand. "Do not move, spirit," hissed Jazintha, as Kaedin started to cloak himself, "or I will end you both."

"Errazure is right," said the ghost as he reappeared. "You do not deserve it. The stone may hold the key to brining me back to life. You only wish to keep it as a family trinket."

"Now this is interesting!" said Errazure with glee, teasing them. "Who shall have it? The proud zharie or the heroic elves?"

"Jazintha, he is trying to turn us against one another," said Kamina. "This is what he wants."

"Then lets us leave!" she said. "Quicks."

"Not until you agree to give up the stone," said Kaedin.

"Never. It will seal my reigns over my peoples," said Jazintha. "I will unites them and succeed where my father cannot."

"Once we have defeated Malenek, we will give it back, you have my word," begged Kamina. "Please, Jazintha, it could bring back my mother." As Kamina pleaded with her, the zharie struggled against own selfishness, imagining the lengths she would go to if there was a chance she could revive her own mother.

She lowered her dagger.

"The spoilt zharie has a conscience after all," remarked Errazure. "How very disappointing. I am afraid, however, that I am having a little fun with you. Forgive me, I have been stuck here a very long time, and entertainment is in short supply." The shaman whispered an enchantment, and the Jewel of Gianna flew from Jazintha's hand to his own. "The stone will remain here with me while Malenek cleanses Emdara. And I am afraid you three will have to stay here with me as well."

"Over my deads body," said Jazintha.

"So be it," said Errazure. Jazintha attacked first, yelling a short-lived war cry as she charged at him with her curved daggers. A blast of silver light shot out from Errazure's fingertips, launching her into the ceiling. The grains of sand tightened around her, enveloping her body, sinking upwards.

"Do you dare try and steal the stone?" Errazure asked the young elf.

"She does not," said Kaedin, standing behind the shamen, "but I do." Kaedin had used Jazintha's attack as a distraction to sneak behind the desert mage. His ghostly fingers snatched for the stone, and he managed to hold it in his grasp. The spirit enjoyed a fleeting moment of exultation before he sensed something was wrong. A surge of power built up within the Stone of Spirits. It discharged a violent blast of energy that sent Kaedin crashing through the walls of the palace and out into the desert. The residual explosion pinned Kamina and Errazure to the ground, weakening the magical integrity of the palace. The walls of sand wobbled, while the ceiling and columns started to crumble.

Kamina's bond with Kaedin was stretched tight as he was repelled out of the tomb. She lost her grip on Ascara as the strength was sapped from her body, collapsing like the palace around her. She felt nauseous, her vision blurry. The dark presence of Errazure loomed over her, holding the stone in his hand, admiring its beauty.

"It is designed to protect itself from the spirits," he explained. "They cannot touch it. It simply will not allow them to, as if it were alive, judging them." Kamina realised he was fixated on the stone, talking to it and not her. Above them, Jazintha struggled to free herself from the quicksand ceiling that had almost consumed her.

"Why do this?" the elf asked weakly. "Why create the spirits?"

"The spirits are just a tool, like this sword," he said, picking up Ascara from under her fingertips. "It is the ætherghouls that are the key. The souls trapped within their rotting bodies will draw Yannah closer to Emdara, and eventually engulf it. We will all be at one with Gianna."

*

Out in the desert, Kaedin's faint ghostly hand appeared from the sand he had fallen into. He climbed back from under the desert floor and sprawled over the sand. His insubstantial form was unable to feel the severe heat radiating off the surface, only the pain of his fraught bond with Kamina.

Kaedin gazed back towards the palace of sand, which was beginning to subside. He scurried back towards the tomb to save Kamina before it caved in on top of her.

*

"Imagine it," droned Errazure, undaunted by the sand palace falling apart all around them. "Imagine a world without the confines of this fleshy shell and all the sin that resides within. Of course you cannot. The only world you know is the forest of Elgrin. You cannot conceive how man and the other races fight and feud over land and coin, things that do not matter in the greater scheme."

"You are full of lies!" yelled Jazintha from above, spitting sand at him. "How would you know of such things?"

"Once again the answer is the Mother Goddess Gianna," he said.

"She would never do such a thing!" insisted the zharie, although her voice betrayed her faltering beliefs. How else had Errazure survived if not with the help of a god? Jazintha thought.

"Soon, you will be able to ask her. When the bonds between this world and the next are weakened, Gianna will take over he who controls the spirits."

"Malenek," said Kamina.

"He will be her vessel," revealed Errazure. "Together they will guide us into this new era of existence."

"But why would she need a body?" asked Kamina. "You said our souls would be free of the flesh." The shaman's mouth moved as if to answer, but he was temporarily stumped by the elf's question.

"See!" cried the zharie. "He lies! Gianna would never harm a living soul."

"Gianna has grown tired of those who squander her gift of life!" Errazure yelled suddenly, still ignorant to the subsiding walls of sand. "She has been wearied by those who hoard the wealth of the land for their own greed! But I cannot expect a spoilt zharie who lives on a pedestal built by slaves to understand this."

"What about my brother? Why send Jaelyn to kill him?" Errazure laughed manically as he peered down at her with astounded eyes.

"It is ironic that you ask such a question. Gianna prophesised that there existed one being so powerful and evil that they alone could stop our plan, and so Jaelyn was dispatched to kill them."

"Kaedin is not evil!" screamed Kamina, her strength flowing back to her. She could feel Kaedin closer now, saw his light as the spirit phased through the wall.

"My dear child," said Errazure, kneeling down by her side, his rough hand clutching her smooth face. "Jaelyn was not sent to kill your brother. He was sent to kill you."

Kamina's heart sank with guilt. At the outset she had blamed Kaedin for being targeted, for being bonded to her, for making her come on this journey with Callaghan. But now, if Errazure's words were true, it meant that her brother was a ghost because of her. A goddess had deemed her so evil that a Zalestian had journeyed halfway around Enara just to kill her. Even though her strength had returned, Kamina was paralysed by this revelation. She felt Kaedin's ethereal glow on her face, the spirit standing by the wall, having heard Errazure's confession. It was like watching him die all over again, but this time from the inside, his dreams of being special, of being tied to the rangers and their adventures, dashed by this desert shaman.

"No," she whispered.

"Yes," affirmed Errazure, rising up again. "And since he failed, it is up to me to rid the world of your evil." The shaman picked up Ascara with the intention of driving it into the elf's heart, with Kamina powerless to stop him. He would have succeeded had it not been for the swift intervention of Kaedin, who forced his ghostly fingers inside Errazure's head.

"You are lying!" screamed the spirit. Ascara and the stone both dropped from the shaman's hands. Kamina caught the blade between her palms, its tip almost piercing her chest. The stone fell to the sand, rolling away along the slanted floor. With Errazure stunned by the spirit invading his thoughts, the spell holding Jazintha disintegrated. The zharie plummeted to the ground with a painful thump.

Kaedin skirted the edges of Errazure's thoughts, swimming in the dark mists. He was no longer a passenger to some malevolent force; he was in control, searching tirelessly through the shaman's secrets. He saw Gianna visiting Errazure in the desert, reviving him. Kaedin witnessed the sand palace being constructed with a mere wave of Gianna's hand. He rifled through a cascade of images; he saw the Stone Sect finding the shaman, watched Errazure training Jaelyn in the ways of magic, and finally heard the revelation.

"There is one in Emdara who can still stop our plans. She needs to be stopped."

She.

It was all true.

"Get... out... of...my... head!" cried Errazure. He summoned all his magic, insulating his body with the silvery glow. The spirit was shocked by a bolt of magic, forcing his hand out of the shaman's skull. Errazure spied Jazintha chasing after the Stone of Spirits. He cast furious hexes in her direction, striking the sandy floor in front of her. Vague shapes emerged from the sand, neither man nor beast, but ungainly deformities with limbs. They clumsily lashed out at Jazintha, blocking her path to the Stone of Spirits. She defended herself against their attacks with her daggers, slicing into their bodies, but like the palace, the sandy beasts were unscathed.

With the warrior zharie occupied, Errazure slipped past his abominable creations and scooped up the stone. Kaedin snapped out of his stupor and pursued the shaman. Errazure thrust the stone in the ghost's direction. Kaedin dodged his reach, but he was incapable of snatching the stone back.

"Kamina!" shouted Kaedin. "He is getting away!" Kamina picked herself up, clutching Ascara's hilt as Errazure fled further into the depths of his crumbling palace. She started to give chase, but spotted Jazintha in more immediate danger. One of the sand creatures smacked the zharie into the wall with such force that she lost hold of her daggers.

"Kamina!" repeated Kaedin, but she turned her back on him, rushing to Jazintha's aid. The elf sliced through the sand creatures with Ascara, cutting off their arms.

"I did not needs your helps!" exclaimed the zharie as she gathered up her daggers from the ground.

"You are welcome," replied Kamina sourly. Both turned to pursue Errazure, but the palace shook again, more violently than before. Lumps of sand crashed down from the ceiling as the subsiding accelerated. From the bowels of the decomposing building they heard Errazure's mocking laugh.

"I would rather be buried alive with the stone than have Gianna's plan ruined," he yelled, echoing up to them.

"We have to go after it," declared Kamina, but Jazintha stood in her path.

"If we do we will die," she retorted as the sand started to sink below her feet. She grabbed the stubborn elf by the arm, but Kamina would not move.

"We did not come all this way to leave without the stone!" exclaimed the elf.

"Kamina," said Kaedin solemnly. "It is not your fault." His words shot into her troubled heart, and she submitted to Jazintha's strength. They fled the chamber as the ceiling collapsed. The trio sprinted through the hallway of columns that crumpled all around them, the floor sinking beneath their feet. Kamina could see the exit in sight, but it was lost in the haze as they were consumed by a cloud of sand.

CHAPTER THIRTY-FIVE
THE STONE OF SPIRITS

KAMINA AND JAZINTHA EMERGED FROM THE SAND CLOUD, coughing and spluttering as they dusted themselves off. Kaedin's spirit remained unaffected, watching as the air cleared around him. They stared back at the sunken sand palace, now nothing more than a large divot in the desert floor, another unremarkable part of the Darosa wastelands. It was as if their encounter with Errazure had been erased from existence, and the Stone of Spirits along with it.

"We have to dig it up," Kamina said eventually. Her words were laced with a new found conviction sparked by the shaman's revelations.

"It is buried too deeps," said Jazintha. "Besides, we haves no tools."

"Then we will dig with our hands!" she exclaimed. The elf retraced her steps until she was convinced she stood where the sand palace had fallen, and where Errazure had surely suffocated under the weight of his own tomb.

"It woulds take days!" implored the zharie, following her. "We woulds die before we evens reach halfway," Jazintha paused to scan the desert for something that may aid their survival, while Kamina stared at the sand at her feet. She glanced up to find Kaedin lingering where they had left him, clearly troubled by Errazure's confession concerning Jaelyn's target.

"Kaedin," she called out. "What happened when you touched the stone?"

"At first, nothing, but then…" Kaedin struggled to find the right words to explain the sensation he had experienced. "It felt as if I was suddenly somewhere I should not be, as if it were alive, judging me. It was as if the stone was rejecting me, and then I felt a force rip me away."

"Maybe Gianna thinks you unworthy of touching her jewel," said Jazintha.

"You are missing the point," said Kamina. "We do have something to dig with." They turned to Kaedin, who was slightly unnerved by their synchronous smiles. Only when Kamina nodded down at the sand did he finally latch on to their intentions

"No," he stated. "No no no no no."

"Kaedin, the force did not just repel you. It hit all of us. It weakened the walls of the tomb. You could blast your way out."

"Do you not understand!?" snapped the spirit in a harsh, despondent tone. "Did you not hear him? It was not me Jaelyn was sent to kill. I was not meant to be like this. It was you, so why do you not go and get it? Or you," he sneered, turning on Jazintha, "if I am so unworthy of your precious Gianna."

"But…" Kamina faltered. "But you said…"

"I lied," he confessed. "Can you not comprehend what it is like to know that you are dead because of a mistake?" Kaedin immediately regretted lashing out at her, the one person who loved him most in this world

Kamina stood open mouthed, unable to answer or shed any more tears. She had not travelled halfway around the world to come so close to her prize, to bring Kaedin and Talia back from dead, only to be thwarted by the shallow depths of sand that separated her from the Stone of Spirits. She slid down onto her knees and started to dig with her hands cupped like a spade.

"Kamina, I am sorry." She refused to listen to the sullen spirit, too busy clawing her way into the sand. "Kamina?"

The fate of the world is at stake, yet all you care about is how it affects you!" It was her turn to lash out. "I am sorry the world does not revolve around you, Kaedin. I am sorry you are not the centre of everything. I am sorry you are not evil enough to have an assassin sent to kill you!" Her arms were already starting to ache, but Kamina would continue until she found the Stone of Spirits or death found her. She did not even stop when Kaedin stood before her, digging through his transparent feet. Kaedin allowed his ghostly form to descend down through the sand. His eyes pleaded for forgiveness before his head disappeared entirely under the surface. She stopped her futile attempt to dig out the stone and joined Jazintha, who had sidled away to safety.

"Maybe he coulds not finds it?" suggested Jazintha, impatiently waiting for something to happen.

An explosion of sand and energy slammed the pair onto their backs. Amidst the blast, Kamina was sure she had heard Kaedin scream.

"Kaedin?" she called out as she picked herself up, fatigued by the strain of her spirit bond. She could hear his faint voice growing louder as he fell from above, the repulsion of the stone having shot him straight up into the sky. The spirit plummeted down into the dry, sandy hole. Kamina stepped up to the precipice of the pit, much bigger than before, and saw the ghost partially submerged at its centre.

"Did it work?" he grumbled.

"It is a start," she replied.

"You will needs to do its several more times," added Jazintha, appearing by her side. Kaedin mumbled something inaudible even to Kamina's ears, as his body receded back down into the gritty sand. The girls withdrew, awaiting the next explosion. Kaedin was forced to continue this action six times, and each time Kamina was stung by their spirit bond being stretched to its limit. The constant force was more taxing with each turbulent attempt to reach the stone, but she held on for both their sakes.

"I found it!" they heard him shout after the sixth attempt. Jazintha helped her up as they ambled towards the rim of what was now a large crater. Parts of the sand palace remained intact, jutting out of the pit. At the centre sat

Kaedin, staring at something shimmering in the light of the twin suns. The two girls raced down the steep slopes towards the stone, but paused as they reached it. The Jewel of Gianna was still clutched by Errazure's dead hand. The appendage had twisted and withered, now a proper reflection of the shaman's true age.

Kamina edged cautiously towards the skeleton hand, expecting it to jerk back to life and snatch the treasure away. She clasped the stone in her hand and tried to pull it free, but the shaman's dead fingers were locked tightly around the prize. Kamina yanked at it harder. The hand broke apart, decomposing to into dust as she fell. Kamina lay back and stared at the beautiful jewel, admiring the silvery white energy waltzing within.

She had found the Stone of Spirits.

It was almost impossible to believe that such a small object, so minute it could be held in her hands, had the power to thwart Malenek's entire army of sprits and ætherghouls. And yet, holding it now, she felt an intense closeness to Enara, the energy within pulsing through the crystal shell. With the stone now in her possession, she would soon be able to help save the world and free Talia from her prison.

Jazintha snatched the Jewel of Gianna from the elf's delicate hands. Kamina rose slowly, as the warrior zharie pointed one of her dagger at her. She held the stone high up in her other hand, in case Kamina should attempt to steal it.

"I am sorries," she said, "but this belongs to my family."

"Jazintha, we need it to defeat the spirits," said the elf. "You would never have found it without us."

"And you wills be welcomes in Zatharu as heroes. You can stays with us untils the threat in your country is over."

"Do you not understand?" she pleaded. "It will never be over. Did you not hear Errazure? They plan to turn the entire world into spirits!"

"They wills not succeed. What he claims is impossible!" But the zharie's voice wavered. She waited for Kamina to respond, but the elf was too busy gazing at something above her. Jazintha felt the stone plucked right out of her fingertips. She jumped round, dagger aimed upwards, only to be met by another ghost.

"Nothing is impossible," said Callaghan, holding the stone in one hand, and a rope ladder in the other. The ladder stretched high into the sky, where a fantastic sight greeted the desert trio. It was like a ship of the ocean, hovering in mid-air, bobbing in the blue sky.

"It is called a norora," said the ranger as he dropped down onto the sand. "A very impressive Zalestian invention." Jazintha was so shocked at seeing him there, she momentarily forgot about the stone. Their eyes met briefly, hers full of overwhelming emotion, while his were filled with regret that he could not return the affection. He simply bowed for the zharie.

"Jazintha Zaleed Zharie," he said. She did not have time to reply, as

Kamina interrupted their moment, springing towards the ranger with such force that she almost bowled him over.

"I thought you were dead," she whispered, hugging him tight. Since their arrival in Zalestia, Kamina had been forced to be strong, to dig deep inside herself and discover the qualities needed to complete this quest. Now that Callaghan was here, now that he was alive, all she wanted to do was collapse in his safe arms and let him protect her, at least for a little while. His rough hand stroked her soft blonde hair, comforting her.

"And I you, my little friend. I am glad it is not so." He glanced over to Kaedin, who wore a wide grin on his ghostly face. Callaghan smiled back at him, happy to see they had survived the desert.

"How did you find us?" he asked.

"We spotted explosions of sand in the distance," said Callaghan.

"Promise you will not leave us again," pleaded Kamina, gazing up at him with her wide green eyes. Despite himself, she saw his hesitation, the edge of his lips contorting against his smile.

"It would seem you do not need my help," he said, turning their attentions to the jewel in his hands. "So this is the Stone of Spirits?" Kamina nodded, but Jazintha was quick to interject.

"It is the Jewel of Gianna!" she stated. "It belongs to my peoples."

"That is something to discuss with your father," responded the ranger. "He awaits us above. Come." He offered Jazintha the rope ladder. The zharie showed off her superior strength and skill, ascending to the airship with agility and speed. Callaghan held the steps for Kaedin, but the ghost could not clutch the rungs long enough to ascend.

"I will run," he said finally, tired of falling on his face.

"It will take too long," urged Callaghan. ""Besides, the bond between you and Kamina would be stretched far too thin." Kamina had an idea, and whispered it into Callaghan's ear. The spirit watched the ranger glance between himself and the stone.

"No," protested Kaedin, backing away from them.

"Time is of the essence, Kaedin," stressed Callaghan.

"Stop being such a coward," Kamina added. "You've already done it six times."

Kaedin begrudgingly submitted himself to be zapped by the stone again. He took hold of the rope ladder and elevated himself. Callaghan tapped his feet with the jewel. A rush of energy propelled him upwards, past the blur of the rope ladder and through the norora. He popped out of its roof and into the air, shortly falling back towards the ground. He focused his energy to land on the outer hull of the norora, before slowly phasing though it. He emerged in the cabin of the airship, discovering he had to concentrate more than usual just to stand on its deck.

"We meet again, young spirit," bellowed the voice of Zahyr Zaleed Khan. "You always make such grand entrances." Kaedin stood before Zahyr, embarrassed by the mocking leer painted across the Khan's face. The spirit scanned the dark interior of the norora. While the outer hull was comprised of gruzalug shell segments, the inside was fashioned like the lower deck of the *Arad Nor*, fitted with a floor of light wood. There were triangular portholes dotted along the walls, and at the centre sat a bizarre fusion of metal and glass. The chaotic contraption housed glowing green rocks, which were being licked by a fire, pumping a faint turquoise gas into the fabric balloon above.

"Do you have it?" asked the Khan as Jazintha clambered into the craft.

"The ranger has it," she said. Kamina and Callaghan eventually joined them inside the norora, the ranger closing the hatch behind them.

"Let me see it, Callaghan," said Zahyr. "Let me feast me eyes upon the jewel once more." The ranger, aware of the skado lurking in the shadows, handed the stone over to him, despite Kamina's shaking her head.

"I am proud of you, my daughter," roared the Khan, embellishing Jazintha for the benefit of the Amarosians. "You have returned to us our dearest treasure, stolen from us so many years ago. Let us speed home so we can spread this news far and wide across Zalestia."

"Zahyr, I will need the stone back," stated Callaghan.

"But it is the Jewel of Gianna?" urged the Khan. "Where is your Stone of Spirits?"

"They are one and the same," said Jazintha.

"How do you know this?" asked Callaghan.

"We met Errazure Ecko," replied Kamina. "He told us as much."

"It cannot be so!" exclaimed the Khan, scaring the elf slightly, but Jazintha intervened.

"It is true, father. He claimed its power kept him alive all this time."

"This complicates things, Callaghan" said Zahyr. "You think the Jewel of Gianna is a weapon?"

"I do," replied the ranger. "We know it repels spirits, but that cannot be all there is to it. Malenek would not be so concerned with it otherwise. May I?" Zahyr grudgingly gave back the Jewel of Gianna. The ranger studied it, mesmerised as Kamina had been by the lively energy within.

"What else did Errazure say?" he asked. The desert trio shared secret glances. Kaedin stepped away to the opposite end of the norora, sulking into transparency. "What has transpired to make him so distant?"

Kamina repeated to Callaghan and Zahyr what Errazure had told them; that it was she who was the target of the assassination, not Kaedin. It was she who posed a threat to their plan.

"A self-fulfilling prophecy," said Callaghan.

"A what?" she asked.

"A prophecy was made that you would thwart this plan, and yet, had you never been singled out, you may never have been caught up in these events. Do you not see, Kamina? By targeting you, they created the very person the prophecy had warned them against."

"It should be me," she murmured. "I should be the spirit."

"No," he said in his warm, husky voice. "Things happen for a reason. Had events not played out exactly as they have, you may never have ventured here to find the stone. Now that you have, we stand a real chance of stopping Malenek and his spirit army. Focus on that."

"So what do we do with it?" she asked. Callaghan's brief smile faded

"I have no idea, although seeing it… it looks similar to Ascara's jewel."

"Perhaps it requires an incantation as well," said Kamina.

"Yes, but that knowledge has been passed down by the rangers. This may require a different prayer, but it cannot hurt to try." The ranger, attempting to evoke the magic of the Stone of Spirits, started to whisper Ascara's words against its smooth surface.

"Acsentio…"

"Wait!" exclaimed Kaedin. "We do not know what the stone does. It might send me away to Loria."

"It might equally return you to this world," said Callaghan. "We must try, Kaedin."

"Then please just let me have a moment." The ranger assented with a polite nod. The spirit stepped over to one of the portholes, watching as the sand passed by below. Kamina joined him, unsure what to say, and so stood in silence until he spoke.

"If this is it," mumbled Kaedin so only she could hear. "If this is to be my end in this journey, then I want you to find Nyssa. I want you to tell her I am sorry. Tell her I wish we could have been rangers together."

"I will," whispered Kamina. "Kaedin, I wish it had been me that Jaelyn hit with the spell."

"Let us do this," he declared, ignoring Kamina's words as he returned to Callaghan.

"Are you sure?" asked the ranger. The spirit rattled a tense now. His form fluctuated erratically as Callaghan lifted the stone close to his lips.

"Ascentio Risaar Emanos."

They watched with anticipation as the light within the stone tingled slightly, but beyond that, there was nothing. The tiny sliver of hope Kamina had allowed herself now disintegrated like Errazure's cursed hand. It was not just her hope, but Kaedin's as well. He continued to watch the Stone of Spirits intently, while Kamina hung her head low.

"Perhaps it has to be someones bonded with a spirits," said Jazintha, joining them as they strived to unlock the secrets of the stone. Callaghan handed the artefact to Kamina. The elven girl closed her eyes, praying to the Elementals that it would work.

"Acsentio Risaar Emanos." Again the light within sparked, more alive, briefly remembering its purpose, but forgetting just as quickly, the flicker lost in the swirling light.

"What if it is not Risaar we should be praying to?" asked Kaedin. Kamina repeated the invocation with the names of the other Elementals – Ygrain, Aquill, and Whirren – but each attempt only wrought further disappointment.

"Your Amarosian words will not work!" exclaimed Zahyr, insinuating himself into the huddle of adventurers. "It is the Jewel of Gianna!" Callaghan nodded for Kamina to try what the Khan was suggesting.

"Acsentio Gianna Emanos," she whispered. The words provided the same stunted reaction within the stone as before. Kamina's jubilation at finding the jewel quickly soured into frustration.

"No no no! You still use Amarosian words!" snapped the Khan, snatching it from the elf. "We are in Zalestia." He tried offering various Zalestian prayers to the jewel in Gianna's name, but his words failed to do anything.

"Father, there is somethings I must tell you abouts Gianna," said Jazintha, staring up into Zahyr's wide, displeased eyes. "Errazure claimed she is behinds the spirit army, and that she will use Malenek as her vessel here on Emdara."

"Do not dare speak out against the gods!" he roared. "Especially Mother Gianna!"

"But it is true!" she retorted. "How else do you explains it?"

"Your daughter is telling you the truth," stated Kaedin, hovering near the leery Khan. "I entered Errazure's thoughts and saw his memories. He was visited by a being of light. She said her name was Gianna. It was she who singled out Kamina to him."

"Nonsense!" exclaimed Zahyr, "Gianna would never betray us."

"What if it was not Gianna?" posed Callaghan.

"What are you suggesting, ranger?" asked Zahyr.

"It is evident now that some unseen adversary has been manipulating events, lining up the pieces for years, decades even, pushing them to action. The being that visited Errazure claimed to be Gianna, but what if it was not?" Zahyr's eyes sparkled with the fire of an idea.

"Azik," he whispered, forgetting his daughter's blasphemy.

"The Betrayer," said Jazintha, sharing the same thought as her father.

"Did you not say that Malenek though Azik's equal was Risaar?" Kamina asked Callaghan, recalling his history lesson in Calisto.

"Beyond the imagery of fire, they are very different," said the ranger. "Azik was originally the God of Joy, but betrayed Gianna, his mother, and killed his father, Egoras. Risaar stood equal among the Elementals."

"Gianna casts Azik down into Haegor, where he was forced to remains, watching those who sinned burns for all eternity in the eternal flames of the underworlds," added the zharie.

"But without fire we would have no warmth," said Kamina. "Risaar granted us this gift." She indicated Ascara, only now realising she was still in possession of the sword. She hastily handed Risaar's blade back to Callaghan.

"In Zalestian lore," he explained, taking the sword, "man stole the fire from the gods, which is why the underworld is imagined as a furnace. It represents their fury at the theft."

"And now we have stolen their wings!" laughed Zahyr. "How do like my flying ship, little elves? I named it after the Goddess of the Wind. She will honour us with a speedy flight."

He moved to the centre of the craft, bellowing orders at his men. They pushed the controls and levers. The flames increased in height, and the rocks glowed green. The resulting jolt of gas thrust the norora ahead at an even faster pace. The small band of adventurers adjusted to life sailing through the skies, watching the sand dunes drift by below. The distance did not seem so great from above, thought Kamina. Their trek through the desert wastes was made to feel small and insignificant.

"The legends say thats the entrance to Haegor is in the Darosa Desert," noted Jazintha, watching the dusk sky turn red above the dunes. "What if Azik found a way out?"

"Or what if someone set him free?" thought Callaghan aloud. He recalled the story Ajarone had told him about the Stone Sect. Could they have used it to unleash a god? While they had managed to find the Stone of Spirits, they now had more questions than answers.

Soon they could make out the deep green of the jungle canopy, and in the distance, the citadel of Zatharu. Jazintha realised that this was not their final destination.

"Where are we going?" she asked her father.

"It is a secret," he replied, smiling as he admired the Jewel of Gianna.

CHAPTER THIRTY-SIX

THE PIT AND THE PAST

THE NORORA CARRIED THE REUNITED ADVENTURERS TO THEIR final destination, a small fortified compound hidden within the dense jungles north of Zatharu. It was far enough away from the citadel that no keen-eyed citizen could see the strange airships taking off and landing, even if they were high up in the palace.

The sky ship slowly descended, landing within the walls of an open roofed structure. The passengers peered out of the portholes, gawking at the fleet of nororas that filled the hanger. Callaghan counted at least fifty ships, possibly more, all in the late stages of construction. Zahyr barked at his pilots as they fumbled the landing, touching down with a sudden jerk.

"They need to be more careful," he translated into Amarosian.

"How long has this been here?" asked Jazintha as they disembarked from the craft.

"And why do you need so many?" inquired the ranger, slightly unnerved by this secret compound.

"It was built on the ruins of an old zirkesh several years ago," replied Zahyr, "and we need as many as we can lay our hands on."

Various building crews buzzed around the hulls. Kamina was shocked to see that these were no ordinary craftsmen, but slaves bonded by chains. They were watched over by a merciless squad of zeetoo. More sentries were stationed further out of the compound, armed with a bola to stop any escape attempts without killing the slaves.

"This is why the gruzalugs attacks us," said Jazintha, glancing over the rows of the desert snake shells. "You have been hunting thems here."

"Their armour is incredibly light and dense," he explained. "No spear or arrow can penetrate it. They are perfect for our purposes."

"This is an invasion fleet," said Callaghan.

"No, it is an annihilation fleet!" roared the Khan. "Ever since I inherited the throne of Zalestia, I have devoted my life to two things - finding the Jewel of Gianna, and defeating those who dare insult our gods and kill my own blood." He dazzled them with Jewel of Gianna, locked in his vice-like grip. "Today, I have achieved the first. It can only be a sign from the Mother Goddess that we will soon realize the second."

"Zahyr, you cannot do this," urged Callaghan.

"I can and I will!" he snapped back. "The Amarosians have spent all their strength building defences around their coast. They expect the fight to come from the sea, not from the skies!"

"Please Zahyr, allow me to use a norora to return with the stone and save us from the spirits. Instead of conquering Amaros, you could be something much greater."

"And what is that?" he asked.

"Its saviour."

"Ha! Playing to my vanity will not quash my need for vengeance, Ranger of Ishkava," said the Khan. "Malenek's plan will fail, and when it does, I will swoop in and finish what he has started."

"And if Malenek succeeds?" asked Callaghan. "You will be gifting him the ability to bring the spirits here."

"The Amarosians have an entire army against a handful of ghosts. All they have to do is kill one man, and like that, they all disappear."

"You do not know that for sure," said the ranger, trying to convince him of a nobler path, but the Khan was toying with him.

"We should find out," said Zahyr. He subtly nodded to Mazban Zool, who had shifted behind Kamina like a shadow. He flashed a blade from his shawl and held it to the side of her neck. The skado surrounded the group, armed with scimitars. Kaedin made to dash towards Kamina, but Zahyr stalled him with a pointed finger. "Do not move, spirit, or your sister's throat will be cut and you will cease to be."

"Not before I kill you," said Kaedin.

"Zahyr!" yelled Callaghan, withdrawing Ascara. "You go too far. They are innocent in this." Those within the norora hangar, zeetoo and slave alike, paused to watch the situation escalate.

"Father, what are you doing?" quizzed Jazintha.

"I thought you would be proud?" replied Zahyr, confused by his daughter's demeanour. "The entire armada will be complete in a matter of days. You will live to see your country victorious over our enemies."

"Or see your friends and family fall to the spirits," countered Callaghan, seething at Zahyr's ignorance and betrayal.

"Watch your sharp tongue, ranger, or it will feel a sharper blade cut it out. On the subject of blades, give me your sword, or my mazban will put an end to their precious bonded lives." Gazing into Kamina's wide, frightened eyes, Callaghan could see no alternative. He slowly handed Ascara to one of the skado, who delivered it to Zahyr. The Khan admired the red ruby encrusted in her hilt. He then dealt his daughter an unexpected blow to the face with the handle. She stumbled to the ground.

"That is for stealing the blade from me, and a kind reminder, my daughter, that I am your Khan."

"I am sorry to displease you, my Khan," said the zharie, her cheek stinging with pain and embarrassment.

"You will return to Zatharu and remain in your quarters until I command otherwise," he ordered.

"Yes, my Khan," said Jazintha, before being ushered away by an armed escort of zeetoo. She allowed herself one last apologetic glance back at Callaghan and Kamina.

"What shall we do with them, my Khan?" asked Mazban Zool. Zahyr pondered this for a moment.

"The pit," he instructed finally.

"Move!" screamed the Khan's subordinate. He marshalled the prisoners out of the hanger to a small flat plain at the far corner of the compound. There were several wells dug into the ground, each covered by a heavy stone grate. Two zeetoo heaved one of the grates aside. They tied a long length of knotted rope to the grate, throwing it down into the dark depths of the shaft.

"You are making a mistake, Zahyr," said Callaghan. "We must stop Malenek. He is only a pawn in a much larger game."

"A game I will win," said the Khan, smirking at the ranger.

"How do you expect to win when you do not truly know your opponent?"

"One does not need to see one's opponent to defeat them," said Mazban Zool, interjecting on the Khan's behalf.

"You do not even know the rules," the ranger said in riposte. "How do you know you too are not being manoeuvred into this course of action?"

"I make my own rules!" roared the Khan. "Soon I will rule all of Emdara. I will keep you alive long enough to witness it. Your fate after that will depend on you." With this last threat, Zahyr Zaleed Khan left them in the hands of his ominous mazban.

"Down," directed Zool. Callaghan glimpsed at his surroundings again, trying to judge if he could somehow turn the tables on Zool and his armed zeetoo, but the mazban would kill Kamina before the ranger could even reach him. Callaghan took hold of the rope, and descended into the depressing pit.

"You go next," commanded the mazban, pointing at Kaedin.

"We need to go together," replied the ghost, indicating Kamina.

"If you insist," he said, shoving Kamina down the hole. Her sudden screams echoed out of the pit. She snatched at the snaking rope, but it blurred by her. The elf's short fall ended when Callaghan caught her in his arms.

Above them, the spirit screamed at the mazban as he tried to tackle him. The distance from Kamina weakened him. He started to fade against his will, disappearing into the ground as he lost coherence.

"Join your friends or I will make sure this well is filled with water once more," threatened Zool. Kaedin crawled back to the hole, plummeting down into the pit. His luminescence streamed down the walls in a circle of light, landing at the bottom unharmed. The mazban loomed over the hole, sneering at them. He spat down the well as the zeetoo retracted the rope. The spittle struck Callaghan. He wiped it off as the grate scraped back into place. Pinpoints of light beamed through its holes, marking their only way out of the tall prison.

Jazintha sat mournfully inside a britzka as the men harnessed rhenzos to the front. Her father approached the carriage, leaning inside the window.

"What fate have you bestowed on the Amarosians?" she inquired softly.

"Mazban Zool is placing them in the pit."

"If that is what you believe they deserve for retrieving the Jewel of Gianna, then it is a fitting punishment," she said, not wishing to aggravate her father any further.

"I thought you hated everything about Amaros?" said Zahyr. Although he knew she chose her words carefully to pacify him, shame still dirtied his daughter's pretty face. "We are about to deliver a decisive blow in this endless war, yet you have the look of someone who has already lost."

Zahyr's hand graced his daughter's chin, tilting her head up, forcing her to look at him. Jazintha gazed into his old, brown eyes, filled with decades of hurt and despair, pain he held the Amarosians accountable for. What if the ranger was right? Jazintha thought. What if my father is being manipulated into this? She would like to have believed that he had been swayed towards this course of action, that he was not as bloodthirsty as he claimed. He was blinded by his vengeance, unable to see the harmful repercussions of his actions. He had used Callaghan to rescue her, and the elves to recover the Jewel of Gianna, but now he tossed them all aside. There was no honour in that, and yet she had always considered her father to be an honourable man.

"What if we could be their saviours, instead of their conquerors, like the ranger says?" she asked, appealing to his humanity. "Surely this is worth more?"

"My noble, naive daughter, if we offered them our assistance, they would take it, but after the threat has passed, the offering would be forgotten under the weight of this war, a war which has ravaged us since before you were born. No, they would soon forget our helping hand, but not the crushing fist that will rule them!" He slammed his own fist down against the door of the britzka, right in front of her face. Jazintha placed her hand gently on his, finally seeing sense in her conflicting emotions. She could not allow her beliefs to be swayed by his brute force. She stared back at her father with the face of a hardened, yet compassionate zharie.

"The ranger saved my life once from the rebels. The elves likewise in the desert. They found the Jewel of Gianna, yet you reward them with imprisonment while you go off to destroy their lands?" She could see her father's temper flare, but she was yet to deliver her final blow. "Is this what my life is worth to you?"

Zahyr was left speechless. He eventually found his tongue, ordering the zeetoo to transport Jazintha back to Zatharu and out of his sights. As the britzka disappeared into the jungle, Zahyr Zaleed Khan was left standing alone holding his two prizes; the sword of Risaar and the Jewel of Gianna.

"It is done, my Khan," Zool informed him, watching the britzka rumble away.

"She will see," he muttered, still staring at the treasures in his hands "Any chance for peace has long since passed. This war will end with only one victor. Come, tonight we drink to Kratoz, God of War. May he bless our next battle with his blackened blood."

*

Kamina sprawled over the pit's dank floor far below the ground, resting her back against the damp, mossy wall. She was exhausted from their momentous march into the Darosa Desert. Callaghan scoured the surface opposite her, searching for hand holds to climb. Kaedin glowered beside her, his eerie, inescapable eyes glaring down, boring into her head.

"What is it?" she asked, unable to suffer the spirit's silence any longer.

"This is all your fault," said the spirit. "You allowed yourself to be caught off-guard…"

"Kaedin."

"…and now we are stuck in this hole!" he continued.

"Kaedin!" repeated Callaghan, more firmly this time. "Enough of this. It is nobody's fault except mine. I should never have trusted Zahyr. Besides, you are wrong. Only Kamina and I are stuck. This was not the only well in the vicinity. Perhaps you could use your unique gift to scout around us, see if there is anything that might help our predicament." Kaedin resisted the urge to reply, storming off through the wall without a sound. With the spirit gone, Callaghan sat next to Kamina, the pair hunched against the wall.

"He is just upset," said the ranger. "Errazure's words have clearly unsettled him."

"He has every right to be," she sobbed. "He is a spirit because of me. Because I am evil."

"Kamina, you are the furthest thing on Enara from evil," Callaghan said, amazed at the words spilling from her innocent little mouth.

"Errazure said I was evil. Jaelyn travelled around the world just to kill me. He would not have done so unless he believed the same."

"They have been tricked into believing this," he said.

"Have they?" exclaimed Kamina, startling the ranger. "How do you know for sure? When I saw Zahyr with Jazintha, I realised I do not know who my father is. What if he was evil? Kaedin said our parents… my grandparents were killed by raiders, but Talia survived… what if they kidnapped her and… and…"

"Kamina…" objected Callaghan, but she ignored him.

"…what if Errazure was right?" she prattled on. "What if I am going to destroy the world?"

"Kamina Elloeth, I do not believe you have a bad bone in your entire body." He graced her blushing cheek with a gentle finger. "You have sacrificed so much in order to save a country of people who fear and hate your kind." She gazed up into his blue eyes, trusting and warm "It does not matter who your father is. Talia raised you, and she raised you well. You have a good soul. Trust in that."

"He is right," said Kaedin, re-emerging from the wall. "This is not your fault." The spirit indicated his ghostly body. "You did not arm Jaelyn with magic or send him to Elgrin. You are as much a victim as I am."

"You should not have been snooping," said Kamina, wiping her tears away, "but I am glad you were."

"I was not snooping," he said. "Your voices carry through the walls. They were impossible to escape, but... I heard something else."

"What was it?" asked the ranger. The spirit squirmed anxiously. "What did you hear?"

"As I entered the wall, I was surrounded by darkness. I could hear your voices, but there were others, more distant. I was not just hearing them, Callaghan, I was feeling them."

"The other spirits?" he guessed. Kaedin nodded, clearly troubled by the reoccurrence of this connection.

"How is that even possible?" asked Kamina. "You are bonded to me, not Malenek?" Her last words carried with them a hint of annoyance, as if her brother had somehow betrayed her.

"Kaedin and the other spirits reside in the same plane of existence, somewhere between our world and Illyria," deduced Callaghan. "It is possible that this is where the connection comes from."

"But why now?" Kaedin asked. "We are as far from Amaros as we could possibly be."

"Perhaps they are reaching out, trying to find you?" proposed Callaghan.

"Or because the spirit world is getting closer to our own," suggested Kamina. "Like Oldwyn said."

"This may offer us an unforeseen advantage," said the ranger.

"We are stuck in the bottom of a well with no hope of escape," replied the spirit. "What advantage can if possibly give us?"

"There is always hope, Kaedin," stated Callaghan. "You said you could feel them. Can you see where they are?" The spirit closed his eyes and focused on the spirit army marching across Amaros. The strands of energy that held his form together pulsed like a heartbeat.

"Caspia," he murmured, opening his eyes. "They have entered Caspia."

CHAPTER THIRTY-SEVEN

THE ENEMY WITHIN

WARNING BELLS TOLLED THROUGHOUT THE CITY OF CALISTO, as watchmen spread word of a small regiment approaching from the west. Duke Garstang, recently arrived back from Gorran, joined Craecoran Gemmel as their men rallied to their stations. They all feared that the worst had finally arrived; that the contingent of men advancing towards them were not men at all, but vengeance spirits.

"Let us hope the mage has prepared his magics by now," said Duke Garstang. As he spoke, Ramiro and Cohen were rushing to the library where the cyclops had hidden himself away.

"Oldwyn!" exclaimed Ramiro, descending into the obscurity of the lower levels ahead of the aged Cohen Hesh. "The spirits are upon us!" Amidst the few candles flickering in the darkness, they discovered Oldwyn Blake slumped over a desk, snoring loudly. He had surrounded himself with odd stacks of books and scrolls. "Oldwyn!"

The mage barely stirred. The infuriated ambassador seized the nearest book and slammed it down upon the desk. Oldwyn woke with such force that he almost toppled backwards. The staff rolled from his hand, landing at Ramiro's feet. The cyclops' watched as the ambassador picked it up. He recognised the dazzle of magic in the man's eager eyes.

"Ramiro, give me back my staff," said Oldwyn softly. The ambassador was transfixed by the green emerald embedded in the staff's crown.

"Ambassador Messer," urged Cohen. The call of his formal title broke Ramiro from his spellbound state.

"What? Oh yes," he muttered, handing the staff back to Oldwyn. He resisted letting go, his fingers wrapped firmly around the dark Elgrinwood. Oldwyn gave it a final, defiant tug to release the ambassador's grip.

"The spirit army is upon us and you dare to sleep!" he moaned, recalling what was happening outside the city. "The only reason I let you leave the Black Tower was because the ranger promised you could help defeat this army. It is time to make good on that promise."

"I am not ready," said Oldwyn. "Nor do I need to be. It is not Malenek that approaches Calisto."

"What?" asked Cohen. "Then who?"

"A lost son of this city, returning home," replied the mage. Before either Cohen or Ramiro could make sense of this riddle, a sedcoran dashed down the steps searching for them.

"Ambassadors, the army outside… they wave a flag of peace," he said.

They followed the messenger back to the western gate turret. A host of archers were spread across the city's perimeter wall, the aim of their arrows trained on the approaching men. As Ramiro and Cohen joined Duke Garstang and Craecoran Gemmel, they spied the flash of a white flag, waved by the bold leader of this rancorous rabble.

"Who are they?" asked Ramiro.

"Marauders, ambassador" said Duke Garstang.

"Scum," spat a nearby soldier. The sentiment was echoed in the emotions of the men manning the wall.

"It could be a trap by Malenek," grunted Gemmel, his eyes betraying his bloodlust.

"Malenek has no need for traps, craecoran," said Ramiro. "His army can walk through the bloody walls. Open the gates."

"But Ambassador Ramiro, those men are thieves and deserters," protested Duke Garstang.

"Most of them have bounties on their heads," added Gemmel.

"All the more reason to find out why they risk coming directly to our front door," he stressed. "As soon as they enter the gate, have your men surround and disarm them."

"As you wish," replied Craecoran Gemmel through gritted teeth. "Raise the gates!"

The marauders warily marched through the gateway and into Calisto, all too aware of the tense bowstrings of the archers above. Once inside, Vangar and his men were greeted by a contingent of armed corans, led by Craecoran Gemmel himself.

"On your knees!" he yelled. The marauders grudgingly obeyed. Those that did not were treated to the blunt end of a sword. Crowds of curious citizens and refugees converged near the gates to see what the ruckus was about. When all the marauders had been searched by the corans, it was deemed safe for the ambassadors to address them.

"Who is in charge of these men?" asked Ramiro.

"That would be me," stated Vangar. He rose to meet the ambassador, but he reconsidered when the sharp end of Craecoran Gemmel's sword was shoved in his face.

"Did you hear anyone give you permission to move, deserter?" Gemmel shouted rhetorically, putting on a show for his men. "That was always your problem, wasn't it, Innes? Never could take orders." The other marauders shifted restlessly, but Vangar kept calm. This was exactly the reception he had been expecting.

"What is your name?" asked Ramiro, ignoring the mutual enmity.

"I am sure your courteous craecoran here can tell you," he said with a wry smile.

"This is Innes Vangar, ambassador," Gemmel informed him. "He led a mutiny on a ship in Zalestia," he added with scorn.

"The *Haelion*?" recalled Ramiro, realising now why Gemmel's words were spiked with such animosity. "That was some time ago."

"Almost fifteen years," Vangar clarified.

"You've amassed a long list of crimes since then, haven't you, Innes?" said Gemmel, lingering on the last syllable of Vangar's first name, relishing the sound. "Not only in Caspia, but Heroshin, Legoria, even Rundhale. The Nkar-Lek probably want you too. Perhaps you care to explain to the ambassadors why you have slithered out from whatever rock you were hiding under? Or why they shouldn't let me execute you right here?"

"Would these executions be scheduled before or after Lord Malenek's army of spirits arrive?" asked Vangar cheekily. "Because if it is after I think we best be on our way."

"I can do it right now!" threatened Gemmel.

"Enough!" barked Ramiro, stiffening at the mention of Malenek. "What do you know about the spirits?"

"We encountered a ranger travelling with one," said Vangar. "He warned us of an impending attack by an army of ghosts. Naturally we didn't believe him, but we ventured to Gorran and saw the army for ourselves. They killed those who were so blinded by their greed that they refused to flee."

"So you admit you tried to loot Gorran?" quizzed Gemmel. "No doubt you have come here to do the same."

"I'm afraid not, Craecoran Gemmel. We were only in Gorran to take a peek at your wife's frilly bits and bobs. Lovely lace she wears, by the way." The other marauders chuckled, joined by a few of the craecoran's own men.

"I'm going to kill you!" hissed Gemmel.

"Yes, so you have said. Repeatedly. It's getting a little boring, truth be told." Vangar was enjoying riling up his former superior officer, but he gently pushed Gemmel's sword out of his face so he could address the ambassadors. "Despite the reward for our capture and almost certain execution, we have come to offer you our help, to fight the spirit army alongside you."

"What can a traitor offer that the entire army of Amaros cannot?" Craecoran Gemmel laughed out loud, as did some of his men. However, his smirk faded as a disconcerting smile crept across Vangar's scarred face.

A skilfully aimed arrow cut short the residual laughter, as well as a tuft of Craecoran Gemmel's greying hair. It shot right across his head, planting itself between the craecoran and Vangar. The soldiers scanned the surrounding buildings, spotting an Etraihu archer reloading his bow. Before Gemmel could order his own archers to retaliate, shouts of confusion screeched from all directions. A number of the spectating civilians were attacking his men, swiftly disarming most of the corans guarding the marauders.

Vangar surprised the ill-prepared craecoran, stripping him of his own sword and holding it to his throat. He gazed into Atticus Gemmel's eyes, as wide as an injured animal expecting death, but the fatal strike never came. The leader of the marauders offered the craecoran his sword back. Vangar's men followed his example unenthusiastically.

"We offer you a small band of men smart enough to outflank you inside your own walls," said Vangar. "And we didn't even need an army of ghosts to do so." He plucked the arrow embedded in the ground, fingering Gemmel's tuft of hair. "We also have the best archer in all of Amaros."

They gazed up at the building behind them where the archer was positioned. His bow was lowered, but an arrow rest on his string, ready to fire. The Etraihu's long, black hair danced on the breeze like the cloak of Death himself.

"Ariel Atari," whispered Cohen.

"Your reputation precedes you, Ariel!" Vangar shouted up to his friend. The Etraihu of the Coru tribe made a mocking salutation in reply.

"Given the threat we face, his skills would be most welcome," said Ramiro.

"Ambassadors, might I have a word in private," said Duke Garstang, after registering Gemmel's insistent glare. The two ambassadors stepped aside to join the military leaders.

"These men are not to be trusted," said Garstang. "Making a deal with them would be like making a deal with Malenek."

"They are here to hinder our efforts," added Gemmel. "I guarantee it."

"If that were true they would have already killed us," retorted Ramiro, growing tired of the craecoran's incessant malice.

"Only because you ordered they be allowed into the city in the first place!" Gemmel snapped back.

"You will address me as ambassador," hissed Ramiro. "In spite of their past, the marauders are here because they fear for their lives and wish to fight for them. The best chance to do that is if we work together. I would rather you spend more time thinking about defending my city than your own stubborn pride, is that understood, Craecoran Gemmel?"

"Yes, ambassador," he replied.

"Are you sure this is the wisest course of action?" asked Cohen.

"I am talking about a temporary truce to face an extraordinary enemy," reasoned Ramiro. "If we survive the onslaught of the spirits, then we can reassess our position."

"That is not good enough," argued Duke Garstang. "I want your word that those men will face charges for their crimes."

"If we survive, so be it," Ramiro agreed eventually, the weight of deceit weighing heavily on his conscience. "Do not breathe a word of what we have spoken about," he added, deliberately staring at Gemmel.

They returned to Vangar and his awaiting men. "We think it best that we accept your offer to aid Amaros and Calisto in this time of need," said Ramiro. "We therefore suggest a temporary truce." Vangar offered his hand, which Ramiro shook, but the others refused.

"We face a common enemy," added Duke Garstang, "but that is all we have in common." Vangar withdrew his hand with a cynical shrug.

"How would you like to proceed?" asked Cohen, keeping the peace.

"I would ask that my men and I first be granted a warm meal and a strong drink."

"Our city is not some whorish inn," warned Gemmel. "Nor will we help your men get drunk."

"It is merely to replenish our strength so we may build traps beyond these walls," said the marauder.

"Your traps are for robbing travellers on the road," said the craecoran, mocking him. "They will be useless against the spirits."

"We are not targeting the spirits," explained Vangar. "We are targeting the man who controls them. Malenek will be expecting to encounter your armies. He knows your tactics, as do I, which is why we were able to infiltrate the city so easily. He will not be expecting the marauders." Duke Garstang and Craecoran Gemmel exchanged a silent shrug, which was as much of a compliment as Vangar was likely to receive from the pair. "What are your evacuation plans?" he asked.

"Evacuation?" repeated Gemmel. "We are not planning on losing this city."

"I doubt you were planning on having a haircut today either, but it happened," grinned Vangar, still holding the tuft of hair.

"Your point?" asked the craecoran, snatching the clump of his own hair back from the marauder.

"The city is at breaking point with refugees, yet you have a fleet of empty warships anchored beyond the curved cliffs. Start sending people over by boat. In the event that we do lose the city, they can sail to Heroshin."

"Agreed," said Ramiro, Vangar's plan being the most sensible one he had heard of late. "Craecoran Gemmel, consider all available boats at your disposal."

"But ambassador, it will cause panic among those left behind," said Duke Garstang in protest. "There will be unrest."

"Then you oversee this task yourself to ensure they do not riot," replied Ramiro. "Craecoran Gemmel can show Vangar and his men to the mess hall. Make sure they have whatever they need."

"Thank you, Ambassador Messer." As Gemmel grudgingly guided the mob of marauders to have a decent meal, Ramiro and Cohen headed back to the council chambers through the boisterous, packed streets of Calisto.

"I must ask again, Ramiro, are you sure that this is the wisest move?"

"Look around, Cohen," he replied. "All these people and no-one thought to evacuate them. We have grown stubborn and conceited. The marauders live to survive. We could use some of that instinct."

"Agreed, but making a fool of Craecoran Gemmel..." Cohen started to say, but paused when he heard Duke Garstang chasing after them.

"Ambassadors," he said, catching up to them. "I must protest against using the ships for evacuation. Not only will it send out a negative message to the men, but also the citizens. We do not have nearly enough boats to carry people, or supplies to feed them while they are stranded at sea. There will be mass panics and rioting."

"I think you underestimate the people in this city," said Ramiro. "Fill the ships with women and children, no one will oppose that. The safety of our citizens is more important than the fragile egos of your men."

"They are afraid, sir," he said bluntly.

"They are soldiers," retorted Ramiro. "Lead them as such." He turned to leave, but Cohen did not follow.

"I will stay and help Duke Garstang with the evacuation plans. It may appease the men if they see an ambassador making these decisions."

"As you wish," muttered Ramiro as he left. Duke Garstang and the Heroshin ambassador were led by two soldiers down through the cliff tunnels to the docks.

"If I may be so bold, Ambassador Hesh," said Garstang in low tones, "I noticed you did not agree with Ambassador Messer either."

"He is a staunch leader who loves his city," replied Cohen, choosing his words carefully, "but I fear he has lost focus and will do anything to save it."

"Unfortunately, he has great sway in the ranks," added the duke. "He was an ataincor, like his son…" They paused in their gait. Cohen motioned the soldiers to continue ahead so they could converse in private.

"Are you suggesting that if he did not have the respect of the men, you would do something?" asked Cohen.

"The truth is that he has lost some in recent weeks with the freeing of Oldwyn Blake. There are rumours swirling the barracks. They say Ambassador Ramiro secretly worshipped the cyclops' staff."

"Oldwyn Blake has been and always will be an unstable element," said Cohen. "Ramiro's reliance on a man he reviles, who killed his only son, shows just how far he is willing to go. And all the mage seems to be doing is sleeping. I fear we may be doomed."

"And I fear we will not survive the spirit assault if Ambassador Messer is the one giving orders," declared Duke Garstang,

"What are you suggesting?" asked the ambassador.

"I would call a vote of no confidence in the Alliance."

"Such a move would take time, certainly more than is in our grasp. Miden Lome has not handled the situation at all well, and Arkes Da'ri is still in Rundhale. I am afraid for the moment there is nothing we can do to remove him."

"There is something," whispered Duke Garstang. "We could arrest him."

"This is madness!" hissed the ambassador "On what charge?"

"That he has lost all reason," replied Garstang. "We could have a physician or a priest diagnose him."

"None would dare do so," said Cohen, "and no citizen would believe it."

"Then we frame him for a crime. Something believable." Duke Garstang saw a flash of inspiration appear on Cohen's face, but it faded into a frown. "You have thought of something, ambassador?"

"No, it was stupid. This is stupid," he protested. "We cannot arrest an innocent man for a crime he has not committed, let alone an ambassador."

"We can if his actions lead to our annihilation," said Duke Garstang. "It is our only option if we are to save this city. You know I am right, Ambassador Hesh. Please, tell me how to do this."

"Right now we are all relying on Oldwyn Blake to protect us from the spirits," said Cohen. "If Ramiro were to attack him, seeking revenge for his son, he would be placing us all in danger. But you must promise that no harm will come to him."

"I promise you," vowed Duke Garstang, "but I will require your help to sway the others."

"And Ramiro will be released once this storm has blown over," stated the aged ambassador, ill at ease with their scheming in the shadows.

"Of course," he replied, although none too convincingly.

*

Ambassador Ramiro had discovered a barrage of problems awaiting his return. The refugees were crowding Caspia's streets and had been forced to take shelter wherever they could. He had called leaders within the merchants guild and the shipbuilders together with Chief Councillor Glin Corag to see if they could set up temporary accommodation within their warehouses. The merchants were worried about thieves but agreed to help, as did the shipbuilders, although they warned that their yards were littered with sharp tools and were no place for families. As the groups left to arrange these plans, Ambassador Hesh rushed in.

"Ramiro," he wheezed. "There is trouble with Oldwyn Blake."

"What in the name of the Elements has he done now?" he muttered, hurriedly followed Cohen Hesh through the university district to the library, accompanied by their bodyguards.

"You men best stay here," advised Cohen as they reached the building. "We do not wish to agitate the cyclops any further." The men stood guard at the entrance as the pair of ambassadors descended into the dark depths of the library once more. When Ramiro arrived at the bottom first, he found Oldwyn Blake politely conversing with Duke Garstang.

"Ah, ambassadors, do join us," said the mage.

"I do not understand," said Ramiro. "I was told there was a problem."

"I am afraid there is," replied Duke Garstang. "You." He attacked Oldwyn Blake without warning, swiping away his staff. The cyclops tried to fight back, but Duke Garstang knocked him out with a swift blow to the head.

"What are you doing?" exclaimed Ramiro.

"I did nothing," stated Duke Garstang. "You attacked him in a fit of rage, still angry over the death of your son. Is that not what you witnessed, Ambassador Hesh?" Ramiro cottoned on to the fact he was being set-up, staring at Cohen in disbelief.

"I am sorry," muttered his fellow ambassador.

"This is an outrage!" Ramiro said, seething. "How dare you betray your people like this!"

"It was not us who made a truce with Vangar and his bunch of thieves," snapped Duke Garstang "It was you who shook the traitor's hand."

"I will do what it takes to save my city and all those within her walls."

"So will I," said Duke Garstang. "Ambassador Messer, you are under arrest."

"No-one will believe you."

"They will believe what we tell them," replied Cohen Hesh, as he sidled up beside Duke Garstang. The Heroshin ambassador produced a hidden blade, and thrust it into Garstang's back. Cohen wrestled the staff from his hands as Garstang felt the sting of betrayal and his life slipping away.

Ramiro caught the dying dignitary as he collapsed against him. His hands were blooded from the wound, as the light left Duke Devon Garstang's sorry eyes. Cohen loomed above him, the staff in his hand, while the cyclops' mage lay unconscious behind him.

"You?" quizzed Ramiro. Cohen Hesh dropped the façade of a helpless old man. He leered as he lashed out at Ramiro with the staff. The green crystal cracked the Caspian ambassador in the head. He fell down, suffering the daze of concussion. In his distorted vision he witnessed Cohen cutting himself several times, imitating defensive wounds on his hands and arms. Ramiro tried to scramble up the steps, but he was disorientated, his feet unsure in the dark. A gush of warm blood matted his hair as he fought to stay awake.

With the stage set, Cohen called for the bodyguards. He spun the story of Ramiro Messer's betrayal, conspiring with Oldwyn to kill himself and Duke Garstang. The Heroshin ambassador cast the net wider, accusing Vangar Innes and the marauders of colluding with the schemers. The soldiers carried Ramiro away as he drifted into the abyss of unconsciousness. He struggled to speak, his words garbled by the pain in his head. The guards dragged him up the steps, with orders to lock both him and the cyclops back in the Black Tower. His mumbling grew inaudible, as he submitted to the darkness infringing on his thoughts.

The last vague image ingrained in his memory was Cohen Hesh holding the staff he had managed to keep safe for so long.

CHAPTER THIRTY-EIGHT
FIGHT OR FLIGHT

K AEDIN'S ETHEREAL GLOW SHIVERED WITHIN THE DARK WELL AS he focused all of his energy into the connection he shared with the spirit army in Amaros.

"They are in Gorran," Kaedin said as he emerged from the linked trance.

"How do you know it is Gorran?" asked Kamina. "You have never been there."

"I just know. I can tell you exactly what it looks like. Every street, every alley, every building." The spirit was clearly thrilled by the new knowledge gleaned from Malenek's ghosts.

"You must try and sever this link between yourself and the other spirits," said Callaghan.

"But why?" urged Kaedin. "We know exactly where they are now. We can keep track of them."

"And they us," noted Callaghan. "Who knows what influence they will be able to sway over you if they become aware of this connection, if they are not already."

"But they know so much. I am learning from them…"

"Kaedin, enough!" he snapped, rising to face the apparition. "If Malenek is already in Gorran, I fear we are too late."

"Then it was all for nothing," muttered Kamina, slumped on the floor. "It is over." Despite herself, she began to sob again. The ghost glared at Callaghan, a momentary look of defiance, before continuing.

"Malenek will not arrive in Calisto for at least another three days," revealed Kaedin.

"Why so long?" asked Callaghan.

"The spirits are a burden to him," he explained. "They are exhausting him of all of his energy. He travels slowly and rests often. There was some sort of altercation in Gorran. I think Malenek was injured."

Kaedin's news replenished the ranger's optimism. "Do not give up hope just yet, my little elf," said Callaghan. He knelt beside Kamina, wiping away her tears. "Rest for now, save your strength." He took off his cloak and folded it up into a pillow. Kamina lay down on the uncomfortable rocky floor, curling her body into a tight ball, the temperature beginning to drop in the twilight.

*

Kamina's sleepy eyelids shut out the murkiness of the Zalestian hole. When she opened them again, they were bathed in the warm, iridescent glow of Elgrin Forest, the twin suns sparkling through the evergreen leaves.

"Wake up, or you will miss the end of the story," teased Talia, against whose arm Kamina slumbered. She turned the heavy page of the book in front of her, revealing an illustration of various races at war. Some Kamina recognised; the elves, the humans, and what she assumed to be centaurs. Others she did not, like the swarm of small, dark creatures, tall white giants, and some mysterious blue-skinned beings.

"The various races fought over the power of the Elements," read Talia. "Some retreated in defeat, some were lost forever, and some grew more dominant." Her delicate fingers hovered over the army of men. "In the chaos, the gifts of the gods were lost."

Kamina could tell it was a dream from the tiny details. She was her own age, and not the little girl this fictitious Talia mistook her for. The story that she told was one Kamina had never heard of before. And yet, seeing Talia here now, so real, and so beautiful, she could not help but to embrace her in a tight hug, hoping never to let go.

"I know you are my mother," she whispered. "I wish you had told me."

"You are no daughter of mine," rasped another voice from her past, only this one more recent. Kamina realised the person she was cuddling was not Talia, but Errazure Ecko. He shoved her down onto the forest floor. The Zalestian shaman rose up, looming over her. The suns disappeared, replaced with sinister storm clouds. A vicious wind howled through the forest, carrying with it fire and sand, ripping off the leaves and branches from Elgrin's trees. The forest was submerged in sand, while the tree trunks were fraught by fire.

"You are evil!" he denounced, unsheathing the sword nestled by his side. She was horrified to see it was Ascara.

"I strike you down, enemy of Emdara!" he screamed, thrusting the sword into her heart.

*

Kamina woke with a start, gasping as the pain from her dream remained wedged in her chest. She was paralysed, her body drained of energy.

"Are you feeling weak?" asked Callaghan, sat next to her. Kamina managed to nod. "It is the strain of your bond. Kaedin is exploring the walls to try and find a means of escape."

"I feel cold," she said, shivering. He propped her head up on his shoulder, and used the pillowed cloak to cover her body. It eased her burden slightly, but stuck at the bottom of the dark, dried-up well, there was little else he could do.

"We are never going to get out of here" muttered Kamina, a cold shudder jolting her body.

"Have some faith," replied the ranger, although even his voice faltered as their hopes of escape swiftly faded.

Kaedin was also suffering from the tension of the spiritual tether as he drifted through the solid ground, a sensation he was still not entirely comfortable with. He had spiralled out from their cell without any luck. He had even managed to climb higher, reaching the surface, but the bond had been stretched too far for him to enact any sort of plan. The spirit was about to return to Kamina when he heard the faint reverberations of an unfamiliar voice through the rock. He followed the sound until he emerged into another shaft, much like the one they were being held prisoner in, but bigger, almost homely in a way.

"A firentazme!" exclaimed a voice. Kaedin spied an aged Zalestian with a zany face, crowned by a mop of straggly grey hair. His body was crooked, and yet he moved with an unexpected dexterity. The man's excited eyes were made bulbous by a contraption he wore around his head. It was comprised of two glass orbs that dangled in front of his face, through which he gazed at the ghost. Unlike those Kaedin had encountered before, the man was not the least bit afraid of him. He circled the spirit, studying every inch of his ethereal form.

"I am not a firentazme," replied Kaedin, struggling to concentrate as the madman danced around him, occasionally waving his hand through his intangible body. "Do not do that!"

"I am sorry, I did not mean to hurt you," he said in flawless Amarosian, recoiling from the spirit.

"It does not hurt," said Kaedin, who felt slightly guilty for snapping at this meek old man. "It is just... uncomfortable."

"I will not do it again," promised the stranger, retreating into the room. It was littered with bizarre constructs and creations; fusions of glass, metal and wood. The walls were reminiscent of Oldwyn Blake's prison cell in the Black Tower, etched with designs and schematics in black chalk. They were scrawled all the way up to the only exit, a grating in the ceiling exactly like theirs. However, the man did not seem to be here against his will.

"You are a prisoner," said Kaedin, although his hesitation made it sound more like a question.

"Not at all," he replied. "Ah, here it is." His old hands picked up a large square metal frame, fitted with a bulging, convex lens. He held it close to Kaedin, magnifying the strands of energy that fused together to fashion his elven form beyond death.

"Tendrils of energy..." muttered the man. "Magical resonance... fluctuating frequencies... What are you?"

"I am a spirit," replied Kaedin. "Of vengeance," he clarified, unsure if there was any other kind.

"Oh, I know that," chuckled the man, placing the large lens down. "But what were you before you crossed over?"

"An elf," remembered Kaedin. He had allowed himself to be judged and seen as a spirit for so long, he had almost forgotten that he was still an elf. "Who are you?"

"My name is Leotori Nazaroto. I invent things."

*

The britzka carrying Jazintha bounced along the northern jungle pass through the dead of night. The zharie was kept awake by her inner turmoil, torn between her loyalty to her father and her friendship with the people of Amaros. The Khan was fuelled by blood thirst and vengeance, and while he deserved some sort of reparation after all these years, she could not deny the right course of action as he blindly did. The entire world was in danger, and the Amarosians were helpless to defend themselves without the Jewel of Gianna. She had not believed Kamina and Kaedin when they had first spun their fantastic story of spirits and ætherghouls and the end of Emdara. Yet after their trek into the Darosa wastes and their confrontation with Errazure Ecko, the truth was undeniable.

Before Jazintha arrived at a resolution to act, she was snapped from her melancholy thoughts by a commotion outside. Shouts and yells surrounded the britzka. A spear shot through the side of the carriage, narrowly missing her head.

They were under attack from rebels.

Jazintha escaped the confined space of the britzka, readying her daggers to defend herself. Her zeetoo guard were overrun, and she could not face off against so many enemies on her own. She sprinted back towards the norora compound, kicking and slashing at anyone who dared to stand in her way. She fought well, but was wrestled to the ground by several rebels. Even in defeat she struggled, not willing to be taken prisoner again, but they overpowered and disarmed her. A hand snatched at her hair, wrenching her up. The zharie of Zatharu came face-to-face with the leader of the Jalenari rebels.

*

Kamina's strength returned as Kaedin toiled back through the rock and into their tall cell.

"Did you find a way out?" Callaghan asked, but Kaedin shook his head.

"There is no way out except the way we came in," he said, signalling the stone grate high above their heads.

"Why were you gone so long?" asked Kamina, her face pallid with worry.

"I met another prisoner," explained Kaedin. "His name is Leotori Nazaroto. He is the inventor of the flying ships."

"The man that invented the nororas would be of great intellect," commented Callaghan. "Surely he could figure a way out of this chamber?"

"If he knows of one he did not tell me. He seemed quite content in his cell. He and Oldwyn Blake would be the best of friends," the ghost joked. Callaghan was less than amused. Before Kaedin could wipe the smile from his face, they heard someone above shove the stone grate aside, the heavy grill clawing into the ground. Two silhouetted faces appeared over the edge gazing down at them. A length of rope whipped against the wall of the well as it unravelled towards them, dangling just above their heads.

"Climb!" hissed a voice they immediately recognised as Jazintha's, tinted with her trademark hostility. "Quicks!"

"You first, Kamina," said Callaghan, picking her up and lifting her so she could grab the rope. "Kaedin, climb with her through the wall." The spirit scaled up the side of the well, keeping an even pace with Kamina. Callaghan shimmied up close behind her, eventually reaching the surface and their freedom. The prisoners had presumed that Jazintha was acting alone, and were surprised to find a group of rebels awaiting them.

"The rebels rescues me," the zharie explained. "I believes you know their leader." The ranger spun round and was shocked to see Ajarone still alive.

"My friend," said Callaghan, grasping his arm. "How did you survive?"

"Hazkeer chased me to the edge of a cliff on his muzzled Xanzasaur," recalled Ajarone. "I threw my spear. He thought I had missed, but I cut the ropes binding the animal's jaws shut. It quickly devoured the man who saw fit to ride its back. Since I had defeated Hazkeer, the mantle of Jalenari leader fell to me. My first priority was to aid you in your journey back to Amaros. A spy within the walls of Zatharu told us you and the Khan had journeyed north. On the way we encountered the zharie's caravan and confronted them."

"Confronted?" mocked Jazintha. "You were surprised by our appearance. Were it nots for your whimpers about the ranger you would be foods for the creatures of the jungle."

"So what made you join them?" asked Callaghan.

"I have not joins the rebels!" she snapped back.

"We have come to a certain understanding," explained Ajarone. "The zharie agrees that the spirit army must be stopped."

"Enough talks," scowled Jazintha "We must gets you backs to Amaros."

"We cannot leave!" exclaimed Kamina, the small elf surprising even the staunchest rebel warrior. "Not without the Stone of Spirits."

"Kamina is right," said Callaghan. "If we escape without the stone, our journey will have been for nothing."

"I do not knows my ways around this place," confessed Jazintha.

"I might know someone who does," said Kaedin. The spirit tried to decipher which direction he had travelled when he encountered Leotori Nazaroto. The others followed him as he scanned the ground, looking for another stone grate. Eventually he stumbled upon the entrance to the well that

Leotori called home. Callaghan and Ajarone hastily shifted the cover plate out of the way.

"Are you sure we can trust him?" asked Callaghan.

"No," said Kaedin. "Leotori, it is Kaedin."

"The spirit?" echoed a reply from the gloom.

"Yes! You must come with us." They threw him the rope. There was a long, indecisive pause before they felt tension upon it. The troop pulled him up, and soon the aged, crazy Zalestian appeared, gazing up at his rescuers through his handcrafted glasses.

"Oh, hello there," he chirped politely, as if out for a leisurely midnight stroll rather than in the midst of a prison break. "My my, there are so many new faces."

"Hello," said Callaghan as he helped the inventor out of the hole.

"An Amarosian human," commented Leotori, inspecting the ranger from head to toe. "A fine specimen as well."

"Leotori, I am Callaghan Tor..." he began to say, slightly bemused.

"Can we saves introductions until laters?" hissed Jazintha.

"Jazintha Zaleed Zharie!" addressed Leotori, bowing before her. Jazintha allowed herself a hypocritical moment of fame.

"Gets up, please," she insisted. "We need to know where my father resides in this place."

"He has a private yurt on the opposite side of the norora compound," said the inventor. "He sometimes invites me there to discuss my designs. We drink jalajala juice fused with zojo. Very potent. Good for the soul."

"That is where the stone will be," said Jazintha over Leotori's ramblings.

"Are all of the nororas able to fly?" asked Callaghan.

"Ha ha, no no no no no," assured Leotori. "Only the prototype. The others still require the final adjustments we have made in recent weeks. You see it was all to do with the fuel injection ratio to the weight of the jalaaroca burned. It gives off a unique gas..."

"If we get you to the prototype, could you fly it to Amaros?" demanded the ranger impatiently.

"No," replied the inventor curtly.

"But you invented them?" quizzed Kamina. A zany smile broke across Leotori's face as he glanced between the pair.

"We Zalestians have a saying. In Amarosian it means, ask stupid, idiotic, dumb question, get back stupid, idiotic, dumb answer. A joke." Kamina scowled, but Callaghan knew they did not have the luxury of time to feel insulted. He was distracted by a movement in the dark. A zeetoo had spotted them and raised a warning horn to his lips. The ranger snatched Ajarone's spear and hurled it through the air. It broke the guard's horn, but not before he trumpeted out a brief alarm.

"We must act quickly!" urged Callaghan. "I will take Leotori to the norora and get her ready to fly. Kamina, you and Kaedin must find the stone."

"And whats of me?" asked Jazintha.

"You will help Ajarone distract your father and his men."

"I would be more usefuls beside you," she insisted.

"No," said Callaghan. "We need to draw your father from his quarters. I imagine your reappearance will do just the trick."

"As you wish, ranger," sulked the zharie. She led Ajarone and the rebels to face off against the zeetoo reacting to the horn.

"You two go that way," Callaghan said to the elves. "Sneak around the compound. We will approach from the far side. Meet us back at the norora." Kaedin nodded, fading into the night air.

"This way," whispered the invisible spirit, leading Kamina through the trees that skirted the norora bays. They heard a lot of commotion, but thankfully very little fighting. As they reached the opposite side of the compound, Zahyr emerged from his personal yurt, drawn out by the ruckus. He yelled something in Zalestian at an approaching zeetoo. While the elves did not fully understand the reply, they managed to distinguish Jazintha's name from the jumble of foreign words. The men hesitated, too scared to attack their ruler's only daughter. Zahyr sighed and shot back into the yurt, shouting at someone within. When he appeared again, he was armed with the ranger's stolen sword.

"He is taking Ascara with him," noted Kaedin.

"We must get the stone," insisted Kamina. "That is all that matters."

"Wait here," he said. Kamina hid amongst the trees while Kaedin invisibly floated through the fabric walls of the yurt. She did not have to wait long for his return.

"Well?" she asked.

"It is there," he confirmed, "but there are two soldiers guarding it. There is no way to retrieve it."

"I have an idea," said Kamina, smiling.

"No," Kaedin replied. "Not again."

*

Zahyr and his men marched out to meet the troop of rebels. He was dismayed to see that the messenger had not been mistaken, and that this miniscule mob was indeed led by his seditious daughter.

"Jazintha, what is the meaning of this nonsense?" he barked at her.

"I cannot stand by and wait for the world to end," she said. "Father, I am asking you to reconsider the ranger's request. Allow him and the elves to take the Jewel of Gianna to Amaros."

"And if I do not?" he asked with a smirk. "Are you and these pathetic insects going to stop me?"

"Not just us," she said.

Zahyr and his men cowered as an explosion of spiritual energy blasted his private yurt apart. The two guards watching over the Jewel of Gianna were trapped under the heavy canopy as it collapsed. The wave struck the nearest norora to the yurt, hurling it against the compound wall before it exploded in a ball of green flame.

"Secure the jewel!" he screamed at his men. They ran back, trying to free the two zeetoo from the tangle of fabric and wood that had enveloped them. They tore away at the pieces of yurt, desperately seeking the Zaleed family treasure, but it had already been acquired by a light-fingered elf after her ghostly brother had touched it.

A norora buzzed as it filled with gas in preparation for take-off. Zahyr spied Leotori Nazaroto helping Callaghan ready the prototype for launch. The landing from their journey to Darosa had bent the back rotor, which the old inventor was diligently trying to fix. The Khan marched towards them, but he was stopped by his daughter, the cold metal of her daggers tickling his throat.

"Let them go, father," she said.

"You know I cannot." He thrust his head back, cracking her in the nose. Jazintha tumbled to the ground, her twin blades nicking his neck. He wiped the blood away, peering at the red stains on his fingers as he loomed over his daughter. He was distracted as the mechanisms of the norora began to whirr.

"Stop the norora!" yelled the Khan. He snatched a spear from one of the zeetoo, and hurled it at the renegades. The ranger dived out of the way, but the old Zalestian was too slow. It snagged Leotori's shoulder, pinning him against the wall. Kaedin and Kamina ran to rendezvous with Callaghan, but a relentless volley of spears, darts, and poison arrows prevented them from reaching the norora. Zahyr caught sight of the jewel clutched in Kamina's hands. He stalked towards them, armed with Ascara.

Callaghan was cornered, striving to escape the barrage of missiles and usher the elves into the safety of the norora. The Zalestia ruler charged at them. The ranger scooped up a wayward spear, ready to reclaim his sword. However, the clash never came.

"Attack!" roared Ajarone, causing Zahyr to halt his advance on the norora. The rebels overwhelmed the zeetoo guards, freeing the slave workers and gifting the Amarosians a window to escape.

"Kamina, get inside the norora!" shouted Callaghan. The elf disappeared inside the sky ship, its hull shielding her from the unremitting fusillade. The ranger returned to Leotori flanked by Kaedin. The inventor was hung on the wall by the spear like some dirty rags hung out to dry. Callaghan was about to yank it out, but Leotori's hand grasped his arm.

"Leave me," murmured Leotori. "You must leave me."

"But we need you to fly the norora."

"Callaghan, get into the norora and seal the door," said Kaedin. "I know what to do." As another salvo of spears narrowly missed him, the ranger heeded the ghost's words, crawling under the norora and inside its impenetrable cabin, closing the hatch.

"I need you to think about flying the norora," said the spirit, edging his fingers towards Leotori's head.

"It will take too long to explain," gasped the inventor. "It is very intricate. Up is down and down is up, left is right and right is wrong. And that is to chance the directional variant. The mixture of fuel and flame is a very tricky equation, very tricky indeed, very volatile if not done correctly…"

"Leotori," said Kaedin, cutting the inventor's ramblings short. "I do not need you to tell me. Just think it. This will feel a little strange." With that hasty warning, the spirit reached into Leotori's mind, and searched for the secrets of flight.

From inside the norora, Callaghan and Kamina watched the rebels battle against Zahyr's men, while the Khan himself faced off against his own daughter. Kaedin trailed into the norora and began working the controls with his limited touch. The fuel started to burn faster, the jalaaroca gas pumping into the balloon until they had lift.

"You did it!" exclaimed Kamina, as the ship started to rise.

"What about Leotori?" asked Callaghan. Kaedin shook his head.

The brief battle paused as both sides watched the norora drifting up above them. Zahyr stood in defeat, the Jewel of Gianna lost to him, but there was still the consolation prize of Ascara.

"I still have your sword, Callaghan!" He held it aloft, bragging to the ranger. Zahyr's narcissism proved to be his weakness once more. With the sword exposed and her father distracted, Jazintha flipped onto her hands and sprung up, kicking Ascara out of his hand and into the air. The zharie caught it in a graceful flip. She sped along the compound, trying to catch up with the norora. Her father howled at his men to tackle her, but they were kept at bay by the Jalenari rebels.

Callaghan opened the hatch and descended down the rope ladder dragging along the ground. He wrapped his legs around one of the rungs, reaching out to her.

"Give me your hand." Jazintha stretched out her hand, but the norora was picking up speed. "Hurry!" he yelled.

"Take the sword!" she cried, throwing Ascara up to Callaghan's waiting hand. He caught it, but reached down again for Jazintha. Her fingers were so close to his, all she needed to do was make one final leap.

Mazban Zool fought off the rebels with a vicious flare. He snatched a bola from one of his injured opponents, and whipped the weapon around his head, before unleashing it with deadly accuracy. It wrapped around Jazintha's legs as her fingertips touched Callaghan's. The zharie stumbled, crashing to the ground in a cloud of dust. The ranger remained on the rope ladder as the norora gained altitude, watching helplessly as Jazintha writhed on the ground, until Zalestia vanished from view in the vapour of the clouds.

Jazintha glanced skywards, smiling when she saw the Amarosians escaping into the clouds of the night sky. She struggled to free herself, wriggling out of the confines of the bola. She hastily threw it at Zool, who avoided her attack. He plucked a small blowpipe from his belt and shot a poison dart at Jazintha. The needle struck her neck. The zharie slowed, staggering until she slumped to the ground paralysed. She sprawled over the dusty floor, her muscles twitching in spasm. The fighting came to a swift conclusion. Soon the dark shadow of her father loomed over her.

"I am okay," squealed Leotori in the distance. The inventor was bleeding heavily from his wound, using the spear that had injured him as a walking stick. "It is just a flesh wound."

"Have the inventor attended to," ordered Zahyr as Mazban Zool joined him. The Khan glared down at his daughter. "Then have him finish the norora fleet. And round up all those rebels still alive. I have use of them."

"Yes, my Khan," said Zool. "Do not fear, the effect of the poison is only temporary."

"I am not worried," replied Zahyr, kneeling next to Jazintha, stroking her face. "She has a far worse fate in store for her."

CHAPTER THIRTY-NINE
THE PILGRIMAGE OF THE ELVES

TENSIONS WERE AT AN ALL-TIME HIGH AMONG THE CORAN THAT manned the outer wall of Calisto. Duke Devon Garstang had been killed by the unlikely pairing of Ambassador Ramiro Messer and the cyclops mage Oldwyn Blake. On the orders of Ambassador Cohen Hesh, now head of the Alliance, Craecoran Gemmel was leading the hunt for Vangar Innes and the other marauders. They were believed to be in league with Messer, Blake, and ultimately Lord Malenek. When all this was happening behind the walls of the city the coran were sworn to protect, they could not help but wonder why defend it at all.

A spotter's cry signalled movement to the north. Everyone seized on the shouts and screams that the spirits were approaching, but it soon became apparent that this was another false alarm. The group that was following the path of the Ico were not ghosts or ætherghouls.

They were the elves of Elgrin Forest.

They moved with elegance, not hurried or in the rigid precision of a marching army, yet in harmony, as if in time to a piece of music only their pointed ears were privy to. As the elves neared the northern gate, the archers noted that a small band of humans accompanied them, walking and trotting on horses out with the main procession.

Craecoran Gemmel broke off the hunt for the marauders and made his way to the northern wall, gazing down upon the eldest elves who led their kind to Calisto. At first neither party spoke, until Ambassadors Cohen and Narain arrived, the latter feeling it was his duty to address the elves.

"My name is Isan Narain, Ambassador of Legoria."

"I am Abbal Eredu," said one of the elves, possibly the eldest of them all. "We have come to Calisto seeking refuge from the army of *gwann'gul* that spreads across Amaros."

"How do we know we can trust them?" whispered Hesh.

"The ranger did so," answered Isan, "and so will I."

"If it is our trust you question, then please speak to the humans we have harboured in our care on the way here," shouted Endo Eredu, who had heard the ambassador's whispers on the wind. Two human children, a boy and a girl mounted upon a grey-speckled mare, stood alongside the outspoken elf.

"It is true, Mr. Ambassador, sir," shouted up the boy. "A lady elf saved us in Perhola, and then Master Endo killed one of them beasts."

"They are the children from the seeing spell," Isan realised. "Raise the gates." Cohen conceded the point, but the elves arrival had unnerved him. Malenek had said the creatures of Elgrin would be left alone. He wondered what had changed in his master's plan, or if the priest had lost control of his ghoulish forces.

The elves entered the city of Calisto and were not surprised, or in any way offended, by the lukewarm reception that they received.

"Welcome to Calisto," said Ambassador Narain, cordially offering his hand in friendship for Abbal to shake. The elder elf was not accustomed to the human greeting. Isan's hand hovered between them, while Abbal offered him a courteous bow. "I am afraid the city is already overcrowded with refugees from Gorran and other towns and villages, but we will do our best to accommodate you all."

"Do you have a plan?" asked Endo.

"A plan?" repeated Isan, puzzled.

"To fight the *ackran-fay* and the *gwann'gul?*"

"Excuse my son," said Abbal. "He believes we should have defended our own borders." Given the strained tensions he was currently sensing amidst the elves, Ambassador Narain decided it would be best not to explain the events of recent days; Ramiro's betrayal, the re-incarceration of Oldwyn Blake, or the ongoing hunt for the marauders. He instead focused on the positive.

"The ranger Callaghan Tor journeyed to Zalestia to seek out a relic which may help our fight against Malenek's forces. He is aided by a young elf and her spirit companion." Isan hoped the fact that Kaedin and Kamina travelled with Callaghan would allay some of the elves' understandable fear. Instead, many of their number were aggravated by the news, except for an elder female, who smiled upon hearing that her kin were alive. He could not help but smile back, mesmerised by her aged, yet eternally bright, emerald green eyes.

The humans that had travelled with the elves received a warmer welcome. When word spread that elves had entered Calisto, Norrek accompanied an insistent Nyssa to the northern section of the city. Torg tagged along with his superior and his curious daughter, exercising his injured leg. The Tilden guard was taken aback when he spotted his horse being ridden by two children.

"Plagacia?" he said, patting her head. She neighed in recognition, nuzzling him. After the mare's manic adventures halfway across Amaros, the horse waved her tail, pleased to see her master's familiar face.

"How is it you came to ride this horse?" Torg asked the children.

"The elf lady gave her to us," replied Kiki.

"Talia Elloeth," recalled Ponyo. "She saved us." He stroked the horse again. "Plagacia. So that's your name."

"I told you it wasn't Shadowlance," said his sister with a smirk.

"Where are your parents?" asked Nyssa.

"They..." started the boy, but they were interrupted by someone shrieking their name.

"Ponyo! Kiki!" shouted a thin woman rushing over to them.

"Auntie Poppel!" exclaimed the children, almost falling off Plagacia to greet her with a momentous hug.

"I thought I had lost you!" she cried. "Where is your mother?" All Kiki could do was shake her head in reply. "Well never mind. I've got you now. And who is this?" she asked, eyeing Torg.

"Torg Magnale, miss," he replied. "Guard of Tilden."

"It was his horse that saved us," said Kiki. Poppel glanced at the horse, and remembered the mare the elf had ridden. She grabbed Torg in an unexpected embrace.

"Thank you," sobbed the woman. Torg glanced at Norrek and Nyssa, who both grinned.

"You should thank the horse," Torg said eventually.

"Then thank you, horse," said Poppel, patting Plagacia, who snorted, scaring the woman. "Never really liked horses me, but I'll make an exception for this one."

"You look famished," Norrek said to the children. "Come, we will get you some food."

"You can tell us all about your adventures," added Nyssa.

"You as well," Torg said to his hungry horse, leading Plagacia to the stables.

*

With the arrival of the elves, Vangar found the diversion he had been waiting for. Without warning, most of his men had been arrested along with Ambassador Messer, and now only a handful remained free. He needed answers, and the only man who had any was locked in the Black Tower. The barracks were now deserted, with the majority of soldiers defending the walls, while those in reserve had been ordered to the northern gate to help with the incoming elves. Only a few trainee coran remained, and two of those were positioned in front of the Black Tower.

"Gentlemen," said Vangar, greeting them. "Before you thrust your weapons at me, you should know that my best archer has two arrows trained on your jugulars. If you so much as twitch for your swords, he will let them fly right through your throats."

"You're bluffing," scoffed one. "He can't hit us both at the same…"

A pair of arrows buried themselves into the wooden beam directly above both guards.

"I assure you, he can," said Vangar, who had signalled Ariel Atari behind his back. "Now, I'm just going to take these keys, and go inside. You be good little soldiers and stay here. Oh, and smile for my friend." The marauder let himself into the Black Tower, leaving the two guards wearing fake, unbearable smiles.

"Ramiro," hissed Vangar as he snuck up the spiral steps, knocking on each passing door.

"I'm Ramiro," shouted one.

"No, I am," yelled another.

"Who is there?" mumbled the ambassador's voice eventually, locked in the penultimate cell, directly below Oldwyn Blake's current quarters.

"It is Innes Vangar," he said, trying the various keys in the ambassador's cell door.

"Locked you up as well, have they?" asked Ramiro.

"Not for a lack of trying, but it is only a matter of time. Ambassador Hesh has unleashed his ugly hounds on our trail. We need to know why?"

"Cohen killed Duke Garstang," revealed Ramiro. "He framed me and Oldwyn for it."

"Hesh killed Garstang?" Innes was shocked at the idea of the old man killing anyone.

"I believe he is in league with Lord Malenek," said Ramiro. "With the cyclops incarcerated, the city is defenceless."

"None of these keys work," said Vangar, having tried the full set.

"Cohen must have taken it," guessed Ramiro. "My freedom does not matter. You must break Oldwyn out of here. He is the only one who can defend us from the spirits." Vangar climbed to the top of the steps, but discovered the rusty key snapped in the lock.

"The key has been broken in the lock," he shouted down the steps. "There is no way to get in or out of there."

"Then we can only hope the ranger returns in time," prayed Ramiro. "It is clear to me now that Cohen supported Callaghan's quest so eagerly in order to get rid of him. He knew it was an impossible journey."

"The ranger is an expert in the impossible," remarked Vangar, recalling his dive off the Finsing Falls.

"Cohen would have a contingency for his success," cautioned Ramiro. "We need to warn the ranger. You and your men must procure a ship. Sail out of Calisto and await his return. Not too far though, for it is a great sprawling sea and you may miss him."

"Ambassador, are you telling me to steal?" he asked, a certain glee infecting Vangar's voice.

"You are a thief, are you not?" said Ramiro. The marauder could not tell if he was joking. "No, I want you to borrow one. Return with it intact so that it can be used to ferry my citizens to safety when the spirits eventually arrive."

"I will make sure of it," replied Vangar. "You have my word as a thief."

"Vangar, before you go… if we were successful in defeating the spirit army, Duke Garstang and Craecoran Gemmel would still have brought you to justice," confessed the ambassador. "I agreed to it. I am sorry."

"Do not fear, ambassador," he said, "I suspected as much. But seeing as you are in prison and I am not, we shall leave that conversation for another time. Keep well. We will try and free you soon."

"May the Elements guide you," whispered Ramiro.

Vangar skidded back down the steps. As he reached the last, he heard the voice of a sedcoran addressing the two guards on the other side of the door.

"You men heard?" said the lanky sedcoran. "Bleedin' elves have come here seeking sanctuary. Can you believe that? Was quite a sight."

The two corans said nothing, but kept their painfully fake smiles in place.

"Well, carry on," said the sedcoran, slightly perplexed. Vangar waited until his footsteps had thumped away.

"Well done men," said the marauder sarcastically, locking the door and replacing the keys on the coran's belt. "I would not move for a while if I were you. And please make sure Ambassador Ramiro is well taken care of when you find the key to his cell. Trust me, he'll soon be free, and will remember those who helped him."

The marauder disappeared out of the barracks, leaving the two corans rigidly standing guard. After a few moments, one took a chance and stepped forward. Another arrow shot into the wooden beam above him, splitting the first right down the middle. The coran jumped back to his post, retaining his awkward smile.

"That should do it," said Vangar, grinning next to Ariel Atari. "Now, let's go steal us a ship."

The two marauders cautiously made their way down to the docks, gathering some of their men along the way.

"Where is Creevy?" asked Vangar, noticing his surgeon missing.

"Arrested, along with most of the others," answered the bushy-bearded Dappin Creig. "We're all that's left."

"Dappin, you used to be a sailor, did you not?" asked their leader, looking over his shoulder.

"Many moons ago," muttered the marauder.

"I want you to take Terris and Tig and steal a ship, the fastest you can find," said Vangar. "Sail out half a day on a direct heading for Zalestia, and wait for the ranger to return."

"The ranger?" asked Dappin. "Why?"

"Because if he comes back here he'll be walking into a trap. Tell him Garstang is dead, and that the mage and Ramiro are in jail, framed by Hesh."

"And what makes you think he'll believe us?" quizzed Terris Todd. "Last time we met him we weren't exactly friends."

Vangar mulled this point over. "Tell Callaghan I did as he asked, and what I predicted has come to pass," he said. "He'll like that. It almost rhymes."

"What are you going to do?" asked Dappin.

"Keep the soldiers that are following us occupied long enough for you to escape. Now go!" The trio of marauders sprinted down through the caves and along the esplanade, while Vangar, Ariel and the remaining marauders turned to face a squad of soldiers led by Craecoran Gemmel.

"Surrender yourselves and your weapons!" he demanded.

"On what charge?" asked Vangar.

"You are suspected of conspiring with Lord Malenek, Oldwyn Blake, and Ambassador Messer."

"Atticus, do you honestly believe Ambassador Messer would conspire with Malenek? Do you think he would do that to his own city?"

"No, but I think you would, thief," responded Gemmel. "Now put down your weapons. Or don't. I'm just aching for an excuse to kill you." Ariel tightened the string of his bow. Vangar stole a quick glance at the docks. He spied Dappin casting off a rope and manoeuvring a borrowed ship into the bay. Vangar rest a calming hand on Ariel's shoulder.

"Do as he says," he ordered. The archer slowly let the elastic energy expel as he aimed the arrow down. The soldiers surrounded them, roughly binding their hands behind their backs. Their captors kicked and shoved them back to the upper city level. When they reached the top, Vangar struggled to gain a better view of the bay, falling to the ground. From this awkward angle he spotted the pirated ship as it escaped the crescent bay and raised it sails.

"Is that the rest of your mob, Innes?" Gemmel asked, picking him up.

"Might be," said Vangar, sporting a wry grin.

"Cowards."

"When they come back, we'll see how cowardly they are," replied Vangar. He received Gemmel's boot in his face as a reward for his insolence.

"You won't be alive long enough," remarked the craecoran with a threatening sneer, dragging the marauder back to the barracks.

PART THREE

Recent events have left me feeling tired - the elves, the journey to Hylan and the frozen wastelands of Araneque have all taken their toll. I find myself doubting all that I believe in. The strange occurrences of recent days have festered in my mind like a resilient weed. Which deities do I now place my faith in? What plan do I follow? Each choise differs wildly, and each with its own sacrifice. I shall have to ponder this further ~

I was ready to give the men of Enara another chance, to become head of a church that could unite two lands at war, but then I was paid a visit by a young farmer, his lands recently raided by thieves, who not only stole food and money from him, but also the lives of his wife and children. He sought his vengeance while their blood remained warm, and their spirits will be watching over him in Illyria, proud that while he could not save them, he saved another victim of the raiders.

The farmer has lingered in the castle for over a week now. He is but a shell, filled with rage and anger, although his brief time with the elves has brought some light to the darkness within. I have counselled him in the hope these emotions will soon leave his soul, or if not, that he can control them, wield them. I suggested he journey to Mount Ishkava and seek out the Rangers who reside there. He is soon to depart Mytor on route to Hylan. I hope it is not the last I have seen or heard of Callaghan Tor.

As I watched him leave, I felt sorrow, for I realised his story has swayed my mind to the dark truth I fear to face, that Enara cannot be saved. She deserves a new beginning, a better beginning. Even if the vengeful farmer becomes an Ishkava Ranger, it would take a thousand like him to stem the tide of man's insolence and greed. I will wait to hear more of the plan of which the Zalestian spoke of.

Balen Malenek

Excerpts from the private journals of Balen Malenek, dated fifteen years ago.

CHAPTER FORTY

DURU UMBIN

The crumbled ruins of Duru Umbin marked the border between Caspia and Rundhale, home to the sparse Etraihu tribes in the west, and the centaurs in the east. The hoofed horse masters were the reason the giant defensive wall had been built by man in the first place, when their land had bordered the kingdom of Heroshin. At that time, King Bryce Anselm had deemed it necessary to protect the city of Gorran when it was still under his domain, even if it meant barricading the human Etraihu tribes as well. In the war that saw Caspia seize Gorran, the centaurs took advantage of the men battling amongst themselves and demolished a large section of Duru Umbin to the south, using the new gateway to attack both depleted forces. The rest of the wall, mainly to the north where the peaceful Veyo tribes resided, was left by the Caspians to deteriorate over time.

"The Etraihu were telling the truth," said Rynn, a rugged centaur hiding among the stone ruins. He was joined by several others, all gazing beyond the remnants of Duru Umbin at a strange, unnatural sight. The eerie glow of the spirit army illuminated the chilly night as they began their mass exodus from Gorran, accompanied by thousands upon thousands of ætherghouls.

"They may have spoken true words, but they themselves do not attack these abominations," remarked Abryr, an older centaur, his long shaggy black hair streaked with grey, framing his scarred face.

"That may be soon to change," said Tyrys, a younger centaur, his amber eyes directed not at the ethereal glow of the spirit army, but along the stretch of ruined wall. Two distinct tribes of Etraihu approached the ranks of centaurs that were formed behind the scouting party. The first were the Rhae, known to be wild but cunning, clad in thin leather armour. The second were the Braig, feral in nature and often incommunicable, adorned in the full hides of animals they slaughtered on the Rundhale plains, believing this would imbue them with the power of the beasts that they wore.

"The Rhae and the Braig march together," noted Rynn, slightly surprised.

"And with a ranger," said Abryr, spotting the hulking frame of Dash Cole, dressed in his traditional ranger's attire, while his hair was moulded into a spiked mohawk.

"It is a night of most unusual sights," replied Tyrys. The scouts watched as the men met their fellow centaurs, inevitably followed by some scuffling and conceited remarks.

"Stay here," ordered Abryr to Tyrys, while he and Rynn descended the low slope to their gathered clan. Abryr trotted to the front, glaring at the more savage Braig with his amber eyes until the bestial men backed away.

"Master centaur, I am Dash Cole of the Ishkava Rangers," he said. "This is Havek, leader of the Rhae tribes." The Etraihu nodded curtly at the centaur.

"I am Abryr," he replied, taking stock of the Rhae leader.

"These are strange times," said Havek. "Perhaps we should waste less of it with staring contests and start talking about how to strike at these spirits."

"Agreed," said Rynn. "You have seen them then?"

"Aye," muttered the Rhae next to Havek, a gangly man named Fisko. "We spied them leaving the gates of Gorran after the suns set."

"We propose a temporary pact to try and tackle this threat," said Havek.

"A threat brought by a man," said Abryr. "Why should we trust you?"

"He is a madman from Mytor," replied Havek. "He is not Etraihu, he is certainly not Rhae, and I do not take kindness to your suggestion, hoof-walker."

"Please, we require discussion, not blame," said Dash. "We must carefully consider our strategy. The message we received from Arkes Da'ri mentioned only what my fellow ranger Callaghan had informed her. The spirits themselves are unstoppable. No weapon can harm them, not even Risaar's fabled blade. The ætherghouls are fast and savage…"

"Much like our friends here," Havek said, indicating the Braig. The centaurs remained sombre, not sharing his sense of humour.

"…but unlike them," continued Dash Cole, "the ghouls are dead, their souls trapped within the rotting flesh. For them to be rendered inert, those souls must be freed by destroying the body that holds them prisoner."

"What about the man who leads them?" asked Abryr. "Lord Malenek?"

"He is vulnerable," said the ranger. "The Caspians believe if he dies, so too will the spirits that are bound to him."

"Then why not just kill him?" growled a new voice to the fray. A snarling Braig named Ridig circled nearby, sniffing around them.

"He wears a suit of armour, and is guarded by the spirits, as well as a… bodyguard," said Havek.

"A stone man, possibly a Moltari golem," added Dash. The ranger noticed that this news caused more concern among the centaurs more than the existence of the spirits.

"We must devise a plan to draw as many of the spirits and ætherghouls away from Malenek as possible," said Abryr, "while another group flanks west and takes him out."

"A diversion," stated Havek. Abryr nodded. "I like the way you think, horse master."

"Enough talk!" moaned Ridig. "More kill!" He launched into an animalistic cry that was mimicked by the other Braig, before charging over the rocky ruins of Duru Umbin.

"Wait!" yelled Abryr, but the Braig had already given away their position. The Rhae ran after their Etraihu cousins. Left with little choice, the centaurs followed.

The Braig charged towards the nearest ætherghouls, raising their oversized weapons and whooping a war cry in the faces of their enemies. They were unafraid, even of this undead scourge, but in the ætherghouls the beastly Braig had met their match. Yet not a single one of them was killed by the undead. The ætherghouls dragged human and centaur alike back to the spirits, who reached into their bodies and snapped their souls. The Braig had no word for retreat, but the remaining Rhae accompanied the centaurs back to Rundhale, sullied with defeat.

From a distance, Malenek and Gort watched as the first ætherghoul centaur bleated into existence and joined their ranks.

"It seems the centaurs are more man than beast after all," said Malenek, eyeing the creature curiously as it bucked and stumbled like a newborn foal.

"Should we change our plans?" asked Gort, as the ætherghouls made short work of those who continued to fight, refusing to run away.

"No," murmured Malenek. "The Etraihu are too few and sparse, and by the looks of things the centaurs will prove difficult to capture. We must strike Calisto, in case Callaghan succeeds in his search for the stone."

The attack served to delay them until dawn, when the spirits were satisfied that all those who opposed them were now ætherghouls, save for those few who were fortunate enough to have fled. Malenek gazed over the ruins of Duru Umbin as the twin suns rose up, casting the ancient stone in shades of lavender. The remains were a decaying legacy of man's need to divide land and war with others. Soon, these would be unfamiliar concepts of an old, forgotten world. He turned Shento east, and his weary horse trotted behind the growing army of ætherghouls marching towards Calisto.

CHAPTER FORTY-ONE

FLASHBACK OF A FARMER

THE STOLEN NORORA SAILED HIGH INTO THE NIGHT SKY, SO CLOSE to the twin moons of Ygrain and Whirren that Kamina believed she could reach out of the triangular porthole and touch them. She could just make out the moonlight shining on the sea below, the surf gently breaking against the Zalestian coastline. Behind her, Callaghan and Kaedin worked the levers that controlled the various rotors and wheels responsible for manoeuvring the airship. The ghost instructed the ranger which ones to pull when he could not focus his spiritual energy to the task. He kept a watchful eye on the fuel that burned to raise them up like a bird, mindful of Leotori's warnings.

When Risaar revealed itself, the red light glimmered upon the blue ocean. Callaghan said his morning prayer with Ascara, although after the explosion in the norora hanger he decided against igniting her blade.

Few words were exchanged between the trio over the course of the morning. Kaedin concentrated on keeping them aloft, while Kamina and Callaghan stared out of the rear portholes, watching as Zalestia disappeared behind them, growing smaller and smaller until it was a hazy blur on the horizon. Each separately wondered what cruel fate Zahyr Zaleed Khan would bestow on the brave Jazintha Zharie.

The ranger had discovered some supplies left over from the norora's expedition into the desert wastes. He shared them with the drained elf, her mind still dwelling on the words of Errazure Ecko.

"You know," said the ranger between mouthfuls, "it is bad luck to travel in an unnamed vessel."

"But it has a name," replied Kamina. "The norora."

"That is what it is, like a ship or a horse, a man or an elf," he explained. "It needs an individual name, something to give it character and purpose." Kamina mulled over this problem as she chewed on some soft, spongy bread. She thought of naming it after Talia, who she felt deserved some recognition for her sacrifice. But then she thought of Jazintha, who had fought against her own father to engineer their escape.

"I cannot decide between Talia and Jazintha," confessed Kamina.

"Why not both?" suggested Callaghan.

"The *Talia Jazintha*," said Kamina, liking the way it rolled from her tongue.

"Yes, that is a fine name. We will have Kaedin venture outside to paint it on the hull," he added with a smile.

"Hopefully it will bring us good luck," she said, but any blessing the new name brought proved to be brief.

"You might want to see this," said Kaedin. The pair joined the ghost at the front of the newly named *Talia Jazintha*, crowding around the tiny window to catch a glimpse of the Badlands. The dark storm clouds stretched out across the sky, towering far higher than they had yet soared.

"Kaedin, we need to go up," said Callaghan. The spirit was already working the controls, gradually increasing the fuel consumption of the flames, which in turn burned the green jalaaroca faster. It gave off a faint green gas that streamed up the vent to fill the balloon. The norora slowly started to rise.

"We will not make it," said Kamina. "We have to go higher."

"If we burn it too quickly it could ignite the whole ship!" snapped the spirit, losing concentration and, as a consequence, his ability to touch.

"Let me," said Callaghan, intervening on Kaedin's behalf. He slowly increased the flame, the spirit desperately watching over his shoulder. Kamina gaped in panic as the storm clouds consumed them. Blasts of thunder shook the airship. Lightning zinged and crackled across the norora's bow. She remembered the beating the *Arad Nor* had been forced to endure, and wondered if the norora would contend with the Badlands any better than her sea-faring counterpart. They flew blind through dark grey clouds as the *Talia Jazintha* screaming at full speed through the storm.

"This is not good!" she cried out. With no other option, Callaghan cast aside Leotori's warning. He poured fuel onto the fire, the flames leaping higher, the jalaaroca fizzling under the intense heat. Callaghan and Kaedin jumped back when sparks flew off them, quickly stamping them out before the norora caught fire. The ranger's rash actions caused the sky ship to swiftly ascend, emerging from the charcoal black clouds into the calm night air high above the Badlands.

With danger narrowly averted, Kamina was entranced by the raging storm underneath her feet. From above it was strangely beautiful, she thought, counting the chains of lightning that danced through the clouds. It was after dusk when they passed over the calm centre, the storm swirling around it. Once again she glimpsed the eerie blue luminescence below the surface of the ocean. It had been worth staying awake for, but now her eyes weighed down heavily, forcing her to seek sleep. She lay down against the wall of the hull, wrapping herself up in animal furs. Despite the heat of the burning fuel, the air was colder the higher they climbed. She tried to get comfortable, overhearing Callaghan and Kaedin as they discussed their flight.

"After we pass over the Badlands, we should descend," advised Kaedin.

"To save fuel?" enquired Callaghan.

"No," replied the ghost. "In case we crash." Callaghan could not tell whether the spirit was serious or attempting to make light of the situation. He smiled back nervously.

"When you see Amaros, head north along the coast," said the ranger.

"You mean south?" replied Kaedin, confused. "To Calisto?"

"We are not heading to Calisto," said Callaghan. "Not yet at least. We still have no idea how to use the stone, but Malenek might. He has kept a meticulous journal for most of his life. I am hoping he has unintentionally left us a clue. I doubt he was worried about anyone reading them, which means they should be unguarded." The listless ranger leaned against the wall, stretching his weary muscles.

"You should get some rest as well," said the ghost, indicating Kamina, asleep on the deck.

"No, something may go wrong," the ranger said, staring at the array of intricate controls.

"I will keep an eye on it," Kaedin assured him. "I do not sleep."

"What of the spirits?" asked Callaghan. "Have you felt them since our escape?" The spirit remained ominously silent. "Kaedin?"

"They are getting louder the closer we get to Amaros," he revealed. "It is as if they are on the other side of a doorway that leads into my thoughts."

"You must work hard to counter their influence, to make sure they do not open that door," said Callaghan. "Their power may be amplified by the ætherghouls they have sired."

"I will try," muttered Kaedin, slightly embarrassed that he had to admit this vulnerability to his hero, but if he did not, he risked losing the ranger's friendship, something he had come to value, even as a spirit.

"Until we resolve this, that is all you can do," said the ranger, trying to reassure him. "Wake me if need be." He slumped down alongside Kamina, who pawed the air in her sleep, suffering nightmarish visions. She briefly stirred, but finding Callaghan next to her, instinctively snuggled against him. He placed his arm around her, his protective presence soothing her back to sleep.

"Do you think Jazintha will be okay?" she murmured.

"She is a brave and fearless young woman," he replied, brushing Kamina's smooth blonde hair behind her pointed ears. "I only hope her father can see these strengths. Now go back to sleep." Kamina drifted off into her dreams, as Callaghan continued to brush her hair. His gaze drifted from her innocent face to his own rough hand, focused on the simple band of silver that adorned his ring finger.

"Callaghan..." said a voice, someone long gone from this world.

*

"Callaghan," called out his wife. The young, lean farmer broke from chopping wood and entered the cosy farmhouse. Arayana prepared the evening meal in the kitchen by the window. Her auburn Heroshin hair shone in the daylight streaming through the window. Callaghan snuck up behind her, playfully tickling her and kissing her neck.

"Wash your hands first!" she shrieked as he stole a piece of fruit. "And fetch the children."

"Where are they?"

"Feeding the chicks."

Callaghan ventured out to the chicken hut. Inside he could hear the children giggling along with the tweets of new born chicks and the paternal clucks of mother hens.

"Hutten, Castan, Kamina," he called out. Castan, his youngest son, and Kamina, his only daughter, emerged from the hut. The boy resembled his father, with dark chestnut hair and blue eyes, while his daughter was a miniature version of Arayana. Kamina clutched one of the chicks in her hand.

"Look father," she said, holding the ball of fluff out for him. Callaghan could see what had attracted her to this chick in particular; it had a black streak running over its bright yellow body, from head to tail. "Why is she different from the rest?"

Callaghan took the chick from his inquisitive daughter. It chirruped at him while he stroked its curious mark. "I do not know," he said, handing it back to her. "The Elementals make it so. Where is your brother?"

"Standing beside me," replied Kamina.

"Very funny. Your other brother." Kamina and Castan both shrugged.

"Father!" shouted their missing sibling, his voice tainted by a panicked urgency. Callaghan ran round the hutch to find Hutten staring at the small forest that bordered their land.

What is it?" asked Callaghan, but he soon spotted what had startled his oldest son. Three burly men marched out of the trees and crossed the field towards them. Callaghan discerned the Heroshin colours that marked their uniforms. He kept Hutten close by his side as the soldiers approached them.

"Good day," he called out to them.

"Good day," replied one the soldiers with a wave. "We were wondering if you could spare some food for a few of Amaros' starved soldiers."

"My family and I were just about to have our evening meal. I'm sure we can spare some for you and your men."

"It would be greatly appreciated," said the man, extending his hand. "I am Arghus, Knight of Heroshin."

Arghus and his companions, Humerc and Hishman, shared the food Arayana had prepared, while regaling the Tor children with stories of their lives as soldiers for the king.

"We are on a training exercise of sorts" Arghus informed them. "It is a race, from Hylan to Calisto. We are one of ten teams."

"What happens if you win?" asked Hutten.

"We become Accolades," replied Arghus. "Private guards to King Arthadian himself."

"And we don't need to travel the bloody seas to Zalestia," cursed the broody Humerc, a sentiment shared by the other soldiers. Arayana and

Callaghan shifted uneasily in their seats at Humerc's language. "Sorry," he added. "Talk best left for the barracks."

Later in the evening, as Arayana tucked the children into bed despite their protests, Callaghan opened a bottle of mead to share with the soldiers.

"So why have you yourself not joined the Caspian ranks, Callaghan?" asked Arghus.

"Or do you enjoy the delights of agriculture too much that you cannot bear to leave it behind," said Humerc with a mocking laugh.

"Ignore him," said Arghus. "He cannot handle his drink."

"No, I will answer," stated Callaghan. "I am a father first, Humerc. I would not leave my young children to fend for themselves."

"Or your wife without a husband," jeered Hishman, the shortest of the three. Callaghan noticed that his uniform was too big for his frame. On further inspection, he noticed Humerc's was slightly too small, the seams on the arms of his shirt almost bursting.

"And what will you do when the Zogs invade Amaros, and come to your farm?" asked Humerc.

"I will defend my family and my lands," Callaghan retorted. Inside his head, doubts began to form as he recast his thoughts over their story.

"How will you do that, when you have not even trained as a soldier?"

Callaghan corked the bottle of mead. "Please, kindly finish your drinks and leave. I will not be insulted in my own home."

"He knows we're not soldiers," said Hishman. Callaghan's startled expression gave away the truth.

"Then I'm afraid we cannot leave," stated Arghus. "What gave us away?"

"Your uniforms do not fit," Callaghan admitted, "nor your demeanour, or your story."

"Well it was true that the knights who wore these uniforms were on a training exercise," confessed Humerc, feeling the threads. "Before we killed them."

"Please, just leave," begged the farmer, edging towards the room where his children slept.

"I'm afraid we cannot do that," said Hishman, mirroring Callaghan's movements. "You know too much."

"I know nothing," he pleaded.

"The man who hired us would disagree," said Arghus.

"Please, my children are innocent. Please do not harm them." Callaghan could see now that these were mercenaries with no conscience, no soul, focused solely on the coin they would earn. He hurled the bottle of mead at Humerc, smashing him in the face. He grabbed his chair and tried to tackle Arghus, but knight or not, he had been trained to fight. He tackled Callaghan with ease, the humble farmer falling to the floor. The last thing he heard was Arayana and his children screaming, before Humerc's giant boot ploughed into his face and turned his world black.

Flames licked Callaghan's face as he coughed himself awake, the acrid smoke infesting his lungs. Across the floor he saw the vacant eyes of Arayana, his wife's body violated and slain. He crawled under the table, grabbing her cold hand tight, overwhelmed with tears of anger and rage.

"Hutten," Callaghan wheezed, picking himself up and dragging his beaten body into the children's bedroom, while the house burned and collapsed all around him. "Castan," he called out. "Kamina!" He found them positioned together on a bed, the two brothers framing their sister in the middle. They looked so peaceful, as if they were just asleep, were it not for the marks around their mouths, signs that they had been smothered. Callaghan reached out to touch them, but he recoiled in grief. He did not wish to feel their cold skin as he had with Arayana.

He did not wish to know their death.

The roof began to give way. Callaghan protected the bodies of his children from any falling debris. The cottage would soon collapse completely, but he would not allow his family to be harmed any more than they already had. One by one he carried the children to the window, forced to drop them out onto the ground like chopped wood. Callaghan fought through the fire to reach Arayana's body. The children's room caved in behind him, burying him in dust and stone.

He lay stunned, wondering if he should just let the smoke and flame consume him, so he could join his family in the next life. His thirst for vengeance pushed him to survive, just a little longer. He hauled himself up, and staggered over to his wife. He dragged Arayana's body through the inferno and out into the chilly night air. Exhausted, his body finally gave way, and he fell with her into the grass. The young farmer lay helpless, unable to do anything except watch in disbelief as his home, passed down from his father and his father before him, crumbled in a cloud of ash and embers.

By the time Risaar dawned upon the smouldering ruins, Callaghan had buried the bodies of his family. He bandaged his wounds as best as he could. Armed with his axe, he followed the trail of the fraudulent knights, vengeance coursing through his veins.

*

Callaghan emerged from his recurring nightmare, his forehead clammy with a cold sweat. Tears mapped the tracks they had followed many years before. He reached under his shirt and pulled out the ring on his neck chain. It matched the one on his finger, the metal of the two bands kissing as he held it in his hand.

"What is wrong?" asked Kamina, waking to see Callaghan's tears falling from his face.

"Nothing," he said, hiding Arayana's ring and sniffing away his tears. "I was just thinking of another life. Foolish thoughts," he added, chastising himself for indulging in past memories and clouding his judgement.

"I had a nightmare too," she admitted, hoping to make the ranger feel better. "It is always the same. Talia is reading me a story, about the four Elementals, but at the end, she turns into an ætherghoul... or Errazure Ecko... or..."

"Talia was a fine woman," said the ranger. "You should not forget that."

"You always speak as if you knew her," Kamina noted. "Before you met her in Tilden, I mean." Callaghan knew he had to tell Kamina the truth, to reveal to her what Kaedin could not, but he struggled to work out where to begin. He was saved from making the painful admission when a flame flickered past the norora's bow.

"Callaghan!" cried Kaedin. "We have company!"

*

"I'm telling you, I saw something," said Terris Todd, having glimpsed a silhouette pass by Whirren and Ygrain.

"In the sky?" questioned Dappin Creig, the former fisherman who had been placed in charge of the expedition.

"Probably just a cloud," said Tig Norden. "This is useless. They could be anywhere in this bleedin' ocean. Or worse."

"That's why we didn't stray too far from Calisto," Dappin reminded him.

"Will you just fire an arrow up there, Tig," said Terris. Tig looked to Dappin for approval.

"Can't do no harm," he said with a shrug of his shoulders. "All we're doing is waiting."

"Waste of a good arrow if you ask me," muttered Tig, dousing a prepared fire arrow in oil. Terris opened a lamp, allowing Tig to set it alight. He shot the flare into the dark gloom. They stared in disbelief as it illuminated a ship hovering in the sky.

"By Risaar's beard!" Tig whispered.

"Shoot another one!" shouted Dappin. Tig's second arrow sailed closer to the flying ship than the first. The brief streak of light revealed more of its shape and form, and the fact that it was much larger than it had initially appeared, or much closer to them.

"Arm yourselves!" ordered Dappin, as they felt the draft of the unknown ship descending upon them. It was so close they were able to see its underside in detail. Tig fired an arrow right at it, but it bounced off, ricocheting into the ocean.

"Do not shoot!" shouted someone from the ship.

"Show yourselves!" Dappin yelled back.

"My name is Callaghan Tor of the Ishkava Rangers." A wave of relief drifted across the skeleton crew.

"I am Dappin Creig. I was sent to find you by Innes Vangar."

"Why would Vangar wish to find me?" questioned Callaghan.

"We took your advice and headed to Gorran. We saw the spirit army, and headed to Calisto…"

"Not that we were scared!" shouted Terris.

"No, to help, but then… well…" stammered Tig.

"Oldwyn Blake and Ambassador Messer were imprisoned for the murder of Duke Garstang," Dappin said, cutting to the chase. "Most of the marauders have been rounded up too, including Vangar. They're accused of spying for Lord Malenek. Vangar aided our escape so we could find you. He needs you to return to Calisto and reason with Ambassador Hesh."

Callaghan opened his mouth to speak, but the news from Calisto was nothing short of astonishing. He paused to try and piece it all together. He could not believe that either Oldwyn or Ramiro would murder someone, let alone collude with one another to do so.

"How do I know you are Vangar's men?" he asked eventually, the brief memory of Bosk Finney bristling against his mind. "How do I know you do not work for Malenek?"

"Vangar said you might think that," Dappin called out. "He told me to tell you that he did as you asked, and what he predicted has come to pass." Callaghan recalled their brusque exchange at the peak of Finsing Falls. He had told Vangar to journey to Calisto. The marauder had said they would all be arrested and executed.

"Callaghan, what do we do?" asked Kamina. The ranger was considering all of their options. Without Oldwyn and his magical staff, they would not be able to hold off the spirits, but unless they figured out how to use the Stone of Spirits, they would not be able to defeat them.

Two goals. Two ships, but Callaghan had to go to Calisto.

The sky lightened, heralding Risaar's dawn. Callaghan turned to Kamina and Kaedin in the dim glow of the morning. "I am sorry my friends," he said. "I must leave you once again."

"But…"

"Do not protest, Kamina," said the ranger. "I am not asking you to hide away. I am giving you a mission. You must reach Malenek's castle in Mytor, find his journals, and discover the secret of the Stone of Spirits."

"I cannot," she panicked. "I cannot do it without you."

"You have already accomplished much without me, my young friend," he said. "It was you who slayed a gruzalug and found the stone. Have faith in yourself. You have the heart of a ranger, Kamina Elloeth, remember that. And if you get scared, think of Talia." Kamina tried to find some argument to counter him, but she could not. The very mention of her mother's name brought forth a renewed sense of courage inside her.

"And just in case you run into any danger, take this." The Ranger Elite handed her Ascara. "Risaar's blade will protect you where I cannot."

"But it is yours," she said.

"Then you had better return it to me," he replied with a farewell smile. "Kaedin, take good care of her."

"I will," was all he could say. The ranger braced himself in the door, allowing himself one last look back at his young companions.

"Good luck" he shouted above the roar of the winds. He dove off the norora and into the sea. The elves watched as the ranger resurfaced and swam to the ship, aided on board by the marauders. Callaghan waved at them as the ship raised it sails, arcing around and heading back to Calisto. On the *Talia Jazintha*, Kamina waved back while Kaedin manoeuvred the norora away, heading north-west, but he struggled to do so alone.

"Kamina, I need your help." She approached the controls, realising she should have paid more attention when Callaghan and Kaedin were flying. "Pull that lever towards you," he said. Kamina grabbed one. "No, not that one!" he shouted, moments too late. The norora began to swoop toward the water. Kamina quickly remedied her mistake, and moved her hands to the correct lever.

"You may have the heart of a ranger," he commented, "but you still have the mind of a child."

"You are just jealous," she barked back as she swung the norora around.

The sails of the borrowed schooner filled with a strong wind, now in a race against Malenek to reach Calisto. The sodden ranger watched the norora navigate north across the sky.

"May the Elementals keep them safe," he prayed.

CHAPTER FORTY-TWO

THE WALL OF THE MIND

THE BORROWED SHIP SAILED BACK INTO CALISTO'S CRESCENT BAY, heavier one ranger than when they had left. While there were a few boats bobbing out at sea, Callaghan was dismayed to see that the vast majority of vessels were still docked.

"So much for an evacuation," muttered Tig.

"Well at least there's a welcome party," noted Dappin sourly, having spied Craecoran Gemmel and a squad of armed corans waiting for them. The skeleton crew lowered the sails and allowed the momentum to guide them into the docks, where they were quickly detained.

"You three are under arrest," yelled Gemmel.

"Under what charge?" asked Callaghan, his appearance catching the craecoran by surprise.

"Theft, conspiracy to murder, and being general miscreants," he said.

"We didn't steal the ship. We borrowed it," said Terris, echoing Vangar's words. "Not a scratch on her that wasn't there before."

"Take them away," ordered Gemmel, before turning to Callaghan. "Ambassador Hesh asked me to escort you to the council chambers if you arrived back, sir."

"Am I under arrest too?" asked Callaghan.

"Things have happened while you were gone, ranger" he said. "The ambassador will want to tell you himself."

"Then let us not keep him waiting." As Craecoran Gemmel led the ranger up the cliff paths to the council chambers, neither noticed two men spying on them, hidden in plain sight amongst the crowds of refugees. One was tall and pudgy, the other his opposite, small and lean.

"What shall we do?" asked the tall one.

"Follow them," replied his partner. "Something is wrong. We must not reveal ourselves until we are certain of Callaghan's fate."

*

"Thank the Elements for your safe return, Callaghan!" exclaimed the aged ambassador, as Gemmel ushered the ranger into Cohen's office. "Thank you, craecoran. Please wait outside." The highest-ranked soldier in Caspia was offended by his sudden dismissal. He marched out into the hall, slamming the door behind him.

"You have the marauders to thank as well, but instead you have had them arrested," stated Callaghan, making no attempt to hide his disdain.

"No doubt by now you have heard of the tragic death of Duke Garstang," said Cohen, ignoring Callaghan's tone. "He fell afoul of a plot between Ambassador Messer and Oldwyn Blake. It seems the marauders are also in league with them."

"Ramiro and Oldwyn seem an unlikely pairing for a partnership," Callaghan noted, growing suspicious of Cohen as he tried to push this wild conspiracy theory.

"Indeed, they fooled us all," said Cohen. "It seems Malenek's influence reaches far and wide."

"That aside, if the marauders are involved, why did they search for me?"

"That I do not know," said Cohen, worried as the ranger tugged at the threads of his hastily-woven fiction. "All I know is that Duke Garstang uncovered evidence of their involvement."

"What sort of evidence?"

"Secret messages sent by herks," said Cohen. "His archers shot them down before they could be delivered."

"Where are these damning messages now?" asked the ranger.

"I am afraid they were in Duke Garstang's possession. I do not know where he may have kept them, and we have been too busy to spare anyone to search his quarters. He showed me one in Ramiro's handwriting. It mentioned he had failed to stop you travelling to Zalestia." Parts of what Cohen said made sense to Callaghan, but he still had trouble believing all that the ambassador claimed. Yet how else could Cohen have known about the traitor aboard the *Arad Nor*, unless…

"Did you find the stone?" enquired Cohen. He could see the ranger dwelling on the details and hoped to distract him, but in doing so, he revealed his true self to Callaghan.

"No," the ranger lied. "The Zalestians proved to be very hostile."

"What of the elf and her spirit?"

"They perished in the Badlands," continued Callaghan. "Our ship was struck by lightning and the elf… she could not swim." The ranger watched as the ambassador pretended to be sympathetic, as he piled lies on top of lies.

"Then we are done for," muttered Cohen. "It seems our only option may be to negotiate a surrender."

"There is no negotiation with Malenek," warned Callaghan. "He is too invested in his plan now, pushed into this madness like an unwitting pawn."

"My brother always described him as fair and honest," said Cohen. "Hopefully he will show this to be true."

"Volan told you this?" he asked. The ranger watched as Cohen realised which lie he had tripped up on. "You said you had not seen him in years?"

"I may have exaggerated," tried Cohen.

"Was it before or after he had even met Malenek?" The two men stared at one another across the table.

"Let us not play games any longer," Cohen said, dropping his mask of deception. "When did you know?"

"When you asked about the Stone of Spirits," said Callaghan. "It should have been your first question, but instead you were too busy laying the roots of your deceit."

"It changes nothing. Oldwyn and Ramiro are locked up, and Lord Malenek will soon be here to lead us into a new world."

"It was you who persuaded Volan to join Malenek," deduced Callaghan. "You sacrificed your own brother."

"Yes," admitted Cohen, still embittered by the decision. "We needed a ranger to wield Ascara's magic. I had hoped Malenek would convince you to join our cause, but as soon as I saw you here, I knew Volan was gone."

"Since we are being so honest, how long have you been involved?" asked Callaghan.

"Almost as long as you have been a ranger, my boy. I met Malenek in Hylan when King Arthadian made him an honorary Lord. He confided in me about his plan, part of it anyway. I was intrigued. I had grown bored of the royal court and the endless plots and betrayals that lay within that family, although they did come in handy when I framed Ramiro and Oldwyn for Garstang's murder."

"You killed Garstang." The ranger was distraught by this realisation. The thousands of deaths at the hands of the spirits and ætherghouls were tragic, but those individuals murdered by Malenek and his collaborators seemed the greater crime, a futile act with no reparation.

"A necessary evil, to remove your friend Oldwyn from the equation," said Cohen. "You only have yourself to blame. We did not think you would succeed in freeing him."

"But you voted for it," recalled Callaghan.

"We had hoped news would spread and that people would flee here, but Oldwyn's seeing spell worked far better than a lone messenger might. Besides, it was the best way to send you off on your suicidal mission to Zalestia. Once you were gone, I could deal with the cyclops alone. Now there is nothing to stand in the way of the vengeance spirits." Callaghan managed to hide his hopeful thoughts of Kamina and Kaedin.

"So what happens now?" he asked.

"You could tell people the truth, but I doubt they would believe you," said Cohen. "I assume you will not reconsider joining us?"

"No, although I assume if I do not then I will be arrested?"

"Yes," said Cohen. "Ah, the truth can be so refreshing sometimes."

"For a politician, I imagine so," retorted Callaghan.

"And I assume you will not go down without a fight?" the ambassador finally asked.

"Let us find out." Callaghan lunged for Cohen Hesh, his former friend, now a betrayer like his brother. The ambassador managed to scream before the ranger could reach him. Craecoran Gemmel burst in and tackled Callaghan to the floor. The craecoran's men beat him down before dragging him away.

"He is deranged!" proclaimed Cohen. "He has returned empty handed, in league with the Zalestians. He wishes to dismantle the Alliance. Lock him up in the Black Tower."

"But it is full, ambassador," said Gemmel. "We had to place most of the marauders in the old gaol."

"Here," said Cohen, offering the craecoran a special cell door key. "Lock him up with Ramiro. The traitors can enjoy each other's company. And break the key in the lock like you did with the cyclops."

Craecoran Gemmel led the way as his men forced the ranger along the streets to the barracks, next to which stood the bent, ugly prison. Soldiers and citizens glared at him, ashamed and betrayed as Callaghan was hauled through the gates to the Black Tower. He even recognised a few of the faces within the crowd, including Norrek Melo, his daughter Nyssa, and their friend Torg.

"Tell me why, ranger?" Gemmel demanded as he pushed Callaghan up the spiral steps. "The others I understand, but you, you are of Ishkava."

"Ambassador Hesh is the one in league with Malenek," he replied. "Not I, Ramiro, or even Oldwyn. Can you not see he has manipulated events to betray this city, this country, by having these people arrested? Without us, you are defenceless against the spirits."

"We do not need the cyclops to defeat the spirits," bragged the craecoran as they arrived at Ramiro's cell.

"Cohen is playing to your arrogance," said Callaghan as Gemmel unlocked the door. "He killed Duke Garstang to remove Oldwyn and leave this city vulnerable."

"No!" exclaimed the craecoran, pointing at Ramiro, who lay slumped on the cell floor. "He killed the duke, a man who I considered a friend. Him and that one-eyed freak!"

"I did not," murmured Ramiro, too weak to stand. "The ranger is telling you the truth, Atticus."

"I offer you a prediction," said Callaghan. "Cohen Hesh plans to surrender, to submit to the spirits without any struggle." Gemmel considered what they were saying, but he was interrupted by a sedcoran clamouring up the twisting staircase.

"Craecoran Gemmel, sir. The spirits have been spotted approaching from the west."

"Craecoran, listen to me," urged Callaghan. "You must free Oldwyn."

"I have my orders," he stated, slamming the thick door in Callaghan's face. The wronged prisoners heard the key twist in the lock. A moment of contemplative silence passed before the soldiers descended down the steps.

"Are you all right, ambassador?" asked Callaghan, examining Ramiro.

"Nothing a decent meal and a walk in the fresh air would not cure," he replied. "Did you find the Stone of Spirits?"

"Yes," whispered Callaghan, "but Cohen thinks otherwise." The ranger continued to relay his adventures and those of Kamina and Kaedin to Ramiro. "The elves are on their way to Mytor as we speak."

"Then let us hope Malenek has left them something to find," said Ramiro. "And that someone in this city starts to see sense."

"I believe they already have," said Callaghan, smiling as he realised that Gemmel had disobeyed Cohen orders.

He had not broken the key in the lock.

He had in fact left it there.

*

Craecoran Gemmel pounded up the steps to the wall above the western gate, where he laid his eyes upon the spirit army for the first time. Strange storm clouds followed them across the land, darkening the skies as the blight of thousands of ætherghouls marched towards Calisto. Behind them he could make out the silver ethereal glow of the vengeance spirits, and somewhere in their midst, Lord Malenek.

"Pray the Elements be with us," murmured Gemmel.

"Craecoran, you are just in time," said Ambassador Hesh. "I was bringing the others up to speed." Gemmel marched over to meet the group, including Ambassadors Narain and surprisingly, Lome, still shaken by recent events. Unbeknown to them, Norrek Melo had left Nyssa in Torg's care and followed Gemmel from the Black Tower. He now drifted through the soldiers ranks, trying to get within earshot of the meeting.

"The Ishkava Ranger Callaghan Tor returned without the artefact he claimed would stop the spirits," continued Cohen. "He has been brainwashed by the Zalestians. He attacked me in my chambers."

"Callaghan?" questioned Narain. "I cannot believe it so."

"It is true," said Craecoran Gemmel. "I was there."

"Then we are done for," muttered Lome, quivering against a wall for support.

"I do not wish to admit it, but Miden may be right," said Cohen. "Our only hope may be to negotiate with Malenek for our surrender."

"We can still fight them!" roared Gemmel, livid at the mere thought of submission to the spirit threat.

"With what?" asked Ambassador Hesh. "We have no weapons that can harm the spirits."

"As I understand it, we don't need to harm the spirits," replied the craecoran. "We only have to take out Malenek and the spirits disappear."

"Malenek is behind those," stated Hesh, pointing beyond the wall at the ætherghouls in the far distance.

"Those we can fight," growled Gemmel.

"If we fight them we will lose," Cohen hit back. "They outnumber our forces three-to-one. Our only option is to surrender."

"If that is true, then I retract my request for refuge in Calisto," said Abbal Eredu. The leaders of men had not perceived the small party of elves that had made their way to the western gate. Their hearing was far greater than Norrek's, who though closer had struggled to make out the conversation.

"Elder Eredu," said Isan Narain, descending the steps to meet the elves. "We are merely discussing strategy."

"It sounded more substantial than that," snapped Endo, accompanying his father and the other elders.

"Forgive our intrusion, Ambassador Narain," said Abbal, "but my son speaks the truth. If you plan to surrender to the spirits, allow us to leave. We will return to Elgrin Forest."

"Elder Eredu, please reconsider your request," urged Narain.

"Ambassador Hesh," said Lashara. "You said the Ishkava Ranger Callaghan had returned empty handed. What is the fate of my kin, Kaedin and Kamina Elloeth?"

"I am sorry, by Callaghan informed me that they lost their lives at sea," recalled Cohen. "I am sorry." Lashara closed her eyes and uttered a prayer, but her grief was interrupted by shouting from the look-outs on the north wall. While the elders remained to comfort Lashara, Endo followed Narain as they ascended the wall and ran round to view the territories to the north. Unnoticed in his uniform, Norrek tagged along behind them. He stood terrified alongside Calisto's soldiers as more ætherghouls emerged from the swamplands, dragging several Ogarii they had captured with them.

"They must have followed us along the river," said Endo.

"What are they doing?" asked Narain.

"They're going to turn those Ogarii into ætherghouls," Gemmel said. They watched as the giants of the swamps were dragged across the plains to meet the spirit army, who had paused to allow their forces to regroup.

"I do not think it is safe for you to leave, Master Eredu," said Isan, traumatised by what he was seeing.

"I concur," whispered Endo. "It seems the fates of our two races are once again entwined."

"Tell the men to lower the gates, and signal our intention to surrender," ordered Cohen. The ambassador's words evoked Callaghan's recent warning to Craecoran Gemmel.

As the soldiers stared blankly out upon the fields, Norrek slipped away from the men, determined to do something. He was not going to let his daughter become one of those things. He marched to the Black Tower, his mind set on freeing the ranger. Before he even set foot in the barracks, Norrek was seized into an alley. He tried to fight back, but his tall, burly assailant had him locked in his grip.

"Do not fight us," he heard another say, finding a short man beside him, two hatchets tucked into his belt, which he tapped with his hands.

Norrek stopped struggling when he realised who these men were.

*

Ramiro was huddled in the corner in the cell, while Callaghan explored the walls and door, searching for some weak spot.

"You are wasting your time," said the ambassador. "No one has ever broken out of here. Not even Oldwyn."

"I heard that," bellowed the mage from his cell above.

"It is good to hear your voice, Oldwyn," Callaghan shouted up.

"And yours, my friend," bellowed the mage, his words echoing through his floor to their ceiling. "I am glad you survived the voyage to Zalestia."

"I met someone on my travels who knew you," said Callaghan. "Gigondas."

There was no reply from above.

"Why did you not tell me about them?" he asked. "Gort and Gigondas."

"Why did you not tell the elf that you knew her mother?" replied Oldwyn.

"That is not a fair comparison," said Callaghan, struck by a short pang of regret for not speaking to Kamina during their time on the norora.

"Who are these people that you speak of?" asked Ramiro, frustrated that the pair were talking in private riddles.

"Malenek's stone bodyguard and his brother," he explained. "How is it they came to be in your care, Oldwyn?"

"Now is not the time," stated the mage sharply.

"Now is all the time we may have," replied the ranger.

"As you wish," replied Oldwyn with a heavy heart. "Ambassador Messer, I would ask that you cover your ears."

Ramiro did no such thing, staring at the ceiling with disdain.

"Years ago, I had a vision of another mage, a Zalestian assassin, sent to kill a creature of Amaros. I intercepted him, and managed to thwart him, but his targets were struck by a rogue spell, leaving Gort and Gigondas in their deformed state."

"Why was a mage sent to kill them?" asked Callaghan, who was beginning to see similarities between this story and that of Kaedin and Kamina, of history repeating itself. "Why are they so important?"

"It concerns a prophecy lost long ago," reminisced Oldwyn, "cast in an age before man held dominance over these lands."

"What did it say?" asked Ramiro, now intrigued by the story.

"You are not meant to be listening!" exclaimed the mage.

"Oldwyn, what was the prophecy?" asked the ranger insistently.

"*Four children born of day and night,*
Their arrival heralding the end in sight,

One wields Whirren's breeze,
The second Risaar's light,
The third Aquill's grace,
The last Ygrain's might."

"Is that it?" asked Ramiro. "What does it mean?"

"That four children will be born on the same night, each possessing the power of an Elemental," Oldwyn explained. "Some translations suggest they would be sent as our saviours in Enara's darkest days, while others intimated they would foreshadow the end of all things, that these four would carry out our final judgement and execution." Callaghan wondered if this was the same prophecy Jaelyn Zsatt had mentioned in his conversation with Malenek. Could Kamina or Kaedin be one these children?

"And you believe that Gort and Gigondas are part of that prophecy?" quizzed Callaghan. "Do you think it means now?"

"I do not know. I never had the chance to discover more than that, did I ambassador?" he asked rhetorically. As Ramiro shrugged off the mage's stinging words, there was a muffled commotion from below. Footsteps pounded up to their cell, and the key twisted in the lock. The door opened to reveal the friendly face of Norrek Melo.

"It is good to see you again, Master Melo," said Callaghan.

"And you, ranger, although I do not come alone." Norrek stepped back to reveal two men who Callaghan instantly recognised as fellow Ishkava Rangers.

"Gregor!" he exclaimed, seizing the arm of the tall man in the traditional ranger welcome. "And Jochan!"

"Flint and Sprong at your service," said the smaller man.

"I am afraid now is not the time for pleasantries," urged Norrek. "Ambassador Hesh has opened the gates and is signalling our intent to surrender to the spirit army."

"The last door is sealed shut," grumbled Gregor Sprong. Callaghan ascended past him and found the key broke in the lock. He battered against it with his shoulder, but try as he might, the door refused to budge.

"Do not concern yourself with my freedom, Callaghan," said Oldwyn from behind the slab of steel. "Leave me here, but you must bring me my staff."

"Cohen took it," recalled Ramiro as Norrek helped him up from the floor. "It could be anywhere."

"And he is unlikely to tell us its location," added Callaghan.

"I suggest seeking out the Witch of Anawey," shouted Oldwyn through the door. "I sense her latent magic somewhere in the city. I believe she can help you find it."

"First we must confront Cohen and Gemmel," said Norrek. "We must close the gates."

"We cannot go up against Caspia's armies with only a handful of men," warned Flint.

"Luckily for us, I know where to find some more," said Callaghan.

Callaghan led Ramiro, Norrek and his fellow rangers through the streets of Calisto. They kept an eye out for any soldiers, but most had been called to man their posts along the city's perimeter wall.

"Who is the Witch of Anawey?" asked Ramiro.

"The elven warrior who wielded Oldwyn's staff before he did," explained Callaghan. "When the elves retreated from Legoria to Elgrin Forest, it was she who was charged with destroying Anawey, hence the name."

"But those events happened over nearly two hundred years ago," pointed out Norrek.

"The elves live far longer than us men," revealed the ranger. "Some used to believe that their lifetime was eternal."

"How did Oldwyn come to possess the staff?"

"Don't you know your ranger history, ambassador?" quizzed Jochan Flint. "When the elves gave up Legoria, they also gave up their magic. They held humans in contempt, but still trusted a few. One such soul was an Ishkava Ranger named Mondo Blake, and so the elves bequeathed the staff to him."

"Bequeathed?" said Gregor. "That's a big word for a small man."

"Well between the two of us, only one of us can read," griped Jochan.

"I knew Oldwyn's father was a ranger, but I did not know he had powers of magic," said Ramiro, ignoring the bickering rangers.

"He didn't. Oldwyn got that from his mother's side, but we don't talk about that," warned Gregor Sprong. To make his point, he waved his weapon of choice, a sharp spiked club, in Ramiro's face.

They had made their way to the council chambers, one of the few areas of the city that contained trees. It was here that they found the elves, in congregation around the trunk of a large Caspian oak.

"Ranger," called out Endo Eredu, who had spotted the party flitter into the park. "I was led to believe you were arrested."

"I made my own release. Ambassador Hesh is not to be trusted."

"We are aware of this fact," said the elf. "He intends to surrender the city to Lord Malenek."

"We aim to stop his plans," said the ranger, "but we need your help."

"We have not raised arms in over two hundred years, ranger, and we will not do so now," said Abbal firmly, interjecting before his son could answer. "The elders have spoken on this subject."

"Then allow me to speak with the Witch of Anawey," he requested.

"That name is an affront..." Abbal started to protest.

"...But one I was quite fond of," said Lashara, interrupting him as she appeared by his side. "It has been a long time, Callaghan Tor."

"Lashara," said Callaghan, slightly surprised.

"I learned from Ambassador Hesh that you led my grandchildren to a watery grave," she said. Lashara shrugged off her frail form as if it was camouflage, revealing the danger she still posed, even now.

"Forgive me, it was a necessary rouse," he explained. "Kaedin and Kamina are alive. The Stone of Spirits is in their possession." This joyous news brought a smile to Lashara's face. Word spread through the congregation of elves that Kamina was alive. The elves' chanting changed in tone, from slow and melancholy to something more joyful altogether.

"Where are they now?" she asked.

"They have travelled to Mytor to try and uncover the secrets of the stone," revealed the ranger. "We must delay the spirits to allow them time to return."

"And you wish me to help?" she asked.

"Oldwyn Blake said we should seek you out. We need to find his staff. He suggested you may be able to help locate it."

"Mondo Blake's son," whispered Lashara. She looked away from them, as if seeing something they could not, but her eyes swivelled back, directed at Ramiro. "You," she said finally. "You have touched Voleski."

"What's Voleski?" he asked, surprised by this revelation.

"She means the staff," whispered the ranger.

"It likes you," she said, smiling at the ambassador, something which unnerved him further. "I will need your help to find Voleski again. Come with me." Lashara took Ramiro's hand and led him into the crowd of chanting elves. The rangers and Norrek started to follow, but the crowd closed around them, making it clear that they were not welcome.

"Callaghan, I will find the staff," shouted Ramiro. "Go. Free Vangar and his men." The small band sped towards the old gaol, as the ambassador was drawn further within the mass of elves. They stopped abruptly as Lashara turned to him, her face intimately close to his own. Her old yet soft hands explored the wrinkles and dimples of the ambassador's face.

"Close your eyes," she whispered. "Picture Voleski in your mind."

Ramiro did as she asked. He drifted back through his memories, seeing the staff in the hands of Cohen, and before that, safely locked up in his basement. The elves surrounding them started humming a distinctive prayer, drawing him out of his thoughts.

"No," said Lashara, her fingers applying pressure to different parts of his face. "Do not picture where it was. Picture where it is. Open your mind to its power." Ramiro focused harder, and from the darkness he saw the staff, no, not saw, nor even felt. He could not describe what he was feeling, other than... wet.

It was underwater.

"I know where it is!" he exclaimed. Ramiro hurried through the gathering of elves, followed closely by Lashara. He ran to the bridge that crossed over the end of the River Ico to the Elemental Church. From here, he could see the entire bay.

"It could be anywhere," he said.

"No," said Lashara, "You stand where he stood. Where would you throw it?" Ramiro turned to face her. Behind Lashara, the rush of the Ico roared over the edge, transforming into the waterfall that gushed down into the bay. They glanced over the railing, down the long flowing stream of water.

"There?"

"There," said the Witch of Anawey.

"It will take too long to fish out," groaned Ramiro. Lashara smiled at him, and he knew what he had to do. He clambered up onto the railing, but paused as fear took hold. The old elf gave him a nudge, and Ramiro followed the staff down the waterfall, plunging deep into the water.

*

"You took your time," said Vangar, as Callaghan and his fellow rangers appeared with keys to the gaol cell.

"I was busy breaking out of the Black Tower," he replied as he unlocked the cell door. "What were you doing?"

"Discussing politics with my colleagues," said Vangar, signalling his fellow marauders. "More specifically, expostulating about Ambassador Hesh's unscrupulous policies."

"Then let us go voice those opinions," said Gregor. Vangar gazed up and down the tall brute, armed with his spiked mace.

"Another ranger," noted Vangar. "I like this one better than you, Callaghan. He looks more fun."

*

Craecoran Gemmel watched the progress of the spirits and ætherghouls from the wall, as the ambassadors continued to debate the details of their surrender. He kept a keen eye on Malenek's stone bodyguard, pacing along the loose groups of ætherghouls, keeping them in order like a dog herding sheep.

"We must evacuate," insisted Isan Narain. "We can speak to Malenek when our people are safe."

"No, there is no time to evacuate," argued Cohen Hesh. "If we are seen to be running away, the spirits will storm through our walls. We must open the gates and negotiate with Malenek in good faith."

"Lord Malenek is a man of faith," said Miden Lome, still traumatised by the seeing spell. "Let us speak to him."

"Then it is decided," said Hesh. "Open the gates."

"Ambassadors, I must object," grumbled Craecoran Gemmel.

"The decision has been made, craecoran" stated Hesh firmly, betraying his infirm charade. "You will follow it."

The soldiers at the gate reluctantly started to open them. They were taken by surprise when Callaghan and Vangar marched towards them, backed by a small platoon of men, a mix of marauders and Tilden guards loyal to Norrek.

"Do not open those gates," shouted Callaghan.

"Arrest those men!" shrieked Cohen Hesh. The soldiers surrounded the insurgents, but dared not attack the trio of rangers, especially the colossal force of Gregor Sprong. "Now!" he yelled, seeing their hesitation.

"Craecoran Gemmel," shouted Callaghan, "Do you believe me now?"

"I am beginning to," he grunted, glaring at Cohen.

"This is madness!" exclaimed Ambassador Hesh. "Arrest those men!"

"Belay that order," blasted Gemmel. "Do you have a plan, ranger?"

"The same as before," Callaghan yelled. "Oldwyn will protect the city, until we can use the Stone of Spirits."

"But you said…" The ambassador's words trailed off as he realised the ranger had tricked him. "You lied?"

"Only after you did, ambassador."

"Then where is it?" he probed "Where is this fabled stone?"

"Somewhere safe," said Callaghan.

"You're bluffing!" exclaimed Cohen. "You failed, and now you're trying to cover it up."

"He is not!" yelled Ramiro. The Caspian ambassador silenced the crowds as he squelched towards the gate accompanied by Lashara. He was soaking wet, but held Oldwyn's staff triumphantly in his hands. He was accompanied by Lashara. "You are the only liar here, Cohen Hesh. Craecoran Gemmel, close those gates. And arrest that man for the murder of Duke Garstang!"

"With pleasure." The craecoran marched towards Hesh, but the aged Heroshin ambassador surprised him, spryly slipping from Gemmel's grasp and stealing a horse from a startled sedcoran. A team of corans closed the gates, but not before the disgraced and treacherous Cohen Hesh could escape, leading his stolen steed out to meet the spirit army.

"We must get the staff to Oldwyn before Cohen reaches Malenek!" warned Callaghan. Ramiro and Callaghan darted through the streets towards the Black Tower, followed by Flint and Sprong.

"Callaghan, wait," shouted Vangar, chasing them with Ariel Atari. "Oldwyn's door has been sealed shut." In his haste, the disconcerted ranger had forgotten this fact. He instinctively reached for Ascara, whose magical blade could break down the door. He remembered too late that he had gifted the sword to the elves.

"It will take too long to break through," said Ramiro.

"Ariel has an idea," Vangar said, speaking on his mute friend's behalf.

When they reached the barracks, the Etraihu archer unfurled a length of rope he had spied earlier. He tied it to an arrow, and shot it up at the highest cell of the tower. His expert aim saw the arrow shoot through one of the narrow slits, bounce off the ceiling, and return out of another. When the heavy arrow brought the rope down to them, it formed a simple pulley.

"Good aim," said Callaghan. The ranger grabbed hold of the rope, while the others took a firm grip of the opposite end, ready to hoist the ranger to the top of the tower.

"Callaghan," said Ramiro, stepping up to the rope. "Please, let me." Callaghan passed the staff to the ambassador. The ranger fell in line behind Ariel. With the aid of Vangar, Flint, and the sheer strength of Sprong, they launched Ramiro high into the air, all the way up to Oldwyn's cell. The cyclops appeared on the other side of the restricted window.

"Give me the staff," urged the mage. Ramiro stretched the staff to the narrow slit, but it was too small to cram the weapon through.

"It will not fit!" he exclaimed. Oldwyn's thinned fingers extended out and graced the jewel of the staff. A spark of magic broke apart a section of the sill, wide enough to work the staff through. Oldwyn took hold, but Ramiro kept a grip of the other end.

"Oldwyn, I am sorry," the ambassador said sincerely. "Truly I am."

"As am I, Ramiro Messer," replied the mage. "Perhaps in another life we would be friends. Now leave me."

"But Oldwyn…"

"Leave me!" he boomed in a voice that rattled Ramiro's spine. The ambassador signalled for the others to lower him down. As they did, the rope frayed on the stone of the narrow window. It snapped, whipping away from Ramiro as he fell. Oldwyn intervened, quickly casting a spell that caused the ground to rise up below the falling ambassador, making a slope that he clumsily slid down.

With Ramiro safe, the mage now he turned his attentions to the spell he had to perform, his last spell, the one that he had spent years etching into the walls of his cell in the Black Tower, written in blood and tears.

The others helped Ramiro to his feet, as a green glow pulsated out of the tower's slits and cracks. An explosion of magical energy slammed them all to the ground. They rolled out of the way as fragments of stone from the top of the Black Tower rained down around them, hot to the touch.

Oldwyn now stood on the airy platform, with no walls to confine his magic, only the sight of the sprawling city below, the land ahead, and the skies above. He chanted his last spell, over and over, the magic growing stronger within his staff.

"Do it," Callaghan whispered from the ground.

Oldwyn finally brought the staff crashing down upon the floor. The stone chimed like metal, the sound reverberating up the length of the wooden staff to the jewel at the top. The pent up magical energy poured out from it, casting a net that expanded out over the entire city and beyond.

*

Malenek ordered his men not to attack the lone rider who approached them at speed from Calisto. He was disappointed to discover it was Cohen

Hesh, clearly distressed.

"My Lord," he said, but his failure was evident from the green flash of light that expanded out over Calisto, forming a magical barrier around the city.

"How did this happen?" asked Malenek.

"It was Callaghan," explained Cohen. "He has the Stone of Spirits." This unwelcome news enraged the priest further.

"You have failed in your task, ambassador," he asserted, "but you can still be useful. Your soul will bring us closer to Illyria." Malenek nodded to Martyn Keyll. Without hesitation, the spirit broke the soul of Cohen Hesh from his body. They watched as the old ambassador transformed into an ætherghoul, joining the ranks of thousands. However, the spirits were distracted by something else, their collective stare turning as one to the north.

"What is it?" asked Malenek, oblivious to whatever they could sense.

"The other spirit," said Keyll. "He has returned."

"Where is he now?" asked Malenek. The spirits focused their concerted energies on the one who was bonded to the elf.

"He travels to Mytor," said the spirit.

"Stop him," ordered Malenek. "Now!"

CHAPTER FORTY-THREE
LIGHT IN THE DARK

THE NORORA SOARED HIGH ABOVE THE CLIFFS OF CASPIA, streaming north towards Mytor. The elves used the rugged coastline to maintain their course, a dividing line between land and sea that would lead all the way to Malenek's castle. Kaedin kept his eyes fixed ahead, trying to spot their destination. Kamina gazed south towards Calisto, thinking of Callaghan.

"I wonder if he made it," she thought aloud.

"Let us hope so," Kaedin replied, "otherwise our journey will be for nothing." He adjusted the controls to raise the norora slightly, but his energy refused to focus, his hand trembling.

As if to answer Kamina, a small green flash pulsed in Calisto, followed by a shimmering light far in the distance.

"Did you see that?" she asked in awe, as the green light glittered in the sky. "Oldwyn's spell must have worked! Kaedin, did you see…?" Her question was cut short as Kaedin collapsed to the deck, gasping in pain as his ethereal form shook in an uncontrollable spasm.

"Kaedin?" she said meekly, taking a step towards him.

"Stay back!" he growled in a voice not entirely his own, raising his hand to keep her away. "It's them." He struggled to fight the unwavering army of spirits that invaded his thoughts. They probed his mind, a relentless assault on his individual psyche. He had to exert all of his energy just to keep them locked out of the door to his soul. His body lost its tangibility and slowly started to slip through the norora's hull.

"You have to fight them, Kaedin!"

"I cannot," he wheezed, hunched over in pain. There were too many thoughts striking out at him in the dark place his mind was dragged to. They pulverised him with an endless wave of voices, overpowering him. His feet sank through the deck and into the skies the norora sailed through. If he continued to resist, he would plummet down into the ocean and Kamina would die.

With that thought, he focused his energy on his physical form, submitting to the onslaught of the spirits.

The voices stopped.

"Kaedin?" asked Kamina. The ghost rocked himself back and forth, humming an old melody. She stepped closer, kneeling beside him.

"Kaedin?" she asked again.

He suddenly lashed out at her. Kamina shrieked, staggering backwards, to avoid his deathly touch. The spirit slammed his hands down on the cranks and levers repeatedly like a wild animal, destroying them. He bashed at the fuel containers above. Flares of gas sparked out of the cracks. The ghost focused again on Kamina, edging back towards the rear of the ship.

"Kaedin, please stop!" she begged. The spirit stalked towards her swinging his fists. His movements were clumsy, as though he were a puppet from the teacher's show being poorly controlled. She ducked out of the way, scrambling back long the length of the ship, hunted by the spirit. Kamina was shocked as Kaedin's form flickered, revealing the faces of the various spirits who sought to manipulate him.

"Get out!" Kaedin yelled as he clawed at his head, as he lurched towards her. Kamina was backed into a corner, trapped by the forces holding Kaedin hostage.

"Kaedin, I know you are in there. You have to fight them. You have the strength, I know you do," she cried as the spirit loomed over her. "Fight them!" He clenched his fist, readying another attack. Kamina squeezed her eyes closed, holding her hands up in a futile defence against the ghost.

The strike from the spirit never came. Kamina opened her eyes. Kaedin hovered above her, having returned to his senses. He stared at her hands, at the scar on her palm. The spirit held up his shaking hand, showing her his matching scar.

"Are you... you?" she asked.

"I am," he replied. The pair shared a thankful smile, having prevailed against the spirit forces, but an unhealthy shudder from the norora interrupted their fleeting victory. The ship shook as it ascended too quickly, causing Kamina to lose her balance. Kaedin rushed to the controls as she tried to stay on her feet.

"Kaedin, what is wrong?"

"The release valve is broken!" he exclaimed. "There is too much gas. It is going to explode!" The jalaaroca fumes hissed out as Kamina experienced an unpleasant pop in her ears. The animal skin inflated beyond its capacity, causing them to soar higher into the sky.

"We need to jump!" she yelled, fighting against the turbulent jerking of the norora to reach the hatch. Kaedin traversed the deck with relative ease. Kamina grabbed his ghostly hand as he hauled her to the door. They gazed out of the porthole, only to find they were far too high to bail out of the airship.

You will not survive," said Kaedin. The spirit scanned the norora, trying to think of some way to save them. They had to lower their height, and release the gas. "Kamina, you have to deflate the balloon."

"But the norora will crash!" she exclaimed

"We can bail out before it does," he said. "You must hurry."

Kamina staggered over to the stern of the ship. She unsheathed Ascara and used the blade to cut through the roof of the gondola. She squeezed through the hole, but was immediately blown back by the prevailing winds. She tried again, forcing herself to lie low on the roof. The winds howled around her as she gripped Ascara with both hands, afraid the sword would be sucked from her grasp. Kamina stretched Ascara up, trying to pierce the balloon with the tip of the blade, but it was out of reach. She tried again, rising her body up slightly, but she could not compete with the vigorous airstream.

Kamina crawled to one of the thick ropes that secured the balloon to the rest of the ship. The lissome elf fought against the sheer wind to slink slowly upwards. She thrust Ascara at the balloon, finally cutting a hole. The gas vented out, but she struggled to keep hold of the sword. The blade cut into the rope, causing it to fray. Kamina lay flat on her stomach as the threads of the rope sprang loose one at a time. The norora started to level out, allowing Kamina to wriggle back through the hole.

"You did it!" exclaimed Kaedin. Kamina dropped inside the gondola, but her expression made him regret his moment of optimism.

The fraying rope snapped.

The norora lurched sideways. Kamina was tossed across the floor as the cabin twisted in the sky. She hit the side of the hull hard, her face pressed against a porthole. As the ship spiralled downwards she could see it was heading directly for the black cliffs and the perilous rocks at their base.

"Kaedin!" she cried, but he was preoccupied with trying to remain inside the ship. The norora pitched unpredictably as another rope unravelled. The spirit struggled to maintain his form, sinking halfway through the deck. He managed to pull himself back into the cabin, teetering towards the door.

"Kamina, get to the hatch." Against the fear of death and the force of gravity, the elf climbed up the tilted floor until she reached Kaedin at the doorway. She secured Ascara to her belt before throwing open the hatch door. Even as the wicked winds lashed her hair against her face, she saw the black mountains of Mytor. They were close enough for her to make out Malenek's castle nestled near the coast, high above the seas.

"Kamina, jump!" Kaedin screamed. "Now!"

"No, wait!" She had to time hear leap perfectly, otherwise she would end up scattered upon the rocks at the foot of the cliffs.

"Kamina..." Kaedin grimaced as the gondola lurched towards the cliffs.

"Not yet," she said, but Kaedin knew they were out of time.

"Now!" He pushed his sister out of the norora. Kamina plummeted past the tall black cliffs and plunged into the cold waters below, narrowly avoiding the treacherous rocks. She swam to the surface just in time to witness the norora slam into the side of the cliffs. The remaining fuel and gas ignited, blowing it apart in a tremendous explosion. She ducked back underwater as parts of the ship crashed down around her, swimming out of their way.

Kamina struggled back to the top, gasping for air. She spotted Kaedin sat in the charcoaled remains of the norora's hull. It would never fly again, but appeared to be seaworthy, bobbing up and down upon the surface.

"We really should stop travelling in ships that burst into flame" she said as Kaedin helped her climb into the vestige of the hull. She slumped into the wreckage, coughing up water. Her frantic hands checked that Ascara was still by her side, and that the Stone of Spirits was safely tucked away in her pocket.

"You pushed me," she said sourly, glaring at Kaedin.

"I had to," he said, looking down at his feet. "I promised Callaghan."

"Are you okay?" she asked.

"No," he sighed. "I can still hear them."

"The spirits?" she asked.

"Yes. No. Not just them, the ætherghouls," he revealed. "I can hear their trapped souls, well not hear exactly. I can feel them striving to get out from under the skin. There are so many…"

"You must stay in control," she said, her lower lip quivering. "I cannot do this without you."

"They seem to have subsided for the moment."

"Good. Now, how we will get to Mytor?" They both gazed up at the craggy, impassable cliffs looming above them.

"We should paddle along the coast," he suggested. "Perhaps we will find a path within the cliffs."

"And what if we do not?" she asked. "Should we not go back to Caspia?"

"By then it may be too late, if it is not so already. This is all my fault." Kamina allowed Kaedin to bathe in his pity as she searched the surrounding sea for a makeshift oar. She tried to fish out a smouldering bit of wood, but it was still blisteringly hot. She ripped off part of her robe and snatched it out of the water. They sculled along the sea, making sure not too drift to close to the cliffs for fear of being smashed against the rocks.

"There." Kaedin pointed at the cliffs, sparking Kamina's waning interest.

"What is it?" she asked. "I do not see a path."

"No, there," he repeated, wagging his finger downwards towards the base of the black cliffs. She had not spotted it at first, but as they neared it became more obvious that there was a large, cave sucking in the sea like a giant, rasping mouth. "It may lead to the top."

"I do not think we have a choice," Kamina said. The current of the cave was too strong for her single oar to contend with. She used it as a rudder, guiding the dingy through the entrance as waves crashed against the rocks all around it, like teeth broken from the cave's mangled jaw.

The water within the cave was calmer, the diminished waves pushing them further inside. The darkness was dispelled by Kaedin's silvery glow, illuminating the cavern with a magical radiance. Kamina's fearful imagination cast faces in the shadows of the stalactites, horrible ghoulish expressions mocking them. The makeshift boat came to an abrupt halt as it struck an incline. They climbed out, peering up the dark slope that greeted them.

"I guess we go this way," said Kamina. "You first."

"Why me?" Kaedin squealed.

"Because you are a spirit and I need you to light the way," she replied.

"That is a wise suggestion," he said with a modicum of surprise.

The cavern wound upwards, narrowing into little more than a crawl space. This was no problem for Kaedin and his ability to walk through solid rock, but Kamina had to wriggle and writhe through them, worried that she may become stuck. She removed Ascara and slid the sword in front of her, scuffing her hands and knees on the rough rock. As she twisted through an extremely tight spot, she was suddenly cast into darkness. Kaedin's light disappeared, followed by a short scream.

"Kaedin?" she called out, pulling herself along. "Kaedin!"

"I am fine," he replied eventually. "The cavern opens up again. Watch for the gap." Kamina squirmed another short distance before she felt the weight of Ascara's blade tip over the edge. She wormed her way out, throwing the weapon down to Kaedin who did not think to catch it. The sword clanged at his ghostly feet.

"Watch it!" he exclaimed. Kaedin's outburst echoed around the vast cavern, his voice reverberated from one end of the chamber to the other.

"The sword cannot hurt you." Kamina whispered, picking up Ascara.

"This place must be huge," he said, ignoring her. His ethereal light barely penetrated the gloom of the gigantic cave. Kamina held Ascara's jewelled hilt to her lips.

"Ascentio Risaar Emanos." Nothing happened.

"What are you doing?" asked Kaedin.

"We need light," she said.

"Only a ranger can wield Ascara," said the spirit. Kamina glared at him, his disparaging remarks prompting her to try again.

"Ascentio Risaar Emanos!" she shouted. Her words echoed all around them, but there was no spark of a flame.

"Told you..." derided Kaedin, but he was cut short when the symbols etched into the sword's surface started to glow. Kamina watched in wonder as she felt heat emanate from the metal, but just as quickly, the magic faded. Ascara's blade remained cold steel.

A blast of fire erupted from the other side of the cavern, allowing them to see the true size of the chamber, if only for an instant.

"Was that me?" whispered Kamina.

"I do not believe so," Kaedin replied. They heard something pound towards them at a fast pace, wheezing and snarling in the dark. The charring, acrid breath of the creature stirred memories of the shadow that had attacked the *Arad Nor*.

The dragon.

Razor sharp teeth reflected Kaedin's glow. Kamina sprinted to the shelter of a nearby stalagmite as fire erupted from the ugly mouth of the dragon. The spirit was too slow and was caught in the scorching blast.

"Kaedin!" she screamed as he was enveloped in the flames. Kamina balked at the intense heat, shielding her eyes with her arm. When the flames evaporated, Kamina peered out towards the dragon. Kaedin stood unharmed, although his usual silvery glow took on a brief fiery orange hue.

"Ha!" he shouted at the dragon, pointing at its massive, bewildered face. The creature fired another blast at Kaedin, but it proved as futile as the first, although Kamina was forced to hide behind the rocky column again. The spirit, bolstered by the dragon's failure, marched towards it. The intimidated creature tried to back away from Kaedin, but the beast was not built to retreat.

"Kaedin?" Kamina hissed, but there was no response. She cautiously emerged from behind the barricade to be greeted by a strange sight. Kaedin was stroking the dragon. What was even stranger was that the scaly creature seemed to appreciate it, in the same way Eshtel used to enjoy her brushing his fine chestnut coat. The dragon growled as it caught sight of the elf and the blade that she carried.

"Put it down. He is harmless," said Kaedin. The dragon droned playfully.

"He?" she asked. Kamina now noticed that the animal wore a tight golden collar around its neck, sharp on the inside so that it cut into the dragon's scaly skin. "He destroyed the *Arad Nor*."

"I am sure he was ordered to," said Kaedin.

"Then read its mind," she said. "Like you did with Ramiro and Leotori." Kaedin gazed into the dragon's huge red eyes, unwilling to stretch inside his monstrous head and probe his mind.

"Ramiro did not exactly enjoy the experience," Kaedin replied.

"Then do it gently!" she hissed.

"I am sorry," he said, stroking the dragon, before sliding his hand through the scaly surface and into the creature's thoughts. The images appeared not as before in a shroud of mist, but as though he was peering into a broken mirror... the *Arad Nor* on fire from above... an ugly man ordering the attack... being whipped at his hand... stabbed with a gold edged knife... Malenek's angry face... a Mytor woman, lying dead... a young Zalestian boy...

Kaedin fell back to the floor, knocked out of the dragon's mind by the intensity of the thoughts themselves. The dragon squealed and roared in pain, one giant claw landing right next to Kaedin. Kamina moved to attack, but Kaedin raised his hand, signalling that she should stand down.

"Do not strike," Kaedin murmured. "He is in pain. So much pain." His new pet snarled hot breath over the spirit who could not feel it. "He was ordered to attack us. He is a prisoner."

"But he is not in chains," noted Kamina.

"No, he has been here most of his life, dependant on his captors. He is too afraid to leave." Kaedin paused as he tried to unscramble the thoughts he had gleaned from the dragon. "I think he is from Zalestia."

"Like the other creatures we saw there," said Kamina, Ascara still raised.

"No, there is something different about him." Kaedin slowly stood up and calmed the beast with his touch. "Come closer, he will not harm you."

Kamina sheathed Ascara and charily moved towards them. The dragon cocked his head up when she appeared beside Kaedin, but as she began to caress the beast's head as he did, an enjoyable rumble rose from the dragon's throat. Kamina stared at her own reflection in the creature's huge eye as it fluttered its large, leathery wings.

"This must be how Malenek visited Errazure Ecko," Kamina guessed. The mere mention of the Zalestian mage angered the beast. "It is okay," she said soothingly. "He can harm you no more. He is dead." This revelation caused the dragon to erect its full mass and roar into the cavern, shaking the walls. To Kamina it looked as though the creature was laughing at the news, gloating about Errazure's demise.

"If that is true, we cannot be far from his castle," he whispered.

"Kaedin, we are already under it."

CHAPTER FORTY-FOUR

THE GREAT DIVIDE

T**HE PROTECTIVE SHIELD THAT** O**LDWYN** B**LAKE HAD CAST OVER** Calisto was barely visible to the naked eye, the magic stretched so thin as to make it almost imperceptible. There was a green tint to the light that flowed through, but every so often a flash of energy sparked across the net like sheet lightning in a storm.

The spirits had commanded the ætherghouls to test the barrier. Those that had tried had managed to pierce through the thin layer of magic, only to combust in a brief blaze of green flame, freeing the soul within the undead slaves. The magical net rippled when they did, as if the ætherghouls had disturbed a wall of water, before it returned to its invisible calm state. The spirits, while not suffering the same fate as the ætherghouls, were unable to touch the partition without being repelled by the magic that held it in place.

When these facts became evident to the soldiers watching from the walls of Calisto, they let out a celebratory cheer. Their optimism was boosted further when Malenek ordered his men to retreat from the magical obstruction. Only Gort remained, staring through the green tint of the spell to its source on top of the Black Tower.

"Father," he whispered into the ether.

*

"This is not a victory," warned Callaghan as the soldiers celebrated around them. "Oldwyn does not have the strength to maintain this spell for long."

"Then what do we do?" asked Ambassador Narain.

"We evacuate those who are not able to fight," answered Ramiro. "The rest of us must make a stand against the spirits."

"You will not win if you fight as you normally would," said Callaghan. "We must devise a strategy to reach Malenek. If he dies, the spirits will hopefully die with him."

"It will be near impossible to reach him through that battalion of beasts," said Flint. Sprong nodded in agreement.

"The quickest way would be to have the archers take out the ætherghouls, and send riders to charge through the rest," suggested Craecoran Gemmel. "Hopefully one would get through."

"The archers will not stop the ætherghouls," said Callaghan, exposing the flaw in the craecoran's plan. "And even if you made it through them, the spirits would spook the horses. All you would have is injured men thrown from their steeds, who would then be turned into our enemy."

"We need more numbers if we are to have any hope of survival," said Vangar.

"We could try again to persuade the elves to join our cause," said Callaghan. "We stand a greater chance with them on our side. Ambassador Messer, given your recent time with Lashara, I would ask that you accompany me to try and persuade them to fight."

"I have another issue that requires my attention," said Ramiro. "Excuse me." Without further explanation, he walked away, leaving the other leaders to figure out a plan.

"I greeted the elves when they arrived," said Ambassador Narain. "I will gladly accompany you."

The ranger and the Legorian ambassador headed towards the grounds of the council chambers, leaving Vangar and Craecoran Gemmel to stand in silence amidst the revelry of the soldiers.

"Just so you know," muttered Gemmel, "if we survive this, I'm going to have your head."

"Atticus, we are not going to survive this," replied the marauder. He peeled back his eye patch, revealing the scorched scar from the attack that claimed his eye. "But some of us might. I will make preparations for the evacuation." Gemmel grabbed Vangar's arm as he made to leave.

"Tell me why," said the craecoran. "Why did you steal the *Haelion*?"

"Another time maybe." He shrugged Gemmel's hand away as he headed for the docks.

*

High above them, at the top of the Black Tower, Oldwyn focused all his energy on maintaining the protection spell that encircled Calisto. As a consequence, he could hear every sound in the city; every heavy footstep, every tense hand gripping the wall, every stolen laugh and sacred breath reverberated through the ground and into his body.

"Father," he heard Gort say at the edge of the barrier, the net of magic catching the sound of his words like a conduit to his mind.

"Gort," replied the mage. "What are you doing?" His words, no more than a whisper, travelled through the staff and along the wave of magical energy, echoing out to the stone man's ears.

"Helping build a better world," grunted the stone giant.

"No, my child," replied Oldwyn. "You are helping destroy this one."

*

Callaghan and Isan Narain raced to the council chambers. The elves were still praying in the park that surrounded the structure. The mass of tall, slender bodies parted as the ranger approached with the ambassador in tow. They wandered among the elves, calmed by their peaceful chanting. The partition led to the nine elders, formed in a circle around a large Caspian oak.

"You have very few trees in this city," observed Abbal Eredu, breaking from his prayers. "It is disconcerting."

"What brings you to us, Ranger of Ishkava and Ambassador of Legoria?" asked Lashara.

"I think you know what I have come to say," replied Callaghan.

"We told you, we will not raise arms," stated Abbal firmly.

"With all due respect, Elder Eredu, we need every able body to fight for our freedom, for our very existence."

"With the same respect, Ambassador Narain, we renounced those ways hundreds of years ago."

"Then you will be a little rusty," said Callaghan, trying to placate them with humour. "The elves are fast and strong, and we need that advantage to overcome the ætherghouls."

"We provided you with sanctuary when you requested it," added Isan.

"Had we known your shelter was contingent upon killing, we would not have done so," countered Abbal.

"Do not do it for us," said Callaghan. "Do it for the elf who currently searches for a way to defeat the spirits."

"Kamina," whispered Lashara.

"She has done your people proud," said the ranger, rallying them to their cause. "We must make sure her continuing efforts are not in vain." The nine elders glanced between one another, arriving at some unsaid agreement.

"We will consider your request, Callaghan Tor," said Abbal.

"I would ask that you consider it quickly. I fear we have little time left."

*

Ramiro Messer had donned his old armour, which still managed to fit despite lying in storage for many years, ever since he had won his seat on the council. He had wandered aimlessly through the city, watching as women and children fled to the docks, while all able-bodied men remained behind.

He ended up at the Calisto cemetery, a labyrinth of tombstones, crypts, and mausoleums, stacked on ancient catacombs. He entered the section devoted to the military and knelt down by his son's grave, marked with the insignia of the Caspian army. Most of the headstones bore the same stamp, representing soldiers who had given their lives in service to their country.

"Reynard," he started to say, but beyond his son's name, no other sound emerged. Ramiro could think of nothing else to say, his mind blank. He simply knelt there, and thought of his son.

*

"You left us," grunted Gort.

"I was held captive, here in this city," replied the mage. "The first thing I did after I was freed was to search for you. I would never leave you, or your brother. But you did, Gort. You left Gigondas."

"I... I..." stammered the giant. "We could not wait forever! I came back for him, but he was gone."

"He found life at sea upon a ship," Oldwyn revealed. "And death."

"You are lying," the stone man shouted.

"You master is to blame," revealed mage. "He sent his hidden beast to sink the ship carrying Callaghan Tor to Zalestia, the same ship that counted Gigondas as a member of the crew."

"I... I passed on that order," confessed Gort, his loyalty to Malenek torn by this devastating news.

"You were not to know," whispered Oldwyn, trying to console the rocky brute despite the distance between them. "But you can still make amends." Gort turned and gazed back at Malenek, surrounded by the spirits. He contemplated seeking his own vengeance, the irony not lost on him. The priest glanced at him from far away, and Gort knew he could not. Malenek had been there for him when Oldwyn had gone. He had helped him seek answers to his parentage, although he had ultimately found none. The stone giant had been abandoned over and over again. He would not do the same to his master.

"No," said Gort eventually, turning to face Oldwyn's magic once more. "This world is a cruel place. We deserve a better one, and have come too far to fail here."

"It is never too late," affirmed Oldwyn.

"You are just trying to use me!" blasted Gort, pointing a large, accusing finger towards the top of the Black Tower. The giant realised he had accidently thrust his arm through the magical barrier, seeing the green glow upon his rocky limb.

"Gort, what are you doing?" shouted Malenek. The giant did not reply. He cautiously stepped through the barrier, unaffected by the magic. He found a large boulder about the size of a man's head, half-buried in the ground at his feet. Gort reached down and dug it out with one mighty hand.

*

"What in the name of the Elements is it doing?" asked Craecoran Gemmel, as he and the Calisto garrison watched Malenek's servant step through Oldwyn's shield. With one step the stone giant had splintered the optimism of the soldiers. Even the peculiar pair of rangers, Flint and Sprong, were shocked that he had penetrated the protection spell so easily, completely unaffected by the magic.

The brute picked up a large rock in one hand. He started to spin round, building up momentum, faster and faster, until he suddenly stopped. The missile flew out of his mighty hand, hurtling towards the city. It shot through the sky, high above their heads, heading towards the top of the Black Tower.

"No," whispered Gemmel.

*

Ramiro was lost in the haze of old memories, rekindled since his encounter with Kaedin's spirit. He had spent so long remembering Reynard as a murdered ataincor that he had forgotten him as a young boy. He reminisced about a time working at the docks in his younger days, his son no taller than his knee. The boy had gawked in wonder at the ships he built and at the burly, giant craftsmen who were in Ramiro's construction team. He had used a piece of scrap wood to carve a wooden soldier for Reynard. Ramiro recalled the statue in its most intricate detail. He had always been good with his hands. Ramiro realised he had not carved anything since his son had been taken from him. If I survive this onslaught, he thought, I will make something new.

Ramiro rose up from Reynard's grave, kissing his hand and laying it on the slab of stone that bore his son's name. As he turned to leave, he was distracted by a projectile arcing across the sky, heading straight towards the Black Tower.

"No," he gasped.

*

"Do you think they will join us?" asked Isan, as he and Callaghan rushed back to the edge of the city to re-join Craecoran Gemmel and the rangers.

"The elves are as proud as they are wise," replied the ranger," but despite their composure, as a people their passion runs deep. I can only hope..."

His words were cut short by a whooshing sound above. They spotted the rock shooting across the sky above the city's rooftops, on a collision course with the crest of the Black Tower.

"No," whispered Callaghan."

*

The cyclops mage watched as the rock thundered towards him, sent by someone he had once called son. Oldwyn was too weak to move, leaning on the staff to support his waning stance. He closed his giant eye and whispered his last words into the green jewel.

"I am sorry."

He lost hold of the staff as the boulder struck his body. The bludgeoning thud sent him tumbling over the edge, plummeting down to his death. Time slowed in all of Enara. Oldwyn Blake's life, longer and more eventful than most, flashed before his eye. All eyes in Calisto, and some far beyond, watched his body flutter down through the air. His fall was soon ended by the ground below, breaking his soul from the mortal coil. His spirit drifted and dispersed, journeying across the great beyond and into Illyria.

CHAPTER FORTY-FIVE
THE PRIEST'S JOURNALS

At the far end of the dragon's lair, Kamina and Kaedin discovered a set of cold, slippery steps worn into a narrow rocky pass, snaking upwards into the heart of the castle.

"This must be it," said Kamina, drawing Ascara as she slinked up the steps. The awkward pang of her bond being stretched caused her to stop. Kaedin was not following her lead. She crept back down, spying her ghostly companion soothing the dragon's scaly head with his spirited hand.

"We will return to free you," Kaedin whispered. He could not be certain he would fulfil this promise, but the passion of his pledge underlined his intentions. The dragon sensed his doubt, releasing a pessimistic groan tainted with loneliness. The brooding beast retreated into the darkness of the cavern, spitting a sulking fireball towards the spirit as he did so. The ghost returned to Kamina, the sorrow gleaned from the fragments of stolen memories weighing heavily on his heart. He ascended the steps in front of her, leading the way.

The stairwell was rough, twisting at odd angles, until finally the elves found a heavy door set within the rock. Beyond it they could hear what sounded like an ætherghoul wailing. Kaedin faded into thin air and drifted through the door, searching for the source of the deafening noise. The man he had seen in the dragon's memories, Salamon Silnor, was attempting to sing a limerick, his hand drumming on an empty cask of mead. He was swaying and swirling as he did so, as if dancing with some unseen damsel. Kaedin stifled his laughter and returned to Kamina.

"The dragon's tormentor is the only one I can see," he reported back. Kamina used Ascara to cut through the lock, and together they explored the castle in secret. They climbed upwards through the levels, Kaedin flitting through the walls, attempting to find Balen Malenek's study. They reached a landing, where Kamina spotted an unassuming wooden door.

"This one," said Kaedin, poking his transparent head through the wall. She entered the unlocked study and laid her eyes upon Malenek's impressive library of books and scrolls. She stood in awe as she imagined all the stories and legends that were held within their words, bound to parchment, palimpsest, and paper. One of the walls was at odds with the room, an empty space that had perhaps once been home to a painting.

"Stop gawking and start looking for a book about the stone," said Kaedin.

"You could help," she shot back, approaching a bookcase.

"Perhaps you have not noticed, but I am limited in what I can touch," remarked the ghost.

"You can read the spines and the words within" she said. Kamina flicked through various journals, opening them so Kaedin could scan their words.

"Anything?" she asked on their fourth attempt.

"Nothing about the stone," he sighed. Kamina slammed the journal shut. She paused as she noted one of the journals was out of place, jutting out from the line of other volumes. Kamina plucked it from the shelf and opened it. The pages fluttered open to where they had been pressed on their last reading, by the very man Kamina had killed in Elgrin Forest.

"What about this one?" she asked the spirit. Kaedin scanned the words with a look of surprise on his face. "What is it?"

"This... this is about Callaghan and..." his words trailed off as he continued to read.

"What does it say?" she demanded.

"Kamina, you do not wish to know..."

"Read it!" she shouted at him. Kaedin exhaled any protest he was about to make as he read Malenek's words to her.

"I was ready to give the men of Enara another chance, to become head of a church that could unite two lands at war, when I was paid a visit by a young farmer. His lands had recently been raided by thieves, who not only burned down his farm, but also stole the lives of his wife and children. He sought his vengeance while the blood of those he loved remained warm. Their spirits will be watching over him in Illyria, proud in the knowledge that, while he could not save them, he saved another victim of the raiders, one of the elves who had visited me recently. The raiders had already slain the female, Sharla, but her husband Kaman was still alive, suffering mortal wounds. He used his last breath to beg the young farmer to save his daughter, Talia, still trapped in her feverish slumber. He took her back to what remained of his farm and looked after her day and night, until she awoke several months later. This was the redeeming mission of Callaghan Tor. His whole existence was channelled into his love and devotion for that pretty young elf. She saved him from the dark, vengeful path he was set on, and in return he loved her like a husband..."

Kaedin stopped reading as tears teemed down Kamina's face, turning the last line over and over again inside her head.

He loved her like a husband.

"Does this mean...? Is Callaghan my...?" she stammered, quivering. Clunky footsteps from the narrow corridor outside cut short the stream of questions overwhelming her mind. Kaedin evaporated into thin air as Salamon skulked into the room, but not fast enough. He gasped, startled by the spirit and the small elf holding the journal.

"What are you doing in here?" he shrieked, trying his best to intimidate the young elf. However, Malenek's servant was unarmed, whereas Kamina was in possession of Ascara, the sword that had created the spirit army in this very castle. Salamon eyed the blade with a sense of vague recognition. He stepped back in retreat as Kamina thrust the sword threateningly towards him

"What do you know about the Stone of Spirits?" she yelled. Salamon quickly scurried out of the study. Kamina chased after him, Ascara in one hand and Malenek's journal in the other. She pursued him down the steps and into the main hall, Kaedin not far behind. The young elf sped through the large entrance hall, bearing down upon the foul smelling servant, but he found protection behind two armed guards. Kamina slid to a desperate stop.

"I thought you said the castle was empty?" she hissed at Kaedin, as the guards raised their weapons; the first revealed a sword, while the larger of the two unfurled a spiked morning star.

"Get her!" shouted Salamon. Kamina turned on her heels and darted back through the castle, eluding the slow guards by hiding in a small store room.

"I have an idea," whispered Kaedin, still invisible. "Stay here." He drifted off before she could argue. Her bond to the spirit was stretched to its limits, draining her energy. She struggled to hold Ascara as footsteps thudded nearby, ominously pausing in their stride. The door was suddenly wrenched open. Kamina shoved her way out, kicking one of the guards in the knee. She doubled back, hoping to reach the main gates of the castle and escape. The stretched bond with Kaedin sapped her strength, causing her to collapse in the main hall, the metal gate still too distant to reach.

The guards bore down upon her. Kamina deflected an attack from the sword, only to be forced to roll back to avoid the mace. She dropped Malenek's journal, the book lost as the guards traipsed past it towards her. She searched for another exit, but the two guards and Salamon ensnared her in a circle. The repulsive servant had collected a meat cleaver from the pantry, tossing it from one hand to the other, toying with her. Her life-force drained to the point she could no longer point Ascara's heavy blade, the tip of the sword falling to the floor. Sweat poured from Kamina as she struggled to keep hold of the hilt. Salamon sneered at her as he picked up Malenek's journal.

"This does not belong to you, little elfling." He smacked Kamina's face with the book, and she thudded to the floor. "Where is your spirit now?" he sniggered, raising the cleaver to strike.

A sudden resurgence of strength allowed Kamina to lift Ascara just in time to defend herself. Her blow knocked the cleaver from Salamon's hands. She rose to her feet, the strain of the bond now lessened. The beating of wings swooped around the castle, as Kamina realised what Kaedin's plan entailed.

"He is very close," she said, smiling. "And he is bringing a friend." Malenek's minions now registered the whooshing beat of wings closing in on them. Kamina leapt aside as the dragon crashed through the large main doors, breaking off a large chunk of the castle wall along with it. Kaedin hugged the dragon's head, one of his hands delved deep into the creature's mind, controlling his movements. The guard gripping the mace moved to attack, but he was gobbled up by the dragon's giant jaws. His weapon thudded against the floor as the animal chewed on his limbs. The second was caught in one of the beast's claws. The dragon hurled him against a wall, breaking his back, before trapping Salamon under the same talons. The creature crushed his captor against the flagstones, leering at him.

"Please," he begged, squirming, "I fed you. I looked after you." His beseeching only enraged the dragon further. It arced back its head and then roared at Salamon, igniting a long volley of fiery breath. Malenek's journal lay near Salamon's hand. Kamina scooped it up and dived out of the way, narrowly avoiding the intense blast. When she looked back, Salamon's body was nothing more than blistering, broiled bones. The fiery behemoth turned its red eyes upon her. Kamina was sure the dragon was deciding whether or not she would make an appetising meal.

"Kaedin," she said meekly.

"Do not worry, I am in control," replied the spirit. The dragon bucked like a large horse, kicking out the metal gate, which clanged down the abyss immediately outside. "Well, mostly," he added with an unsure grin.

"We need to go back to the study and find out about the stone," said Kamina, dusting herself off.

"There is no time," said Kaedin, gazing through the dragon-shaped hole in the entrance and beyond, to the other side of Amaros. "The spirit army marches on Calisto."

"But Oldwyn's spell…"

"Oldwyn has fallen," Kaedin revealed.

"All the more reason we need to find out how to use the stone!" she insisted, marching up the stairs to the study.

"There are thousands of books!" shouted Kaedin. Kamina stopped on the steps. "If we stay here and search, the fight may be over before it has begun."

"What are you suggesting?"

"We go now, and hope the sight of the stone is enough to distract Malenek." Kamina withdrew the Stone of Spirits from where it was hidden within her Zalestian robes. She gazed at the swirling white and silver magic swirling within, hoping it would provide her with an answer.

"And if it does not?" she asked.

"Then the dragon will," he said defiantly. The beast roared in agreement.

"But once we near the spirit army…"

"…it will only be a matter of time before I succumb to their wrath," said Kaedin. "I know. It is a risk we must take."

"It is decided then," she said, slipping Ascara into the sheath on her back. "We must go." Knowing the fate of Enara was at stake, Kaedin nodded. Kamina pocketed Malenek's journal before climbing up onto the dragon.

"Hold on," said the ghost. Kaedin directed the dragon out of the castle. The beast spread its giant wings and dove down into the abyss. He swooped up, beating his wings as they shot out of the gorge and into the grey clouds above, setting them on a direct course to Calisto and their destiny.

CHAPTER FORTY-SIX
THE HEAT OF BATTLE

Callaghan hovered over Oldwyn's corpse, which had been moved inside the mess hall of the barracks. The ranger lay the faithful staff, the weapon Lashara had called Voleski, beside his friend's body. He carefully closed the cyclops' large eye.

"Your sacrifice will not be in vain," he whispered as he covered the body with a thin sheet. The ranger let out a scream of rage, upturning another table nearby. His chest heaved with anger, exhaling the malevolent emotions until he calmed down. Flint and Sprong stood by the door, watching their fellow ranger overcome his furor.

"Callaghan, we must lead these men against Malenek," said Jochan Flint. "They are lost and scared. Their own leaders have betrayed them, but they believe in you."

"They believe in Ascara, in magic, and I have none," he replied, eyeing Voleski. He thought of wielding it, but like the Stone of Spirits, he did not know how. "We cannot win against an army of spirits."

"Maybe not," said Gregor Sprong. "But we can damn well try, and those men out there, they will follow you."

"Why?" asked Callaghan.

"Because I will follow you. And do you know why? Because you are the Ranger Elite. They gave you the sword because you deserved it, not because you needed its fancy magic."

Callaghan composed himself, channelling his fury into his desire to win this fight. "Then let us do so," he said. "Let us send these spirits back to the beyond."

He led the pair of rangers out of the building. The legions of Amaros' army awaited them, joined by the marauders and other volunteers who wished to fight. In that moment, Callaghan wished he had Ascara, not to battle the spirits, but so her inspiring flame could cast light at the shadowy fears that vexed the faces before him.

"It might be prudent if you say something," whispered Vangar, hovering near the ranger.

"What would you have me say?" the ranger replied softly. "I am as scared as they are."

"Then might I suggest a lie," said the marauder.

"Right, men," screamed Craecoran Gemmel, when it became obvious

Callaghan had nothing to say. "Get to your posts!"

The sedcorans and ataincors barked orders at their squads, leading them to their positions. The archers lined the walls as the infantry spread out behind them, ready to attack should the enemy breech the city. Ramiro and Isan joined the rangers at the command centre upon the wall, both ambassadors dressed for battle. The legions of ætherghouls swarmed towards the city, past the line where the magical border had held them at bay. Malenek and his ever present spirits remained at a safe distance. Some of the ætherghouls fell victim to the marauder traps, finding death at the bottom of spike-laden pits.

"Nicely done," Gemmel muttered to Vangar.

"Was that a compliment, Atticus?" he asked. "By the Elementals, it must be the end of the world!" The craecoran snorted at the marauder's joke.

"Archers, light your arrows." he screamed. The ranger had been right, arrows would not kill the ætherghouls, but fire might. "Fire!"

Thousands of arrows flared high into the air. Gravity dragged them back towards the ground, striking their targets and setting them ablaze. Rows of ætherghouls burned, but those hit writhed around manically until the flames were doused. They crawled back up, staggering onwards with scorched arrows poking out from their putrid, charred flesh. The archers fired another volley, but in vain.

"This will not work," said Flint. "We cannot hide here until we have no more arrows."

"Even if we hold the ætherghouls at bay, Malenek need only wait for the cover of darkness to move closer. The spirits will pass through the walls, and we will be done for," said Callaghan.

"Then it is agreed. We must take the fight to them," urged Gemmel.

"Raise the gates!" yelled Ramiro. As they marched down the steps to lead their men out onto the battlefield, they were greeted by a welcoming sight. A large contingent of elves coursed through the streets of Calisto, led by Endo Eredu. They joined the human soldiers at the western gate as it was hoisted open.

"The elders have decided that we must lend our support to those who have sheltered us during these difficult times if Kamina Elloeth is to have any hope of succeeding," said the elf.

"I am glad," replied Callaghan. "Craecoran Gemmel, these elves have no weapons."

"Then let us find them some quickly," he roared. "This way!"

*

The dragon shot through the skies, urged on by the spirit upon its back. Kamina held onto its scaly hide behind Kaedin, shielding herself from the cold, ferocious winds. She dared to peek out from behind the dragon's head, and saw strange storm clouds forming over Caspia. Below them, she glimpsed

Lake Comodo, no more than a puddle from this height. She followed the winding path of the River Ico all the way to Calisto. Outside the city, she could see thousands of men, specks from this distance. Some were lined up outside the city, but most were swarming towards them.

The ætherghouls were marching upon the city.

"Do you see them?" shouted Kaedin about the wind shear. Kamina nodded, trembling with apprehension.

"Are you ready?" she asked.

"No," he replied honestly. "You?"

"Not really," she replied. Kaedin grinned as he commanded the dragon to descend towards the city.

*

The armed warriors of Calisto hastily formed into lines outside the walls of the city. The archers continued to fire, slowing the ætherghouls' advance, even blasting some into the great beyond. The wide-eyed soldiers watched as the living corpses stalked towards them, all except the marauder scout Terris Todd, who had spotted something in the skies.

"Look!" he said, pointing. Callaghan could make out the shape of the dragon. At first he thought that they were doomed, before he heard the faint cry of his name.

"Callaghan!" yelled Kamina. She hurled Ascara down towards them. Its blade struck the ground between Calisto's forces and the advancing ætherghouls. The dragon then swept along the ground, scorching the land with a salvo of fire. The men cheered as the ætherghouls burned in the dragon's breath. The ranger ran out and plucked his faithful sword from the ground. He whispered into the red jewel of her hilt, summoning her power. Ascara's blade blazed like the battlefield behind them.

"That dragon carries a child of Elgrin on its back," affirmed Callaghan. "She has journeyed around the world to find a way to defeat this army. What do you say we give her a hand?"

"For Kamina," said Endo Eredu.

"For Kamina!" repeated Callaghan.

"For Kamina!" the men yelled in reply.

They marched out towards the line of dying fire.

"I hope that was not a lie," Vangar shouted brazenly.

"Ask me again when this battle is won," replied the ranger.

*

"You missed Malenek!" Kamina yelled, as the dragon swooped up into the air, swinging around for another attack.

"Have you ever tried to control a dragon with your mind?" Kaedin screamed back, as he steered the flying behemoth round for another pass. He set his sights on the cluster of spirits and the armoured human at the centre of the scourge.

Malenek struggled to control Shento, the horse riled by the dragon descending towards them.

"Bring them down!" he barked at the spirits. They focused on Kaedin with such force that it struck the lone spirit like a spear penetrating his skull. He seized up in agony, screaming out, unable to remove his hands from the dragon. The creature shared the spirit's torment, roaring in the throes of this mental anguish.

"Kaedin!" exclaimed Kamina, but it was too late. The spirit could no longer control the beast. The dragon crashed down onto the battlefield, ploughing through scores of ætherghouls.

No, thought Callaghan as the dragon crashed down. Not at this final hour.

He commanded the men to move forward and rescue the elf, but the ætherghouls overwhelmed them. The undead picked off the soldiers and dragged them back across the ground to their ghostly masters. The spirits broke their souls and sent them back to fight their former comrades.

Ramiro ran towards the downed dragon in search of Kamina, cutting through the enemy with his son's sword. He had almost reached the dazed beast when he was tackled by an ætherghoul, one he barely recognised as Cohen Hesh, scratching and tearing at his face. Ramiro jabbed his sword into the side of the abomination, freeing himself. The ætherghoul was still alive as he stood up, stabbing at it again and again until it was finished.

An almighty roar made the ambassador turn round. The dragon rose up, no longer under Kaedin's control. It blasted fireballs at the soldiers and ætherghouls without discrimination. Ramiro leapt out of the way as one exploded by him. He fell with a thud, and his world turned dark.

Upon hearing the explosions, Kamina stirred from the daze of the crash landing. She stumbled to her feet, unable to hear, the sounds dull and far away. A faint whooshing noise grew louder. She glanced up as the dragon's giant wings flapped above her. The injured beast tacked awkwardly through the skies as it flew away to its freedom.

Her ears popped with an eruption of noise; soldiers yelling, arrows flying, ætherghouls screaming, and men dying. She was trapped in the middle of a battlefield.

A small squad of spirits advanced through the fighting towards her. Kamina reached inside her robes for the Stone of Spirits, but it was not where she had left it. She patted herself down as it became apparent the jewel was no longer in her possession. She scanned the surrounding area and spotted it glistening in the mud. Kamina scrambled through the legs and bodies of the fighting warriors. She was almost upon it when it was kicked away by an unwitting soldier. She scurried after it, but found a spirit in her way. It spotted her and reached for her soul, only to be thwarted by Kaedin. He was able to tackle Kamina's attacker, wrestling in the same plane of existence. With the threatening spirit distracted, Kamina lunged for the stone, grasping it in her hands. She thrust it against the enemy spirit. The stone's forbidden touch hurtled him away, while the residual blast knocked down those around them.

"Run," Kaedin groaned, struggling as the other spirits contended for command of his soul.

Malenek felt the stone's presence when Kamina struck one of the spirits bonded to him. He suffered the pain as it was thrust upon them, weakened as the tethers stretched out in different directions. His forces were overwhelming those of Calisto, but not fast enough. They had to breach the city and end this.

"Gort, Martyn. Break the gates," he commanded. "Use the Ogarii."

"But my Lord…" objected the stone man.

"I will be fine," Malenek assured him. "Go."

Callaghan searched for Kamina, but instead spied the stone giant lumbering through Calisto's soldiers, knocking them aside as he barrelled towards the city accompanied by two ætherghoul Ogarii.

"Stop them!" he yelled. Flint and Sprong answered Callaghan's call. Gregor swiped up a dropped sledgehammer and thrust it at Gort, knocking him down in his tracks. The giant picked himself up and met the burly ranger's gaze. Gregor was a mountain among men, but he was no match for the gargantuan Gort. He swung the weapon again, but Gort grabbed it and tossed it away, hurling the ranger to the ground. Flint appeared from behind, hacking away at Gort's leg with his hatchets, but the blades only managed to chip his thick stone hide. He kicked the little ranger away, and then proceeded to lead the two Ogarii as they careered towards Calisto's walls. The archers fired at him, but their arrows bounced off his rocky hide. Gort charged towards Calisto, picking up speed before slamming into the wall with his shoulder. His first attack dented the outer stone, the shockwave causing those standing at the top to lose their balance.

Martyn Keyll commanded the Ogarii to mimic Gort's actions. The brutes slavishly pounded at the wall, shaking those who stood upon it. The archers managed to down one of the Ogarii after several successive shots to the head. Craecoran Gemmel gathered a squad of coran and retreated to the wall to challenge the brutes, managing to slay the downed Ogarii, but it was not enough. Part of the wall collapsed around them, allowing Gort and the ætherghouls to clamour through the rubble and breach the city.

On the battlefield, Vangar and Ariel Atari worked as a team. The archer slowed the ætherghouls with his arrows, leaving Vangar to finish them off with his sword. They both paused as Malenek's bodyguard broke down part of the outer wall. Vangar peered across the battlefield to Malenek's position. With the stone giant gone, the priest's only protection was a small troop of vengeance spirits.

"If we get close enough, can you make the shot?" Vangar asked Ariel, who nodded sternly in reply. They fought their way through the ætherghouls while avoiding the spirits, until Ariel was almost in range. He made a quick sprint and then leapt up upon the back of an ætherghoul, using it to springboard high into the air. As he soared over the battle, he managed to make two shots. The first missed, deflected by a spirit, but the second struck Malenek's armour, knocking him off his horse. Vangar and Ariel's stealthy manoeuvre brought with it unwelcome attention from the spirits. They retreated back as the ghosts gave chase.

Malenek thudded to the ground. Over the clangs and screams of the fighting he heard Shento neigh hysterically and gallop away. The priest rolled out of the way of his hooves, watching through his visor as the horse fled.

Once inside the city, Gort and the remaining Ogarii bound up the steps, knocking the archers from their perches along the wall. The ætherghouls began to swarm through the crack below them, invading Calisto's streets. As the stone giant swatted a pair of soldiers over the edge, he witnessed the Etraihu archer's assault on Malenek, leaving his master unprotected on the ground. He leapt down, crushing a soldier beneath his feet. Gort pounded back through the battlefield, but he was stopped by a strike from Craecoran Gemmel's sword.

"Where do you think you're going, golem?" he grunted.

As Atticus Gemmel prepared to face off against the stone giant, the ætherghouls poured into the city. They clashed with the soldiers on the streets, including Ambassador Narain. He was untrained in how to use a sword, and fell back as an ætherghoul attacked him. Isan tried to push the undead beast away, but it snarled and scratched on top of him, too heavy for him to hold off for long.

A small green burst of magic struck the beast. It exploded into a pile of ash, the trapped soul glowing for an instant above Isan before evaporating into the ether. The ambassador turned to see who had cast the spell, only to discover it was Lashara Elloeth. She stumbled, weakened by the exertion. Isan caught her and led her to safety.

"Thank you," he said.

"I did not realise I still possessed its power…" she said, but her words trailed off as something caught her eye. Isan followed her gaze and spotted several objects in the sky over the sea flying towards them.

"What in the name of the Elements is that?" asked Isan. Lashara shook her head in uncertainty.

They were not the only ones to have noticed the strange objects in the sky. Terris Todd had also spotted them with his keen eyes, as he managed to free the soul trapped inside an ætherghoul.

"Callaghan!" the marauder cried, pointing at the skies. "Is it more dragons?"

"No," replied the ranger, discerning the shapes of the Zalestian norora fleet. "Something worse." He feared Zahyr had followed through on his plan to launch an invasion, but his immediate concern was the Stone of Spirits. The ranger heard the neigh of Malenek's horse as it fled from the fighting. He saw the priest pluck Ariel's arrow from his armour, having to remove the plate on his leg. He was exposed and vulnerable. Callaghan cut his way through the ætherghouls towards his old friend, hoping to bring a swift end to this madness.

Kamina was lost in the throng of battle, desperately searching for the ranger. She helped a nearby soldier escape the clutches of a spirit by using the stone against it. The act did not go undetected, and she was quickly pounced on by an ætherghoul. The creature sliced at her with two hooked hands, causing her to drop the artefact. Kamina defended herself against the ætherghoul, whom she now recognised as Maulin Lamn, the marauder who had kidnapped her. She dodged his deadly hooks as they dug into the ground by her head.

"Maulin!" shouted a voice from the battlefield. An echo of recognition caused the ætherghoul to glance up. Vangar's boot collided with his face, kicking the ætherghoul to the mud. Kamina scrambled for the stone as Vangar brought an end to the sad life of Maulin Lamn, lobbing his head clean off, freeing his soul from the rotten flesh. Ariel seized Innes' shoulder and pulled him away from the reach of one of the spirits. The pair of marauders were surrounded by the spectres, closing in on them from all angles. The young elf jumped in front of them, saving their lives by striking the spirits with the stone. Vangar caught Kamina as she was bowled over by the blast of energy.

"We must get you to Callaghan," he said. Vangar was forced to unceremoniously drop her to the dirt as a slew of ætherghouls attacked. "Go!" he yelled at her, fending them off "We will hold them here." Kamina darted away, scooping up a soldier's lost sword for protection.

The ranger had fought his way to Malenek at the edge of the battlefield. A small squad of the spirits were still present, protecting the priest. They spotted Callaghan approaching and moved to attack him, but halted when Malenek spoke.

"Let him through," he said, his voice weak. The spirits parted for the ranger, who cautiously walked through them towards Malenek, hunched over in his armour. "That is far enough, Callaghan."

"It is over, Balen," he said. "We have the Stone of Spirits." Even through the visor of his helmet, Callaghan was able to see how pale and fragile Malenek had become. His pursuit of peace through the spirits had almost consumed him. He could barely stand, and yet he managed a weak smile.

"You have the stone, but you do not know how to use it," said the priest, nodding to one of the spirits. The ghost stepped forward, and Callaghan immediately recognised him.

"Kaedin?"

"The boy is under our influence," Malenek muttered. "I know all of his secrets. He will not attack me, but he is going to attack you. It is ironic, since for so long he has desired to be you." Kaedin clumsily lurched towards Callaghan, still resisting the controlling influence being exerted over him by the other spirits.

"Kaedin, you can fight this," said Callaghan, pointing Ascara at him. As Kaedin reached for him, he waved the sword through the spirit, disrupting his energy. "Concentrate!"

Kamina rushed to help Callaghan fend off the spirits, but as she drew closer she was shocked to see Kaedin attacking the ranger. A loud droning from above heralded the fleet of nororas nearing the battlefield. Distracted by the flying contraptions, Kamina did not hear an approaching ætherghoul until it was almost upon her. She swivelled round, sword raised to face the snarling beast, but the elf lowered her weapon.

"Talia," said Kamina, her sword falling to the ground. The ætherghoul cocked her head, the name a faint memory, but it was a fleeting hesitation. The creature snarled at the elf, leaping to attack her. Kamina shielded herself, but the ætherghoul's strike did not come. She withdrew her arms from her face to see Jazintha hanging from the rope ladder of a norora, her twin daggers hoisting Talia's ætherghoul in mid-air. The zharie dropped the ætherghoul, somersaulting down onto solid ground.

"Jazintha!" exclaimed Kamina "You are alive!"

"My father's punishment," explained the Zalestian briefly, as she was joined by Ajarone and the other rebels. Talia's ætherghoul rose up again, injured but still snarling. Jazintha moved to strike again.

"No," cried Kamina. "She is… she was my mother."

"Then free her froms this suffering," said Jazintha, handing the elf a scimitar. The zharie left Kamina, as she and the Jalenari rebels joined the fight. Kamina gazed into the eyes of the injured ætherghoul, slithering towards her. Tears welled up in her eyes as she raised the sword.

"Goodbye," she whispered, her lips quivering as she plunged the blade into the ætherghoul, striking the heart. The creature shrieked one last time as its body disintegrated into dust, the particles dancing around Kamina in the wind. For a brief moment she touched Talia's soul, a white flash in the air, and heard her mother whisper her name one last time.

"…Kamina…"

CHAPTER FORTY-SEVEN
THE SECRET OF THE STONE

"...Kamina..."

The horrific sights and sounds of the battlefield bled out into the serene silence of her dreams. Kamina found herself in her recurring vision once more, only now in this bright, idyllic version of Elgrin Forest, she was an outsider. She saw her younger self nestled on Talia's knee, being read a story.

Talia turned the page of the storybook that rest on the child's little lap. Kamina stepped closer so as to better see the illustration. It depicted a Zalestian man, an Amarosian woman, a female centaur and a strange blue creature. Light radiated from each pair of their clasped hands. Behind each Kamina noticed there was the faint outline of one of the four Elementals.

"It was my hope that the power would come into the hands of those who it was meant for, to be used for good, but it was not to be," said Talia. "However, not all hope is lost," she added, looking up at the battle-weary Kamina. She was shocked to find her younger self staring up at her as well.

"You are not Talia," she said, sure of her words yet unsure why. The figure in front of her placed the child down and rose up from the fallen tree she sat on. She was the perfect imagine of Talia, flawless, as found in Kamina's fondest memories.

"No," replied the woman, shaking her head gently. "I am not."

"Then who?" Kamina asked. The being that masqueraded in Talia's form simply smiled.

"You know who I am," she replied, tapping Kamina's right temple with the lightest touch. "It is all up here."

"You are one of the four Elementals," Kamina guessed. "But which one?"

"You already know this as well," said the goddess. "You hold my power, my essence, in your hands." Kamina gazed down to find the Stone of Spirits wrapped in her fingers. She held it up, gazing inside at the amazing swirls of silver energy flowing within the jewel, as if being blown by a breeze.

Breeze.

Air.

The Goddess of Air!

"Whirren!" Kamina exclaimed, but then frowned. "I tried the enchantment with your name. I tried it with all four of the Elementals."

"We go by many names," she hinted, stepping towards Kamina, stroking the elf's hair as she gazed deep into her eyes. "The spell will work with the right one."

"Why can you not just tell me?" demanded the elf.

"Because it is important you do this on your own," she replied.

"But why me?" pleaded Kamina, feeling time slipping away from her, as the details of the dream faded. "Why not Callaghan, or an ambassador or a soldier or a...?"

"You will see, in time." She kissed Kamina on the forehead, and the world melted into a silvery white. "Think about where you found the stone."

*

The dreamscape shattered as Talia's spirit disappeared. Kamina was thrust back into the battle by the atrocious cries of soldiers being twisted into ætherghouls. She gazed at the stone, furiously searching her mind for an answer to the Elemental's clue. She recalled the first time she heard Callaghan say the magical enchantment, and explaining what it meant.

"Ascentio Risaar Emanos."

But she had tried that with Whirren's name.

"Think about where you found it?"

In Errazure's Tomb. In the Darosa Desert.

In Zalestia.

"We go by many names."

The names of the Zalestian gods. Kamina scanned the battlefield for Jazintha, but she had lost sight of her. Perhaps one of the other Jalenari rebels would know. Some were still climbing down the ropes from the nororas.

Kamina recalled what Zahyr had said about the flying ships.

"I named them after the Goddess of the Wind..."

Norora? No that was not it. What was it?

Then she remembered the storm in the Darosa Desert, and Jazintha's outburst.

"Orora is very angry!"

Orora.

Kamina raised the Stone of Spirits to her lips and whispered the words.

"Ascentio Orora Emanos."

There was no reaction from the jewel. Kamina was about to admit defeat when a single light within the crystal twinkled, like the brightest star on the darkest night. She watched as the light pulsed, growing stronger, until the Stone of Spirits shone like a beacon of radiant light. The young elf could feel the energy of the stone surging in her hands, along with the elation of unlocking its secret. The magical glow was reflected in the stream of joyous tears that ran all the way down her face until they met her rapturous smile. The power was infectious, and for a brief moment Kamina could feel all of Enara, all of the life force that nourished the world in the palm of her hands.

A tendril of the silvery white light shot out through the skirmishes.

Callaghan stabbed again at Malenek through Kaedin, whose ghostly hand reached for Callaghan's heart. The ranger thrust his sword through the spirit, causing him to lose focus of his form. The bolt of ethereal energy from the Stone of Spirits struck Kaedin, surrounding him. His ghostly wisps gained weight and form, glowing bright until Kaedin's spirit was restored, made flesh once more.

The ranger flashed an astonished smile as he saw Kaedin's real face, firm and full of colour. The elf's jubilant surprise soured into gut-wrenching agony. They both stared down to find Kaedin skewered through the stomach by Ascara.

"No," said Callaghan. He withdrew the sword and caught Kaedin's limp body. "I am sorry," muttered the ranger, as the former spirit now struggled to breathe.

Malenek, aghast at Kaedin's miraculous return to life, scanned the battlefield for the Stone of Spirits. He saw it still glowing brightly in Kamina's delicate hands.

"Get her!" he cried to his remaining spirits. They moved as one with the army of ætherghouls, chasing after the young elf. She fled through the skirmishes, hunted by the spirits. They turned those soldiers she passed into ætherghouls, overwhelming the remaining forces fighting for Calisto. She dared to steal a glance back at Malenek's forces pursuing her, not spotting the spirit who had outflanked her until the last moment. The apparition snatched for her soul. His fingers slipped through her skin, knocking the wind from her. She managed to thrust the Stone of Spirits at him before he could separate her spirit from her body. The spirit was blasted away by the magic, while the discharge floored those fighting nearby.

The strain of Malenek's bond to his spirits was stretched too far. With each strike Kamina dealt them with the stone, their master was dealt a matching blow. He was battered by the supernatural forces he had wrought into this world. The priest sprawled backwards, unable to breathe. He watched the unnatural storm clouds swirling above him, and knew that he was too close to fail, that he could still deliver them all to Illyria.

"No," he hissed, crawling to his knees, using his sword for support. "It is nearly done."

Callaghan watched Malenek shudder on the ground, his skin growing paler, the grip on his sword shaking as he was ravaged by the pain of others. The ranger lay Kaedin down upon the ground and marched over to the priest, Ascara in his hands. The ranger loomed over Malenek, the eyes of his former friend and confidante pleading for mercy.

"We are so close, Callaghan. Can you not feel it?"

"No, I cannot," he replied, raising his sword. "May the Elementals forgive you."

An ætherghoul pounced on Kamina. She fell awkwardly, fracturing her leg. She screamed out in pain, trying to fight off the beast. Her screams distracted

Callaghan, who tried to spot her amidst the chaos of the battlefield. Malenek seized the opportunity and thrust his sword at the ranger. He was denied his strike by Jazintha, who blocked him with her daggers, kicking the priest down.

"Glads to see me?" she asked Callaghan. They were interrupted by the arrival of Gort, who had managed to overpower Craecoran Gemmel. He stampeded into Callaghan before batting Jazintha across the ground with the swipe of his massive arm. The pair picked themselves up as the stone man guarded Malenek, ready to defend him against anyone who would make an attempt on his life.

Kamina crawled away from the ætherghoul as it rasped after her. It seized her broken leg, but before it could drag her away, the abomination was run through by the blade of Craecoran Gemmel. He was bruised and bloody from his run in with Gort, but managed a terse grin for the elf. The smile was wiped away as his face contorted in agony. One of the spirits chasing Kamina gripped Gemmel's heart. She tried to save him, but she fell over on her injured leg. She looked on in horror as the spirit snapped the soldier's soul.

It was the soul of Atticus Gemmel that tipped the balance in Malenek's favour. Enara shook as the barriers between worlds blurred. The ground cracked open, swallowing men and ætherghouls alike, screaming as they plummeted to their doom. The supernatural storm clouds that had gathered above the battlefield gained weight, ripping the sky apart.

"What have you done?" Callaghan screamed at Malenek, above the roar of thunder and the quakes from below.

"I have afforded us all a second chance," shouted the priest, as Gort helped him to his feet.

The world began to break apart. Those still alive on the battlefield, even the ætherghouls, stopped fighting. They all gazed up at the supernatural storm clouds, scarred by thick, red lightning. The flashes remained in the skies longer than usual, as if illuminating a fissure in the sky that had always existed, unseen until now. The deafening thunder that followed reminded Kamina of the Badlands. Still clutching the stone in her hands, she crawled onwards, determined to reach Malenek and finish this, while others froze to watch the world be torn apart.

"What is happenings?" Jazintha begged Callaghan, but it was Malenek who answered.

"The world as we know it is at an end," proclaimed the priest. Jazintha gritted her teeth in anger and lunged for him, but another shudder from the ground sent her tumbling sideways. Thunder boomed as a bright spark of red lightning struck the ground and ripped it open. It ruptured the retinas of those who bore witness, momentarily losing their vision in the flash of intense light. The acrid stench of lava choked their lungs, as a torrent of wind swirled across the battlefield, carrying with it a single scream thousands of years old. It died down, leaving them in a blind, vacant void.

When those still alive recovered their vision, they spied a lone figure standing in the crater where the lighting had struck. This was a being not of flesh and bone, but of raw, magical power. A sense of awe seized both sides of the battle. The crowds parted as the divine being drifted towards Malenek.

"Gianna," announced Malenek, bowing before her. Something akin to a smile appeared on the being's bright face.

"You are not Gianna!" shouted Jazintha, picking herself up.

"And who are you, so arrogant that you challenge a god?" boomed the being's voice.

"If you are an all-knowing god, then you should know I am Jazintha Zaleed Zharie!" The being softly stepped over to the zharie, and graced her beautiful brown face with a glowing hand.

"Such a pretty thing," it said. The glowing white hand suddenly snatched Jazintha by the throat.

"No!" begged Malenek. "You are the bringer of peace! You will unite us and deliver us to Illyria. Please Gianna!"

"She is right. There is no Gianna," said the being, chuckling to himself. "Only Risaar!" A wrath of fire spread from the ground, engulfing the glowing body Malenek had mistaken for the fabled Gianna. Gone was the beautiful, mesmerising glow, leaving only the darkest red flames. Risaar's eyes burned yellow, while his flaming mouth showed a forked tongue of orange fire. Warriors on both sides of the war clutched their weapons in fear, sharing the same trepidation; that their armaments would not even scratch an Elemental, and they did not wish to die trying. The Amarosians recognised Risaar's name, but the Zalestians knew him as something else.

"Azik," said Jazintha, as the flames from Risaar's body scorched her face. "The Betrayer."

"Ah, my other name, one I am not fond of!" He threw Jazintha down onto the battlefield, like a child angry at a toy.

"But... It cannot be." Malenek faltered. His plan was collapsing all around him along with the rest of the world. Risaar stalked towards the priest, leaving a trail of burning footprints in his wake. With each step, Risaar's fire dulled, still weak from his escape to Enara.

"Thank you for freeing me from the prison my siblings deemed so fit to abandon me in," Risaar said. "As a reward, I shall use your body to burn this precious world to a cinder." His flaming finger brushed a frightened tear from Malenek's pale cheek.

"But you built this world," he begged. "You are the warmth, the first light of day."

"You do not believe the words coming out of your mouth," said Risaar. "I helped create this world, only to be banished from it. And now, I am going to destroy it all!"

Before a scream could escape Malenek's gaping mouth, he was enveloped by Risaar's blazing energy. Balen Malenek cried out from the inferno seeking help and forgiveness. Gort attempted to breach the barrier of fire, but the heat was so intense that nothing could be done. The flames wrapped themselves around Malenek's body, absorbing the power until he was no longer human. His skin mutated into a hardened molten-grey. Symbols splintered into his body. The cracks revealed the fire surging deep within. The demi-god fell down on all fours, weak from the transformation. The panting and cries of Malenek bled into the dry cackles of the Fire Elemental.

"Are you all right, my Lord?" asked Gort, stepping closer to the hunched being. The stone man was bewildered by what had just happened. The spirits bonded to Malenek squirmed, uneasy by the forging of a new being that they were linked to. This had not been part of the priest's plan. They should have all arrived in Illyria by now.

They should all have been forgiven.

"I... we are fine," rumbled Risaar as he erected himself up next to the stone beast. The god, growing accustomed to his new shell, cast his burning eyes upon Gort. The sight of the stone man enraged the Elemental, grimacing down at the giant.

"What is wrong?" said the stone man.

"Son of Ygrain!" exclaimed Risaar. He slammed a fist into Gort's face, a fierce crack of stone breaking stone. Malenek's servant was caught unaware, crashing down upon the field. Risaar turned his attention to Callaghan and Jazintha, who shielded Kaedin, protecting him from the Elemental's ire.

"You are not Risaar," shouted Callaghan. "Risaar would not do this."

"What do you know of it, mortal?" Risaar asked rhetorically. "I am Risaar, or Azik if you prefer," nodding to Jazintha as he said so, causing her to flinch. "The most powerful of the four elements, the brightest sun, betrayed by his brothers and sisters!"

"The other gods would not allow this," protested Jazintha. Risaar leaned close to her.

"The other gods are all dead," he said as he leaned closer to her. Risaar relished the fear that flickered over her face, but he could not leave it at that. He struck her with such force that she soared into the air, crashing down amongst the fallen soldiers.

"Jazintha!" screamed Callaghan.

"Do not waste your screams, ranger," said the demi-god. "I should be thanking you. Had you not used my blade so contently, the walls of my prison would not have weakened." Risaar reached down and seized Ascara from him, "I would not have been able to communicate with this world and plot my freedom were it not for you. But you have served your purpose, ranger." The Elemental raised Ascara to strike him down, but Callaghan did not budge.

"Ascara will not hurt me," he said, refusing to break his stare with Risaar.

"No," replied Risaar. "She will kill you!" Ascara's blade burst into flames without words or enchantments. Before the deity could make good on his threat, Kamina pressed the Stone of Spirits against his leg. He gazed down at the elf child, who with a broken ankle had crawled through the statue-like spectators towards the being that inhabited Malenek's body.

"Ascentio Orora Emanos," she murmured. Magical energy surged from the stone, streaming out and striking all of the spirits bound to Malenek. Its power was immense, magnified by the number of vengeance spirits it seized hold of. They were transformed as Kaedin had been, back to flesh and bone.

The aftershock exploded out of the stone, hurling Kamina and the Elemental apart. As the bright wave of light crashed into the ætherghouls, it reduced them to ash, freeing all the souls within. The armies were knocked from their feet and hooves. The stone's blast expanded outwards and upwards, ripping through the sky and into the fleet of nororas, disrupting their engines. Some were out of its range, but those breached by the energy blast crashed down upon the battlefield or exploded in the sky.

The stone's shockwave rippled out of existence, and then there was silence, save for the wind.

CHAPTER FORTY-EIGHT
RISAAR'S BLADE

For a brief moment, in the aftermath of the supernatural explosion from the stone, those that remained upon the battlefield lay perfectly still. Flames flickered around them, as the dust of the ætherghouls drifted like ash on the breeze. Gradually soldiers on both sides stirred to life. Kamina picked herself up and surveyed the scene. Malenek's army had been reduced to just one hundred former vengeance spirits made whole. They were no longer able to snap the souls of their enemies and turn them into ætherghouls under their command. As this reality dawned on them, the leaderless mortals began to flee from Calisto.

"Kaedin!" she called out, limping among the dazed and confused. "Callaghan!"

"Over here," replied the ranger, raising an arm. Kamina hobbled towards him and found Callaghan huddled over her brother, still alive despite his wounds. "If he were not an elf, he would surely be dead," said Callaghan, smiling with relief. Kamina returned the smile, but it was short-lived, as she saw something stir on the ground.

Risaar rose up behind the ranger, his mighty grey hands gripping Ascara. The blade surged alive with fire. Callaghan felt her flames lashing out behind him. Before he could react, Risaar plunged the sword through the ranger's back. Callaghan grunted as he felt the searing heat burst through his body. He tried desperately to say something, but the air rushed out of his lungs. The deranged demi-god twisted the handle, making Callaghan's pain all the more excruciating in the final moments before he died. The ranger's body was jerked like a puppet, Risaar toying with him until he became bored. He tossed the ranger from his sword.

Callaghan's body slumped to the ground next to Kaedin, rasping his last few, precious breaths. The last thing the ranger saw was the elven boy, barely conscious, watching helplessly as his hero died. Callaghan stretched out his fingers. Kaedin grasped his hand. He felt Callaghan's grip tighten ever so slightly and then release.

Kamina's scream was caught in her throat, but someone else cried out.

"Callaghan!" yelled Jazintha as she sped across the battlefield. The zharie fell by the ranger's body, gathering him up in her arms. She kissed his forehead as she cradled his face in her hands.

"No," she whispered. "Don't go. I loves you." His limp body flopped lifelessly in her arms. As Jazintha's tears fell on Callaghan's ashen face, Kamina focused on the Elemental demi-god looming over them.

"Why did you kill him?" cried Kamina. "You are defeated. Your army has deserted you."

"Malenek's army is defeated," Risaar said. "I am not!" He pointed Ascara up into the air. A bolt of fire shot up from the blade and into the sky, turning the abnormal storm clouds a dark, bloody red, followed by an insidious crackle of thunder. The skies flashed and rained fire down upon them. Those soldiers that could not avoid the blasts were consumed by Risaar's flames, their last moments spent shrieking in agony as they fled on fire across the fields. The balls of flame blasted the buildings of Calisto and struck the sea, destroying the boats and ships that carried innocent evacuees.

Jazintha was not so helpless. Enraged by the death of the ranger who had saved her life and captured her heart, she clutched one of her curved daggers and threw it at Risaar. It struck the demi-god's wrist, lava blood dripping from the wound. The force knocked Ascara from his hands. The sword's flame evaporated as it fell upon the muddy battlefield, but the rain of fire continued.

"Unlike your pathetic ranger, I do not need Ascara to kill you!" roared Risaar. The cut Jazintha had inflicted healed itself immediately. His hand shot down and seized her by the throat, lifting Jazintha up and throttling the life from her body. An arrow zinged across the battlefield and pierced Risaar's chest. The demi-god glanced round to see Ariel Atari shoot another, this time striking his arm. Risaar dropped Jazintha, smirking at the Etraihu archer's expression of defeat as he snapped the arrows off. His fiery blood dissolved the arrowheads and healed the wounds they had created.

While Risaar was distracted, Kaedin staggered to his feet and glanced over at Kamina. He could see Ascara lying behind her. Although they no longer shared a spiritual bond, she gathered what he meant for her to do. Kaedin collected a Zalestian spear from the ground and charged, roaring a battle cry as he rammed it through the demi-god's molten-grey skin.

"Still alive, little elf?" said Risaar. "I hope that was not your best shot." With his attentions on Kaedin, Kamina grovelled to where Ascara had fallen. She plucked the blade from the ground and wiped the mud from the red jewel. Kamina watched its fire dancing inside, praying that the sword would finally obey her command. She staggered over to Callaghan's body and gazed into his dead, vacant eyes.

"I am sorry," she sobbed, as she dipped her hands in his blood.

Risaar yanked the spear from his torso and snapped it in half. The wound sizzled with fire, and healed like all the rest. "My turn," he growled. Risaar raised both of his hands above his head, a piece of the spear held in each, preparing to thrust them down and skewer Kaedin.

Kamina manoeuvred behind Risaar. With both bloody hands gripping the hilt, she plunged Ascara upwards into the very being who had forged the fabled blade. The sword burst out through Risaar's chest, nearly striking

Kaedin on the opposite side. Surprised, the powerful brute dropped the spears, twisting round to face Kamina.

"When will you learn, I cannot be harmed by your puny weapons?" boasted the arrogant demi-god with a scornful laugh.

"What about your own sword?" said Kamina. Risaar gazed down, realising too late that it was Ascara's steel that penetrated his new body. Kamina leapt up and grabbed the blade end of the sword. It cut into her hands, but she did not care.

"No," he groaned.

Kamina screamed out the incantation before he could strike back.

"Ascentio…"

Please let this work.

"…Risaar…"

Orora, make this work.

"…Emanos!"

This time Ascara heard her words. Flames burst out from the red hilted jewel and along Ascara's blade, burning Risaar from the inside. Kamina held on, screaming in pain as the red hot metal seared her hands. The God of Fire screamed with her as his innards were superheated by the charge. Kamina refused to let go, watching the fire consume Risaar, the ferocious flames causing his body to crack and burn. The intense heat scorched her face. She closed her eyes and turned her head away, but never once did she consider releasing her grasp of the blade, not until it was over.

Not until he was dead.

"Kamina!" she heard Kaedin cry. "Let go!" But she could not. Risaar was still alive. Just a little longer, she thought. She felt Risaar try and grip her arms, but his limbs were weak, his fingers disintegrating. She felt another set of hands on her. Kaedin ripped her away, freeing Kamina's hold of the blade. As they tumbled to the ground, Kamina opened her eyes just in time to see the flame surrounding Ascara implode inside Risaar. He screamed out one last time before exploding in a flash of red flame, filling the air with embers. The rain of fire ceased as the ominous storm clouds dissipated.

Risaar had been defeated.

It was finally over. Kamina lay on the ground, breathless, watching the supernatural sky dissipate into the usual shade of blue. She felt the warm breeze on her face once more. Despite the devastation and the loss she had endured, the young elf had the strangest sensation of serenity.

Somehow she knew that everything was as it should be.

Kaedin hobbled over to her, helping her up. They gazed at each other, both bloodied and burned, but alive. They loomed over what was left of Malenek and Risaar, a smouldering pile of ash. Ascara lay next to the remains, remarkably unscathed by the ordeal.

Other sights and sounds filtered through their shock. The remainder of the former vengeance spirits retreated, along with Gort. Vangar, sporting several wounds, announced their victory. Those able to cheered, while some, like Jazintha, cried over those they had lost. Kamina watched the zharie cradle the ranger's dead body. Kaedin knelt down next to her, sharing in her grief. Kamina picked up Ascara and scanned the battlefield.

"What are you looking for?" Kaedin asked wearily.

"Nothing," she replied, wiping away a tear.

CHAPTER FORTY-NINE

THE RANGER'S FAREWELL

THE BATTLE-WEARY ELVES SLUMPED AGAINST ONE ANOTHER AS they staggered back to Calisto with the other injured warriors.

"I think this belongs to you," said Kamina, slipping off the tweed bracelet that Nyssa had gifted Kaedin, which Callaghan had then given to her after Kaedin's death. He smiled as he fastened it around his wrist, wondering if he would see her in the city.

The citizens and refugees had returned from the ships and safe houses to welcome them back with heroic cheers. Kamina could not entertain their joy, or partake in their relief. Her bravery had died with Callaghan, and in the aftermath of the battle she had succumbed to shock, separated from herself.

The Elloeths were reunited with their own kind. Several elves were marked by the fighting, including Endo Eredu. As soon as Lashara spotted her great-granddaughter, she scooped Kamina up in her arms. The little elf, feeling completely safe, cried upon her shoulder.

Kaedin saw Nyssa helping her father Norrek, equally bloodied by the battle. He staggered over to them. Neither could quite comprehend how the elf was there, having last seen him as a spirit. Norrek welcomed him like a son, but Nyssa was still afraid, until she saw the bracelet, her gift to him, secured upon his wrist. She embraced him in her arms and kissed his lips, Norrek loudly clearing this throat several times as she did so.

Not everyone had fared as well as they had. Vangar and Ariel had found Ramiro alive on the battlefield, but his eyes were scarred blind, scorched by the dragon's breath. Kamina watched as they carried him inside the barracks, repurposed to house those in need of a doctor. Ariel turned and caught her gaze, her face still bloodied, her hair matted with dirt and sweat, the opposite of her appearance the first time they had encountered one another. The Etraihu archer stared at her as though he had seen a ghost. Kamina glared at him, remembering the loss of Eshtel, until she could bear to look no longer.

*

Despite the many factions and races occupying the city, they came together in the evening to celebrate the fact that there would be a tomorrow. They partied from the town square down to the docks. Even Jazintha and the other Zalestians were welcomed, sampling the Amarosian alcohol, weak by their standards. The zharie remained downhearted by Callaghan's loss, but found comfort in talking with Ajarone, sharing their brief memories of the man.

Many of the citizens found themselves in the churches, seeking answers for what had happened, their beliefs shaken by the rumours that Risaar had appeared on the battlefield, intent on destroying Enara. The priests consoled their flock, but even their faith in the Elementals had waned.

Across the bridge the elves prayed in the park, all except Kamina and Kaedin, who had elected to rest their weary and wounded bodies upon the bench overlooking the bay. They lay there until the twins suns arose, Risaar and Aquill casting their welcoming light over the sleeping siblings.

*

Dawn brought with it the first day of peace between the lands of Amaros and Zalestia. Ambassadors Messer and Narain signed a peace accord with Jazintha Zaleed Zharie. They hoped that trade would prosper between their two lands, the Amarosians very interested in the flying nororas.

Most of the daylight was spent burying the dead and assessing the damage done to the city and the country. Messengers arrived from Heroshin and Rundhale to offer their condolences from King Arthadian and the centaurs respectively. The messenger sent from Rundhale was Dash Cole, who had been saved by the centaurs during the ætherghoul attack at Duru Umbin. He was deeply saddened to hear about the death of Callaghan Tor.

That evening, as the suns began to set, a special service was held for the Ranger Elite on the esplanade that ran along the bay. His body was placed in a small boat and pushed off into the water, floating among thousands of small lanterns, each one representing someone lost in the battle. Dash Cole, along with his fellow rangers Jochan Flint and Gregor Sprong, offered a few words about Callaghan. Ariel Atari lit a burning arrow and aimed it at the funeral boat. The archer shot it up into the sky. Kamina watched the flames flicker, reminded of Risaar as it swooped down into the boat, setting it alight. Kaedin shed a tear as he watched it burn, holding Nyssa's hand tight. He noticed that Kamina did not cry, her face cold and apathetic.

"Kamina, Kaedin, I am Dash Cole," said the ranger shortly after the service. "Ambassador Narain informs me that you accompanied Callaghan on his last quest. It was a very brave thing you both did. I am sure he was proud to have you both as companions." Kamina, who had been carrying Ascara around as a constant reminder of the ranger, thought that Dash was going to ask her for it back. She pre-empted the ranger by offering him the sword.

Dash was slightly stunned, his hands hovering over Ascara. He glanced over at Flint and Sprong, who were equally perplexed. Despite a fleeting thought to claim Ascara as his own, to take up the mantle of Ranger Elite, Dash pushed the blade back into Kamina's arms.

"I think he would want you to have it," said the ranger. "Keep it safe."

*

The next day, the refugees prepared for their long trek back to their deserted towns and villages. Likewise, the Zalestians readied the remaining nororas to fly back across the ocean. The fleet of flying ships were docked outside of the city. Kamina and Kaedin joined Ramiro to say goodbye to Jazintha. The ambassador's unfortunate loss of sight was hidden behind a royal blue scarf tied around his eyes.

"I guess this is goodbyes," said the zharie. "Who knows if we wills see each others again."

"I have a feeling we will," said Kamina.

"I hopes you are right. You are like pale sister I never has!" She hugged Kaedin as well. "You do not turn my skin cold anymore, firentazme."

"We look forward to your next visit, Jazintha Zharie," said the ambassador as he offered his hand to thin air. Jazintha guided it in the right direction, shaking it proudly.

"It should nots be too long, although I may have to calms the Khan downs before he comes," she jested before boarding the norora. "He sent us here as punishments. I imagine he expects us all dead."

"Then perhaps this will help bring peace," said Kamina, reaching into her pocket, and producing the Stone of Spirits. Jazintha's face lit up as Kamina handed it to her.

"Thanks you," said the zharie as she graciously accepted the Jewel of Gianna. "This should appease my father." She gathered the elf in her arms and squeezed her tight, before disappearing inside the norora. The Amarosians stepped back and watched the small fleet of nororas soar into the sky, flying above Calisto and out over the seas.

"I wish I could see them fly," said Ramiro, as he accompanied the two elves back to their kin. They were preparing to travel back to Elgrin, along with some of the residents of Tilden. They joined Ambassador Narain as he said goodbye to the elves.

"We owe you all a great debt," said Isan. "Especially you, Kaedin and Kamina Elloeth.

"I hope this marks a new beginning between our people," added Ramiro.

"Perhaps we have hidden away too long," said Lashara.

"We will see what the future holds," said Abbal Eredu. "We shall take some time to reflect on the rash decisions forced by recent events."

"Well, in any case, you are always welcome here," replied Ambassador Narain. "We will even plant more trees."

"That would be… encouraging," said Endo, offering his hand to shake. Ambassador Narain took, it, and felt the strong grip of the elf. He turned from them, following the elders as they led the procession of elves on the long road back to the safety of Elgrin Forest.

CHAPTER FIFTY
RETURN TO ELGRIN FOREST

The humans and the elves kept mostly to themselves on the long march back, save for Kaedin and Nyssa, who were never apart. By the time they reached Tilden and the humans started filtering back to their homes, Kaedin had made a decision. He had gleaned some sense of tradition from conversing with Torg, himself smitten by the Onassis woman Poppel Orta. With this in mind, Kaedin nervously approached Norrek and Nyssa.

"Sir, I would like to ask your permission for your hand in marriage." Torg coughed nearby, stifling his laughter. "I mean, your daughter's hand," corrected Kaedin. Many of the elves paused to watch this unique event. Norrek was astounded, unsure how to react with such a large audience.

"I am not sure I can, Master Elloeth."

"Father!" hissed Nyssa.

"Am I not good enough for her?" asked Kaedin, confused.

"I thought you wished to go join the Rangers of Ishkava?" Norrek asked.

"My recent adventures have shown me what truly matters in life," replied the elf, smiling upon the face of his love. Norrek also gazed at his daughter, and saw how happy Nyssa looked.

"Then by all means," he said, smiling, "you have my blessing."

*

Many of the elves were glad to reach the safety of Elgrin Forest, but Kamina could only think of how empty their home would be now that Talia was gone. Yet as they trundled through the trees, she saw movement in the forest, and an old friend greeted her.

"Eshtel!" she exclaimed, leaving the line of elves to run and meet the chestnut-coloured steed. She nuzzled her face in his.

"How is this possible?" asked Kaedin, who had ran to catch up with her. They examined the horse's hide, and found that the wound left by the Etraihu archer had been patched and healed.

"Someone has stitched his wound and cared for him," she noted.

"Who do you think it was?" he asked.

She did not reply, for she did not care. She was thankful that he was alive and, given their recent losses, that was enough for now.

*

The first union between a human and an elf took place weeks later amidst the tranquil trees of Elgrin, some blossoming with luscious flowers of pink and white. The elves allowed a number of human guests into the forest, a small step towards acceptance between the two races.

As the eldest elf, Abbal Eredu would have been expected to conduct the ceremony, but his disapproval of the wedding had been very vocal. However, given the hardship Kaedin had undertaken of late, the other elders approved, and Lashara had volunteered herself to perform the service. Kamina had been honoured when the couple had asked them to be the ring bearer, especially since elves traditionally did not wear wedding bands. Nyssa had sewn Kamina an elegant green dress for the occasion. The young elf stood back as the couple exchanged vows, in both Amarosian and Elvish. Kaedin looked smart in his formal robe, a combination of cream and Legorian green. Nyssa was even more beautiful than usual, wearing a traditional human wedding dress, passed down from her mother before illness had claimed her life. Norrek shed a few tears as he accompanied her to the ceremony, looking dashing in his official uniform. He wished his wife had lived to see this day.

When it was time, Kamina stepped forward, holding up the emerald green cushion upon which the two metal bands lay. The couple slipped them on each other's fingers, and with one last kiss, it was done. Kaedin was bonded to Nyssa.

Kamina realised she was alone.

*

The wedding celebrations played out into the evening, with light music and dancing. In the midst of the festivities, Kaedin noticed Kamina's absence, although he guessed where she might be. He found her standing before the graves of Kaman and Sharla, once believed to be her parents, in reality her grandparents. They had added a headstone for Talia, though they had no body to bury. Kaedin stood next to her, and placed a brotherly arm around his niece.

*

With the exception of Nyssa now living with them, things in Elgrin Forest returned to a sense of normality. Once in a while some men ventured into the forest to pay tribute to the Elven Heroes of Calisto, the title of a ballad being spread across the continent.

As the weeks passed by, Kamina could not shake the sense of loss, of all those she had encountered on her journey, but especially Talia, and of course

Callaghan. Sitting up in the walkways between the trees, she busied herself stitching a new sheath for Ascara, using some leather Nyssa had bought for the task. She added the final touches and slid Ascara inside and out to make sure the blade fit correctly. As she did, she had the disconcerting sense that someone was watching her. Her hand tightened around Ascara's hilt.

"Kamina!" She twisted round, pointing the blade at Kaedin and Nyssa, who surprised Kamina with a gift.

"Happy birthday," squeaked Nyssa meekly. "Or *Dira Nestyr!*" Kamina lowered Ascara.

"It is a human tradition to give gifts on the day of birth," explained Kaedin.

"Thank you," said Kamina as she took the wrapped present from him, setting it aside. "Both of you."

"Open it," said Kaedin.

"Maybe later," she replied glumly. Nyssa pushed Kaedin to speak with his sister, while she retreated to give them some privacy.

"You have been moping for weeks now," he said.

"Mourning," corrected Kamina. "I am mourning them, Kaedin. All of them." He watched as she tested Ascara's new scabbard again.

"It is ironic," he noted, "that you once wished to have a peaceful and quiet existence among the trees of Elgrin, while I dreamed of excitement and adventure. Now we want what the other once desired."

"I only wish I could bring them back," said Kamina.

"It will be two more years until you reach *Dira Adolyn*," said Kaedin. "Do you intend to mourn them until then?"

"I do not know what to do!" she exclaimed, her outburst not going unnoticed by their neighbours. "I just... I cannot stay here, Kaedin. It is not the same."

"I suspected you had aspirations of leaving," he said. "We should request an audience with the elders."

"They will never allow such a thing," scoffed Kamina.

"They allowed me to marry Nyssa," he said. "Humans and centaurs come to the forest and hail us as heroes, thank us for our deeds..."

"...and Abbal Eredu hates us for it."

"They are nervous with Ascara in the forest," he explained. "They fear her magic may lead to another war, as Oldwyn's staff once did. But they do not wish it to fall into the wrong hands. We could say you are going to return her to the Rangers of Ishkava, and that you may take a while to get there and back."

"Do you think they would?" she asked, Kaedin having convinced her that such a thing may yet be possible.

"I will speak to Lashara and arrange an audience with the elders," he said, rising to his feet.

"Kaedin," she called after him. "Thank you."

"You can thank me by cleaning the storage hut," he shouted back.

*

As Kaedin went off to meet with Lashara and the elders, Kamina stepped inside the storage hut hidden between two trees. It had not been cleaned in quite some time, and there were signs that the wood snakes had returned. She recalled memories of her mother tackling the creatures, but found herself struggling to remember what Talia had looked like. A sudden wind swept through the hut.

"You look sad," said Talia, appearing beside her. The startled elf soon realised that this was not a memory, nor was it Talia, but someone else entirely.

"Orora," she said. The vision of Talia nodded.

"I do not have long, Kamina Elloeth. I know your heart burns with questions, but I can answer only one." The young elf's mind buzzed with what questions to ask, but she could not decide which one to present to the Elemental.

"Why me?" she chose eventually.

"You will discover this in time. You must follow your heart, wherever it may lead. Do you understand?"

Kamina nodded.

And once again, she was alone.

"Kamina," called Kaedin. She spun around to see him framed in the doorway. "The elders have agreed to see us."

*

Kamina and Kaedin joined the nine elders inside the sacred Tree of Edku. They were almost identical, with their slender frames and long hair coloured in various shades of white and grey.

"Kamina Elloeth," announced Abbal Eredu. "You come before us seeking permission to leave Elgrin and trek to Mount Ishkava, so that you may return the blade Ascara to the rangers, is this correct?"

"No," replied Kamina eventually, ignoring Kaedin's expression of disapproval. "I do not plan on merely returning Ascara. I wish to join the Ishkava Rangers."

"You are not yet of *Dira Adolyn*," noted Enia Vale.

"And yet I have travelled across Amaros, over the seas to Zalestia…"

"In the care of the Ishkava Ranger Callaghan," Kais Eladri reminded her in a demeaning voice. "You are still young, Kamina."

Abbal glanced around the circle, as each member cast an unsaid vote. "I am afraid we cannot grant you what you ask," he declared.

"Thank you elders," said Kaedin, moving to leave, but he paused when he realised Kamina had not done the same. A slight breeze swirled around the inside of the tree, and Kamina heard Orora's words again.

"You must follow your heart, wherever it may lead."

"Is there something you wish to add?" Abbal asked, displeased that she had not yet left their presence.

"Yes," said Kamina. "I have no other option but to become an outcast."

"Kamina!" exclaimed Kaedin.

"That is not something to say lightly," cautioned Karris Kolt.

"You have left me with no choice, Elder Kolt."

"If you choose this path, you will never be allowed to return to Elgrin Forest," warned Abbal, intimating that he himself would carry out this decree.

"You threaten me with banishment," replied Kamina, "yet you sought refuge among the humans, who welcomed you and who would welcome me again."

"You should be mindful to whom you speak, child!" snapped Abbal. "You are as arrogant as your mother!"

"Abbal!" exclaimed Lashara. "That is my granddaughter you are referring to, who saved the life of every elf in Elgrin with her warnings about Malenek's plan. We did not listen to her, yet she alerted us again by sending the human children to our care. Perhaps we could all use some of Talia's wayward spirit."

"I apologise," he muttered, "but the elders have ruled."

"I have something to add," said Kaedin, stepping up beside his sister. "This is the advent of a new world, as it was when you chose to abandon Anawey in search of a better life. The time for hiding among the trees of Elgrin is coming to an end. There has to be understanding before there can be peace, rather than fear or anger. Who better to forge those alliances than an elven ranger?" The elders glanced between each other, considering Kamina's wise words.

"We need time to discuss the points you have raised," said Abbal.

"I depart at dawn," said Kamina. "You have until then to decide." With one last glare at Abbal Eredu, she bowed before the elders and left alongside a very proud Kaedin.

CHAPTER FIFTY-ONE

THE PATH OF ONE

Before dawn, Kamina called on Eshtel, who had been running free in the forest. She brushed his fine chestnut coat, careful to avoid the recent arrow wound. She fed him and watered him, while his large eyes questioned her.

"I have to go," she said, holding back tears. "If you do not wish to come, you should tell me now."

The horse was silent and still.

"Then enjoy the forest a while longer, Eshtel," she whispered. "We may never return."

*

The elves gathered by the Edku Tree to say farewell to Kamina Elloeth, daughter of Talia. She was no longer the scared child who had been stolen away by the Ishkava Ranger Callaghan Tor; now she was following in his footsteps. Not all the elves were happy with this decision. Endo Eredu watched the farewell festivities from a distance. She could feel his judgemental eyes, his scrutinising stare that he shared with his father. She ignored him, enveloping herself in the emotions of the moment. The crowd quietened as her great-grandmother approached, bearing the judgement of the elders.

"The elders found your words wise beyond your years, as did I," revealed Lashara. "You will be welcome back into this forest when you wish to return, which you had better do!" She gifted Kamina with spice cakes for the journey, whispering some parting words of wisdom.

"When you wield the sword's magic, be careful it does not control you."

Nyssa smiled through her tears, while Kaedin grasped her in a warrior's embrace. "I am jealous of you," he muttered out of his wife's earshot.

"You have everything you need here," whispered Kamina, kissing his cheek.

"You will always be my little sister," he confessed.

"And you will always be my annoying big brother!" she said, laughing through her tears. She took Eshtel's reigns and led him away through the forest.

"Kamina!" yelled Kaedin. She turned to see him wave, only it was not just a wave. He held his scarred hand high up in the air. She smiled, and did the same, recalling that fateful day in the forest that had changed both of their lives forever.

"No matter how far apart we are, we will always be a part of each other."

After all their adventures together, those words had never been so true as on this day.

*

After a day's ride at a swift gait, Kamina and Eshtel left the safety of Elgrin Forest, heading towards Heroshin. She planned to cross the salt flats of Hyru, the quickest route to Hylan, the royal city nestled in the shadow of the volcanic Mount Ishkava. When she was far enough from Elgrin, and out of sight of Endo Eredu's spies, she stopped and dismounted Eshtel. She closed her eyes and listened to the wind blowing the tall grass around her, felt the breeze brush over her skin.

"You can reveal yourself," she said with some semblance of authority. In the tall grass to her right, the spirit of Callaghan Tor slowly appeared, his solemn gaze fixed on her.

"How did you know I was here?" he asked.

"We are bonded," she replied. "I could feel you, but I assumed you did not wish anyone else to know." Kamina had imagined his unveiling to be more of a joyous occasion.

"No, it was not that," he explained. "I wished for peace after death, Kamina. Not this."

"This world still needs you," she insisted.

"I suspect Enara will soon have a new Ranger Elite," he replied, admiring her tenacity.

"I need you," she finally admitted.

"Kamina, you defeated a god!" he exclaimed. "One whom I placed my faith in every day. You have no need of me."

"I need you to guide me to the Ranger Temple," she muttered.

"You could have found your own way," he said. "You had not even decided on this path when you dipped your hand in my blood." He stepped closer to her. "What is the real reason you brought me back?"

"I… I have already lost my mother," she said, faltering. "I did not wish to lose my father."

"Kamina, I wish it were true, I really do, but I am not your father." She reached inside her bag and revealed Malenek's stolen journal, the book having survived the battlefield.

"I read this. I know the truth," she said wistfully, saddened by his denial.

"Kamina…" tried the spirit, but Kamina clung to her fantastical hope.

"When you met Malenek, you told him how you cared for Talia." She opened the book and read, having had Nyssa teach her the words. "He loved her like a husband… should love a wife, when neither of them had anyone else in the world. With the elven girl finally awakened from whatever sickness had cocooned in sleep, Callaghan thought it safe to take her back to her people in Elgrin Forest. He accompanied her as a protector, where she gave birth to her child, a gift from the gods themselves…"

"You have only read forward from where you found it," said Callaghan. "If you read what comes before, you will see Talia's name appears before my first meeting with Malenek." Kamina flicked back through the pages, until she spotted the Amarosian scrawl of her mother's name.

"As the Zalestian predicted, and against all odds, a trio of elves travelled to Mytor, seeking an audience with myself. The male, Kaman, was angry with me, but his wife Sharla managed to convey the reason for their journey. Their daughter Talia, gravely ill, had mentioned me by name before this fever took its vicious hold of her. Why she said my name I could not say, but I examined the girl at the insistence of her parents, and made a curious discovery." Kamina paused as she scanned the next lines. "She was to be a parent herself. I could only surmise that her illness was the result of bearing a child when she was so young herself…"

Kamina could read no further in front of Callaghan, feeling like such a fool. She had studied hard under Nyssa's tutelage so she could understand the words, but she had not thought of reading the full book. No, she had allowed herself to believe what she wanted to.

"When I rescued your mother, she was already with child," he explained. "She was too young, and she gripped by a fever that threatened them both."

Kamina placed Malenek's journal back in her bag, disappointed by the truth, wrecking her short-lived fantasy that the ranger was her real father.

"Why Malenek?" asked Kamina. "Why did Talia say his name?"

"That I do not know," said Callaghan. "Nor did she remember when she emerged from her fever."

Kamina could not think of anything more to say.

"I did have a daughter once," revealed the ranger. "Her name was Kamina. Talia named you after her when you were born."

"You were there?" asked Kamina.

"Oh yes," recalled the ranger's spirit. "You were a miracle child. In the months and years that followed, in my time training as a ranger, whenever I found my thoughts clouded by darkness, I thought of you. You see, the elves had never heard of a divine birth." Kamina looked up at him, not fully comprehending his meaning. "When Malenek wrote that you were a gift from the gods, he meant it literally. Kamina, you have no father. Talia told me this much."

"But why Talia?" Kamina begged. "Why me?"

"I do not have the answers you seek," said the spirit in earnest. "The Elementals move in mysterious ways. Our adventure together proves this."

"What do you mean?" asked Kamina.

"Orora," he answered. "If Talia had not been attacked by the same raiders who killed my family, I would never have saved her, and you would never have been born, and in turn, you would never have found the Stone of Spirits, or saved the world from Risaar's return."

"Are you saying the gods have a plan?"

"Given recent events, my views on the Elementals need to be reassessed, but I will say this. I may not be your father, but after the death of my family, the only thing that kept me going, that kept me alive, was caring for your mother. You may think many people are dead because of you, but I am alive because of you, as are countless others."

"You are a ghost because of me," she said, ashamed.

"If you are to become a ranger, Kamina, you must look to the future instead of the past. Do not forget the path you have already walked, but do not dwell on it either. Now come, we have a long journey ahead of us."

Callaghan walked a few steps in the direction of Mount Ishkava, before he realised Kamina was not following. He turned to find her walking with Eshtel in the opposite direction, retracing her footsteps back to Elgrin forest.

"Quitting so soon?" shouted Callaghan, chasing after her.

"No," she said. "I am going to Zalestia to fetch the Stone of Spirits from Jazintha and make you whole again."

"No, you are not," he said firmly. "I started this journey looking for an apprentice. I will not delay their training a second time."

"My training will take a long time," she said.

"Years," confirmed Callaghan. "I can wait. There is a certain peace in being a vengeance spirit. It will do for now. Besides, having one may prove handy to a ranger."

"Are you sure?" she asked. The spirit nodded, reaffirming his decision. With that, Kamina mounted Eshtel and turned him towards Callaghan. The horse trotted along with the elven ranger-to-be upon his back and her willing vengeance spirit by his side, as they headed for Heroshin to continue their adventures together.

THE END

A NOTE FROM THE AUTHOR

I hope you have enjoyed reading the first novel in the *Spirits of Vengeance* series. The project has been in development off and on for just over a decade, and if you have laughed and cried along with Callaghan, Kaedin, and Kamina, then I consider it time well spent.

If I could kindly ask that you leave an honest review at the retailer you purchased the book from, as the more people that discover the world of Enara, the sooner I will be able to finish the next instalment in the *Spirits of Vengeance* saga.

Kamina and Callaghan will return in
Spirits of Vengeance: The Assassin of Araneque.

ABOUT THE AUTHOR

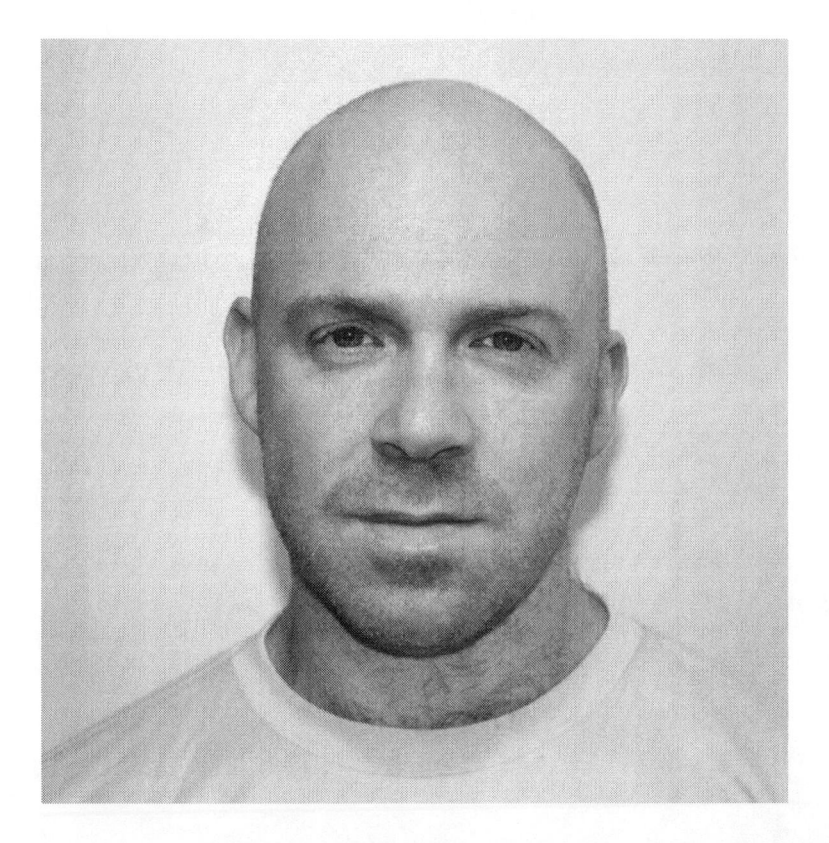

Andrew John Rainnie is a Scottish novelist, screenwriter, and filmmaker. His short films have screened all over the world, and his first book, *My Right Leg Is Tastier Than My Left*, charted his around the world adventures in 2011. When he is not busy writing, he likes to play video games. He currently lives in Glasgow with his girlfriend Lisa. Despite being a dog person, they have two cats, Brando and Niro.

Discover more about Andrew John Rainnie at his official website, www.andrewjohnrainnie.com.

You can also follow his ramblings on Twitter @andrewrainnie.

Made in the USA
Charleston, SC
08 December 2014